Bay State Skye

Janice S. C. Petrie

Bay State Skye

ISBN 10: 0-9705510-4-5
ISBN 13: 978-0-9705510-4-7

PCN Library of Congress Number:
2017906184

Seatales Publishing Company's Website:
http://seatalespublishing.com

Acknowledgments

This is a work of fiction. Although most of the incidents are based on real events, and the settings may be real locations, any similarity to or identification with the name, character or history of any person, product, or entity is entirely coincidental and unintentional.

Thank you to the Cape Ann lobstermen, fishermen, and members of the seafood-processing industry for sharing their stories and passion for their livelihood. This book is dedicated to all the ingenious men and women throughout the ages who have made their living going down to the sea.

This one's for you, Mike. Here's to soaring with the eagles!

Contents

CHAPTER 1

From the pilothouse of the *Anna May*, Jimmy Sweeney spotted a slowly flashing light in the distance that looked like sun glare bouncing off a windshield. It seemed to be reflecting off a boat that was moving in a peculiar way about three hundred yards off the port side of the *Anna May*. The boat appeared to be circling, listing somewhat to its starboard side. Jimmy's curiosity got the better of him, and he turned his wheel left to check out the strange vessel.

The sun was just beginning to set off the breakwater at Gloucester Harbor, and Jimmy was returning to port with his haul. It had been a good day. After a cold spring and summer, when seawater temperatures barely moved out of the fifties, August had finally turned warm. As water warmed, lobsters moved, and pots filled. With last week's nor'easter added to the mix, Jimmy was certain he'd be coming in heavy. His dad had always said, "No one can figure out what makes lobsters tick. When you think you've figured out what a lobster's gonna do, you'll be out of business because they never act the same every year." But today he had proven his dad wrong. Through the years, Jimmy had noted a pattern. When there was a big nor'easter in the late summer or fall, he baited and set his traps right after, and he had a heavy haul each time. It had never failed him in the past, and today was all the proof he needed. He'd pulled 204 pots from the soft bottom just off Thacher Island, and figuring the lobsters to weigh in at around 850 pounds, it was just about his heaviest catch in twenty-five years. It had been a very good day.

Murph Sweeney came up from below with cups of hot coffee for his brother and himself. It was mug-up time, and no one was more deserving of a break than Jimmy and Murph. Murph sat in the chair next to Jimmy, putting a foot on the dashboard. "We're about twenty minutes out. I guess I'll start bailing the holding tanks and getting the lobsters into totes. Hope we have enough totes." Murph grinned as he nudged his brother's arm.

Both men were reveling in their good fortune. It had been a slow summer. Jimmy, who had just turned forty-two last month, had a wife and four kids to support. Murph, who was two years his junior, had to come up with alimony for his ex and child support for his son, which left little for his own expenses. Both men were concerned with paying the mortgage at the end of the month, and if Jimmy lost his lobster boat, he'd be devastated.

"Don't bail them just yet," Jimmy said as he pointed to the listing vessel now coming into full view. "If we get held up here, I don't want the lobsters dropping weight from being out of the water too long."

As Jimmy contemplated how he was going to keep his trawl location a secret from the other lobster fishermen, whose jealousy as they eyed his catch could be predicted, the *Anna May* pulled up close to the strange boat, still under steam. It was sitting low in the water, indicating it might have a significant catch on board.

"*Bay State Skye*," Jimmy said under his breath as he read the name from the bow of the boat. The vessel was a forty-five- to fifty-footer, a dragger that was traveling at about two and a half knots. It was about twice the size of Jimmy's lobster boat. Jimmy steered his *Anna May* into the inner circle of the boat, and suddenly it became apparent why the dragger was moving in a large loop. The dragger net was on deck with the doors still attached, tangled with a ball of four or five muddy, mangled wire lobster pots. The trawl line had been severed in several places, as if someone was trying to free the pots from the net. There was a trawl line hanging over the rail attached to a few more pots. The line was pulled tight from the weight of the traps, which had caused the dragger to list somewhat to one side. But there didn't appear to be anyone on deck.

Jimmy managed to pull alongside the vessel, and Murph tied off the *Anna May* to the cleats of the dragger. After jumping on board, Murph made his way to the pilothouse, carefully stepping over the mass of tangled traps and netting, to throttle back the dragger's engine to idle and disengage its transmission. There was nobody manning the pilothouse.

The two boats were bobbing in the water, back-and-forth and to-and-fro, like tops being pitched in all directions. Jimmy boarded the dragger, stepping over the steady stream of salt water coming from the hose that kept the dragger deck from becoming slick. He opened the door to the lower deck, calling out and listening to hear if anyone answered. There was no reply. Then he opened the hatch on deck to the fish hold and peered down to see if anyone was icing the fish down. There was no sign of activity. There was no one on board. A ghost ship, perhaps, but there were signs of illegal activity everywhere.

"What the hell?" Murph asked as he reached into the holding tank, which was brimming with lobsters. He pulled out a three- to five-pounder. "This guy's been dragging soft bottom for lobsters and caught someone's trawl in his net. I bet there's thousands of dollars' worth of pots and trawl line mangled in this mess. Draggers aren't allowed to take more than a hundred pounds of lobsters in a day. This holding tank must have at least five hundred pounds. And we're busting our asses to lay line and bait traps? How can we compete with this? He'll flood the market with these, and our price will drop a quarter."

Jimmy was as disgusted as Murph. Shaking his head, he said, "I don't think this guy's ever going to get to market. Where is he?" He stepped close to the rail and looked into the dark water below, adding, "Maybe he got what he deserved. A hundred and ten feet down, no one's going to find him."

"Well, I say good riddance to him," said Murph, picking up some of the tangled line, noting several places where it had been severed. "A dragger man pulled over the rail?" Murph asked. Then he added with an audible chuckle, "Oh, wouldn't that be good."

Jimmy looked out beyond the bow, noting the location of the dragger. "He's dragging within state limits. He should know better. No wonder he picked up a trawl line. He dragged straight through the center of the buoys, the silly bastard." Then looking at Murph, Jimmy said, "Do you know who owns the *Bay State Skye?*"

"I thought it was one of the Golini brothers, but I could be wrong," Murph replied, rubbing his stubbly, sandy-blond beard. "That doesn't make sense, though. Billy Golini is a decent family man. He wouldn't be dragging within the limits."

"Well, from what I know of Billy Golini, he's a hell of a fisherman," Jimmy remarked. "And judging from what's down in the hold, this guy's got to have something on the ball."

Murph and Jimmy both made their way to the fish-hold hatch and climbed down the ladder. There must have been fifty totes below, all diligently iced down. Each tote held a hundred pounds of fish, and they were what fishermen called bullets.

"Look at these fish," Murph said as he stuck his thumb in the gill hole of a gorgeous haddock to lift it in the air and show Jimmy. "Clear eyes, the butter still on them, every scale in place. Rigor hasn't even begun to set in. They're the very definition of a bullet, and there must be at least five thousand pounds in here!"

Jimmy looked at some of the totes underneath. There were codfish, haddock, flounder, and a few hake and pollock. "Quite a catch," he remarked. "Any dragger would have been racing to market with a catch like this. What the hell was he doing dragging for lobsters, the greedy son of a bitch? We must be wrong about the owner. This couldn't be Billy Golini's boat. I can't see a Golini brother dragging soft bottom for lobsters with his fish hold full like this. Well, let me get on the radio and notify the Coast Guard."

Murph put an arm out to stop his brother. "I was thinking that maybe we should fill a few of our totes with some of these primo lobsters. We'll leave the beat-up ones—you know, the culls and pistols—but a few of the lobsters that still have both claws aren't going to be doing this boat any good. We could float them overnight and gradually bring them to market with our own over the next few days. After all, we recovered the boat. It eventually would have sunk if we hadn't found it, and the whole catch would have been lost."

"They aren't ours to keep, Murph," said Jimmy.

Jimmy normally never would have considered Murph's idea. But after he thought about it, he said, "We could actually be doing the owner a favor—that is, if he's even alive. Well, I suppose even if he were dead, we'd be helping his legacy. If we took everything but a hundred pounds, at least he wouldn't be over the legal limit of lobsters allowed for draggers. That way, he wouldn't get a hefty fine for ignoring the limits, and he, or his widow, would get the full value of his catch."

"That's just what I was thinking," said Murph. He playfully nudged his brother as he passed by.

Murph gathered several totes and began culling out the lobsters. He was sure to leave a few good ones to counter the many one-clawed or clawless lobsters he was leaving behind. Dragger nets had the reputation of beating the hell out of lobsters as they raked the bottom for anything hiding in the sand and mud. But the draggers usually came up with the larger lobsters, which paid off handsomely at market.

After giving Murph some lead time, Jimmy made his way back to the *Anna May* to call the Coast Guard. There was a station right in Gloucester, and they immediately responded by sending out a forty-seven-foot motor lifeboat (MLB) vessel. There was really no need to deploy the MLB, which had the reputation of being able to operate in all kinds of weather, with up to thirty-foot seas. But Gloucester's own congressman, Barry Contoro, was onboard, seeing firsthand the boat that boasted of being able to right itself in thirty seconds. Its thirteen watertight compartments were key to keeping the boat upright, even in thirty-foot surf and winds of fifty knots. Since Congressman Contoro was already on board, he thought he'd take advantage of riding out on this calm evening to the allegedly abandoned boat discovered by two lobstermen. It wouldn't hurt to have his visit to this impressive boat—primarily a photo op in an election year—morph into a full-blown search-and-rescue mission.

As the Coast Guard approached the two boats, Murph waved them in. Four men dressed in navy-blue coveralls and wearing red inflatable vests were visible on the deck. One man remained behind to radio the dragger's information into the Coast Guard station, while the boarding team consisted of two armed Coast Guard officials and the congressman. The rugged six-foot-tall captain, who was clearly in charge, was the first official to board the dragger. His assistant, an ensign, a slightly shorter, younger man, followed him. Both men had dark-brown crew cuts, in sharp contrast to Murph and Jimmy's wavy, sun-bleached hair, although Murph's hair was significantly longer and more ragged than Jimmy's.

The congressman was the last to board, awkwardly placing his foot on top of the dragger's rail and grabbing the ensign's hand to steady himself on the slimy, wet deck. Although he had begun his tour of the MLB wearing a black suit with a cobalt-blue shirt and tie, he had changed his clothes to match the more official-looking blue coveralls and red inflatable vests, similar to what the other two men were wearing. But the congressman still donned the shiny black dress shoes he'd worn at the beginning of the tour, in the absence of anything better the Coast Guard could provide on such short notice.

Congressman Contoro was no stranger to the Gloucester fishing industry. The Contoro family could trace back three generations of men who'd worked the sea, and Barry and his older brother, Al, had spent most of their youth helping out on their father's fishing boat. In the summers, Barry's dad trapped lobsters. But once the water cooled, and lobsters weren't on the move for the winter, he rigged his boat with a long line and a gill net to catch fish while waiting for the ocean to warm. While his brother was enamored of the sea, Barry was never comfortable working in the cold, windswept, unpredictable waters, and he hated coming home with fish scales clinging to his sweatshirt. There was a saying in the lucrative fish business that the money didn't smell, but it was difficult for Barry to get past the stench of his clothes and skin after working with fish all day. When Barry graduated from high school, he broke with his family's legacy to earn a poli-sci degree from Salem State College and run for the Gloucester City Council and then for the Massachusetts State Legislature. Congressman Contoro's discomfort in once again being aboard a fishing boat was palpable, and he was anxious for the discovery phase of the investigation to be concluded so that he could return to the Coast Guard MLB.

Jimmy and Murph were still wearing their waterproof orange bib overall pants, affectionately known as grundgies, which coordinated well with their yellow waterproof jackets, hats, and tall, black commercial fisherman's boots. This clothing was a vital part of any fisherman's equipment. As long as a fisherman remained dry, he could stay warm.

The captain walked up past the winch, just behind the pilothouse, and turned to face the aft of the dragger. His eyes followed the steel cable from the winch to the flat metal trawl doors that were connected to the cable, and he shook his head. In boats that were built in the early eighties, as this one had been, there was usually a haul line and a block attached to an overhead boom to bring in the tail end, or cod end, of the net. But the captain instead saw a ball of cable, tangled with the dragger doors and a group of contorted lobster traps, in a heap on the deck. Their trawl line was still attached in places and was hanging over the rail in other areas on the starboard side. Normally the doors were attached to the net, and when dropped in the sea, the pressure of the water separated the doors that opened the net to receive the catch. Something had gone terribly wrong here.

"Man, he nailed that lobster trawl good, didn't he?" said the captain.

The ensign checked out the trawl. "Doesn't look like any of this is salvageable."

Everyone on board stared at the mangled mess in disbelief.

"Not only is the lobster trawl a total loss, but there's heavy damage to the dragger's trawl reel and the haul line. The chain even snapped, and the boom fell to the deck trying to raise this mess out of the sea. Damned fool. Do we know whose boat this is?" asked the captain, eyeing Murph and Jimmy.

"Not a clue," answered Murph. Jimmy just shrugged his shoulders.

The two Coast Guard men glanced at the checkers on deck, crudely made from planks of wood. The checkers served as bins that were normally used to contain some of the sorted catch before it was transferred to the hold and iced down. But the checkers were empty. Based on the notable fresh slime on the sides of the wooden bins, however, the checkers surely had been used on this fishing trip.

The ensign followed the captain into the pilothouse to check for personal flotation devices (PFDs) that would help the fishermen stay afloat. There were three on board that were easily accessible. Each PFD looked to be the appropriate size for a grown man. The ensign checked PFDs off his list as present and accounted for.

In the same closet that held the PFDs hung three immersion suits, with the regulation thirty-one square inches of retro-reflective material on both the front and back of each suit, all labeled for their boat, the *Bay State Skye*. These immersion suits would have been instrumental in protecting the fishermen from the cold if they needed to evacuate their vessel suddenly, winding up in the frigid seawater. Immersion suits helped to prevent hypothermia and its disabling and disorienting effects, at least for a while. Although the ocean water was a balmy sixty-five degrees that day, the fishermen still would have been at risk for hypothermia if left in the water for too long without rescue. If a person's core temperature were to dip between seventy and eighty degrees, he or she would more than likely appear dead when recovered. This core temperature could easily be achieved in the sixty-five-degree August ocean water. The ensign checked the suits off his list as well.

The twenty-four-inch orange life buoy was hanging on the wall, with at least the regulation sixty feet of line attached. The inflatable life raft was also present and accounted for, as were the required visual distress signals. The *Bay State Skye* had three working fire extinguishers that had been recently inspected. Finally, the required boat registration was easily located in the pilothouse. Everything seemed to be in compliance, with no violations. All was as it should be, which led to the speculation that the boat's occupants weren't wearing any survival gear when they entered the water, if indeed that was where they'd gone.

Then the officers' attention turned to the lobster pots onboard. Glancing at Murph and Jimmy, the captain had the ensign check the ID number on one of the wrecked ones and compare it with the license number on Jimmy's boat.

Jimmy could barely hold his tongue at the blatant distrust and lack of respect the captain showed them, not to mention the lack of appreciation for notifying them of the abandoned dragger. Each lobster fishermen's trap had an identifying tag attached that matched up with the license number of their lobster boat. That way, if a trap was recovered, it could be identified and returned to the owner. Lobster fishermen in Gloucester had had traps recovered from as far away as the British Isles that they never would have discovered without the ID tag.

"Not a match," the ensign proclaimed.

"Do you think we would have called you if we had anything to do with this?" Murph asked.

"Well, whoever was operating this dragger ran it straight through a lobster trawl. That would give the owner of the traps motive for doing away with the fisherman. That's a fact you can't deny. And being lobster fishermen yourselves, I'm sure your sympathies lie with the lobsterman who owns these traps, certainly not with the dragger owner. Nobody would blame you—unless you had a hand in the dragger man's disappearance," the captain speculated.

"Look," said Jimmy, "I was just trying to do the right thing by calling it in. The fish hold is loaded with fresh fish. It should really be getting to market if it's going to be worth anything. And I need to get my lobsters into totes and weighed in."

"Fresh fish?" Congressman Contoro asked in a surprised tone.

"Bullets!" Murph replied.

"How many pounds?" Contoro questioned, clearly interested in the catch.

"Well, there are fifty totes in the fish hold, so I'd guess there's about five thousand pounds down there," Jimmy said.

"Really?" asked the congressman in a strangely excited tone of voice. Jimmy and Murph had somehow caught Contoro's attention.

"Well, why don't you open the door to the hold and climb down to take a look yourself?" asked Murph, a smirk on his face, noting the shiny black Italian leather shoes Contoro was sporting on the deck of a working fishing vessel. One thing Murph knew for sure: the congressman wasn't interested in getting his hands dirty. He was having a hard enough time tiptoeing through the fish guts and blood left on the deck, despite the running deck hose. Congressman Contoro found it best simply to ignore Murph's suggestion.

The fourth man from the Coast Guard MLB, a lieutenant, boarded the dragger carrying a letter-size piece of paper. On it was the name of the owner of the *Bay State Skye* and the timing of its current trip. No one had reported the dragger missing because it wasn't expected in until that evening.

"The *Bay State Skye* is owned by a Billy Golini out of Rockport. His fishing license is up-to-date for 1990, and everything seems in order. He left Gloucester Harbor last Saturday, August 18, and was due back at about dark on Wednesday, August 22," the lieutenant dutifully read from his report.

"That's tonight," the congressman interjected.

"Yes, it sounds like he was heading in," said the captain.

"Any chance of doing a search for the missing man?" Congressman Contoro asked, hoping the suggestion would lead to action on the part of the Coast Guard. The congressman thought his involvement in the incident's investigation could influence a more responsive search-and-rescue operation than the typical quick helicopter survey for survivors in the immediately surrounding waters and islands within swimming distance. The congressman was motivated not only by the fact that a thorough search-and-recovery mission would look good for him politically, but he was also genuinely concerned about the missing fisherman and his family. He knew how he'd feel if his brother or father were missing at sea. He'd want to be sure everything humanly possible was done to find his family members, and how could he not wish that for this missing fisherman's family as well?

"Are you kidding?" Murph exclaimed cynically.

"Fishing's a dangerous occupation, as you well know," the captain told the congressman. "Vessels are loaded with the opportunity for occupational accidents, and the sea is an unforgiving mistress. Fishermen fall, get knocked off deck, or even worse, get hauled off deck when they become entangled in fishing gear."

"That's when you really don't have a chance," added Jimmy.

"Not all accidents can be prevented," noted the captain, "although the actions of a fisherman can make or break him, sealing his fate. From the looks of this deck, I'd say this fisherman wasn't thinking too clearly. He may have gotten tangled in the trawl line as he cut it free and went out with the traps. There's no way he could ever surface in time. Or maybe he got whacked in the head by the boom when it toppled over and wound up unconscious in the water. There are countless scenarios that could have taken place, given all the factors present on this deck."

"Captain," the lieutenant added, "Billy Golini wasn't the only man working the dragger today. Billy's brother, Tony, supposedly went out with him, too. Neither man has turned up on shore. More than likely, he was on board giving Billy a hand."

"Unlikely both men were hauled overboard," the congressman noted.

"Stranger things have happened," remarked the lieutenant.

"I'll tell you what," said the captain, "I'll order a search helicopter to scan the water in the area before it gets dark. But with all the survival gear still on board, the chances of finding either of the Golini brothers treading water on the surface are slim to none."

"Collecting any physical evidence is out of the question; that's for sure," Congressman Contoro added, taking one foot and dragging it through the fish slime, guts, and blood the deck hose was making a futile attempt to clean away. "This scene is so contaminated, there's no way you'd find anything useful." He had given up on salvaging his dress shoes at this point. The whole trip had validated his decision to choose a different career path.

Just then, all five men looked toward land. New Englanders were used to skies staying light well past seven o'clock in August. But this evening, dark clouds were overtaking the skyline, and a rumble of thunder could be heard in the distance. It was common for evening thunderstorms to occur in this area, especially if the day had been quite warm. Although Jimmy and Murph had enjoyed the natural air conditioning of the sea all day, Congressman Contoro knew that most of the day had been in the low nineties. Scattered thunderstorms were almost a given in these conditions.

"We'd better get the *Bay State Skye* towed in, and you two should be headed to dock yourselves," the captain said to Jimmy and Murph. "Can you give me a number where I can reach you two so that each of you can make a formal statement?"

"Sure," said Jimmy. Murph nodded in agreement.

In an instant, a flash of lightning struck the granite rock that hugged the coastline off Halibut Point in Rockport. As the boats made their way to dock, one in tow, the skies opened up, and rain poured down, washing away any clues as to what had actually happened to the two men aboard the *Bay State Skye* that day.

CHAPTER 2

Jimmy cranked up the radio as he headed to the dock at Flannery's Fish House. He had made a deal for dock space at the head of the harbor some years ago, in exchange for selling his entire catch to Flannery's. It was convenient docking right behind Flannery's fish-processing plant. Jimmy didn't have to load his lobsters into a truck and drive them to the dealer like most lobstermen did. Instead, he used a hydraulic hoist to lift the totes to the edge of the dock from his boat, and a forklift from Flannery's would meet him to bring his totes to the scale at the front of the building. Jimmy would get the maximum weight, with his lobsters coming immediately from his boat, and Flannery's would get strong lobsters that hadn't been out of the water for very long. The deal was working well for both of them, and because Flannery's was a fish-processing plant as well as a lobster pound, Jimmy could purchase barrels of bait, which consisted of fish heads and skeletons known as racks, that were by-products of the fish-processing operation. If fish processing was slow for a few days, Jimmy was assured to be first in line to get the freshest bait. Contrary to what most people believed, lobsters were very picky; only the freshest bait would lure them into a trap. Understanding that was what had made Jimmy's family successful lobstermen in Gloucester for three generations. The deal Jimmy had with Flannery's was a pretty fair arrangement, one that other lobstermen would love to have if an opening at the dock ever came up.

Flannery's benefitted from the arrangement not only by receiving the strongest lobsters possible but also because the company could enlist Jimmy and Murph's services to take their most important clients out to get a feel for the romantic vocation of lobstering. Many of Flannery's customers were from landlocked areas of the United States, and this was the first time they'd have an opportunity to experience being out on a boat in the ocean. Jimmy would take them just outside the breakwater, not too far from shore, and stop once or twice to pull a couple of traps on a trawl line. He made sure the traps were full the day before, to ensure the clients would experience the thrill of a substantial catch. With Jimmy's winning smile and his alluring bluish-gray eyes, coupled with Murph's gift for telling a great tale or two, the clients were sure to have a grand first experience at sea.

Murph had just finished filling the final tote with lobsters, making sure he was ready to off-load the catch as soon as they docked. He cringed as he walked into the pilothouse of the *Anna May*. Billy Joel's "We Didn't Start the Fire" was blaring while Jimmy tapped his hands to the strong beat of the tune. Pop songs weren't a favorite of Murph's. Grunge bands were more his style, and he just tolerated Jimmy's taste in music. After all, it was Jimmy's boat, and Jimmy didn't have to remind him that the owner controlled the choice of radio station. Murph had owned his own boat a few years back, but his love for gambling, drinking, and carousing had ended that, with the bank quickly taking possession of the boat and selling it off to repay his loan. It wasn't too long after that when his wife asked for a divorce.

Jimmy called the office at Flannery's from his ship-to-shore line to let them know he was on his way in. He wanted to be sure a forklift would be waiting by the dock when he arrived. It was getting late, and he had a substantial catch to off-load. With a man waiting to operate the hoist, the unloading time would be cut in half.

Jimmy managed to find a spot at the dock just across from where the *Andrea Gail*, a seventy-foot swordfishing vessel, was tied up. She often off-loaded her swordfish to waiting trucks at the dock across from Fitzy's at the head of the Harbor. Bobby Brown owned this boat, along with the *Hannah Boden*, which hadn't come back to the harbor yet. The *Hannah Boden* was often docked at Flannery's, and both boats sold swordfish to Flannery's on a regular basis. The *Hannah Boden's* absence left a little extra room for Jimmy to dock his boat and off-load his catch.

As Jimmy steered his boat close and threw the engine into reverse to help the *Anna May* hug the dock, Murph stepped over the rail to tie the boat to the lower dock cleats. Then he walked to the end of the dock and cautiously navigated the steep gangplank that stretched between the lower and upper docks. It was dead low tide, and a spring tide at that, which was always a treacherous time to navigate the gangplank. Depending on the tides, the lower floating dock could vary significantly in height from the sturdy, upper pylon dock that supported the Flannery's building. At high tide, there was only a difference of about six feet between the lower and upper docks. At this time, the rise of the gangplank was slight, and most fishermen could easily walk up the ramp without holding the railings, which were often smeared with fish slime or seagull droppings. But at low tide, especially during an extreme spring tide, when the moon was full or new, there could be as much as an eleven- or twelve-foot drop from the first to the second dock. That was when the hydraulic hoist became a crucial piece of equipment to unload the boats efficiently. As Murph approached the upper dock, he was excited to see his good friend and drinking buddy, Denny Russo, topside, and he knew right then that the evening was off to a great start.

Denny and Murph had been friends since elementary school. They traveled with the same circle of friends, but unlike six-foot-two Murph, who was a basketball star at Gloucester High, Denny's height barely reached five-four, which kept him off the basketball court and gravitating more toward baseball as his sport of choice.

Both men had turned forty this year, and unlike Murph, who still had a full head of hair, Denny never took his baseball cap off to reveal his receding hairline, which had rendered him practically bald. Murph was the more outrageous of the two men, and Denny had a grounding effect on him. Both men enjoyed a few beers and sharing stories, which was the bonding force that kept them together all these years. That and the fact that Denny's two sons, Irish twins born just eleven months apart, and Murph's son, who excelled at any sport he tried, had all been together on the same Little League team for the last three years.

"I could use a hand down here to hook these totes up," said Jimmy, seeing Denny was ready to hoist the lobsters up. If Murph started to tell Denny the dragger tale, the lobsters could wind up sitting on the deck for a long time.

"Have you heard about the *Bay State Skye*?" Murph asked Denny.

"You mean Billy Golini's dragger?" asked Denny as he swung the hoist's hook over the *Anna May*, getting ready to lower it.

"That's the one," exclaimed Murph like a little boy, unable to contain his excitement at sharing the story of the day.

"Hey, you guys," called Jimmy from the boat, "you have all friggin' night to tell that story over a few beers at Fitzy's. For now, can we concentrate on getting the lobsters off this boat?"

"Yup," replied Murph. He hated taking orders from his brother, but he knew, too, the sooner the lobsters made it to the scale, the more money he'd make. The story could wait—but not too long. News traveled fast in Gloucester, and Murph wanted to be first with the scoop.

Murph was a hard worker and quick to boot. With the anticipation of telling his story to everyone at the bar, Murph was an unstoppable force. The lobsters were unloaded and at the scale within fifteen minutes.

"Quite a haul," Denny remarked.

"You know it!" exclaimed Jimmy proudly. "You can't go wrong pulling pots right after a nor'easter."

Then Jimmy got down to business. "So, what's boat price today?" he asked Denny. Jimmy knew a lot of the dealers from the Gloucester area would consult each other to see how much they were planning to pay their lobster boats per pound.

"I don't know, Jimmy. You should check in the office," Denny replied, attempting to avoid the subject. Denny knew the price had dropped during the day and didn't want to be the bearer of bad news.

"Come on, Denny, fess up. How much are they paying?" asked Murph.

"OK, I hear it's two eighty-five a pound, but don't quote me on that," said Denny.

"Damn it, Denny. That's a quarter drop a pound since yesterday," said Jimmy.

"What can I say? Lobsters finally started moving. Everyone's coming in wicked heavy today," said Denny. "None of the dealers wants to get caught paying too much. If they do, they won't be able to move their lobsters. Then my crew and me will be picking deads out of the holding tanks left and right. Nothing to do with deads and weaks but cook 'em for meat. Can't ship 'em. They'll die, and then we'll catch hell for shipping weak lobsters. You guys are starting to bring in shedders now, too, and those soft shells aren't gonna hold long. Between the shedders, the weaks, and the deads, we'll be cooking and picking meat for months. Frozen meat sells well at Christmas time, but they'd rather sell live lobsters now."

"Well, they'd better be careful. If they get too low, some of us may just drop a crate or two off at another dealer before coming here to dock," said Murph.

"Hey, you gotta do what you gotta do. Just don't let the big guy hear ya," Denny said.

Jimmy patted Denny on the shoulder. "Hey, thanks for waiting around to take in our boat. I didn't mean to keep you working this late."

"No problem, Jimmy. I can always use the OT," Denny called back. "Are you coming to Fitzy's?"

"Maybe later," Jimmy answered, "I thought I'd check out the auction. The dragger should have arrived by now. But you have to put the lobsters away anyway, so you won't be there too long before I come along."

Denny made his first trip with the *Anna May*'s lobsters, carefully balancing the totes on the forklift blades as he drove through the vertical plastic strips that helped to keep the plant's refrigeration from spilling out into the warm night air. Flannery's tried to keep the production floor no warmer than fifty degrees, and all the employees wore heavy, hooded sweatshirts, even on ninety-degree days. Tourists and summer residents would come into Flannery's retail market on a hot August day and, with a sigh of relief, comment on how nice it must be to work in such a wonderful, air-conditioned building. But truth be told, the damp, cold air got old quick, and most of Flannery's workers couldn't wait to get out into the sun and warmth. Winter or summer, it was all the same for people working in the fish-processing plant, and this was true for the retail clerk, the fish cutters, the lobster-room crew, and the office workers. The money was decent, but there were no frills for even the plant manager at Flannery's.

Murph sat in his late-model silver Ford 150 waiting for Denny while Jimmy jumped into his older, less shiny black Dodge Dakota to drive down the street to the auction. Inside Flannery's lobster room, Denny was lowering their run into one of the holding tanks where the lobsters roamed free. When the lobster-room crew came in the next morning, they would go through the run to size the lobsters and separate the cull lobsters, which only had one full-size claw, from the pistols, which were missing both claws, from the rest of the normal, two-clawed ones. If there were any lobsters considered too weak to survive in the tanks, they'd be set aside to be part of a cook later on that day, when all the boat runs had been sorted or culled out.

Jimmy may as well have walked to the Gloucester auction. It was less than a mile away from Flannery's, and apparently, word was spreading fast about the abandoned dragger being towed in.

The summer people, as well as the native Gloucester folks, all came down to greet its arrival home. Summer people arrived to satisfy their curiosity, but the Gloucester residents, many of whom were from generations of fishing families themselves, were there to support the fishing community. It could have happened to any one of their families, and they were grateful to have been spared this time. But Billy and Tony Golini's families weren't so fortunate, and their wives, with a total of five children in tow, along with their mom and dad, were there to witness the arrival of their loved ones' dragger.

Congressman Contoro was clearly visible on the deck of the Coast Guard's MLB, his meticulously styled black hair blowing in the substantial breeze left over from the thunderstorm. He had anticipated a strong press presence at the auction house and made certain his involvement in the search and rescue was a focal point for all who attended the *Bay State Skye*'s arrival. Not only was the *Gloucester Daily Times* front and center, but the Boston papers had also made the trip north for the story. There were even three Boston television stations taking film footage for the eleven o'clock news. Congressman Contoro was looking as presidential as possible, disembarking the MLB once it was securely tied to the auction dock. He shook hands with the Coast Guard captain and his crew, congratulating them on a job well done. Then he approached the waiting family members to express his condolences. He hugged each of the tearful wives and promised to help in any way possible at this terrible time.

Meanwhile, the auction-house workers began to unload the fish. The sun was setting, and they had to call in a crew to take the boat in so late in the evening. The auction crew worked like a well-oiled machine, opening the hatch to the fish hold and hooking up the totes to the hydraulic hoist that lifted each tote to the refrigerated auction-house floor.

"Nice catch," said Gino Benini, the rotund auction-floor foreman, to no one in particular.

"Should we go ahead and sort it?" asked one of the auction-floor workers.

"From what I understand, this is Billy Golini's catch. No need to sort a Golini brother's catch. They always come in right. That's how they've stayed in business all these years. They know the value of their catch before it ever leaves the boat," said Gino.

"The totes are all iced down," said the floor worker. "I'll have the guys throw the totes in the cooler for the night, then." Gino nodded in agreement, and the worker made his way to the totes on the auction floor.

Jimmy had finally arrived, after walking a half mile from the only parking place he could find. He made his way into the auction house and toward the crowd by the back doors where the *Bay State Skye's* catch had just come through. There were several flashes of light from photographers' cameras, and as he pushed through the crowd to get a better vantage point, he could see Congressman Contoro holding a scrod haddock up for the press. Loving the attention, the congressman picked up a second haddock in his other hand, holding them both as high in the air in front of him as he could.

"He doesn't mind getting slimy when the cameras are flashing," Jimmy noted with a smirk.

Then the congressman looked down momentarily, replacing the fish he was holding while studying the tote the two fish had come from, and immediately looked up again with a smile. "As tragic as this day appears to have been for the Golini brothers, thankfully, they've left a substantial catch for their families," he proclaimed. "And I'm going to follow this catch to make sure it's handled with care so that it brings the highest price possible tomorrow morning at auction." Then, looking toward Gino, he said, "I'd like to buy these ten totes of scrod haddock to help out the families. I'll pay whatever price scrod haddock goes for at the auction tomorrow. Could you please have these totes moved into the cooler with my brother's fish from today?"

"Will do," Gino proudly answered, noticeably excited to have all this attention focused on the auction house.

Workers grabbed a forklift and moved the congressman's ten totes to the cooler where his brother's fish from earlier that day had been stored. Most of the draggers would schedule their trips to leave on the weekend to ensure they would arrive at the auction house sometime midweek. A dragger that arrived on a Friday or the weekend, which was a time of low demand, would suffer a substantial loss when selling its fish. Fish-processing plants usually didn't work on weekends because the employee overtime would cut too much into the profit. The dragger's fish would have to be held until Monday morning before being sold, and its lack of freshness would diminish its value. Processors only took fish in on the weekend if its quality was high and its price was low so that the workers' overtime didn't impact the profit from the sale of the fish. Because this was Wednesday, the fish processors would have a keen interest in bidding on the *Bay State Skye*'s catch, with two days left to cut and ship the fish or freeze it for a later sale.

His brother's puzzled look was all Barry Contoro had to see. He knew he'd have to give Al an explanation quickly before he made a fuss. His brother wouldn't want someone else's catch mixed in with his own. Barry took his brother aside—way aside—in the cooler once the totes had been stored and the workers were gone.

"What the hell are you doing?" asked Al. "Have you lost your mind?"

Congressman Contoro put his hand on his brother's shoulder and guided him over to the *Bay State Skye*'s totes. "Take a good look," he said.

Al reached in and picked up one of the scrod haddock. It was smaller, a light two to three pounds, he guessed. "Yeah, they're fresh, but what of it? My fish are as good as these."

"Look deeper," said the congressman.

His brother picked up three or four fish and threw them on one of the other totes. "What the heck?" asked Al, searching deeper in the totes. "These are all market haddock underneath. They all look like they're in the three- to five-pound range. Are all of these totes like this, with a couple of small scrod on top and a whole tote of market haddock underneath?"

"Looks that way to me," said Barry.

"The auction should have caught this. Didn't they wash and size the catch out like they did with mine earlier today? Joe was working the table this afternoon. He did a good job sizing my catch. How could he have made a mistake like this?" asked Al.

"He didn't," the congressman replied with a smile. "The floor workers didn't wash and table them. No one went through them for size. They knew the boat and trusted the Golini brothers to size their fish properly. They always have in the past. I don't know why this time would be different, but it was."

"You can't take these. These markets are worth way more than what you're paying for this scrod haddock. I bet the widows could use the money, Barry. You need to tell the auction about your discovery and set this right," his brother advised.

"Listen, my personal finances are taking a huge hit with the cost of this reelection. I dare say I need the money as much as they do. I'm sure they've both got hefty life insurance policies. What fisherman with a family wouldn't? And the Fishermen's Wives Fund will be there to lend a hand, too. Hell, the boat's got to be worth at least a couple hundred thousand. They'll be fine. Besides, what are we talking, a difference of a dollar a pound? For ten totes, that's one thousand dollars. It'll never be missed. And even if it went to auction, it would have been sold off as scrod haddock, not markets, so the fish processor would have profited from the auction's mistake. Six one way, a half dozen the other, what's the difference?" the congressman asked. "No difference at all, from where I'm sitting."

"I don't know, with the circumstances of coming into this catch, I think you're inviting trouble. It can't be good luck taking advantage of two respected fishermen lost at sea and their families. I believe what goes around comes around, and I don't want anything to do with it. I wouldn't touch the *Bay State Skye's* fish with a ten-foot pole. You're just setting yourself up to experience the same bad luck the Golini brothers obviously did," said the congressman's brother.

"You fishermen are way too superstitious," Barry scoffed at his brother. Then he added in a defensive tone, "Besides, the Golini brothers weren't as pure as the driven snow either."

"No?" asked Al. "But I don't see that it makes any difference."

"They had dragged straight through a lobsterman's trawl line, destroying about seven thousand dollars' worth of traps and gear. Not to mention the bunch of three-to five-pounders they had stolen that were in their holding tanks. So yes, what goes around comes around," Barry Contoro insisted.

"Suit yourself," said Al, "but it's your fish. Keep me out of it. You can't mix it in with my catch. It's already been sized and recorded."

"I know Colbert's Seafood Company in Boston will pay me the auction's market price, no questions asked. I'll arrange for them to pick the totes up first thing in the morning. They sell to high-end restaurants in town that will take nothing but markets that portion out to just the right size for their more sophisticated clientele. Portions that fill the plate, the kind that markets yield with just the right thickness and surface area, sell at a premium. They're gonna love these," Barry gloated, patting his brother on the shoulder as he left the cooler. Al stayed behind, shaking his head in disbelief. He didn't want to be associated with his brother right then.

As the congressman made his way to the auction-house phone to call Colbert's to offer his market haddock for sale, he noticed Jimmy scanning the room for familiar faces. It didn't appear he was focusing specifically on any one person but rather taking account of who had attended the return of the *Bay State Skye* and, more importantly, who had not. While the local fishermen had, for the most part, shown up to support their fallen colleagues, the lack of area lobstermen present spoke volumes.

Jimmy turned on his heels and headed out the auction-house door, bound for Fitzy's. More than likely, word had gotten out about the illegal dragging and molested lobster gear found aboard Billy Golini's boat, and the lobstermen had gathered at the local watering hole to knock back a few cold ones while gathering information. Jimmy's concerned look was a good indication the abandoned dragger he and Murph had encountered earlier that day would have more of an effect on the Cape Ann community than most had originally considered.

CHAPTER 3

Jimmy walked back to his Dakota and drove the short distance to Fitzy's, where he parked next to Murph's truck. He usually went home and had dinner with his wife, Jenny, and his kids after work, but nothing was usual about this day. His plans to see *Ghost* that evening with Jenny had pretty much gone up in smoke with the discovery of the abandoned dragger. Jenny was a real Patrick Swayze fan and couldn't wait to see his latest movie. Jimmy didn't care about it one way or another, but he firmly believed that the "happy wife, happy life" trope was advice to live by. If Murph had taken this tip more to heart, he'd probably still be married. His ex-wife, Donna, always loved him, even after the divorce, but she couldn't stand taking a back seat to Murph's buddies and became lonely in his absence.

Despite an age difference of only two years, Jimmy couldn't remember more than a handful of times he and Murph hung out together, even as kids. Murph had always run with the jocks, which was in sharp contrast to Jimmy, who gravitated more to kids who liked messing around with engines and building things. The two brothers didn't move in the same circles and didn't have a lot in common. If they weren't brothers, Jimmy was fairly certain he and Murph wouldn't be lobstering together. But Jimmy's practical, grounded side tended to complement Murph's energetic nature, which is what made their business relationship click.

Jimmy felt the need to check in on Murph to make sure the dragger story of the day wasn't blown out of proportion. Although they knew a lot about the condition of the *Bay State Skye* when it was found, no one knew for sure what had happened or what had motivated two respected fishermen to behave in the way it appeared they had. Rumors could be damaging, and Jimmy was sure that tales would be flying at Fitzy's. He was thinking of his own family. He would have wanted someone to have his back if he was in the Golini brothers' situation, for the sake of his wife and kids. After all, they still had to live in this community, and it was hard enough losing their husbands and fathers in that way. There'd probably never be an answer to what had happened to the Golini brothers, and that was bound to eat at the family for the rest of their lives. Jimmy wanted to be sure the facts weren't muddied too much with speculation.

Fitzy's was within walking distance of Flannery's, with a view of the Gloucester pier where Flannery's stood. This suited it well because it blended in with the fish-processing plants and other industrial-type buildings in the neighborhood. If summer people were to drive by, which wasn't very likely unless they were interested in exploring the less glamorous side of the fishing industry, they would surely have judged Fitzy's, with its brick front and its tiny windows, a dive. Although lacking in any kind of aesthetic design, Fitzy's had been a popular hangout for locals for many years. Its wood-paneled bar was especially known for the variety of beers on tap, but the fact that Fitzy's had the cheapest drinks in town made it attractive to a lot of hardworking folks from Gloucester. Murph and Denny could always count on finding friends there, which made Fitzy's a fun place to relax and unwind after work. It had a jukebox, a pool table, and all the typical games you'd expect to find at any bar, but the friendly faces and personable bartenders were what kept its clientele coming back most evenings.

Jimmy walked in to see the usual group of homegrown Gloucester fishermen at their regular corner table. But tonight was somewhat different. There were a few faces he hadn't expected to see, possibly drawn to the bar to hear the inside scoop of what had happened to the dragger. Most people knew Murph spent his evenings at Fitzy's in the company of a few fisherman friends who had graduated from high school with him. This evening's overflow of customers probably had gotten word that he was present when the dragger was discovered. Buy him a few beers and Murph was an open book. And tonight, that book would make for extremely interesting listening.

Most people from Gloucester seldom ventured over the Cape Ann Bridge, which was the primary connection to the mainland for Gloucester and Rockport. There was no need to leave their beloved community. The philosophy of most people living on Cape Ann was that if it didn't have it, you simply didn't need it. Murph was no exception, and Denny had a similar mind-set. Denny had actually formulated a triangle of attractions from which he seldom wandered. The first point of the triangle was, of course, home. The second was work. The third was his favorite drinkery, Fitzy's. A triangle like that, according to Denny, was the recipe for a happy life. Of course, on Fridays his triangle became a trapezoid because Fridays were payday, and the bank had to be added so that he could cash his check. Sometimes he would come up a little short at the end of the week, and rather than leave out Fitzy's on Thursday nights, he would borrow money from someone with a little extra to spare toward the end of the week, then diligently pay them back as soon as his check was cashed. Everybody loved Denny, and it was easy to see why.

Murph and Denny waved Jimmy over to their corner table. They'd already ordered a beer for Jimmy, and it was sitting on the table in front of his reserved chair. Jimmy nodded his head to say hello to the other three men sitting there. Taking his seat, he lifted his beer from the table and chugged it down. He hadn't realized how thirsty he was until that moment, and the beer really hit the spot.

"Another beer, Patty," Murph called to the barmaid.

"No, no, no," Jimmy protested, calling to Patty, "I'm good

for now, thanks."

"It's fine Patty," replied Denny. "Bring it on over. It won't go to waste." Patty brought the beer and set it down between Denny and Jimmy.

Jimmy recognized the other three men at the table. All were locals. Two were lobstermen, and reliable ones at that. Interesting they chose tonight to spend with Murph and Denny.

"What are you two doing out tonight?" Jimmy asked the lobstermen. "I'd think you'd be getting some shut-eye so you could head out bright and early tomorrow morning. It's going to be another beauty of a day. You're not a Rizla, after all." He was referring to the series of lobster boats their owners named *Rizla* after their favorite brand of rolling papers made from rice, which were originally intended for rolling tobacco but more widely used by weed smokers.

"That's for sure," answered Sully Sullivan with a loud chuckle, brushing back his curly, reddish-brown hair, which was quickly being overtaken by gray. Sully had been lobstering for many years. Although he was of average size, he was strong, which was primarily a result of the heavy lifting that was part of being a solo lobster fisherman. "Have you seen those guys out there?"

"Yes, I have," confirmed Jimmy with a wry smile.

"All you see is them out there steaming. They run this way, and then they run that way, and you see smoke billowing out the windows of the pilothouse. It's like Cheech and Chong on the water!" Sully's comment produced an audible snicker from the men at his table, which proved contagious to the neighboring tables.

"Well, you can tell one of those guys by the catch they bring in," Jimmy added. "I've seen them come in with barely two hundred pounds."

"Most of those guys just scrape by and go home and live with their parents. It's about all they can do," said Sully. "They get just enough for beer and weed money. They're out at eight in the morning because they have to be in at noon so that they can be plastered by two. That's their reality. Us real lobstermen get in around dark, pushing around six or seven hundred pounds for the day, and they're smashing beer bottles in a rage because they think everyone should be at their level instead of doing any better."

"No damned ambition," said Johnny Higgins, another successful lobsterman who happened to be Sully's best friend. Both their faces were weathered and lined with wrinkles, an occupational hazard brought on by days and years spent in the salty wind and sun. Johnny and Sully were both pushing forty but looked close to seventy to anyone who didn't know better. As with Sully, Johnny's full head of dark-brown hair was quickly graying, but he was in just as good shape as the rest of the lobstermen. It was a perk of their occupation. They looked ancient, but they had the strength of young men.

"I don't think I've seen you in Fitzy's before. I was under the impression you frequented more swanky establishments. Did you get a sudden desire to see how the other half lives?" Jimmy teased.

"Oh, I think you know the answer to that," piped up the third man, Robby Murdock, who owned a popular breakfast and luncheon joint down the street. Although Robby was close to Sully and Johnny's age, he looked amazingly young. His daily jog and an indoor job that kept him hopping were like a fountain of youth. Every short black hair was in place, with not a speck of gray to be found. Each of them—Sully, Johnny, and Robby—had a wife and kids at home, which made it even more strange they'd be out at Fitzy's tonight. "We wanted to get the straight scoop from the horse's mouth," Robby confessed.

"We heard the Golini brothers were dragging for lobsters inside state lines. That's really hard to believe from those guys," said Johnny.

"I know. We were surprised ourselves," said Murph as he got up to use the restroom. "But someone's lost a trawl line worth some substantial dinero, from the looks of it." He headed off down a dark corridor at the other end of the bar and disappeared.

"Did you get what you came here for?" Jimmy asked Sully.

"I'd say so," Sully said with a grin, but then he said, "Jimmy, I'll tell you what. I'll trade you a dragger story for a dragger story.

How's that sound?"

"I'm always interested in a good dragger tale," said Jimmy, remembering how much he enjoyed Sully's company.

"Good," Sully continued. "I had found the best damned lobstering spot I've ever had, inside state lines on soft bottom. I invested just about all the trawl lines and traps I owned in that one place and didn't tell a soul where they were." Sully made a motion with his thumb and index finger at his mouth like he was locking a door, turning the key, and throwing it away.

"A spot like that doesn't come along every day," Jimmy agreed.

"Exactly," Sully said. "So, I was steaming out to my secret location, which shall remain secret just in case lightning strikes twice." Sully paused and grinned, taking a drink of his beer before continuing. "And I see this dragger, right in the area where my traps are. It was Ferrero's boat out of Gloucester, and the son of a bitch had dragged right through my trawl line. As I steamed up to the dragger, the three men on board were busy cutting my traps and line out of their nets and off the dragger doors. So, I yelled to them, 'Hey, those are my traps you've got there!'" Sully took another gulp of beer and, leaning back, continued his story. "And Ferrero called back, with what appeared to be an authentically concerned look on his face, 'You mean these traps here?' He held up one of the traps he was in the process of untangling. 'Yes, that's one of mine,' I called to him. He looked me square in the eye and asked, 'Do you want it back?' And I said, 'Yes, I do.' And do you know what that bastard did? He cut my trap and line free of his dragger door and dropped it in the water, where it quickly sank and disappeared, right in front of me."

"You must have wanted to kill him. I know I would have. What'd you do?" asked Jimmy.

"What could I do?" Sully asked. "I got in my pilothouse and headed back to shore. I'd lost thousands of dollars of equipment that day. It was probably the worst day at sea I ever had."

"Then Ferrero got away with it?" Jimmy asked.

"Not exactly," answered Sully. "I did what any law-abiding

lobsterman would do. I went to the Coast Guard, filed a complaint, and took him to court. They didn't get him for fishing in a closed area, which they should have because he was about a mile inside the line, but there was no way to prove it. But he was found guilty of molesting gear and given a hefty fine, and he lost his license to fish for thirty days."

"At least you got some satisfaction," Jimmy told Sully.

"You'd think so, but he appealed the decision, mainly so he could keep fishing," Sully added. "Well, the following spring, Ferrero was coming back from buying swordfish in Nova Scotia, crossing the Gulf of Maine with a load of illegally bought fish he was taking back to sell as his own catch in Gloucester, when he ran into a bad southwester and capsized, sank, and drowned."

Patty stopped by to bring a couple more pitchers of beer and, having overheard the last comment asked, "What's a southwester? Is that like a nor'easter?"

"A southwester's a strong windstorm," answered Robby, who had lived in Gloucester for his entire life. Even though he didn't fish, he'd heard the term enough to know.

"It's not the rain that keeps boats tied up during a storm," added Johnny. "It's the wind. It can be a perfectly sunny day, and if the wind is high, any experienced fisherman will stay on shore until the wind dies down. Even the fish processors know that if a bad windstorm is predicted, there ain't gonna be a lot of fish around, so they'd better load up on fish early to weather the storm."

"That's right," Sully continued. "There was another boat just in front of Ferrero returning to Gloucester, too. He saw what happened and didn't go back to try to save him. He just didn't care."

"Wow," Patty remarked, hanging around for the rest of the story. "That's harsh."

"Yep," Sully said. "So about four or five months later, the state called me up to see if I was ready to go to court with Ferrero. And I told the person who called that it wouldn't do us any good 'cause he's dead. Do you believe that? They didn't even know. And that's my dragger tale. A fair trade for yours, wouldn't you say?"

"Yes, I would," said Jimmy as Murph reappeared to take his place at the table.

"Took you long enough," Jimmy said to Murph.

"Oh, I ran into a guy I went to school with, Joey Barthelmes. You remember him; he had seven brothers and sisters and lived on Maple Street?" Murph said.

"I suppose you've been telling him about your day?" asked Jimmy.

"A little," said Murph, flashing a sheepish smile. Then he added, "Well, he had heard about the dragger and really wanted to know the truth about it."

"I hope that's all you told him," said Jimmy.

"I don't need to embellish this one. The truth is a great story in itself," said Murph.

Jimmy turned back to Sully. "Well, Ferrero was obviously a snake. What I don't get is why the Golini brothers, who appeared to be honest guys and were well liked in town, would resort to dragging through a lobster trawl. Their boat was loaded with fresh fish. It's got to have been plain greed that made them stop to drag for lobsters within the state line on their way in. They would have known there was a good chance of dragging up some lobster trawls. They were family men. Men like the Golini brothers don't usually do things like that."

Sully sat quietly for a moment, then said in a low voice, "I wasn't gonna say anything, mainly because I'm pretty sure the Golini brothers' families don't know yet. But hell, everyone in town will know before long. I'd just rather it not come from me and would appreciate it if this didn't get around."

Everyone looked at Murph. "I won't tell a soul," said Murph. "I swear. The dragger story is giving me plenty of mileage. I don't need anything else to talk about."

"Well," continued Sully, "the Golini brothers are—or I guess I should say, were—very successful fishermen. When they began to bring in a substantial amount of money, they hired an accountant to handle the financial end of the business. From what I understand, the accountant pretty much swindled the Golinis, leaving them with a lot of debt. I think they were trying to make extra cash any way they could to avoid the inevitable task of telling their families what had happened."

"How did you find that out?" asked Jimmy.

Sully leaned in. "I was waiting to fuel up at Rose's Marine when the *Bay State Skye* was just finishing. When Billy asked to put his fuel on credit, Rose's manager was called over and hesitated to give his approval. Billy insisted he'd always paid his bills and that he was good for it. But the manager told him that hadn't been the case for the last few months since their accountant ran off with their money. Billy's account at Rose's was in arrears, mostly for fuel and supplies, and it was becoming a concern. Normally, I wouldn't say anything, but the family's going to have to be told. Maybe they'll be able to hunt down the crooked accountant and get some of their money back, but so far, the Golini brothers had had little luck on that end, from what I overheard. Billy was pretty agitated, and although the manager at Rose's was being discreet, it was pretty easy to figure out what was going on."

"Well that puts a whole new light on things, don't it?" said Denny.

"You hear about that happening all the time," said Jimmy.

"Poor bastards," said Murph.

"Well, that explains why they were dragging for lobsters, but it doesn't give an indication as to why both men suddenly disappeared," said Johnny.

"Maybe they owed somebody a whole lot of money," said Murph. "Maybe when they first realized their accountant had stolen their life savings they panicked and borrowed money from the wrong people just to keep their boat in the water. The Golini brothers obviously weren't able to pay the money back, especially with the kind of interest those guys want, and so maybe those guys steamed out to encourage the Golinis to pay up."

"It's possible," said Denny, "but killing them guys would make sure they'd never get their money back."

"Maybe they didn't mean to kill them. Maybe they meant to scare them, you know, to let them know they weren't safe, even at sea. And maybe something went wrong and they were forced to kill them. There were two brothers together, and from what I've heard, the Golini brothers wouldn't have backed down from a fight. They would have defended each other and their boat," Murph rationalized.

"Maybe this, maybe that . . . and we're off to speculation land," said Jimmy to Murph.

"It just makes sense," said Murph. "That's what my money's on."

"He's got a point," said Sully.

"Well, the Golini brothers don't need us adding anymore to the story. As you said, Murph, the story is good enough to stand on its own, with no embellishments," said Jimmy. He was beginning to see what Murph liked about Fitzy's. There was a real feeling of camaraderie.

"It's possible, but not probable," Johnny piped up. "Let me tell you a true story of something that happened to me that might shed some light on a more likely scenario."

"We're all ears," said Murph, annoyed that Johnny had blown off his theory as not being probable.

"It was a lousy day, with a lot of tide and chop, years ago, the day I almost got it," recalled Johnny, ignoring Murph's sarcasm. "I had a trawl caught up for a couple of weeks, and I kept hauling from the western end, thinking it would come out, but it didn't. So I told Pat, who was my crew that day, to stand clear 'cause I was gonna set the line back, which would release the traps and trawl back into the sea. My plan was to turn the boat around and try to pull the traps from the other direction, hoping it would free the line from whatever was holding it to the bottom. I unwrapped the line from the hauler to create some slack to lift the line off the upper pulley. But when I flipped the line out from the pulley, a turn of it went around my thumb. I figured it was just gonna slip off, but it got tight instead. Before I knew it, the line had closed around my thumb and was dragging me to the rail of the boat, where the now-freed trawl line and traps were dropping back into the sea. By now, I was hanging over the railing with my feet hovering above the deck. I yelled to Pat to get a knife to cut the line because it wasn't slipping off. He grabbed a knife from a box, but by the time he got it, my hand was in the water. Now I was up on the rail with my feet in the air, and Pat cried out, 'I can't reach you.' And I yelled back to him, 'Then you've got to cut my thumb off—you've got to cut something— because I'm going if you don't.' Just as I said that, the rope let go. I don't know why because when I took my glove off, the middle part of my thumb was the size of a pencil, and the top of my thumb was swollen wide, with blood squirting out of my thumbnail. If I'd gone over, I'd have been dead; Pat couldn't have gotten me back in time. By the time he'd turned the boat around, I'd have been dead. The depths out there were about a hundred and twenty feet. It was February, to boot, and cold. You don't last long in those waters, ten minutes at the most. Hypothermia sets in quickly. The only thing you can do in that situation is to take a couple of deep breaths and get it over with fast. I hope that's what the Golini brothers did. No sense suffering."

Jimmy listened to Johnny's story, nodding in agreement. "It's dangerous, especially if you've got an open stern with the ropes going by your feet. When you're turned and doing something you've got to do, and you're away from the controls, one turn of the rope on your leg and you're out the stern. They find the boat, but they'll never find you. Remember, that happened to old man Benson. They could probably have found his body if they wanted. It would more than likely have been tangled in the gear, but they don't send dive teams out. The state police come out and check the islands, but no one ever goes in the water. You're just gone."

"That was a sad day," Robby piped up. "Benson's daughter was about to be married that Saturday. Benson's future son-in-law went out with the search team in hopes they could find Benson, but they had no luck. The father-of-the-bride had just disappeared, same as the Golini brothers. It's a sad reality of fishing, but it happens all the time."

"I guess we all could tell a similar story," Sully added. "We all love it. But let's face it; if we're honest with ourselves, fishing's a risky business. Even when you're doing everything right, crap can happen."

"I think we're all a little in denial," said Jimmy.

"Hey, do ya think?" added Denny. "Why do ya think I work on dry land? The money's not as good as you guys are making, but for the most part, I know I'm coming home every night."

"Personally," said Murph, "I never think about it. I guess there's a part of you that thinks, that's never going to be me. You learn to trust your luck, I guess."

"That's the least of your worries," said Johnny. "If it happens, it happens. I'm not gonna sit here and worry about it. My attention's focused on the mooring inside Gloucester Harbor that I've been in line to get for about a year. I'm legitimately next in line for it, but the harbormaster's thinking of passing me over to moor a sailboat in my spot instead. It used to be that when a commercial fishing boat gave up a mooring in the harbor, it was replaced by another commercial fishing boat. But now, when a fishing boat gives up its spot, the harbormaster immediately replaces it with a recreational boat, usually a sailboat."

"People have been attracted to Gloucester for years because it's always been a working fishing village," Robby observed. "They love the romantic idea of a working fisherman's port, but they want to get rid of anything that isn't picturesque and touristy, like a working commercial fishing boat or a fish plant. Most of them aren't too attractive, and they don't smell like roses, but they're crucial to the survival of the fishing industry. Local fishermen have lost control of the harbor and the docks to people coming in from outside the area."

"Ain't that the truth," said Jimmy. "Good luck, Johnny. I hope the vote goes your way. We don't need another sailboat moored in the harbor." Jimmy got up and stretched. "I guess I need to get home to my wife and kids. I called Jenny to tell her about the Golini brothers so that she wouldn't worry, but hearing something like that always scares the heck out of families whose husbands and fathers work the sea. I haven't told her that Murph and I found the boat yet. I thought I'd save that for when we were face to face."

Everyone agreed that made sense. They'd enjoyed their evening together at Fitzy's, but the truth was, whether they acknowledged it or not, the fishermen themselves were always reminded of their own mortality whenever there was an accident at sea. It helped to talk the day's events over with friends in the same line of work, though. Tomorrow would be another day, and the buyers representing area fish dealers would be arriving at the auction house at five in the morning to start bidding on the *Bay State Skye*'s catch. That is, all the catch except the ten totes that were bought by Congressman Contoro, which were scheduled for pickup and trucking to Boston first thing in the morning.

CHAPTER 4

Vinnie Andreas pulled into Flannery's parking lot at quarter to five in the morning, parked his truck, and opened the door. He slid off the seat and dropped to the ground, instantly smelling the dumpster located near the back dock that was full of crab shells. Flannery's crew knew enough to call the waste-disposal company as soon as the dumpster was full, but they were at the mercy of the company's pickup schedule. The warm nights and days changed what had the potential to be a great, exhilarating gasp of fresh, salty air into a slight gag as he made his way to the six-wheeler International Harvester truck that waited for him.

August was Vinnie's favorite month of the year to work as Flannery's buyer at the Gloucester Seafood Display Auction. It was easier to crawl out of bed at four thirty in the morning when the air was warm and the sun was beginning to peek over the sea. Vinnie paused for a moment at the dock behind Flannery's to look out toward the breakwater. He had heard about the Golini brothers' disappearance just before going to bed the night before. Having been involved in some facet of the fish business for most of his life, he knew the Golinis and was in disbelief at the possibility they both could be gone.

Vinnie was a Gloucester boy, hailing from a proud, first-generation Greek American family. His grandparents, who hadn't accompanied the rest of the family to America, remained in Patra, and because they were fairly well off, Vinnie never wanted for anything in his life.

That allowed him the luxury of showing his true, devilish nature. Although he was an average-size man, he had a boyish smile, an abundance of energy, and charming dark eyes that could get him out of many a tight spot smelling like a rose. Because of his job, he was in great shape, and when looking at any situation, he always tried to manipulate it to work things out to his benefit, even if it meant the use of shady tactics, his specialty.

He watched the sun come into full view as memories rolled over in his mind. Working with a much younger Billy Golini on the Boston Fish Pier had been one of his most memorable jobs. The work of a lumper was tough, but the pay was good, and the trickery the job allowed was entertaining enough to keep the work from becoming mundane.

The two youths unloaded boats for one of the fish dealers on the pier. The Boston Fish Pier didn't have a display auction like Gloucester had, where the fish from each boat could be scrutinized for quality before the auction began. Discriminating Boston dealers would only buy the top of the catch, which was the freshest, being caught last. This fish wasn't burdened with the weight of the entire catch compressing it, as was often the case with the bottom of the pile, which was caught first. Many dealers would purchase all the fish off the boat, sight unseen, for a better price. Whether a dealer bought from a particular boat depended on its reputation for catching good fish and taking care of it as they headed back to the pier.

Vinnie used a vital tool to off-load boats: a tractor with five trailers trailing behind it. Each trailer contained three boxes, lined up in a row, each box equipped with two metal hooks where a hoist could be connected to lift it to the fishing vessel. Because the entire boat was being off-loaded before the fish were weighed, there was a system in place to simplify the weigh-in process. A lumper from the dealer purchasing the boat's fish would drive the first empty trailer onto the scale, and the scale worker would write down the tier weight, including the boxes, in crayon on the front box. That figure was the designated tier weight for every trailer pulled by the tractor.

It seemed logical. It was a labor-saving procedure that both the boat owner and the dealer could depend on for being an accurate weight for the fish, without having to unload each box of fish onto a scale. But Vinnie's boss had found a way to snag a few more pounds of fish for his company, without anyone being the wiser. Each eight-foot-long trailer had two steel rails at its base to support it. But the lead trailer that Vinnie was using to establish the tier weight for his entire string of trailers had another hundred-pound rail welded onto its base. The four trailers following it didn't have that additional rail. Because the first trailer was the only one weighed, each of the others would pick up—but not pay for—an extra hundred pounds of fish. A fishing boat that had a successful trip could easily come in with upward of ten thousand pounds of fish in its hull, so the difference wouldn't be detected by the boat owner.

Of course, you could simply slip the scale man a few hundred dollars to shave the weight somewhat as well. But that got to be expensive. Everyone played games in the fish business. If you were half-asleep, you wouldn't be in business very long.

Billy Golini was an unknowing pawn in the deceptive practices Vinnie enjoyed, an honest man even in his youth. A few years later, when they both were working for a Boston dealer not located directly on the pier, Billy had caught a trucker attempting to steal a full bag of scallops. It was the middle of winter, and he had been told to help unload a truck from New Bedford that had a fresh load of sea scallops on board. As Billy carefully placed the forty-pound cotton bags of scallops into a tote held by a forklift, he noticed the trucker squirreling away a bag behind a plastic board in the box of the truck.

"Hey, what are you doing?" he asked the driver.

"That one's for me," the driver answered with a shifty smile and a menacing look.

"Oh no, that's not gonna be happening," Billy replied.

"Oh yeah?" The trucker approached Billy, ending up practically chest to chest with him, looking him square in the eye. Billy matched the trucker's glare, even though he had about fifty pounds and a couple of inches on him.

But, as with everything in the fish business, the inside of the scallop truck was wet. Scallop juice had seeped out of the bags, and with the freezing temperatures, it had become icy. Uncomfortable with the closeness of the trucker, Billy took a step backward and slipped on the ice, falling back against the side of the truck. As his feet slipped, Billy's arms reached upward in an effort to regain his balance. As his arms flailed, he accidentally hit the trucker's chest, pushing him slightly backward. The trucker, who was close to the back of the truck, lost his balance and slipped on the ice himself. He landed on his butt and rolled off the truck, falling about five feet onto the icy pavement below. His head slammed back with the force of the fall, knocking him out cold. An ambulance was called, and as it arrived, the dazed trucker regained consciousness. Billy never heard from the trucker or his company again.

A missing bag of scallops would never have been detected because scallops lost weight if they were stored out of water, just as lobsters did. The weight of the scallops loaded into the truck would never match their weight at their destination. Billy diligently brought the entire load of scallops to the scale, including the one the driver had salted away, and weighed them to assure the weight was reasonable compared to what the New Bedford dealer claimed was on the truck. Vinnie respected Billy's honesty but enjoyed a challenging scheme now and then to break up the monotony of the overwhelmingly dull job.

Because the second dealer who employed Vinnie and Billy wasn't located on the Boston Fish Pier, Vinnie's practice of weighing in a heavy first trailer wouldn't work anymore. But that didn't stop him and his foreman from dreaming up a new plan of deception. Dealers not quartered on the pier itself would truck their purchased fish back to their processing plants using large blue plastic barrels. Vinnie would meet a boat at the Boston Fish Pier dock with enough barrels at the ready to take in all the fish bought. The fish was off-loaded from the boat using canvas baskets hoisted from the deck of the boat to the dock. Fish would be emptied into the barrels from the baskets. A full barrel of fish would weigh, on average, four hundred pounds. Barrels weren't normally weighed; a full barrel was usually assumed to be four hundred pounds. Of course, there was dickering between the dealer and the boat owner. If the barrel wasn't quite full, the dealer would insist on shaving twenty or thirty pounds off the load. If there was a significant amount of ice attached to the fish going into the barrel, the weight would be adjusted accordingly.

There were often two or three dealers collecting their fish from the same boat as it was being unloaded. A boat captain would have to keep a sharp eye out, maintaining accurate records of how many barrels each dealer was taking. One dealer might be interested in the top of the catch, whereas another might only want to purchase the flounder or haddock. As Vinnie and Billy filled each barrel from the baskets that were being lowered to the dock, their foreman would occasionally instigate an argument with the boat captain about the quality of his fish.

"Look at this fish," the foreman exclaimed in one instance, confronting the boat captain. "It's garbage. You expect me to pay full price for this?"

"What's wrong with it?" the irate captain fired back. "It's been iced since it was caught. Do you even know what you're looking at? You're out of your friggin' mind!"

"I've been a buyer in this business for twenty years," the foreman shot back as he motioned with his hand behind his back for Vinnie to load three barrels on his truck while he kept the boat captain distracted. Vinnie dutifully rolled the barrels to the truck as the foreman picked up a fish from a canvas basket as far away from Vinnie as possible.

"Smell this!" the foreman demanded as he shoved the fish

toward the boat captain's face.

"Get out of here," the captain cried out as he shoved the foreman and the limp codfish as far away as he could. "If you don't want the fish, leave it. There are plenty of dealers who'd be thrilled to buy fish off my boat!"

"Well, let me see," the foreman said as he began to calm down, noting that Vinnie had managed to get the three barrels into the truck without being noticed. "Maybe it's not as bad as I thought."

"Damned right it's not!" exclaimed the captain, still angry at the foreman's accusation.

"No, I guess you're right," said the foreman as he lifted the fish to his own nose and took a whiff. "It's actually pretty decent," he said and placed the fish in a waiting barrel, putting his hand on the captain's shoulder. "OK, I've got these eight barrels right here. Let's settle up."

The captain made out the slip for the eight barrels, eager to send the insolent foreman on his way. The foreman paid the captain and turned toward his truck, loaded with eleven barrels of fish to go back to the plant. The foreman nudged Vinnie and said, "Remind me to give that boat captain a good Christmas gift. Do you know how much fish we've lifted from him this year?"

"Yep," answered Vinnie with a smile. Then he went to help Billy, who was wheeling the purchased barrels to the truck.

*   *   *   *   *

Vinnie was startled from his daydream by a truck pulling up next to his. It was Jimmy, who had arrived to install a hauler he'd just picked up from Rose's Marine before heading out for the day.

"Hey, Vinnie," Jimmy said as he brushed by on the way to his boat. "Terrible thing about Billy Golini and his brother. Didn't you work with Billy when you both were first starting out?"

"Sure did," Vinnie recalled sadly. "I was just thinking about those days with Billy. He was a good guy. Can't believe he's gone."

Jimmy slapped Vinnie on the shoulder, "He's one of us, no matter what. We grieve one another like family, fishermen, you know? That's the way it is."

"Yeah, it is. Well, I'd better get to the auction. There's a lot of fish down there, not to mention Billy's. Flannery's planning to buy some of *Bay State Skye*'s haddock and flounder. I guess it's their way of helping the family out."

"I'll catch you later, then," Jimmy said as he headed down the gangplank.

Vinnie climbed into the International Harvester, glad that it was summer and the engine would turn over easily. When the weather was cold, the truck needed an electric engine heater to ensure it would start in the morning. Vinnie had driven off with the block heater extension cord still plugged in so many times that the manager began wrapping the extension cord around the driver's side door handle multiple times to remind him to unplug the truck before he took off for the auction.

"Where's my head today?" he asked himself as he climbed out of the truck to retrieve the paperwork waiting for him in the office. He fumbled for the key to the retail door and, once through, turned to punch the alarm code into the keypad. Walking behind the retail counter, he made his way to the small deserted office and grabbed his clipboard. Then he turned quickly to get back to his truck. It was five to five, and he was about to be late to the auction. He wanted to get a chance to check out Billy's fish, partly because he was planning to purchase a good chunk of the catch and partly to satisfy a nagging curiosity about the circumstances surrounding the discovery of the *Bay State Skye*.

Vinnie skipped the road check due to the time. He had a valid reason today, but the truth was, he rarely checked the tires, the lights, the gauges, or anything else he was required to on his class two vehicle. Luckily, the auction was only a short distance down the road and in a matter of minutes, he was pulling in and getting in line. He'd missed his chance to nab the prime spot by the auction house's loading-dock doors. There were five trucks in front of him now, the first from Colbert's Seafood Company in Boston. It was already being loaded with the fish Congressman Contoro had bought from the *Bay State Skye* the evening before. Vinnie stayed in his truck a minute longer because the first truck had just closed its rear doors and was getting ready to leave. As the royal-blue Colbert's truck headed down the main drag toward Route 128, Vinnie and the other three trucks moved up a space.

Vinnie left his truck and hustled in to check out the *Bay State Skye's* fish. Parting the plastic strips to the cooler, he noticed he wasn't alone in wanting to buy the Golini brothers' fish. There were two other buyers standing alongside the row of stacked totes labeled "*Bay State Skye,*" examining the catch. As they walked off, Vinnie made his way down the makeshift aisles, constructed of totes filled with fish from all the boats that had been unloaded and tallied the day before. It had been a busy day, which wasn't unusual for a Wednesday, especially considering a few boats might have delayed their trip out due to the windy conditions of the previous weekend. The *Bay State Skye's* catch was located at the very back of the maze of stacked totes. Vinnie picked up a haddock and, noticing the scales still firmly attached and the clear eyes of the fish, knew the rumors were true; Billy's catch was as good as he'd heard. He returned to the auction floor and sat in his usual seat. Flannery's was a member of the auction, which gave him the perk of having his seat reserved for him. It was nothing fancy, of course. The buyers' reserved seats were actually high school students' desks. His seat had the particleboard half desk on the left, to accommodate his being left-handed.

Vinnie took out his clipboard and looked at the list of fish the buyer from Flannery's Boston division was expecting from the Gloucester auction. The buyer was willing to go as high as $6.25 a pound for market haddock because they had an order for an event at the Parker House Hotel and needed the fish. Because it was summertime in Boston, market and scrod haddock would be an easy sell to the restaurants Flannery's sold to. In addition to scrod haddock, flounder was requested for the retail market in Gloucester, which also sold to stores and restaurants on Cape Ann. The *Bay State Skye* had fifteen hundred pounds of market haddock, another thousand pounds of scrod haddock, a thousand pounds of flounder, and five hundred pounds of hake and cod. Vinnie looked at his price-per-pound limits for the rest of the fish listed, based on how much the buyer thought he could sell the fish for and the percentages of waste he was projecting during the cutting of the fish. The fish was brand new and in great shape, so the percentages were expected to be good with experienced cutters on the line. Once he had decided to bid on all the *Bay State Skye* had brought in, Vinnie scooched down in his chair, folded his arms across his chest, and took a nap.

The Gloucester auction began with bidding on some of the smaller boats' catches that were brought in on Wednesday, earlier in the day. When it looked like the next up would be the market haddock from the Golinis' boat, Marco Sousa, owner of the local Sousa's Seafood, a smaller restaurant, sat down next to Vinnie, nudging him awake.

"Weren't you going to bid on the markets from the Golinis' boat?" Marco asked.

"Oh yeah," Vinnie said as he straightened up in his seat, rubbing the side of his head. "Have they gotten that far yet?"

"Just about," Marco replied with an air of urgency in his voice. "Listen, I really need three hundred pounds of market haddock, but I can't go higher than five seventy-five a pound. If I sit tight and don't bid against you on the markets and scrod, will you sell me three hundred pounds of markets at the price you pay?"

"Sure, I can do that," Vinnie replied. "I doubt they'll get too much more for the markets anyway if you don't bid against me. But I want to be sure Jill Golini and Billy's kids see some money from this. They're probably going to need it."

"I don't care if that family sees a single red penny from the *Bay State Skye's* catch!" Sousa declared. "With what those Golini brothers did to that lobster trawl line! You know whose trawl that was, don't you?"

"I didn't know they'd identified the owner," Vinnie said, a bit taken aback by the vicious tone of Sousa's voice.

"It was Johnny's trawl! He lost a pretty penny out there yesterday. Damn near took out most of his lines and pots. Not a chance of recovering them either. They're just gone. And for what? To pinch a few hundred pounds of illegal lobsters on the way in?" Sousa ended his rant by quietly pounding Vinnie's desk with his fist.

"Wow," Vinnie remarked. "I had no idea. Johnny and I go way back. I spent four years in just about every class in high school with him. We were thick as thieves. Still are, really. That sucks. Does he know?"

"The word around town is that the Coast Guard's going to let him know today. But if I know, and you know, I'm pretty sure it won't be too long before Johnny'll hear about it from someone." Sousa shook his head. "A damn shame. Johnny should be getting the proceeds from the catch, not the Golini families."

This was a substantial dilemma for Vinnie. He knew and respected Billy Golini, but Sousa had a point. And Vinnie had to admit he cared far more for Johnny than he ever had for Billy. Johnny was a true friend, the kind of friend he could count on to help him hide the body, if it ever came to that. He was pretty sure Billy wouldn't turn him in—he hadn't told on him with all his antics at the Boston Fish Pier. Billy had to have known about some of them, even though he hadn't let on. But Vinnie wouldn't have been able to depend on Billy if he got into a real jam. Of that, he was sure.

"You've got a point," Vinnie said. "But the *Bay State Skye's* fish are coming up soon. Do we have a deal?"

"Sure do," Sousa said, patting Vinnie on the shoulder and moving to his appointed seat in the back of the room. The deal had been made in the nick of time; the auctioneer was about to start selling the *Bay State Skye's* fish.

"We're going to start the bidding for the markets at five twenty-five," Gino, the auction-floor foreman, announced. "As most of you already know, we lost two family members yesterday at sea. Billy and

Tony Golini disappeared from their dragger yesterday afternoon. The Coast Guard did a surface search of the waters where the dragger was found abandoned and buzzed the islands, but there was no sign of either man. We're sending the proceeds from the sale of the *Bay State Skye's* fish to the Golini family, so let's try to get them a good return.

"Hmmp!" Vinnie heard Sousa murmur from the back of the room, and he was really glad that was all he had to say.

Gino handed the auction back to Bob, the auctioneer. Bob, a tall, rugged retired fisherman with a weathered face, was fairly fast-talking, and he loved still being a part of the trade. "OK, who'll give me an opening bid of five twenty-five?" Bob asked.

Vinnie raised his index finger in the air.

"I have five twenty-five right there," Bob said, pointing to Vinnie. "Do I have five thirty-five?"

The buyer from Colbert's Seafood Company raised his hand. Vinnie looked out of the corner of his eye to see who had just bid, not wishing to look concerned. Colbert's had deep pockets and was a fierce competitor of Flannery's, with both companies' main branches located in Boston. This might not be good, Vinnie thought to himself. But then he remembered that Colbert's had just picked up the fish the congressman bought the night before, and they wouldn't want to push the price up too high.

"I have five thirty-five from the young man at Colbert's. Do I have five forty-five?" the auctioneer's voice sang out.

Vinnie opened his hand and raised it slightly, just enough to get the auctioneer's attention.

"I have five forty-five from Flannery's. Do I have five sixty? Five sixty anybody? Anyone five sixty?" called the auctioneer.

Vinnie sat deep in his seat, looking as relaxed as he could, counting on Colbert's buyer having been given a limit. Seconds dragged on like minutes until Colbert's rep raised his hand again.

"Damn!" Vinnie said under his breath.

"I have five sixty from Colbert's. Do I have five seventy-five? Five seventy-five?" The auctioneer was looking right at Vinnie. Vinnie glanced back at Sousa, who was sitting in silence, leaning forward, with his head resting in the palm of his hand. The pose was relaxed, but the intensity in his eyes told a different story. He wanted that fish badly, and it looked like it might slip out of reach in the next minute.

Vinnie raised his left index finger again, with his elbow still resting on the arm of his desk. He was trying to look apathetic, like he really didn't care whether he got the fish or not. He had some wiggle room left in the limit for what he could pay, but he wanted to help Sousa out if he could. He knew this was Sousa's last chance.

"I have five seventy-five right there. That's five seventy-five to Flannery's. Do I have five eighty-five?" The auctioneer's voice was excitedly hopeful.

Colbert's buyer glanced at Vinnie and read his nonchalant look. Maybe Flannery's was less interested in buying the Golini brothers' market haddock and more interested in bidding up the price, knowing Colbert's would be stuck paying the auction price for the fish they'd bought from Congressman Contoro the night before. Considering that, Colbert's buyer decided to let the fish go and let Flannery's get it for five seventy-five per pound. Better to do that and pay the same price for the congressman's fish that Flannery's paid for the auction fish, than to take a chance of getting the whole load at a much higher price. This way they'd be able to compete with or possibly beat Flannery's price to restaurants if their cutters were more skilled than Flannery's, which remained to be seen.

"Do I have five eighty-five? Five eighty-five anyone?" the auctioneer sang out, looking directly at Colbert's buyer. The tall, thin man just sat there with his arms crossed.

"OK, five eighty, then. Who will give me five eighty? Five eighty?" the auctioneer pleaded.

Nothing. Nobody moved. Everyone on the floor sat stone still, eyes looking away, focused on the floor, the wall, anywhere but the auctioneer. It was done.

"Five seventy-five going once. Five seventy-five going twice. Sold to Flannery's for five seventy-five," the auctioneer announced, tapping a paperweight to his desk to make it official.

The look of relief on Marco Sousa's face was palpable. He'd gotten what he wanted. He strolled by Vinnie and said, "I'll meet you over at Flannery's in a half hour."

"Good enough," Vinnie replied as he walked by, looking straight ahead. He didn't want the auction house or the other buyers to know the two had made a deal to keep the price low. Vinnie returned to his desk to buy all the scrod haddock and cod from the *Bay State Skye*'s load, along with some hake that was fairly popular with the local old-timers who came into Flannery's retail market. He was outbid on the flounder, so he had to leave that behind. There were more boats due in today, so there'd be another chance to buy flounder at tomorrow's auction.

Vinnie began collecting his totes of fish by the loading dock and walked by a tote belonging to the dealer who had outbid him for the *Bay State Skye*'s flounder. He eyed the flounder as he dragged his tote full of haddock behind him, using a long hook to pull it along. Remembering that Flannery's had promised a couple of medium-size flounder to a school for a fish-printing activity, he reached in and grabbed two fish as he walked by. Tossing the flounder into his tote without missing a step, Vinnie made his way to his truck to wait his turn to load the fish he'd bought. The scraping sound of the plastic tote being dragged across the wet cement floor was uninterrupted during the entire event. Nobody noticed. Not that he cared if they did. He was sure he was just returning the favor for some other time another dealer had swiped a few fish from him.

By the time Vinnie got to his truck, he was next in line. He quickly backed up to the loading dock, waiting to hear the usual thud that indicated he could back no farther. He watched as the auction's forklift operator loaded several pallets of fish totes into the back, then dragged a few of the loose totes into the truck with his hook. Closing the back of the truck, he headed to Flannery's, following the same procedure in reverse when he arrived at Flannery's dock.

"How many pounds of these markets does Boston want?" Vinnie

yelled to the office as he walked through the plastic strips of the large garage door at the loading dock. The small six-by-ten office stood directly in front of him now, and because it was constructed on three sides with a half wall and glass to the ceiling, Vinnie could see the astonished looks on everybody's face.

"What's up?" he said as he entered through the spring-loaded metal office door.

The small office was crowded. Murph and Jimmy were leaning against the ten-foot Formica counter that ran the length of the room, and Denny was at the other end, collecting the lobster order tickets. Flannery's Gloucester plant manager, Paul, and the retail and lobster-room manager, Meredith, were sitting on the tall, uncomfortable stools at the counter, which had a height that was clearly designed for work to be done in a standing position.

Both Paul and Meredith were in their midthirties, but he looked considerably older than she. This was partly because of his curly, salt-and-pepper hair, which was in sharp contrast to her straight, medium-length, light-brown hair, and partly because she was tall and slender, contrasting with his more rugged appearance. Paul's legs were like tree trunks, and his arms were equally muscular. He didn't work out; he just grew up that way. Meredith often told him if there was ever any trouble, she was a runner, not a fighter. Any brawls would be left for him to settle.

Vinnie's greeting was met with a "Shh!" from the room. Everyone was listening intently to the radio.

"At five twenty-five this morning, a truck loaded with fish overturned on the Southeast Expressway by the Storrow Drive exit. It caused a chain-reaction crash involving six other vehicles that all simultaneously slammed on their brakes to avoid the overturned truck and spilled fish. The driver of a white pickup is being cited for a DUI and driving to endanger. According to the fish truck driver, the white pickup swerved in front of him, cutting him off. He turned the wheel to avoid the pickup, and that was when the truck overturned. The good news: there were no injuries. The bad news: this fish is really starting to stink, and with a prediction of ninety-seven degrees today, it's going to be a scorcha! I'm sure they're trying to get this mess picked up as soon as they can. Traffic, as you can imagine, is all backed up. That's it from here." The reporter threw the broadcast back to the station, which promptly went to a commercial.

"Did anyone catch the name of the fish company?" Paul asked.

"I don't think they said," replied Denny.

"Whoa. I guess I'll be taking a different route to Boston. Was he on Storrow Drive or on the expressway near Storrow Drive?" Vinnie asked.

"On the expressway. Sorry, Vinnie. Your day just took a turn for the worse," Jimmy answered. "No easy way around that."

"I'd better call Boston to let them know we're going to miss our early morning flights out," Meredith remarked. "They may have enough lobsters in their pound to fill the early orders if we give them a heads-up. They're just standard chick and pound-and-a-half orders."

"We may have trouble getting the eleven o'clock truck past there, too," Paul noted. "We could possibly do a Logan run ourselves and not stop off at the Boston plant first. We can go through Revere and bypass the expressway—unless that gets clogged up with people trying to get around the accident. What a mess!"

"I don't know if it even makes sense for me to make the trip to Boston," Vinnie said, figuring he'd run the idea up the flagpole to see if anyone saluted it.

"Vinnie, you have to get that fish to Boston to give them a chance to cut it and get it to the Parker House for this evening's event," Paul answered. Then, after pausing to think for a moment, he added, "Come to think of it, traffic should be better by the afternoon. If we cut the fish here instead of Boston, we'll be right on schedule. Let me check to see what else is in that order. I guess the Boston plant hasn't heard about the accident, or we'd have gotten a call by now." He left to use the phone in a more private location to offer Boston a solution.

As Paul was leaving the office, Sully walked through the plastic strips. "Got any bait?" Sully asked as he opened the office door.

"Sure, Sully," said Denny. "Jimmy and Murph get first dibs, but there should be enough for all of you."

"Did you hear the news about the overturned truck on the expressway? It was loaded with fish," Sully said, smiling mischievously.

"We just heard it on the radio," Denny answered. "Too bad."

"Glad it wasn't one of ours," Meredith said. "Our trucks are all still here."

"You don't know whose truck it was?" asked Sully, already knowing the answer.

"No," replied Denny. "Do you?"

"I saw it on TV. They didn't mention the company's name," Sully continued. "But when they zoomed in on the box of the truck, you could clearly see the Colbert's Seafood Company name and the royal-blue color of the box."

"No kidding," said Vinnie, now smiling along with Sully. "You don't suppose that was the truck that left the auction house around five of five this morning with the fish Colbert's bought from the congressman, do you? You know, the *Bay State Skye* fish?"

"I do indeed!" Sully said gleefully.

"Well, I guess they'll be missing the fish I bought at the auction today. Colbert's was bidding against me, and I think he stopped to keep the price of that fish that's stinking up the expressway right now from getting too expensive," Vinnie theorized.

"Why are you so happy?" Denny asked Sully.

"I don't want to see any good come to any of the fish onboard that dragger. I heard Johnny's going to take the loss for the destruction of all that lobster gear. It was his trawl they busted up, you know," Sully exclaimed.

"Yeah, I heard," said Vinnie.

"That's news to me, and I was the one who found the boat," Murph asserted.

"I heard from Marco Sousa down at the auction this morning,"

Vinnie said. "Oh, that reminds me. Don't cut three hundred pounds of the markets I brought in. I promised them to Marco if he didn't bid against me. Five seventy-five a pound, plus the five-cent auction fee . . . worked for both of us."

"I'll let the guys on the dock know," Denny said. "Too bad about Colbert's truck, though. They didn't do nothing wrong."

"Fruit of the poisonous tree, you know," said Sully.

"I guess when the chips are down, I'm in Johnny's camp," Vinnie added. "Sure hope he can recover."

"I guess we've all been there, in one way or another. Maybe we can arrange a fundraiser for him. We can put our heads together at Fitzy's tonight," Murph suggested.

"Well, we've wasted enough time this morning. Denny, can we get our bait? We need to be shoving off," said Jimmy.

"Sure thing," said Denny. Murph and Jimmy followed Denny into the cooler where the bait was stored. They took two barrels for the day and headed out to the back dock. After he sold the one leftover barrel of bait to Sully, Denny headed back to the lobster room to get the crew to cull out the lobsters that had come in on Jimmy and Murph's load the night before, which secretly included about four hundred pounds from the ill-fated *Bay State Skye*'s catch. He wanted to get a cook going with any of the deads or weaks they found. The weather was beautiful again today and most of the lobster boats had already left their dock, so Denny knew he would be slammed with lobsters at the end of the day. He needed to get yesterday's lobsters culled out and tucked away in the holding tanks in anticipation of the next load coming in. There was no time to contemplate the tragedy of the *Bay State Skye*, but as he began to go through Jimmy and Murph's lobsters, Denny wished they had left the Golini brothers' ones right where they found them, back on that star-crossed dragger boat.

Bay State Skye

CHAPTER 5

Vinnie grabbed a forklift and picked up the pallets of fish from his truck that had been earmarked for Boston and brought them into the plant. He stopped at the office to have Denny take the temperature of a sample fish or two and give the readings to Meredith to record. Although the FDA's HACCP program—Hazard Analysis and Critical Control Points—hadn't been fully implemented, Flannery's was one of the seafood plants the FDA was working with to identify critical control points. The arrival of the fish was considered one of them; if the fish arrived warmer than they should have been, bacteria could have already begun to grow, which would lower the safety of the finished product. Pretty much every piece of seafood in the plant would need to have its temperature taken at one time or another—that is, unless it was still alive and kicking. Even the lobsters' temperatures needed to be taken after a cook to be sure they met the minimum temperature allowed to ensure that no harmful bacteria were present.

The HACCP program had its origins in the space program. NASA couldn't risk having unsafe food being launched into space with the astronauts. Once the program was established, it was expanded into the juice and seafood markets. Flannery's welcomed the HACCP program as a way to keep its seafood quality at the highest level because Flannery's often sold to high-end restaurants and was committed to selling quality seafood. Flannery's had actually gone the extra mile to have a full-time lab technician on board to test the bacteria counts around the plant to be sure they were within FDA guidelines.

After the fish were deemed cool enough, they were brought to the cutting line, where the load was dumped, little by little, into a large tank of superchlorinated, potable water. This not only helped to wash the fish but also separated the fish from the ice in which they were packed. Because the fish were heavier than the water and ice, they sank to the bottom of the tank, where a conveyor belt picked up each fish, bringing it to a line where it would be sprayed with more potable water. The spray would wash off any loose scales or ice that was still stuck to the fish.

Having been thoroughly rinsed, the fish would continue their travels with a slide down a chute and onto a rubber conveyor belt to the cutter's line. Each cutter would grab a fish, fillet it, and place the fillets, skin side down, on a higher-level conveyor belt. This conveyor took each fillet through a tunnel equipped with potable-water sprayers on all sides. From the tunnel, the fillet would take a quick ride to the skinning machine, where stainless-steel rollers underneath would grab the tail end of the fillet and pull it through a vibrating blade that would ride along the back of the skin, literally pulling it off the fillet. The blade was so precisely set that it could remove the skin while leaving the protective membrane, which held the fillet together, still intact.

Next, the fillet rode to the candling box, where a worker inspected the fillet for nematodes, which is a classy name for worms. It was typical that this job was given to the new guy because it was the most undesirable job in the plant. Essentially, a candling box consisted of a light that illuminated the fillet from below, and the keen-eyed worker would pluck out any nematodes he found with a pair of stainless-steel tweezers. After a final rinsing at the candling box, the fillet was finally ready to pack.

Workers would take the fillets and size them while checking for any fillets that were too ragged to be used as market fillets, designating them as chowder fish. The good fillets were then packed into rectangular metal cans that held approximately twenty-five pounds each. The fillets were carefully placed on parchment paper in the bottom of the container, with each layer of fish separated by another sheet of paper. After being tagged to identify the date, the product, and the weight, the containers were iced down in a large plastic tote with wheels, ready to be trucked out.

Flannery's cutters were a great group of Portuguese men from the Azores Islands who were very skilled in cutting fish. All the cutters knew one another, and they often socialized together with their families outside of work.

Erico Duarte was one of Flannery's best cutters, and he got along with pretty much everyone. Because of that, he was positioned in the middle of the line, and he was quickly making short work of the *Bay State Skye's* market haddock from that morning's auction. At mug-up time, he took off his gear and headed outside with the rest of the group. The air was a refreshing eighty-two degrees, unlike the chilly forty-eight they'd been working in on the floor that morning.

"Erico, you have a phone call in the office. Erico, phone call," Meredith announced over the speaker system, which had a feed to the outside dock.

Erico hated to go in and cut his break short. He was enjoying the sun on his face and the balmy breeze from the ocean. He could have stayed there all day, really. He reluctantly put down his coffee mug and headed inside to take the call at the floor manager's desk for a little privacy. It was his wife, and when Meredith glanced over at him, she noticed his agitation. He appeared to be shouting into the phone, although Meredith couldn't hear a thing over the sounds of the machinery in the building.

The call was brief. Erico soon returned to his cup of coffee and his friends. A moment later, the bell rang, signaling the end of mug-up time. Each man grabbed his cup and headed back in. They were all looking forward to lunchtime, when they would grab their fishing rods and head to the back of the building to eat their sandwiches and fish off the lower end of the dock. Mackerel and bluefish were hitting right then, and any of the men would have been excited to catch their evening's supper.

Nobody could say what the problem was with Erico and his wife. He was being very vague, even with his Portuguese-speaking coworkers. He was still angry when he got back to the bench. He put his yellow slicker apron back on along with the rest of the guys. It was a necessary piece of equipment; the fish business was an extremely wet line of work, even if you weren't out at sea. Erico picked up his cutter's knife with the nine-inch-long, razor-sharp blade and continued filleting the haddock.

The line had been unusually quiet for a few minutes when Erico cried out, "If she thinks she's going to do that, why I'll . . ." He never finished his sentence. Instead, he picked up a good-size haddock from the conveyor belt, slapped it down in front of him, and raising his hand over his head, slammed the knife down as hard as he could into the fish. The fact that he had ruined the fillets from this beautiful market haddock, ensuring they now could only be used for chowder fish, was only the beginning. In fact, he had done something much worse as well. When he stabbed the fish, his knife came to a sudden halt, hitting the top of the cutting board with excessive force. Erico's grip on the knife wasn't prepared for such an impact, and his hand slid down the sharp edge of the blade, basically filleting the inside of his palm.

Blood poured out of his hand at an alarming rate while Erico remained surprisingly calm, trying to come to grips with what had just happened to him. Workers quickly wrapped the wound with bandages from a nearby first aid kit mounted on the wall. Paul, who happened to be walking by, returning from the lab upstairs, yelled to Meredith to call for an ambulance. Minutes later, Erico was lying on a stretcher being taken to the Addison Gilbert Hospital in Gloucester, with what appeared to be a game-changing injury.

He'd never be able to cut fish for a living again. He'd be lucky if he could ever hold a knife.

His coworkers understood that tempers and knives didn't mix, and although they never expressed their opinion, Paul assumed the cutters were in agreement that Erico's injury was his own damned fault. Nonetheless, everyone was shell-shocked, leading to a much more judicious, slower cutting line. Their precision actually increased due to their more cautious knife handling, but their productivity slowed to a crawl. There was nothing Paul could do but hope and pray they got the fish done in time to ship to the Parker House restaurant and that the mess Colbert's truck had made on the Southeast Expressway would be cleared up quickly so that they could use their usual route to Boston. Not only were the cutters dragging, but they were also down a good man as well.

"This day has been miserable from the get-go," Paul mumbled to himself. His train of thought was interrupted by the ringing of the phone line connected directly to Flannery's office in Boston. Meredith beat Paul to the draw and answered it.

"Hello, Flannery's," Meredith said in as cheery a voice as she could muster, considering that the ambulance had just left with one of their best cutters and it was more than likely the owner of the company on the other end of the line.

"Meredith," Flannery called out in his usual straight-to-the-point manner. "That order for forty-five pounds of fresh lobster meat is a go. Just be sure the priest pays with a certified check."

"OK, thanks for letting me know," Meredith said and hung up the receiver. Then she turned to Paul and said, "Well, that's a little disturbing,"

"What is?" asked Paul.

"Remember the priest from Our Lady of Good Voyage Church who called in an order for lobster meat yesterday?"

"Uh-huh," Paul answered. Then he asked, "What ever happened with that?"

"We've never had an order from him before, and at twenty-five ninety-five a pound, lobster meat is a pretty high-priced item. So I decided to put a call into Flannery to see if he wanted to take the order," Meredith said.

"Why wouldn't he?" Paul asked.

"It just seemed fishy to me . . . no pun intended," Meredith remarked with a smile. Then putting her pencil down, she looked directly at Paul. "The priest was the one who got in touch with us. His instructions were for us to deliver the order to his Chevy Suburban, which would be parked on Taylor, the street that runs parallel to the side of the church, off Prospect. The priest said he'd get the lobster meat to the rectory kitchen himself. I thought the whole thing was odd, so I checked with Denny—he's a local Catholic guy—to see if he'd ever heard of the priest, and he confirmed that Father Florencio serves at Our Lady of Good Voyage. I didn't want to refuse the order if it was legitimate, but I wanted to cover my ass at the same time, so I called Boston to see what Flannery thought about it. He just OK'd the order on the condition the priest gives our driver a certified check. So I guess we're good to go, but quite frankly, I was secretly hoping Flannery would shut the whole thing down."

"Well, if Flannery OK'd it, we should be all set," Paul told Meredith. Then he asked, "Do you have the number for the priest so that you can call to tell him he needs to have a certified check?"

"He said he'd call me back today to confirm the order and delivery time, but I thought I'd call the church's rectory, just to make sure a priest from that parish really had placed the order."

"That's a good idea," Paul remarked. "Can't be too careful."

As the words were leaving his mouth, the phone rang. It was an outside line this time. Paul lifted the receiver.

"Good morning, Flannery's," Paul said.

"Good morning," said the voice on the other end of the line. "I'm calling to confirm my order for fresh lobster meat to be delivered on Friday morning. This is Father Florencio."

"Yes, Father, we were just discussing your order. We've gotten approval from our Boston office with the condition that we're paid by certified check. It's due to the size of the order and the cost of the product; you understand," Paul added.

"Sure, that's no problem," the priest responded casually. "I'll have a certified check ready for you. Would nine in the morning be a good delivery time? I'll be waiting in a black Chevy Suburban parked to the side of the church on Taylor Street."

"OK," Paul said. Then he asked, "But why don't we just deliver the lobster meat directly to the rectory?"

"There's a memorial service being planned for the Golini brothers on Friday morning, and the area around the church parking lot and rectory will likely be crowded with vehicles."

"Oh, I had no idea," Paul said. Then he added, "Isn't it a little early for a memorial? The Coast Guard just brought their boat in last night."

"The actual memorial will be happening sometime before Labor Day," Father Florencio told Paul. "But from what I understand, a lot of the Golini brothers' relatives are here for the summer and scheduled to return home in time for the reopening of school. We anticipate the memorial service to be heavily attended and want to be sure it goes off without a hitch."

Paul thought for a moment and then suggested, "In that case, why don't you come here to pick up your order? We're not that far from your rectory."

"I'm going to be busy all day with the Golini family and only have a brief moment to get away," Father Florencio told Paul. Then he added, "If it's an inconvenience for you to deliver the order—"

"No trouble at all," Paul interrupted, not wanting to lose an order Flannery had already approved. The priest had a plausible answer for everything. "We'll see you bright and early tomorrow at nine o'clock," Paul said and hung up the phone.

"Damn!" Meredith declared. "I can't call the rectory now. If the order's on the up and up, the priest will think I don't trust him."

"Which you don't," Paul pointed out.

"No, I don't," Meredith declared.

"I think we're OK," Paul reassured Meredith. "The priest sounds official. I didn't notice any hesitation or nervousness when he spoke."

"OK," Meredith agreed reluctantly. "I'll go tell Denny he has a forty-five-pound lobster-meat order. I think he's doing a sizable cook today anyway. It's just a matter of getting it picked in time for the morning."

"Sounds good," Paul said.

When Meredith told Denny about the priest's order, he smiled widely. Any chance he had to move some lobsters out of the crowded tanks to make room for the day's incoming load was welcome news.

"I'll pick out a few of the beat-up three- to five-pounders Murph and Jimmy brought in last night and add them to the cook. That should be enough for the priest's order," Denny told Meredith and immediately got to work. When Flannery called a few hours later for an update on the order's progress, Paul was able to confidently confirm it would be ready on time.

"They're working on it as we speak," he told Flannery. "The cook is done, and Charlie and Denny are doing the picking right now. It's still got to cool, but we should have it ready for the morning, especially because it's a local delivery."

"So you're all set?" asked Flannery.

"Barring any catastrophe," Paul replied.

"You mean like the expressway debacle this morning? Wasn't that wild?" Flannery remarked, clearly having some time on his hands to talk.

"Glad it wasn't our fish," Paul said. "It was the rest of the *Bay State Skye's* haddock, you know."

"No, I didn't," said Flannery, although he didn't sound too surprised. "That was one ill-fated boat, wasn't it? I wouldn't have touched any of its fish if it were up to me, but Vinnie had already bid on the fish by the time I heard about it. I'm not superstitious, but to err on the side of caution, I'd have steered clear of it."

"Well, we've got it now," Paul said.

"That's true enough," Flannery agreed. "You have a great day."

"You too," Paul said, hoping from this point on, his day would turn a corner.

Paul went to check on Denny and Charlie to see how the picking was progressing. They were the perfect people to pick lobster meat because neither liked the taste of it. It would be easy to lose a couple of pounds with every cook if the picker was partial to its flavor.

As he entered the lobster room, Paul met Denny driving a forklift on his way out to take some lobsters in from a boat that had just arrived. Paul didn't want to keep the boat waiting, so he waved him on and went out back to the picking room to get the information from Charlie.

Charlie Whalen had been working for Flannery's for about six years. He was twenty-five and taller than average. Growing up in Gloucester, he had played football in high school, and that winning glow still surrounded him. Girls would come into the retail area to get a glimpse of him working in the lobster room. He had no desire to do much of anything else. Life was good for him in Gloucester.

Charlie had the radio up full blast, with Janet Jackson's "Escapades" filling the four-by-five-foot room. As with all potentially HACCP-regulated areas of the plant, this small room, used only for picking lobster meat after a cook, had to be constructed of materials that could be thoroughly rinsed with highly chlorinated water to ensure a bacteria count of low-to-none on all surfaces.

Charlie jumped when Paul entered the tiny room from the door behind him, taking his gloved hand out of his right pocket and pulling the glove off, replacing it with a new one. Paul motioned for him to turn the music down so they could talk.

"Loud enough for you?" Paul asked.

"It's not hurting anything. No one can hear it with the door closed," Charlie answered. Then he added, "And anyway, the beat helps me pick faster."

"Huh," Paul said, amused and a little annoyed by his answer. "Well, if you want to still be able to hear when you're my age, I'd turn it down a bit."

"I hear ya," Charlie replied with a grin. He was just digging himself into a deeper hole as far as Paul was concerned.

Paul shook his head. "How are you and Denny coming on that lobster-meat order?"

"We've got a little over thirty-seven pounds ready. If Denny gets back soon, we should have it done before we leave," Charlie replied.

"Good enough," Paul said. "We're going to have Vinnie deliver it on his way to Boston tomorrow."

"We should be ready," Charlie repeated.

Paul left the picking room and, closing the door, heard the radio turn up full blast again. As he was walking through the lobster room, he met Denny transferring the lobsters from crates to holding tanks.

"We won't go through these till tomorrow. I need to get back to help Charlie with that order if we're going to have it ready to go in the morning," Denny said.

"That'll work," said Paul. "Let me know if you have a problem finishing. We'll need to go into OT if it isn't done."

"OK," Denny agreed. "We shouldn't have to, though. I'll let you know when it's done and in the cooler."

"Sounds good," Paul answered, glad to have someone he could trust overseeing the job. Then he added, "Hey, how do you stand working in that room with the radio up so loud?"

"He turns it down some when I'm there with him. It helps to motivate him, so we don't have to be there so long. It's all good," Denny said.

Paul walked back to the office and picked up the phone to call Addison Gilbert Hospital to complete the accident report on Erico. As he suspected, he was going to be out for an extended time, with a long recovery ahead of him. He was going into surgery that evening and had already had his wife fill out the paperwork for worker's compensation insurance.

Paul hung up the phone and rubbed his eyes. "I have a feeling we won't be seeing Erico again," he said to Meredith. "I may as well let Boston know the accident report and the workman's comp claim will be there by the beginning of next week. No sense putting off the inevitable."

By the time Paul had finished calling Boston, Denny was carrying the bags of fresh lobster meat into the cooler. He waved at Paul in the office.

"All done," he hollered.

"Thanks, Denny," Paul replied, waving back. "Enjoy your evening."

"Will do," answered Denny.

Paul and Meredith packed up and walked out the door, turning back to set the alarm, glad this day had finally ended. The warm air felt especially freeing as they made their way to their cars.

"Tomorrow will be a better day," Meredith called to Paul.

"Could it get any worse?" he called back.

*   *   *   *   *

The next morning, Vinnie headed into the auction house at 5:00 a.m. sharp, determined to win the bid on some flounder. It was Friday, an extremely busy day at Flannery's retail store, and flounder would be in demand for weekend meals from tourists and locals alike. He didn't leave disappointed, taking back five hundred pounds of fresh-caught flounder. Nice stuff. He got back to the plant early, ready to hit the road to Boston before the expressway got jam-packed with people from the North Shore headed to the Cape. When he learned he had to make a delivery to the priest before hitting the road to Boston, he wasn't pleased. He rushed into the cooler, grabbed a bag of lobster meat, and headed past the office on the way to his truck.

"This it?" he called to Meredith through the office glass, holding up a bag.

"That's part of it," Meredith called back, looking up from her desk. "You should have five bags in total."

Vinnie threw his free hand up in the air in annoyance as he rushed back to the cooler to retrieve the rest of the bags.

After putting the lobster meat in the refrigerated box of his truck, Vinnie hastily walked back to the office to confirm he wasn't missing any live lobster orders he needed to take to Boston.

"Looks like you've got everything," Meredith agreed. "Don't forget the payment you get from the priest needs to be a certified check."

"I won't. Hey, did you see the flounder I got for the retail today?" Vinnie asked proudly.

"I saw it when it came through the door to the cooler. Looks great! We'll probably sell out of it today," Meredith said. Vinnie's ability to spot the best-quality fish was second to none. "Oh wait," Meredith called out, "that teacher's picking the flounder up for her school's fish-printing activity today. What did you pay for it?"

"It's on the house," Vinnie answered, remembering those two fish taken with a five-finger discount.

"Really?" Meredith asked. "It's for a good cause, but we need to cover our cost."

"Don't worry about it," Vinnie said. Then he called back as he rushed out the door, "I'm off."

"Have a good trip," Meredith replied.

She looked at the blank invoice in front of her. Vinnie had worked some kind of deal for the flounder, and the less she knew about the details the better. She wrote "no charge" on the invoice and dropped it off in the retail store.

*   *   *   *   *

"Hey, Vinnie," Paul called out, giving a wave in his direction as he headed toward the plastic strips of the dock door to start his day. He heard the toot-toot of a forklift and stepped aside to allow it to pass through the strips and onto the dock. Vinnie waved at Paul and jumped into the cab of his truck, prepared to make his delivery to the priest before heading to Boston.

Paul was just as happy to stay in Gloucester. He had worked at the Boston plant for quite a few years and definitely preferred the rush of the ocean to the rush of the people and traffic he'd left behind. Paul wasn't a Gloucester boy, having grown up in a much more rural setting. His route to work included driving by the mud flats and salt marshes of Ipswich and Essex, which were picturesque this time of year. As he passed Woodman's in the evening, he'd watch the line of customers grow as he inched his way through downtown Essex. Often the line would stretch clear down the main road, filled with a mix of locals and tourists, all waiting to eat a lobster in the rough with a beautiful view of the Essex River in the background. The experience was best when the tide was high. When it was low, an undeniable rotten-egg smell permeated the air. The water was deep enough around Gloucester's Head of the Harbor to avoid the characteristic low-tide odor that often plagued the salt marshes.

Paul seldom stopped in Essex, opting to meet his wife, Sue, and their two kids on the beautiful white sands of Crane Beach in Ipswich, which was on his way home. They often stopped by in the summer to eat a picnic dinner, comb the beach for sand-dollar and moon-snail shells, and watch the sun set. Occasionally a small plane would fly over the beach, and Sue would try to identify the make of the plane as it passed overhead. Paul was trained as an aircraft mechanic straight out of high school and taught her how to distinguish one small plane from another. He'd probably still be working in the industry today, but the major airlines were only hiring military personnel when he graduated. Although Paul took a job for a private aircraft company at Hanscom Field, the minimum-wage salary for three years took its toll on trying to support a growing family. He never cared to be a part of the seafood industry, but when a good-paying job became available, he reluctantly decided to move away from the aviation field. His mechanical ability was invaluable when a machine needed to be fixed quickly, and his ability to organize the workers into a productive team helped him to quickly rise through the ranks to manage the Gloucester plant.

He had no ties to Gloucester and enjoyed crossing the bridge from Cape Ann to leave the peninsula on a daily basis.

Like Paul, Meredith lived outside the Cape Ann area and wound up in the seafood industry after her chosen field had closed. She had earned a bachelor's degree only to find that teaching jobs were hard to come by when she graduated. She would have been better off cultivating a network of people associated with the higher ranks of town administrations, rather than concentrating on earning good grades. Graduating with honors took a back seat to candidates who were politically connected, and she was only able to find aide jobs. Earning a master's degree did little to increase her luck at finding a full-fledged teaching position. When a job for an outreach specialist for the local aquarium came up, Meredith had jumped at the chance. She loved the freedom it gave her to teach, especially since she had a husband and two kids. It was an added bonus that experts in marine biology taught her everything she wanted to know about the sea life she'd be handling. But there were many slow times during the year, and she filled this void working in Flannery's retail. Soon she'd worked her way into the office and then into management.

Although Paul had settled into working in the seafood business, Meredith found it to be a huge conflict with her former position. She had made a career of teaching kids, faculty, and parents about sea animals, and now she was working in an industry that considered sea life food. Flannery's crew understood this and never bothered to initiate her into the fold by dropping a live green crab into the lobster ticket box. Normally they loved to sit back and wait for the inevitable scream or curse from a new employee when he reached in to grab a ticket and came up with a crab instead. When Paul asked Denny why the crew never tried this prank on Meredith, he replied, "That wouldn't of been any fun. She'd of made a pet out of it!"

As he took a seat on his office stool, Paul remembered searching for a haddock stretcher when he first started working at Flannery's. He'd combed the plant for thirty minutes before the guys came clean and admitted there was no such thing. It was a way to size the new guy up, to see if he was a hard-ass or if he had a sense of humor. Paul smiled as an outside line rang. Picking up the phone, he was happy to hear the voice of his good friend Glenn Riley, who owned a small seafood store and restaurant, the Lobster Hut, on Bearskin Neck in Rockport.

"Hey, Glenn," Paul said. "I bet you're busy as hell up there on the Neck with the kind of weather we've been having."

"Sure am," said Glenn. "Hey, I've only got a minute, but I wanted to let you know the young guy you've got working in your lobster room—you know, the good-looking blond all the girls are after?"

"Charlie?" asked Paul.

"That's the one," Glenn replied. "Well, he came in late yesterday afternoon with a Ziploc bag full of what he said was fresh lobster meat and wanted to sell it to me. Of course, I didn't know where it came from or what conditions it was picked and stored under, so I told him that I wasn't interested. He said it was picked that day but couldn't tell me much more than that. Did you have a big order to pick where a couple of pounds wouldn't be missed yesterday?"

"That's disturbing," Paul said, realizing he had a problem on his hands. "As a matter of fact, we did a big cook for a local church order yesterday."

"Well, I'm not interested in getting the police involved or going to court, but I thought you'd be interested in knowing. There's nothing I hate more than a thief," Glenn said. "Hey, I've got a big group of tourists coming in. Don't you just love this time of year? Gotta go."

"Thanks for the heads-up, Glenn," Paul replied.

As he began to hang up the phone, Paul overheard Glenn's bellowing voice declare to his new customers, "How're you doing? Wicked nice day today!" Glenn looked like a cross between a lovable sea captain and a Dickens-style Ghost of Christmas Present. It was no wonder his business was booming so much that he could afford to take winters off.

Paul thought back to when he'd walked into the picking room yesterday. He remembered Charlie jumping when he realized Paul was there. Paul thought it was because he hadn't heard him walk in with the music blasting. But then he remembered seeing Charlie's hand in his sweatshirt pocket. Could he have been putting handfuls of meat into a plastic bag in his pocket as he picked the lobsters? Denny wasn't in the room. He had plenty of opportunity. No wonder Charlie jumped when he realized Paul was behind him.

When Denny appeared outside the office window to collect some lobster orders to pack and get ready for the ten-thirty truck, Paul motioned for him to come into the office. He walked around the outside perimeter and opened the door.

"What's up?" he asked.

"Close the door," Paul said. He waited for the door to shut tightly, then asked, "Have you noticed Charlie acting peculiar in any way?"

"Hey, we're talking about Charlie. What isn't peculiar about him?" Denny joked.

Paul smiled.

"Seriously, you need to give me more to go on," Denny said.

"One of the shop owners in Rockport said Charlie tried to sell him a couple of pounds of fresh-picked lobster meat after work yesterday," Paul said.

"No way," cried Denny. "You mean he was taking meat when we were busting our asses to get that order finished and ready for today? What the hell! Want me to go get him so that you can ask him about it?"

"Yeah, I guess," said Paul, reluctant to have his day go south so soon. He'd barely been at work an hour.

Denny quickly left, returning with Charlie, who seemed to be trying to look bewildered, although Paul was pretty sure he had a good idea why he'd been summoned.

"Do you know why I want to talk to you?" Paul asked.

"No clue," Charlie said, nonchalantly shaking his head.

"I've gotten word that you've been trying to sell some fresh-picked lobster meat to restaurant owners on Bearskin Neck," Paul said as he watched for a reaction. It didn't take long for him to get a response.

"Wasn't me," Charlie adamantly defended himself.

"Come on, Charlie," Paul insisted. "He's seen you before in the plant. He knows it was you."

"He must have me mixed up with someone else," Charlie asserted.

"Let me see inside your pockets," Denny called out without thinking. They weren't picking meat today, and unless he carried a bag as a daily ritual, this was only going to prove Charlie's case. The chance of him having a bag in his pocket today was slim to none.

Charlie gladly turned his sweatshirt pockets inside out. "See," he said to Denny, indignantly. Then he turned to Paul and said, "Happy now?"

"Get back to work. But be forewarned: If I ever catch you taking as much as a lobster knuckle out of this plant, you're finished working here," Paul retorted, knowing it was pretty much an empty threat. In order to bring him up for dismissal and have it legally stand, a cop would have to witness the hand off of the product and the exchange of money—that is, unless the recipient of the product was willing to be an eyewitness. There wasn't much chance of that, and Paul didn't have time to spy on him twenty-four seven, especially at this time of year.

Charlie sauntered out.

"Is that it?" Denny asked.

"For now," Paul said. "Keep an eye on him, will you? I might not be lucky enough to know the person he tries to sell the meat to next time."

"I'll try," Denny replied, "but I can't be everywhere."

"I know. Just do your best," Paul said. Denny left the office and headed out to the loading dock.

Paul couldn't let this go on. Charlie couldn't be trusted. He'd have to find another way to fire him. He left the office and headed for the lobster room. As he rounded the corner, he caught Charlie dropping a cigarette on the wet cement floor next to the tanks and walking away.

"Strike one," Paul yelled over the sound of cascading water from the lobster tanks.

"What?" Charlie asked as he slowly began to turn around.

"You know you can't smoke in here," Paul confronted Charlie. "I'm writing you up."

"That's not mine," he retorted, casually turning toward Paul, staring him down.

"I saw you throw it," Paul replied, meeting his glare. "I'll be out in a minute to have you sign the warning paper."

He shrugged his shoulders and said under his breath, "Whatever."

Paul drew up the warning, and Denny happily took the paper to him to sign.

*   *   *   *   *

The rest of the morning was uneventful. Rosa Santos, who worked the retail counter, gathered the fish from the cooler for the day, which included some premium chowder fish from the *Bay State Skye*'s market haddock that had been cut the day before. Rosa, being Portuguese herself, knew most of the men on the cutting line. Her short dark hair peeked out from under her Flannery's cap as she approached the line.

"Would any of you like me to set aside some chowder fish for your dinners tonight?" she asked in her thick Portuguese accent. "It's a chance to get good fish at a cheap price."

The men, speaking only in Portuguese to keep what they were saying from being overheard, told her, "We don't want anything more to do with that cursed fish from the *Bay State Skye*. We weren't happy Flannery's had bought the fish to begin with. We were taking our lives into our hands cutting it. After all, look what happened to Erico."

She shrugged her shoulders. "Suit yourselves. I don't think the fish is cursed, and deals like this don't come along every day," she said as she hugged the twenty-five-pound plastic container full of fish to her chest. She was strong enough to easily carry fifty pounds of fish at a time, despite her short stature and advancing age. "I'll hold the fish until the afternoon, in case any of you change your minds."

"Don't bother. We won't," the cutter closest to her replied in English. Rosa held back the fish until the afternoon nonetheless.

*   *   *   *   *

When Vinnie arrived back from the Boston plant, Paul asked him, "How'd the delivery with the priest go this morning?"

"Fine. He was waiting for me when I arrived," he answered nonchalantly as he continued unloading his truck.

"Were there a lot of cars in the parking lot?" Paul asked.

"Barely anyone around from what I could see," he replied, grabbing a pallet jack to move the totes of fish out of his truck.

Paul stepped aside to give Vinnie room to maneuver through the loading-dock door, then inquired, "Did you drop the check off in Boston?"

"I handed it to the sales office personally," he answered.

"Did it look on the up and up?" Paul asked.

"Looked good to me," he responded, stopping what he was doing to look directly at Paul. Placing his hands on his hips, he added, "It had a fancy-schmancy bank seal on it and everything. Why? Are you expecting a problem with it? I'm no expert."

"No, no," Paul answered quickly, noting Vinnie's mounting annoyance at all the questions.

Vinnie confronted Paul. "You sound like you don't trust this guy. If you want a play-by-play, I pulled into Taylor Street, right next to the church, and there was a black Suburban parked about a block away. A priest, looking all official, dressed in a black suit with a black clerical shirt and a white collar stepped out of the SUV and handed me a check. I looked the check over, and it looked authentic, so I was satisfied it was the real deal, and I handed the bags of lobster meat over to the priest. I got in my truck, the priest got in his SUV, and we went our separate ways. Now, if you're through giving me the third degree, I'd like to finish unloading my truck so that I can get out of here and begin my weekend."

"I know," Paul said apologetically. "Sorry to be asking so many questions, but it's a lot of money, and our heads are on the chopping block if we screw it up." Paul patted Vinnie's shoulder and added, "Have a good weekend. Thanks for making the extra stop for us."

"No problem," he called back as he hurried through the plastic strips to finish unloading his truck.

Paul had no idea how much trouble he was in until Doug Eklund, Flannery's second-run driver from the Gloucester plant, arrived back from Boston. Doug was responsible for driving the 10:30 a.m. truck, which carried most of the orders for the airport, along with doing a few local deliveries and putting up lobster orders to give Denny a hand. His don't-mess-with-me demeanor, which was normally on display, wasn't really necessary. His six-foot-four frame and athletic build were enough to make anyone think twice before starting a brawl with him. But those who knew him well knew that his wavy, chestnut-brown hair and Dennis the Menace freckles reflected his true personality, which was more mischievously scheming than dangerous. He loved to stir up trouble, then sit back and watch the action. Now, he couldn't wait to tell Paul the bad news.

"Hey, Paul," Doug began, "I think you might be getting a call from Flannery."

"Why would he be calling?" Paul asked, barely looking up from his paperwork. Save the Charlie incident, the day had gone pretty smoothly.

"You know that order Vinnie delivered to the priest this morning?" Doug began, quickly capturing Paul's undivided attention. "Well, Vinnie dropped the check off in the sales office and after a few of the salesmen got done scrutinizing it, they weren't so sure the official-looking seal that was stamped on it meant it was a certified check. So one of them made a run to the bank to cash the check. Guess what?" Doug asked, chuckling and pausing for effect, waiting for Paul's response.

"I hope it didn't bounce," Paul replied.

"Like a cheap red rubber ball," he said, leaning back on his stool and motioning like he was dropping a ball and catching it again.

"No way," Paul gasped, suddenly feeling a tightening in his stomach. "That was over eleven hundred dollars' worth of meat."

"Eleven hundred sixty-seven dollars and seventy-five cents, to be exact," he continued. Doug relished telling tragic news as much as Murph.

Just then, the phone rang. It was the direct line connecting Flannery's office with Gloucester.

"I believe that's the call we've been waiting for," he snickered as he slid off his stool and left the office. His work was done here. He appeared delighted to have beaten Flannery in telling Paul the news.

Paul paused for a moment, mulling things over in his mind. He wished he'd taken Meredith's misgivings about the order more seriously. It was on him that this had gone south. If only they had beaten the priest to the draw and had a chance to call the rectory before he confirmed his order. Priest . . . that was a joke. He had to have been an imposter. This order had been a disaster from the start, right down to the missing two pounds of lobster meat that had headed to Rockport with Charlie.

As the phone rang for the fifth time, Paul stopped obsessing, shook his head, and picked up the receiver. "Flannery's," Paul said in a despondent tone.

"Paul, we have a problem," Flannery blurted out.

"I know. I just heard the whole story from Doug," Paul informed Flannery, trying to save himself from having to hear the unfortunate account of events all over again.

"Good news travels fast," Flannery sarcastically replied. "What's done is done. If that rocket scientist Vinnie knew what a certified check looked like we wouldn't be out almost twelve hundred dollars. But I approved the order, so it's not all on you." Flannery paused and then added jokingly, "Just most of it."

Paul ignored Flannery's comment, failing to see the humor. "We knew it sounded off," Paul admitted, "but no matter how much we checked into it, the guy seemed to be on the up and up."

"Crap happens," Flannery replied.

"Yes, it does," Paul responded, still unable to fathom it happening to him.

"But we're not going to take this lying down. I have a plan to catch that son of a bitch who stole from us," Flannery told Paul.

"I'm in," Paul agreed. Then he asked, "What can I do to help?"

"I want you to call any dealers you know on the North Shore and tell them what happened," Flannery began. "If this so-called priest got away with it once, he may try it again. We're calling around to all the Boston dealers, including those on the fish pier. We're asking them to give us a call if they get a request from a priest wanting lobster meat or shrimp with the same basic setup. Those are the only high-priced items that would make it worth his while to steal and be attractive enough to sell in a hurry. We've already got a call in with both the Boston and Gloucester police. They say if we catch him setting things up with another dealer, they'll accompany us to where the exchange of product and money is taking place and arrest the guy. We won't get our money back, but we'll at least get some kind of justice and keep him from swindling some other fish company. Obviously, he's not a priest."

"Obviously," Paul replied. "I'll get some numbers together."

"I know it's getting late, but can you make the calls today?" Flannery asked.

"Absolutely. I'll get right on it. I'm as anxious to catch this guy as you are," Paul assured him. Then he admitted, "Meredith said the whole thing sounded fishy. Playing Monday-morning quarterback, I should have told the priest we couldn't deliver that much meat on such short notice. I'm kicking myself now."

"Well, let's see if we can catch the guy. At least we'll have some satisfaction," Flannery conceded. Then he speculated, "I can't help but think this wouldn't have happened if the lobster meat didn't have a connection to that star-crossed *Bay State Skye*. I know it's a dragger, but it must have had some lobsters on board if it dug up someone's gear."

Denny walked into the office with the end-of-the-day lobster inventory figures. When he saw Paul was on the phone with Boston, he quietly climbed up on one of the stools and waited.

"I know that boat's gotten under everybody's skin," Paul said, "but there's really no possible way there's a tie-in. We didn't take any lobsters from the *Bay State Skye*. We have to chalk this one up to falling for a good scam artist's con."

"OK, I guess I have to agree that the jinx of the *Bay State Skye* doesn't apply here. You'll let me know if you hear anything?" Flannery asked.

"You'll be the first to know," Paul said and hung up the phone.

Paul turned to Denny and said, "Flannery's convinced everything that's gone wrong in the past couple of days is because we bought fish off the *Bay State Skye*. It's unfathomable to me that the misfortune connected with the Golinis' boat would be contagious to anyone who was in contact with its catch."

Denny slid off the stool and handed his clipboard to Paul. "I probably shouldn't be telling you this because it was kind of told to me in confidence," he started. "But because you were telling Flannery there was no connection to the *Bay State Skye* and the lobster meat, you weren't exactly telling the truth."

"Sure I was," Paul insisted. "The auction house took in all the lobsters from that boat. We've had our hands full with the lobsters our own boats are bringing in."

"That's true," said Denny. "But when Murph saw about five hundred pounds of lobsters on that boat when they found it, he and Jimmy decided to do the family a favor and save the dragger from a fine for being over the legal limit."

"So they took some of the catch as their own," Paul summed up in amazement, seeing where this was going.

"I know it was a very self-serving favor," Denny added. "Nobody knows except Murph, Jimmy, me, and now you. I think I can trust you to keep it under your hat. It was good of them to investigate the dragger and call it in to the Coast Guard. They could have just steamed by and left the dragger drifting."

"I suppose," Paul said. "So some of the *Anna May's* catch really came from the *Bay State Skye?*"

"I'm afraid so," Denny nodded. "So maybe Flannery wasn't as far off as you thought. There's been a lot of talk around town that Colbert's truck overturning in Boston was because of the cursed fish the congressman sold them. I don't know. I'm not superstitious, but a lot of people in this town are. That may be why we got such a good deal on the *Bay State Skye's* fish at the auction."

"Could be," Paul agreed. He had never considered any of that. Living in town had its advantages. Denny was way more up to speed on the local sentiment than he was.

"Let me know if there are any problems with the inventory," Denny added.

"Hey, thanks for letting me know," Paul called to Denny as he walked out.

"No problem. I know I can trust you," Denny remarked. And he was right. Paul wouldn't betray his confidence.

Paul called Meredith into the office to get her caught up on what had happened with the priest's check; then they both called every dealer they knew who was big enough to be a target for the scam the fake priest was pulling. When finished, they joined Rosa in the retail market to help with the Friday crowd. It was just about two thirty in the afternoon when a friendly older couple came through the door. They were new to the retail market, and Meredith, who enjoyed talking to customers, asked if they were visiting from out of state.

"No, we're from Concord. We just drove up for the day," the petite man answered.

"It's a little cooler by the sea on these ninety-odd-degree days," his equally petite wife added.

The couple bought two lobster rolls to eat at Good Harbor

Beach and wanted some chowder fish for their cooler to fry up at home over the weekend. Rosa served up a little over two pounds of the premium haddock chowder fish from the *Bay State Skye* that she had held back that morning. None of the other workers had expressed an interest in buying the fish, and she didn't want to hold it over the weekend.

"That looks wonderful," the wife said.

"Why don't you throw one more piece on the scale?" the husband asked, lifting the visor of his Red Sox cap to get a better look at the fish.

Rosa placed another piece of the fish on the scale, declaring, "That's almost three pounds." The man nodded his head in agreement, and Rosa wrapped and bagged the fish. After paying, the couple went outside to where Flannery's kept the complimentary ice for people's coolers. They filled theirs to the brim and headed back to their car.

"Fifteen more minutes to closing," Rosa said with a smile, but she had barely gotten the words out of her mouth when four separate groups walked through the door, excited to buy fish for the weekend. As the last group was finally waited on, a petite older woman came into the retail store. Rosa recognized her as half of the sweet couple from Concord who had been in earlier. But the woman seemed different this time. She had a dazed look as she approached the counter.

"Could you please call the police for me?" she asked Meredith in a quiet voice, laced with a hint of embarrassment.

"What happened?" Meredith asked.

"We had an accident," the woman said with an amazing amount of composure.

"Oh, I'm sorry," Meredith said as she picked up the phone. "Is anyone hurt?"

"No."

Meredith dialed 911 and explained her emergency.

"Where is the vehicle located?" Meredith asked the older woman, then relayed to the police that the car was at Flannery's, on the other side of the building.

Meredith hung up and, taking the woman by the arm, accompanied her out the door to the other side of the building. Paul, Denny, and Doug trailed behind, curious to see the wreckage. When they turned the corner of the building and could now see the side loading dock, they couldn't believe their eyes. There was an older-model silver Volvo, literally standing on its headlights and front grill, precisely perpendicular to the ground. The car was in perfect condition in every other way, giving the scene the surreal appearance that the car was some kind of strange art sculpture, intended to be viewed in this manner. The old man, equally dazed but unharmed, was standing to the side of his car. He had more than likely sent his wife in to call the police because he was too embarrassed to do it himself.

"How could this have happened?" Meredith asked.

"Actually, quite easily," Doug chimed in. "I bet you've never driven from the back dock to the other side of the building."

"No, I haven't," Meredith admitted. "What's there, a few piles of spare lobster traps?"

"That's about it," Paul said. "Nothing to see, and no way to exit. Well, safely, that is."

The old man had decided to leave Flannery's parking lot by driving around the back of the building on the dock where the boats landed, attempting to avoid the cars pulling in. It seemed an easy way to circumvent the groups of people making their way across the parking lot to the retail store. When he turned the corner to drive around the other side of the building, away from the water, however, there was a kind of optical illusion that could have fooled anyone not familiar with the dock. The side dock was actually raised four and a half feet above the pavement of the parking lot, which was the perfect height for trucks to back in and unload their freight. But because the end of the week had arrived, there were no trucks at the dock. If a driver looked straight ahead beyond the dock, he would think it continued on without a drop because the parking lot made an unexpected dip in front of it. The man had slowly driven over the edge of the dock. His car pivoted on its undercarriage and gently fell to the base, front end down.

"Incredible," Paul observed. Then, approaching the man, he asked, "Are you all right?"

The man quietly replied, "My ego is a little bruised."

Paul smiled and said, "I'm glad you haven't lost your sense of humor. The police are on their way. Would you like to come into the plant and sit until they arrive?"

"No thanks," the old man said. "It's nice standing near the ocean, feeling the breeze off the water."

"If you change your mind, let us know," Paul answered, then turned to greet the police car that had just pulled into the parking lot.

One by one, the crew from the cutting line came out to see the crash. They had been upstairs playing cards in the locker room and had just heard about the accident. It was quite a spectacle with which to end an extraordinary week.

Everyone returned to the plant to close the retail and lock up for the weekend. Paul was glad to see the tail end of this week and get home to his family. Meredith and her husband were getting ready to host a family cookout at their home and were equally excited for the weekend to arrive. As for the Gloucester folks they were leaving behind, the local families were looking forward to getting into their smaller boats to go fishing while dodging the summer people who were boarding their sailboats to go cruising.

*   *   *   *   *

With Labor Day weekend looming, tourists and locals alike were trying to drink up every last minute of summer, knowing the weather would be cooling, the skies graying, and the school year beginning before they knew it. Vinnie arrived at the auction at his usual time, but most boats were still out, taking advantage of the calm seas. Anticipating Monday to be a quiet day for Flannery's retail store, Meredith and Rosa didn't order much fish. Still, the lobster room was busy with orders to ship across the country, trying to get a jump on the Labor Day rush.

The accident from the start of the weekend was a distant memory; the car had been righted and towed away, and any remaining debris had been swept up in anticipation of trucks arriving at the loading dock to pick up their whole fish, bound for New York City and points beyond. The only evidence that the crash had happened at all was the oversize photo on the front page of the *Gloucester Daily Times*. It was normal for this kind of scene to be buried on page six or seven, but the strange manner in which the car was balanced on the pavement had become something of a sensation.

Paul walked into the lobster room to check the quality of the seawater in the tanks to determine whether he needed to pump new water in from the harbor. Often when the tanks were inundated with new lobsters, the water would begin to foam from an influx of ammonia, indicating a change of water was necessary. Because the harbor water was better when it hadn't rained for a while, it seemed this was as good a day as any to change out some water. That way, the water that was pumped into the tank system wouldn't have a chance to become brackish, which would compromise the health of the lobsters.

As Paul turned the corner, he saw Charlie hosing down the lobster-room floor, with his back turned. He watched as Charlie tossed a cigarette butt on the floor and pushed it with the saltwater hose toward the drain that led to the reserve water below. Paul tried to get to the butt before it moved through the grate, but he was too late. Now the filter system would have to pluck out the butt so it wouldn't wind up in the lobster holding tanks.

"Strike two!" Paul yelled to him in disgust. "I'll be out with the papers for you to sign." He turned on his heels and headed back to the office, wondering if he should climb down into the hold to see what other debris might be lurking in the water.

"Son of a bitch!" Paul heard Charlie say as he left the lobster room.

Paul opened the office door without looking and almost ran into Doug, who was checking with Meredith to see if there were any additional lobster orders for the ten-thirty truck.

"We made the cover of the *Gloucester Daily Times*," Doug told Paul proudly.

"I saw," said Paul. "I guess you don't come across a scene like that every day."

"If there's nothing else, I'll be heading out," Doug said.

"You're good to go," Meredith said, but just then the phone began to ring. "Hang on a minute. We may need another order packed."

Meredith answered the phone, and once she was sure there wasn't anything to add to Doug's truck, she motioned to him that he was free to go.

"All set?" Doug said quietly.

Meredith nodded.

Doug left, and Paul had begun to follow him out the door when Meredith called, "Paul, this is for you."

Paul turned around to grab the phone.

"Paul, this is Joe Mancini from down the street at Carrozza's Fish," the man on the line introduced himself. "You called me last Friday to give me a heads-up about the thieving fake priest."

"Of course, Joe," Paul replied. Then he asked, "Have you heard anything?"

"I did," Joe said. "I just received a call from a priest wanting to purchase over a thousand dollars' worth of shrimp. I accepted the order, so I think we're in business."

Paul could barely contain his excitement. "We're going to catch that con-artist bastard after all! Did you set up a place to make the delivery?"

"Same place as you said before, on Taylor Street," Joe said. "This guy's either an idiot or he's wicked confident he won't get caught."

"I'll set it up with the Gloucester cops, OK?" Paul asked. "We'll probably send Vinnie, our driver, with the cops to make a positive ID. Meredith and I both spoke to the priest, but he was the only one who actually saw him."

"The delivery is set up for one this afternoon," Joe informed Paul. "Can your man make it then?"

"He's just pulling in from Boston as we speak," Paul answered. "I'll let him know right now."

"Then we're all set," Joe said. "Let me know if something falls through with the cops. I'll tell my delivery guy to take the check, no questions asked, but I don't want to be left hanging in the wind with this fake priest taking off with my product, too."

"I hear you," Paul said. "I'll make the arrangements right now and give you a call back to confirm everything."

"Ok," Joe said. "Hey, thanks for giving us a heads-up. We might have been standing in your shoes a few hours from now if we hadn't known."

"No problem," Paul said. "We appreciate your cooperation. We need to stop this guy before he cons anyone else."

"Yes, we do," Joe said.

At 12:45 p.m., a plainclothes, dark-haired, stout Gloucester cop, Officer Francisco Martins, accompanied by a reluctant Vinnie, drove past the Crow's Nest Bar in his unmarked car. He turned right to head up to the sprawling Our Lady of Good Voyage church, a well-known landmark, founded in 1893 for the Portuguese population in town. Dedicated to the Madonna, the Catholic church served the largest Portuguese colony on the East Coast, with about two hundred families from the Azores who had settled in Gloucester to work in the fishing industry. The building's architecture was unusual for this part of the country, with its Mission style, complete with a granite foundation and beige-colored stucco covering its exterior to match the style of the churches from the congregation's homeland. Its rose window was a focal point for the second story of the church, and two identical blue-topped bell towers on either side of the central building gave the church an appealing, symmetrical feel. A towering statue of

Our Lady of Good Voyage stood on a pedestal on the peak above the rose window, holding a boat in her left hand, signifying a safe passage.

This felt like anything but a safe passage to Vinnie. He had spent most of his life trying to avoid rides in squad cars, and his discomfort today was palpable. He wiped a line of sweat that dripped down his forehead and into his right eye. It was unclear whether he was sweating because of the warmth of the day or the tension of the event. When Paul had asked him to deliver an order of lobster meat to a priest at the church, Vinnie had had no idea this would also require him to sit in a police car and take part in a stakeout.

"Relax, Vinnie," the policeman told his passenger. "This should be over in no time. I can't imagine a guy playing dress-up as a priest will give us much of a fight. Just let me know when you see his vehicle, and once you positively identify him, I'll take it from there. You just stay put."

"Oh, I intend to," Vinnie said. Within minutes, a black Suburban pulled into a parking space on Taylor Street and backed up to the Carrozza's Fish van, which had been waiting for him.

"Is that the vehicle the priest used before?" asked the police officer.

"Looks like it," said Vinnie, clearly uncomfortable fingering some guy for a crime. God knows he had been responsible for a few illicit acts in his day, and he wouldn't have wanted someone sitting in an unmarked police cruiser pointing a finger at him.

An olive-complexioned, wavy-haired man got out of the car. He looked Portuguese and would have, without question, blended easily into this section of Gloucester. He was dressed just as Vinnie had described, wearing a black sports coat and slacks, with a black clerical shirt and a white clerical collar. He even wore a matching pair of black leather shoes. It would have been hard to distinguish him from any other priest.

"Is that the guy who gave you the check?" the police officer asked.

Vinnie squinted, the glare of the sun affecting his ability to see.

He raised his hand to his forehead to shade his eyes. "Looks like him," he answered. He wasn't the best witness but considering the man had approached the Carrozza's Fish truck on his own and used the same MO as before, there was little chance they were making a mistake. Vinnie slouched down in his seat in an attempt to keep from being seen.

The Carrozza's Fish driver motioned the priest to give him the check. When the priest handed it to him, the deliveryman pretended to scrutinize it, then placed it in his pant pocket and proceeded to give the priest the shrimp order from the back of the truck. Once the priest took possession of the shrimp, Officer Martins sprang into action.

"Stop, police!" he shouted as he stepped from his vehicle.

The priest turned, and with a shocked look on his face, he tried to get to his SUV to flee the scene. But by then, the cop was between him and his Suburban, so he took off running down Taylor Street. He tossed the shrimp to the side of the road and bolted. Vinnie watched with amazement at how fast the somewhat overweight cop was able to sprint behind the thief. Just as the priest had banged a right onto Bent Street, the cop caught up with the thief, tackling him to the ground and handcuffing him. The cop radioed to a squad car in the area, which promptly arrived; the second officer put the man in the back and, siren blaring, took the imposter to the station house to be processed.

By now, shocked bystanders had collected, watching the drama unfold. The Carrozza's Fish deliveryman collected the bags of shrimp from the road. Fortunately, none had broken open in the scuffle.

"There's nothing more to look at," Officer Martins told the crowd. "Go back to what you were doing. Your neighborhood's secure."

The onlookers didn't know what to think. It appeared a man of the cloth had been chased and tackled in the street by some Gloucester cop. The community held a great deal of respect for the Gloucester police, as well as for priests, and it seemed they had just witnessed an unconscionable act.

Officer Martins dropped Vinnie off at Flannery's and filled Paul in on what had happened. Paul thanked him profusely. Although Flannery would probably never see his money again, he would have the satisfaction of knowing the thief was off the streets, on his way to jail. Paul made sure a tote pack with six pound-and-a-half lobsters was ready for the police officer when he left. That was the way Flannery showed his appreciation to anyone who went the extra mile for him. Vinnie went upstairs to the men's locker room and was swarmed by workers on their afternoon break who couldn't wait to hear the details.

As soon as he got word that the thief had been processed, Paul called Flannery to keep him apprised of the afternoon's events. "They got him," Paul told Flannery. "He was arraigned this afternoon, but because it was a nonviolent crime and the dollar amount of the theft was fairly small, the judge let the guy out on bail."

"So he didn't spend so much as a night in jail," Flannery commented, annoyed that there seemed to be no punishment for the crime.

"No," Paul conceded, "but he has a court date. I don't think he'll get away with it in the long run. At least I hope he doesn't."

"Where's the guy from?" Flannery asked. "Is he a Gloucester guy?"

"That's what I would have thought too, but from what the police said, he's a drifter in his midforties who moved to this area for the summer," Paul answered. "He'd been in trouble before, for shoplifting, pickpocketing, and minor things like that. Nothing violent. He was stepping up his game this summer for some reason. I don't know why he set his sights on Gloucester."

"Maybe he thought there were easy marks in Gloucester," Flannery said. Then he added, "At least we proved him wrong. Thanks for letting me know."

"No problem. I'm glad your scheme worked."

*   *   *   *   *

Two days later, on Wednesday morning, a week after making the *Bay State Skye* discovery, Jimmy and Murph headed out to check their traps. It was a wonderfully calm day, and the sun was just appearing over the horizon. There was a mist on the surface of the sea, which gave an eerie feel to Gloucester Harbor. As the sun rose higher in the sky, Jimmy looked toward the Dog Bar Breakwater, which reached all the way to Eastern Point Lighthouse. The breakwater was built right around 1900 by the Army Corp of Engineers partially because the building of the lighthouse in 1832 hadn't totally prevented ships from running aground on Dog Bar Reef and partly to keep the water calm during storms. For Jimmy, the breakwater meant freedom. He was his own man once he passed it, the captain of his ship, in full control of his own destiny, and he liked it that way.

Murph was out on deck preparing to pull the first traps of the day when Jimmy called to him. It was strange to hear from Jimmy that soon after leaving dock, so Murph dropped what he was doing and headed for the wheelhouse. When he opened the door, Jimmy was backing off the throttle. His hand was at his forehead, trying to block out the rising sun.

"Do you see that?" Jimmy asked, his finger pointing to a spot about two hundred feet from the granite breakwater.

"See what?" Murph asked. "I don't see anything. Let's get going. I have plans tonight." He turned to head back out the door.

"Come back," Jimmy urged his brother. "It's right there, floating just to the left of the breakwater."

Murph took a good long look and said, "Yeah, I see it now. What is it? Maybe a dead fish?"

"We need to go take a look," Jimmy said.

Jimmy gave the *Anna May* just enough throttle to slowly advance to the buoyant lump rising and falling in the gentle waves. As they drew nearer, they realized, to their horror, that they had discovered a floating body.

"What the hell?" Murph cried out, nervously running his fingers through his sun-bleached hair, pacing back and forth. "We need to get out of here."

"We can't just leave the body. It will sink eventually, and it might never be discovered," Jimmy told Murph.

"That would work for me, or maybe he'll wash up on shore, which would be the best-case scenario," Murph suggested. He moved closer to Jimmy and, in a quiet voice, as if someone might overhear, said, "You know who this could be don't you?"

"Who?" Jimmy asked.

"It could be Billy or Tony Golini. Do you know how it would look if after finding their boat, a week later to the day we found one of their bodies? We'll be the number-one suspects for sure."

"Would you recognize a Golini brother if you saw one?" asked Jimmy.

"Probably not," answered Murph.

"Neither would I," Jimmy said, grabbing a gaff to pull the body close to the boat.

"We're really doing this?" Murph asked.

"We're really doing this," Jimmy declared.

The two men did their best to turn the body over in the water, preparing themselves for something that, once seen, could never be erased from their memories. They knew they would have to live with the recollection of the face for the rest of their lives. But when they succeeded in turning the corpse enough to see the face, they were relieved to note the soft tissue around the eyes, which was usually the first part of a body to be eaten by sea life, was virtually intact. It seemed the body hadn't been floating in the water for very long.

Satisfied that the body was too fresh to have been one of the Golini brothers, Jimmy called the Gloucester police to report their discovery. They waited with the dead body for an agonizing thirty minutes before the police boat pulled up alongside Jimmy's, with two officers on board. One was Officer David Santos, a white-haired cop nearing retirement who normally handled minor incidents in the harbor. The second was Officer Francisco Martins, the very same man who had apprehended the fake priest con artist earlier that week.

"The *Anna May*," the senior police officer read from the side of Jimmy's boat. "Hey, weren't you boys the ones who found the *Bay State Skye* last week?"

"Yes we were," Jimmy responded confidently, looking the cop straight in the eye. Murph glanced at his brother with a huge I-told-you-so look on his face.

"Either you boys have eagle eyes or you're the luckiest sons of bitches," Officer Martins joked.

"Or the unluckiest," Murph said. Then he added in an annoyed tone of voice, "We should be out there fishing right now."

"We won't hold you up. But we'll need some information before you're on your way," Officer Martins informed the two brothers as he took out a camera and snapped a couple of photos of the scene. "Is this where you first discovered the body?"

"Floating right here, just off the breakwater," Jimmy reported as Murph jumped into the police boat to give the two officers a hand pulling the body on board.

"You don't suppose it's one of the Golini brothers, do you?" Officer Santos asked.

"I doubt it," Jimmy answered. "Look at the way he's dressed. I don't know any fisherman who would go to work wearing a pair of black dress pants and a sports shirt. He'd probably still be wearing his grundgies, too. There weren't any grundgies found on the *Bay State Skye*, and there isn't a fisherman who wouldn't be wearing his grundgies while he worked."

"Good point," said the officer.

"Besides, a man who's been dead for as long as the Golini brothers probably wouldn't be floating," Murph added.

"You'd be surprised," Officer Santos said, leaning against the side of the boat. "I've seen cases when a man hit the sea face-first, and his windpipe closed with the pressure of the water. That kept the air from escaping his lungs and caused him to float for quite a while. In another case, a body had sunk for a time, then suddenly bobbed back up to the surface. The coroner explained that when the anaerobic bacteria inside his gut had eaten any food left in it and even some of its soft tissue, it produced gas. Once there was enough of it, the body rose to the surface again."

"More than I needed to know," Murph declared.

"It's only nature taking its course," Officer Santos stated matter-of-factly. "Now let's have a look at this body."

Murph and the two police officers turned the body over so that it was lying faceup. "We didn't think he'd been in the water very long. None of the soft tissue around the eyes had been eaten," Murph explained.

"I'd say you're right about that," Officer Santos replied as Officer Martins took a couple of photos of the dead man. "Because the body has very few signs of decomposition, it's relatively easy to identify how he died. See the slight bulging of the corpse's eyes and the protruding tongue? That leads me to believe this was a homicide. He's obviously been strangled. See the ligature marks around his neck? Course this isn't the official cause of death. Someone with a higher pay scale will have to make that call. But that would be my guess. What do you think, Fran?"

Officer Martins thought for a moment. "Ya know, I think I recognize this guy. I wouldn't stake my life on it but, he could be the fake priest I collared a couple of days ago for stealing from some local fish companies." He took a closer look, "Ya, I'm sure this is the guy. I knew he was out on bail, but how the hell'd he wind up dead in the harbor?"

"And so the plot thickens," the senior officer remarked. Both cops glanced at the Sweeney brothers.

"Don't look at us," Murph said defensively. "We never laid eyes on this guy until just now."

"We should be shoving off. You can get our contact information from the Coast Guard," Jimmy told the officers. "They have it from the *Bay State Skye* report."

"All right," Officer Santos told them. "Be sure to stay local until we clear this up."

"We have no intentions of going anywhere but fishing," Murph said.

"You know everything we know," Jimmy added.

"That's probably true," Officer Martins said, then added half-jokingly, "but who's to say you boys didn't suddenly go on a killing spree?"

"If that were the case, we wouldn't be stupid enough to keep handing you evidence," Jimmy replied.

"Maybe we should've left the body for someone else to find. We could be pulling traps right now instead of being held up here," Murph fumed as he climbed back into the *Anna May* and gave a big push off the police boat.

"Aw, Fran's just messing with you boys. We really appreciate you helping us out," Officer Santos said.

"We know," Jimmy agreed. "Take it easy."

"You, too," the senior officer replied.

As soon as the *Anna May* was clear of the police boat, Jimmy gave her full throttle, heading past the breakwater and out to open ocean.

*　*　*　*　*

The police boat headed in the opposite direction, making its way toward shore. Officer Martins notified his office that he was bringing in a homicide victim to be sure the coroner was waiting for them. Once docked, the two policemen helped the coroner bag the body. It wasn't long before the body of the fake priest was on its way to the morgue. When it arrived, fingerprints were taken, and sure enough, the corpse was none other than the man who had been masquerading as a priest to steal seafood from unsuspecting dealers.

The two officers were quiet on the ride back to the station house until Officer Santos broke the silence. "I had breakfast at Robby's place this morning," he began, "and while I was there, I overheard

Mrs. Caputo talking to a couple of friends about the fake priest. She seemed to know a lot about what happened, way more than I knew, that's for sure."

"Are you talking about the Mrs. Caputo who hails from the North End of Boston whose family's connection with the mob is pretty well known around here?" Officer Martins asked.

"That's the one," Officer Santos confirmed. He paused for a moment, then added, "I can't help but think the manner in which the thieving fake priest died had all the earmarks of a mob hit. You know, obviously strangled with a thin wire and tossed in the harbor. Quick and easy. I'll bet they won't find a shred of evidence on the body either."

"Wouldn't surprise me," Officer Martins agreed. "What are you saying, that Mrs. Caputo ordered a hit on him?"

"She was sitting at Robby's place eating her ketchup-smothered scrambled eggs, telling her friends that anyone posing as a man of the cloth while pulling a con had no business breathing air on this earth. A crime against God himself was how she put it," Officer Santos recalled.

"I don't know," Officer Martins responded as he pulled the cruiser into a parking space and the two men got out. "I don't see Mrs. Caputo as a murderer."

"She was angry enough to be one," Officer Santos continued. "I didn't have to eavesdrop. Her table was at least twenty feet away from me, and she was so worked up she was actually shouting about it. She didn't seem to be upset about the theft as much as she was mortified that the man had impersonated a priest to commit the crime."

"Her family connections to the mob would make it easy for her to arrange a hit—that's for sure," Officer Martins replied. He noticed Congressman Contoro jogging up the steps of the station house and held the door open when he arrived at the top.

"Maybe we should take a drive over and have a talk with Mrs. Caputo," Officer Santos suggested.

"What do you want with Mrs. Caputo?" Contoro asked.

"We've just come from fishing that fake priest's corpse out of the drink less than an hour ago," Officer Martin told the congressman. "Officer Santos here overheard Mrs. Caputo making some pretty incriminating statements at Robby's breakfast joint this morning."

"From what I've heard, that con artist was a boil on the ass of society. No one's gonna miss him," Contoro said. "But Mrs. Caputo on the other hand, is a pillar of the community, apart from that pesky connection her family has to the underworld. She does a lot of good for our district and works hard supporting a number of organizations that are crucial to the well-being of this city."

"Not to mention her heading a large voting base for you," Officer Martins added.

"Well, there's that too," the congressman agreed, smiling. Then he continued, "Unless that woman strangled the man herself, I'd let it lie. We're well rid of the thief, and we don't want to go rattling Mrs. Caputo's cage needlessly. After all, you don't even know where the man was killed and probably never will. If it was a mob hit, there'll be no evidence to speak of, and nobody's gonna bear witness. Hell, we don't even know where the guy's from."

"We'll see what the chief says," Officer Martins assured the congressman as they parted ways. The two officers headed for the captain's office.

*   *   *   *   *

It was afternoon before the cops called to inform Paul that the thief would no longer be capable of standing trial. Paul actually felt a little bad about what had happened. He wanted the man to be punished for his crimes, but he didn't want to see him dead. He called Flannery to let him in on the unexpected turn of events.

"You'll never guess," Paul said to Flannery, rather subdued. "Nobody could have seen this one coming."

"What happened?" Flannery asked.

"They fished the guy they arrested for stealing our lobster meat out of Gloucester Harbor this morning."

"What happened to him?" Flannery asked.

"There's no official word, but from what I've been told, I think he was probably strangled," Paul responded. "Jimmy and Murph found the body floating by the breakwater and called the police boat in."

"Really? They seem to be Johnny-on-the-spot lately," Flannery joked.

"It would seem so," Paul replied. "But they've had nothing to do with any of it as far as I know. They just seem to be in the right place at the right time."

"Do they know what happened to the thieving bastard, God rest his soul?" Flannery asked with a hint of sarcasm in his voice.

"Police are going on the assumption it was a mob hit, and they'll probably just let it lie from there," Paul speculated.

"It's possible," Flannery agreed. "They had his name from the processing desk and court. Considering how you're telling me the body was discovered, for all intents and purposes, it could have been a hit."

"I don't know anything about the mob, but I guess it's consistent with things I've read and seen in the movies," Paul said.

"Whatever happened," Flannery conceded, "we won't be getting our day in court."

"Which may be a good thing. Vinnie was dreading having to go to court to testify," Paul said. Then he added, "What a terrifying end to a bizarre incident."

"Sure is," Flannery agreed. "I guess the moral to this story is that if you're going to commit a crime, you should stay away from dressing up and posing as a priest."

"Words to live by," Paul quipped and hung up the phone. Then he wondered if there really was something to the talk of a *Bay State Skye* curse. Leaning back in his chair and thinking for a moment, however, he said aloud, "Nah, that's just ridiculous" and got up to take a quick walk out to the back dock.

CHAPTER 6

"Release the deer, everybody. Release the deer," Denny crooned in a suave, soft voice. He was speaking into Flannery's PA system, which could be heard throughout the plant, clear to the outside parking lot. Meredith smiled, whereas Paul shook his head and sighed. Murph, Jimmy and Sully, who had just arrived to pick up bait, looked at Denny, puzzled.

"Flannery just pulled into the parking lot. I'm giving everyone a heads-up he's arrived. You know, like in *Funny Farm*, the Chevy Chase movie from a couple of years ago?" Jimmy and Sully still looked confused, but an expression of recognition swept across Murph's face.

"Oh yeah, when Chevy Chase was trying to sell his house, and he signaled for workers to let deer go on the property as potential customers drove up the driveway. He thought it would make his home more attractive," Murph said, "but wasn't that 'cue the deer'?"

"I changed it to make it my own," Denny replied with a sheepish grin.

"Well, I'd try to hide any deer on my property. Those little buggers will eat every shrub you have down to the nubs," Sully said. "And don't get me started on the ticks."

"Oh, we wouldn't want to do that," Murph commented with a

wide smile. Sully snickered, realizing he was putting a damper on what could only be described as a perfect late-summer day.

"What's Flannery doing up here the Thursday before Labor Day?" Jimmy asked, changing the subject. "I would think he'd be on his way to his home on the Cape this close to the last long weekend of summer."

Flannery usually worked from the main plant in Boston. Although he was in contact with the Gloucester plant by phone several times a day, he seldom visited in person. Jimmy was glad to have happened by on such an uncommon occasion. Flannery's knack for telling an interesting story was well known, and the energetic sixty-five-year-old's reputation for being able to sell ice to Eskimos was well earned. Jimmy was looking forward to seeing Flannery and hearing a few of his tales, even if it meant he wouldn't be getting an early start fishing today.

"They're having a meeting about the gurry plant. Something's got to be done. The rich folks in East Gloucester are complaining about the smell of the fish offal," Meredith said. Then she added somewhat sarcastically, "Guess they haven't gotten used to the scent of fish heads and racks after they've spent a few days out in the air."

"Well, the folks up in picturesque Lunenburg, Nova Scotia don't complain when the whole town reeks of rotting fish from their dehydrating plant. It means the community's thriving, and everyone benefits from the business," Sully added.

"What's up in Lunenburg, Nova Scotia?" Denny asked, reminding everyone that this was way outside his triangle of existence.

"It's an old fishing village that would put you in mind of Rockport. Fishing's the number-one industry in a lot of those seaside Nova Scotia communities. But lately, they've been trying to attract more tourists and summer folks because it's getting harder and harder to make a living solely in the fish business," Paul replied.

"Well, they'd better think twice about that," Murph chimed in. "Johnny was telling us the other night that he's next in line for a mooring in Gloucester Harbor. I don't know if you've heard, but

Bob Carson's *Lizzy Jane* is headed to Florida to do some stone crab fishing and semiretire, so there's a slot opening up for a fishing boat. Normally, it'd be a given that Johnny's boat would get the nod, but the harbormaster's strongly considering putting a sailboat in its place."

"That'd be a shame, especially because he's taken such a hit from the *Bay State Skye* incident. Johnny could use a break, and the community would be better off with another fishing boat in the harbor," Paul remarked.

Denny had almost forgotten about Flannery's arrival, and now he rushed to open the door to head back to the lobster room, doing so just in time to see the plastic strips on the forklift door part to reveal the five-foot-eight, blue-eyed Flannery strolling into the plant. His snow-white hair showed no trace of the chestnut-brown locks he'd had as a youth, and although he wasn't as fit as he used to be, Flannery often claimed his doctor said he had the heart of a thirty-year-old. Although it would be hard to find anyone who would buy into that description, most who knew Flannery would have to agree he had the energy of a man half his age. A slightly younger man, with graying hair and tanned skin, followed close behind him.

Both men headed straight to the office, and as they walked in, Flannery half-jokingly proclaimed, "You lobstermen starting the Labor Day holiday early this year? Or did finding that fake priest's body floating in the harbor yesterday scare you out of the water for a few days? You boys have had quite a week for yourselves, haven't you?"

"Hopefully, that's the last of it. We just want to get back to lobstering. We're here to pick up some bait," Murph said. "Then we'll be steaming out."

"Well, if it's anything like the past week or two, you boys should make a pretty penny to finish up the month of August," Flannery commented. Then, turning to Paul and Meredith, he added, "Paul, Meredith, you remember Wayne Conroy, don't you?"

Paul immediately recognized the name of Flannery's mentor and biggest investor and jumped to his feet to shake Wayne's hand. "Of course we do. We see Wayne's Crab Royale restaurant orders come through all the time. What are you doing up this way? Scoping out another historical building to restore and turn into a restaurant?"

"Not this time. My wife and I are planning to drive up to Acadia National Park today with some friends, and I thought we'd pick up a few lobster rolls for the trip," Wayne said.

"I'll let Rosa know. How many are you going to need?" Meredith asked as she slipped off her tall stool and jumped to the floor.

"Four would be great, Meredith. Thanks!" Wayne replied. "I'm sure we could buy some lobster rolls on the way, once we've crossed the border into Maine, but I've told my friends how great your lobster rolls are, and we all agreed we shouldn't settle for anything less than the best!"

"Well, thank you, Wayne," Meredith said, impressed that a multimillionaire like Wayne Conroy would be so gracious and that he even remembered her name. "I guess we can't take all the credit. We buy our rolls fresh every morning from a local bakery. But you can thank Jimmy and Murph for the lobster meat. The batch we're using today came from that huge catch they had a week or so ago. You remember, Jimmy, that Wednesday catch you came in with after finding the *Bay State Skye*?

"Hard to forget that day," Jimmy answered.

"We froze a lot of that meat right after the cook, but we've gone through so many sandwiches in the last week, we had to let some of it up again," Meredith added. "The tourist season started off slow because of the cold start to the summer, but now it seems we're making up for it."

Meredith called to Rosa as she left the office. Once the door had closed, Flannery turned to face Jimmy and said, "Terrible thing about the *Bay State Skye*. Lucky you happened by when you did. Did you know the Golini brothers well?"

"I didn't really know either of them, other than by reputation, which up until this incident was pristine. But Vinnie knew Billy

Golini pretty well," Jimmy said.

"Yeah, Vinnie worked down at the Boston Fish Pier with him for a few years straight out of high school. Stand-up guy, as far as I've heard," Murph said. Then he added, "I can't believe they're gone."

"What the hell happened out there?" Flannery directed his question to Murph, figuring he'd get more information from him than he would from Jimmy.

Jimmy quickly intercepted the question, much to Murph's relief. "We don't know. The boat was abandoned," he replied.

"And really messed up," said Murph.

"Are you men sure you didn't off the Golini brothers," Wayne teased, a gleam in his eye, "considering what they'd done to your friend's gear and all?"

Murph couldn't keep quiet. "I might have been tempted," he admitted, "but there was nobody there to off!"

"Strangest thing I've ever come across," added Jimmy, still somewhat troubled by the memory of it all.

"But after hearing about the Golini brothers' financial woes, it was pretty easy to see how this could have happened," Sully piped up, in an awkward attempt to stick up for his friends.

"What do you mean?" Flannery asked.

"Well, the word around town is they owed a lot of people money since their accountant took off with their family's life savings, and they were having trouble paying their bills. That could explain why both of them disappeared in such a curious way," Sully explained. "Someone might have tried to collect a debt, and things got ugly."

"Though it could have been simply that one of the brothers became tangled in his gear and was hauled overboard. The other brother would have jumped in to try to free him, as Murph or I would in the same situation, and neither survived. Everything on the deck was helter-skelter. It was pretty clear they were trying to free their dragger doors from the lobster gear when something happened," Jimmy added, trying to bring everyone back to reality.

"It's one of those things that's probably going to remain a mystery, which is too bad for their families. I'm sure they'd like to have some closure, if nothing else," Paul concluded.

"Lots of bad things can happen out there, but I've never felt freer than when I'm sailing. I bet that's why you've chosen the profession you're in—am I right?" Wayne asked the three lobster fishermen, trying to bring a little levity to the conversation.

"I guess you're right about that," Jimmy replied with a smile. Murph and Sully agreed.

"I was accepted into Yale on a full basketball scholarship," Murph added, "but it wasn't for me. I quit before the first semester was over. I've always known the sea is where I belong."

"The sea is alluring—that's for sure—and every so often it can render a miracle," Wayne added. Jimmy sat up, hoping that finally, the focus would be off his brother and himself.

"Wayne's quite a sailor, you know," Flannery said, seeming genuinely enamored with his longtime friend.

"Several years ago, I bought a forty-foot fiberglass sailboat that was built back in 1977. It has two masts and a flying jib on the front. Ever since then, I've been hooked," Wayne began. "I named her the *Liberty*, and we sailed her on Lake Saint Clair and the Great Lakes for years while I was building up my restaurants in Dearborn and Troy. Her mainsail is a brilliant yellow, which matches her yellow hull. Everyone would recognize her crossing the finish line without even needing to try to make out her name on the side of her bow. Man, don't I love the rush of a good sailboat race!"

"That's something Murph has always talked about doing," Jimmy said.

"You know it," Murph agreed.

"Well, we've been focusing on building up the Crab Royale restaurants on the east coast of Florida lately, so what could be more perfect than to bring the *Liberty* down to southern Florida?" Wayne continued his story. "Several months after the *Liberty* arrived, my wife, our seven kids, and a couple of friends joined me for a sail off the coast of Jupiter. It was a beautiful day, with a pretty good chop.

We were enjoying the warmth of the sea when, with absolutely no warning, a rogue wave came over the stern of the sailboat. While the boat and everything in it was being tossed around, everyone scrambled to find something to grab hold of, anything to keep them from getting swept overboard. As I grabbed a rope on the port side of the sailboat, to my horror, I saw my twelve-year-old son being washed overboard and into the sea. It happened so fast; there was no way to catch him." Wayne's voice cracked, obviously still shaken by the gravity of the event.

"Could anyone else on board skipper the boat besides you?" Flannery asked, unsure what he would do in the same situation.

"That was the problem. Your first instinct is to jump in after your child, but then there would be no one left to bring the *Liberty* in if I didn't surface again. That would endanger everyone. So I stayed put. The boat was listing to the port side pretty profoundly, so I reached my arm over the side, trying to grab hold of any part of my son. And you know what? My hand connected with his wrist, and I lifted him back into the boat," Wayne said with a smile as he slapped his hands to his knees.

"No way," said Murph, finding himself completely drawn in by Wayne's story.

"Somebody was looking down on you," Sully said, shaking his head.

"I was never one to believe in divine intervention before, but that day made a believer out of me!" Wayne added. "What were the chances that when I reached my hand in, my son would have been right there? He went over the port side of the boat to be sure, but nowhere near me or I'd have caught him before he hit the water."

"That's incredible," Flannery said. "I'm glad he lived to tell about it—both of you, really. You were better off not jumping in."

"You're not kidding. But how would you know?" Wayne added.

"Well, most of us don't think of it this way, but water is as treacherous as fire," Flannery added. "When I was a kid, my younger brother and I were in a small boat off the Dorchester boatyard. It was a beautiful day, and just like that, storm clouds rolled in. The seas picked up and in a matter of minutes, waves swamped our boat. We were both tossed into the water, but luckily our boat floated just below the surface. We were bobbing in the water for a little over an hour, and even though we had the good sense to stay with the boat, it was amazing how quickly the water zapped our strength. Luckily, a pleasure boat spotted us as they headed in and picked us up. If they hadn't happened by, I don't know if I'd be here today."

"Storms can come up quick. I guess anyone who's spent time on the water will have at least one of those stories," Sully admitted. "I almost rolled my last boat over in a freak January storm."

"Really?" Paul asked. Paul had been selling Sully bait for going on fifteen years and never knew.

"Yep, there was a cold front coming in that was supposed to have fifteen- to twenty-five-mile-an-hour winds with it. But an unexpected snow squall line came with the front, and in about five minutes, the wind picked up to about fifty miles an hour. I got everything buttoned up when I saw it coming and started heading home, but I didn't have enough time. Within minutes, the waves became like mountains, churning. Usually you know whether you should ride down the wave or turn around and ride up over it, but in this situation, I couldn't tell. The water was too agitated. There was one time when I surfed down a wave and the bow dug in, and the stern started lifting in the air. One side of the boat actually went in the water."

"Were you in the shoals?" Flannery asked Sully. Flannery knew of many fishing boats that got into trouble when they hit rough weather in shallow water. The waves would kick off the seafloor, sending the boat over the wave's top, and once on the other side, the boat's bow would go speeding straight into the ocean floor. From there, the boat usually would break up or flip. More than one fishing boat had been lost in that scenario.

"No, I was about ten miles offshore in about three hundred feet of water," Sully answered. "But the waves weren't uniform, so I didn't have time to steer straight down into them. I hit them more diagonally. When the stern came up, my lobster tank—which had five hundred pounds of lobsters in it—slid across the deck a few feet. With all that water and weight, it didn't help."

"How'd you get out?" Wayne asked, his eyes glued to Sully.

"Luck," Sully answered. "The wave that lifted the stern also broke all over the deck. I was knee-deep in water, but it seemed to have helped weigh the stern down and deplete the energy of the surge at the same time."

"I know that all too well!" Wayne admitted.

"Did you have any reservations about going back out there?" Flannery asked.

"Yeah, what did you think after all that?" Paul chimed in.

"Well," Sully said, pausing for a moment. "I started thinking that I needed a bigger boat. It wasn't too long after that I found the forty-two-footer I have now."

"How big was your other boat?" Wayne asked.

"Thirty-seven feet," Sully replied. "But the boat I have now is a little wider too."

The office door opened, and Meredith came in with a bag full of lobster rolls. "Why do I think I've just missed some great stories?" Meredith asked, looking at the astonished expressions on everyone's faces.

"Don't worry—I'll fill you in later on," Paul assured Meredith. She handed the sandwiches to Wayne.

"Thank you much," Wayne said, reaching for the bag. "What do I owe you?"

Before Meredith could get a word out, Flannery said, "Not a thing. I hope you have a great trip. Don't fall in Thunder Hole!"

"I'll try not to," Wayne called back as he walked out the office door and disappeared through the plastic strips of the loading-dock door.

Jimmy's curiosity got the better of him, and turning to Flannery, he asked, "So are they thinking of closing down the gurry-processing plant for good?"

"No, no, no," replied Flannery. "We just have to find a better way to handle the gurry. As I'm sure you all know, East Gloucester serves partly as a bedroom community for Boston. The people living there come to Gloucester because they think they love the fishing industry. It's romantic. They see the boats, the fishermen, and it's wonderful. But they forget that fish smells. Course fresh fish doesn't smell. But after the fish is cut, the gurry, the offal, the fish that's left, the heads and bones? Something has to be done with these processing by-products. And so they sit over at the gurry plant, waiting to be processed."

"Do you know who owns the gurry plant?" Jimmy asked.

Flannery looked in Jimmy's direction and, shaking his head, explained, "Our old gurry plant in Gloucester is run by a chicken farmer from down Maine named Henry Putnam who, from what I understand, is related to the Golini family who owns that damned *Bay State Skye*."

"Really?" Murph asked. "How are they related?"

"I think they're first cousins," Flannery answered. "Henry was always more of a farmer than a fisherman, but he saw a cheap way to produce chicken feed from collecting and processing gurry, so he invested in the plant. He probably wouldn't have thought of the idea if he hadn't had cousins working in the fishing industry. Not only does he use the processed gurry for his own chickens, but he also supplies chicken feed to many farms in his area, and he owns the plant. All the fish waste from Boston, some from New Bedford, and of course, most from Gloucester, is delivered to the Gloucester gurry plant for disposal. The problem is that there are big storage areas at the plant for the gurry with no refrigeration. This stuff would come in totes, great big totes, and it would sit out there in the warm, humid air in the summertime, and bacteria would build up. The smell would be bad enough when the fish were just sitting there, but when it was placed in the oven to cook and heat was put to it, I don't have to tell you the smell was atrocious! Course they have to cook the gurry to dehydrate it. There's no getting around that."

Everyone nodded in agreement. Flannery went on, "Well, unlike the fishing villages of Nova Scotia where real fishing people reside who know that the smell of the dehydration plant means prosperity to all who live there, the residents of East Gloucester, who came up from Boston for romance, not for the smell of rotting fish, felt this situation was intolerable. A couple of weeks ago, it all hit the fan, and the residents just wanted the smell to stop and the gurry plant shut down. There was hell to pay, and the state of Massachusetts stepped in and said that unless the odor from the plant could be taken care of, they were going to close the plant. And they did. Course if the plant's closed, that's it for the fishing industry in the state because there's no place for us to get rid of our gurry."

"What's being proposed?" Jimmy asked, acting as the spokesperson for the group.

"Well, we're having a big meeting of the Gloucester Fisheries Association tonight to see if we can't put our heads together and come up with a solution," Flannery answered. Everyone in the room knew that this was a critical issue for the fish processors, not only in Gloucester but in Boston and New Bedford too.

"It's been a few weeks since any gurry has been processed. I'm sure the gurry from as far back as the *Bay State Skye* and beyond is sitting up there in the plant. We need to do something—and soon," Paul added.

"Oh, that's got to smell ripe, for sure," said Murph.

"Good luck tonight," Paul said.

Flannery nodded and went upstairs to his office. He opened the locked door and glanced out the row of windows revealing a picturesque view of Gloucester Harbor. Then he got down to the business of planning out exactly what he was going to say at the meeting.

As evening approached, Flannery left his office and walked down the dark corridor to his private bathroom, past the eerily quiet men's locker room. The fish cutters and other workers went home at three, having worked a full eight-hour day by then, starting at six thirty in the morning. Flannery's private bathroom had become the women's bathroom/locker room because there was no separate facility for women in the plant. With only three women working at Flannery's, it wasn't cost-effective to have a separate women's locker room added on, especially because Flannery was seldom at the Gloucester plant. The original bathroom plans called for the installation of a phone on the wall inside the stall so that Flannery would never be out of reach, but that detail hadn't been carried out when the plant was built.

Flannery opened the door to a bathroom very different from that which he had envisioned for himself. His senses were immediately overwhelmed by the sickeningly sweet smell of perfume that had been heated to about eighty degrees. The only female fish cutter had turned up the electric heater to warm herself after being out on the chilly production floor all day. The perfume she had sprayed on her skin in an attempt to cover the fishy odor still lingered heavily in the room. She had forgotten to turn the heat down before she left, and Flannery made a mental note to talk to Paul in the morning about checking the bathroom each night before he left.

Flannery headed down the linoleum staircase to the fish-cutting floor. As he passed the office, he waved to Denny, who was waiting for the last few lobster boats to arrive with their catch. He would have preferred to have been waiting by the back dock with a fishing rod in his hand and a line in the water, but he had to be within earshot of the phone to pick up when boats called in on their ship-to-shore lines.

Denny waved back and hollered, "Good luck!" as he watched Flannery part the plastic strips of the dock door. Denny wasn't sure that Flannery heard what he had said, but he noted the determination with which Flannery left the plant. Hopefully, the gurry situation would be settled tonight. Denny's livelihood was riding on it, and he had two young boys to feed.

*   *   *   *   *

Flannery didn't have too far to travel to the Gloucester Fisheries meeting. They were always held at Cameron's, which was right across the street from Harbor Loop, less than a mile from Flannery's Fish House on Main Street. As he stepped out of his white Lincoln Continental with all the bells and whistles, Flannery glanced up at Cameron's iconic sign. The sprawling eagle resting on the opening blue scroll that revealed the restaurant's name in large, red, sans-serif lettering gave an appealing, patriotic feel to this popular local hangout. The sturdy brick building was built to weather any storm, being so close to the harbor, and Cameron's slogan, "Where the Natives Dine," was, for the most part, true.

Flannery walked into the lobby and was immediately met by Congressman Barry Contoro. Barry had been courting Flannery for a while, hoping for a sizeable campaign contribution. The congressman gave Flannery a hearty handshake and escorted him into the small function room where the meeting would take place. The walls were an aqua blue, possibly an attempt to mimic the color of the ocean water that the famous Fisherman's Memorial statue overlooked just a short distance away on the boulevard. But in reality, even on the calmest days, the sea here was a deep, midnight blue. As Flannery entered the room, he noticed the table on one end where the officers of the association would be seated. There was room for five or six people at that table, including the president, the vice president, the secretary, and the treasurer, among others. Congressman Contoro and Flannery made their way to one of the smaller rectangular tables near the front, on the right-hand side of the room.

After a brief discussion of the congressman's take on the *Bay State Skye* tragedy, which didn't reveal anything more than what Flannery already knew, the congressman made a trip to the bar to pick up drinks for Flannery and himself. He returned with a couple of beers, and placing one in front of Flannery, he asked, "So you're not a Gloucester native. How the hell did you manage to wind up in the fish business?"

Flannery retorted, "You're a Gloucester native from a long line of fishermen. How the hell did you wind up in politics?"

"Touché!" replied the congressman as he raised his glass in the air. Flannery reciprocated the move, and they both took a good swig of beer, then put their glasses down on the table.

"I've always been on the processing end of the fish business, not on a boat like you were. I guess the *Bay State Skye* is a reminder of just how dangerous it can get out there," Flannery said.

"That's the truth, but I didn't leave the sea because I was afraid. There was a real sense of freedom, mixed with a feeling of suspense, as you steamed past the breakwater and out to open ocean. When you were lucky enough to bring in a substantial catch, it felt like you'd won the lottery. What I didn't like was the smell, the slime, and the general working environment on the boat. I never could get used to it," the congressman replied in earnest.

"I hear you. I was working for a stationery company in Boston straight out of high school," Flannery began. "I checked the orders as they came through and did some bookkeeping. It was a good job, but when the accountant left, they didn't hire a new one, and I wound up doing all the accounting too. Soon after, the office manager reduced my vacation time from two weeks to only one, so I went to Peterson's Employment to look for another job. I was in luck. Colbert's Seafood Company was looking for an office worker. On my lunch break, I walked into the fish market at Colbert's, and the smell of fish hit me. That made me pause for a moment, but I finally made my way around back. They were unloading barrels of fish from a truck, and I immediately decided this was not for me. Printing wasn't great, but this was worse. I resigned myself to go back to the stationery store. A week or so later, I was told I had to work a half day on Saturdays. That's when I went back to Peterson's Employment and asked if the job at Colbert's was still there, and they said it was. I applied and got the job as their new billing clerk. Soon I drove the trucks and made deliveries when I had some spare time. I went from making twelve dollars a week to making nineteen dollars a week. My mother loved the money! I was sixteen at the time and had to help take care of the household since my father wasn't around. When I first started, the guy in the fish market asked if I was the new guy, and when I said yes, he gave me some lobster meat and a bag of chips to take home. My mother had never tasted lobster meat in her life. Oh, did she love that job!"

Flannery took another swig of beer and continued. "But not long after, the war started up, and I joined the navy to do my part. When I got out, I had taken my SATs and was all signed up to go to Boston University in the fall. But I made the big mistake of going back to Colbert's to see the guys because I had just gotten out of the service. Colbert grabbed me and asked me to look at the new cutting line he was designing. He wanted my opinion. I didn't know anything about cutting lines, but I drew something up anyway and returned the next week. Colbert loved the changes and handed me a week's pay. Now instead of nineteen dollars a week, I got thirty-five dollars a week. That was enough to raise a family on back then. I went home and gave my mother the money. She looked up at me in amazement and asked, 'How can you not work for this nice man?' So school went out the window. I was able to go nights, but it wasn't long when I started training with Fred Maloney down at the Boston Fish Pier to learn how to buy fish. And that's how a boy from the inner city of Dorchester wound up in the fish business."

"Isn't it strange the way things work out. Everything seems to line up and push you toward where you're destined to be," Barry said, as if thinking out loud. "I was having trouble getting press coverage for my reelection campaign, when what appeared to be a routine tour of a Coast Guard MLB that would have normally attracted little attention turned into involving me in the whole *Bay State Skye* incident that everyone's been talking about since. And to think, I almost told the Coast Guard I wasn't interested. I would have been kicking myself now if I'd turned it down. You just never know."

"That's the truth," Flannery replied, and both men took

another drink of their beer.

By now, almost everyone had arrived for the meeting, and people were beginning to make their way to their seats. Even though the group was called the Gloucester Fisheries Association, it wasn't only fish processors who attended. This association was a community of all businesses that had any connection to the fishing industry, which in Gloucester was pretty much everyone. There were fish processors, to be sure, but there were also bankers, lawyers, store owners, and of course, politicians and a representative from the Chamber of Commerce, among many others who attended these meetings. There were about fifteen people in attendance for most meetings, but for a meeting where something controversial was being addressed, there could be upward of twenty-five people present. This was one of those meetings. The room was packed.

The association president rose, who was none other than Robby, the restaurant owner who occasionally stopped by Fitzy's to have a beer with Denny and Murph. In a small organization like the Gloucester Fisheries Association, pretty much everybody had been president at one time or another. This was Robby's turn, and he called the meeting to order. The secretary, who worked at Gorton's Seafood, then rose to recite the minutes from the last meeting. Once he had finished, it was time to pause for dinner.

Everyone immediately dug into the roll basket and ordered their meals off the menu. Cameron's boasted of having fresh seafood from the boats, and most of the plates were packed with baked stuffed fillet of sole, baked haddock, broiled sea scallops, or shrimp scampi served over fettuccine. There was a murmur in the room while everyone caught up with what was new in their colleagues' lives. Even though everyone had worked a full day, their hunger didn't trump the desire to catch up on the local-interest stories. Of course, the hottest topic was the discovery of the *Bay State Skye* and speculation on the fate of the Golini brothers. This was the first meeting since the abandoned dragger was discovered, and nearly everybody in town had developed a theory.

As dessert was being served and the meeting was called back to order, talk turned to the closing of the gurry plant, which was of profound interest to everyone in attendance. After several people rose to speak about the shutting down of the gurry plant and the impact it was having on the fish processors' ability to continue doing business, Flannery had his turn to speak.

"This is ridiculous," Flannery began his well-thought-out address. "We're in the fish business, a business where we have to cut fish, we have to dispose of the gurry, and we're depending on a chicken farmer from Maine to take care of our future! And the way it looks right now, we're not going to have a future because we can't handle fish without a gurry plant. We've got to stop this. We've got to take this thing over."

Then Flannery pulled out the statistics that included how much gurry was cut, the temperatures that it needed to be stored at to prevent a foul odor, and all other pertinent information. He concluded with, "Look, the future of the fishing industry should be in our hands. We're the fish processors. We're the ones who pay the boats for the fish. We should be the ones who run the gurry plant. We should take it over. We should buy out Henry Putnam, get him the hell out of it, and we'll run it ourselves. I move that we set up a New England Fish Processors' Association to take the gurry plant over."

Flannery returned to his seat with a big round of applause. Virtually everyone was on board. The decision had been made. The New England Fish Processors' Association was born, and Flannery was asked to take the helm. Flannery agreed, without any hesitation. Just as Robby was about to motion that the meeting be adjourned, Congressman Contoro rose from his seat.

"I have a quick announcement before we leave," Barry declared, and Robby motioned to the congressman to continue. "As we all know, the Golini family suffered a tragic loss with the discovery of their abandoned dragger a couple of weeks ago. While none of us can bring back the Golini brothers, we may have an opportunity to raise some funds for the Golini family this upcoming weekend. I thought we could add a few features to our traditional Labor Day weekend Gloucester Schooner Festival in remembrance of the Golini brothers and raise some money at the same time—you know, get everyone involved in a community spirit, while the tourists and summer folks are still in town."

"What did you have in mind?" Robby asked.

"We already have the Parade of Sail on Sunday morning to attract people to town," the congressman answered. "I was thinking of a fishing contest. We could hold it at Lane's Cove. I hear the bluefish are hitting in the waters between the Ipswich and Essex Rivers. If we charge for each entry and give out a cash award for the three largest bluefish caught, the leftover cash could go to the Golini family. It might help them get back on their feet, and it would give the local fishing families an activity in which they could participate. Heaven knows there aren't too many locals, save East Gloucester residents, who are polishing up their schooners to take part in the Parade of Sail. I was also thinking we could set up a tent selling cups of homemade chowder, strategically placed where spectators would be watching the Parade of Sail. That could be lucrative, especially if the ingredients were locally donated and the people manning the booth were volunteers."

"I suppose a few of us who sell homemade chowder could join together to make a few batches for the event. That is, if the processors in the area are willing to donate the fish," Robby agreed.

There was a murmuring in the group until Robby called for a vote. "All in favor of setting up a fishing contest and a booth to benefit the Golini family say aye," Robby announced, and the whole room seemed to be in agreement.

"Opposed?" Robby continued. The room was still.

"The ayes have it," Robby declared.

"I'm sure I can send a volunteer and some chowder fish your way," Flannery piped up. "But what about the *Bay State Skye*? From what I can see, she's tied up at the dock across from my plant, and nothing's being done with her. I would think the family would get a pretty penny if they sold her." Many of the others in attendance nodded their heads in agreement.

Congressman Contoro fielded the question. "You would think so at first glance. But the *Bay State Skye* suffered significant damage that day, and it's going to take some money to fix her up. Couple that with the superstitious nature of fishermen, and the ill-fated *Bay State Skye* is going to be a tough sell to anyone local."

"That's a shame," Flannery remarked. "I hope she's not destined to sit at the dock and eventually sink out of sight. She's too nice a boat for that." All in attendance agreed. It wouldn't be the first time a boat was abandoned and eventually decayed to a point where it rotted and sunk at a dock. More boats suffered that fate than one would think. The owner gets arrested, can't afford the upkeep, or simply gets tired of fishing and walks away. Flannery recalled a boat, fittingly named, *The Grim Reaper*, that had sunk at the very same spot where the *Bay State Skye* was now docked.

"If there are no further announcements?" Robby asked as he looked in the direction of Barry Contoro. Barry looked down at his beer glass and smiled. Certain that everyone had finished, Robby continued, "Then this meeting is adjourned. Have a relaxing and safe Labor Day weekend, everyone."

The next day, Flannery's phone was lighting up. The excitement in Gloucester was clear as word of the fishing industry owning its own gurry plant spread. A number of Gloucester Fisheries Association members called Flannery to congratulate him and voice their concerns about the gurry-plant closure. Flannery assured them that as soon as Labor Day weekend was over, he'd be hitting this problem head on. The gurry plant would have his undivided attention because he needed this plant up and running as much as all the other fish processors did.

*   *   *   *   *

Just before Flannery headed off to his home on the Cape to spend Labor Day weekend, he put in a call to Paul to let him know that he'd promised some chowder fish and a couple of workers for the congressman's seafood booth at the festival.

"I doubt you're going to get anyone to agree to work that booth," Paul informed Flannery.

"I'll pay any employees time and a half to work the holiday. They won't have to volunteer," Flannery told Paul.

"That's not the problem," Paul continued. "Most of your employees' sympathies lie with Johnny and the lobstermen. They won't be on board with anything that helps the dragger that destroyed virtually all of Johnny's gear. The Golini brothers put Johnny out of business at the peak of the season."

"I can understand that, but we have to send someone for at least a few hours. Maybe Doug would do it. He likes the OT. I know he occasionally takes lobster boats in, but mostly he drives a truck," Flannery suggested.

"I need Doug here to deliver and collect for the Labor Day retail orders," Paul said. "I'll ask around and see who I can round up. Time and a half will definitely be an incentive. Rosa might be interested. She has no loyalty to the lobster fishermen, and Meredith and I could take care of the retail while she's gone."

"See what you can do," Flannery said, a little disappointed but understanding the dilemma. "We'll need to ship some fish over to the booth. It's really short notice so whatever you've got that you can spare would be fine. Don't give them too much, though. If the family makes a lot of money from this event, they could walk away from the *Bay State Skye*, and that would be a shame. They need to use the money to do any repairs needed and ship the boat out of state to sell, if need be. I don't want to see it slowly sink into the harbor like *The Grim Reaper*. What an eyesore that was! If they need the money, they'll have to sell the boat."

"I'll get right on it. When will the booth be ready to take deliveries?" Paul asked.

"Call Congressman Contoro. He's in charge," Flannery said.

"OK," Paul answered. "Have a good Labor Day."

"You, too," Flannery said, knowing that his Labor Day weekend would be much better than Paul's holiday. Flannery was lucky to have someone as competent as Paul to handle things.

Paul asked around to see if anyone would be interested in earning a little OT for a few hours of work at the booth. His big mistake was asking Denny as he was taking in the lobsters from the *Anna May.* Paul wasn't dumb enough to ask in front of Jimmy and Murph, but word traveled to Murph in lightning speed, and Murph confronted Paul.

"You've got to be kidding me!" Murph blurted out as he walked through the plastic strips at the dock door. "They're planning a fundraiser for the Golini family? What about Johnny? He's going to lose his boat if he doesn't get back to fishing soon. That mortgage isn't going to pay itself!"

Paul met Murph at the door and walked back out through the plastic strips to the scale on the dock. Murph followed close behind and, moving to the other side of the scale, stood next to his brother in a display of solidarity.

"He's got a point," Jimmy said to Paul, trying to defuse the situation.

"I can't believe those guys are doing that," Denny added. "They've got to know it's only going to divide the people in Gloucester."

"They're already polarized enough, I know, with the whole gurry problem," Paul said sympathetically. "I think Congressman Contoro feels a real connection to the Golini family since he was on the MLB when the call came in. Johnny lost gear, which is devastating to be sure, but the Golinis lost two husbands, and their kids have no fathers now."

"Well, when you put it that way," Denny said.

"But maybe we can do something to help Johnny. There's nothing saying we can't have a fundraiser, too, and the proceeds will go to Johnny," Murph declared. "All the victims of this tragic event need to be helped, not a select few."

"What did you have in mind?" Paul asked, almost afraid to hear the answer.

"We could set up a booth selling just lobster rolls. We'll go to Virgilio's and see if they'll donate the sub rolls, and we'll take lobster donations from all the local lobster fishermen. They'll be happy to help out, once they hear the proceeds are going to Johnny."

Just then Sully pulled up. He jumped out of his truck and pulled a crate of lobsters off the back and set it on the dock. Sully listened intently as Murph continued.

"Then," Murph said, "we'll resurrect the greasy pole. Who says it's just for Saint Peter's Fiesta! If we put the word out, I'm sure we'll get some takers. We'll charge a fee to enter and give out prize money for the winners, and the leftover money will go to Johnny."

"I'm in," said Denny. Denny loved the thrill of navigating the wooden pole, smeared with grease, in an attempt to grab the flag at the end before falling into the harbor. "The water's warmer now than on June 29. I bet a lot of people will be psyched to have a second chance at it."

"Well, somebody's got to be able to go lobstering after you two get yourselves killed," Jimmy joked. "I'll run the lobster-roll booth, but count me out for the greasy pole."

"How about you, Sully?" Murph asked, half in jest, knowing Sully never participated in the event, even when he was younger.

"You have a better chance of seeing unicorns and dragons than seeing me up on that greasy pole this weekend!" Sully retorted in a gruff voice.

"Afraid of heights?" Denny teased as he brushed by Sully to mount his forklift.

"No, afraid of bruised ribs and broken bones!" Sully quipped.

While Murph, Denny, and Sully were focused on the fun side of the event, Jimmy was thinking of the marketing end of putting something like this together on such short notice. "If we're really going to do this, we need to get some signs up. We've got just a day to prepare and get the word out," Jimmy said.

"You're my last boat," Denny said to Jimmy. "As soon as I get these guys in water, I'll go around to some lobster dealers and collect some donations."

"Can we do a cook at Flannery's?" Jimmy asked Paul. "It will take us forever trying to cook as many lobsters as we need on a stove top."

"I don't know how great an idea it is to be supporting both sides. There's a good chance we'll be hated by virtually everyone in Gloucester," Paul said.

"You're in it anyway," Murph added. "After all, some of your employees are heading the activities for Johnny."

"I guess that's the truth," Paul said. "I just better not get my ass in a sling after all this."

"You won't," Denny said. "It's all us. You had nothing to do with it. People don't need to know the details."

With that, Denny rushed to get the *Anna May* lobsters in the tanks and headed out to ask dealers and lobstermen for donations. Jimmy called his wife, Jenny, and asked her to start making some signs. Jenny called Murph's ex and Denny's wife to help her. Before long, there were three signs on posts, hammered into the grass on the first and second Gloucester rotaries on Route 128. The signs were strategically placed in front of the professionally designed banner that Congressman Contoro had mounted on each rotary. The handmade signs, made with markers and poster board, were far more eye-catching than the congressman's vinyl banners. They had a homespun, comedic feel to them, and people laughed as they slowed to navigate the busy rotaries on their way into Gloucester. The older children joined their moms to help with some of the slogans and artwork to give the signs a more contemporary feel. Denny's oldest son was especially proud of his signs: "No bruises? No problem! Come try out for the greasy pole, and we'll hook you up," "Celebrate Labor Day! Grab your Captain America costume and try your luck at the greasy pole," and "The greasy pole wants you! Bathing suits optional."

Denny had managed to collect enough lobster donations to make about five hundred lobster rolls. His biggest donor was Glenn from the Lobster Hut on Bearskin Neck in Rockport. Glenn always contributed generously to most local causes, but this weekend he was in an extra-generous mood because the film *Mermaids* was being produced on the North Shore of Boston. Most of the filming was being done in the Rockport area, and that meant the cast would be having dinner in the Lobster Hut's tiny upstairs restaurant, which overlooked the Motif One. It had become a tradition that the cast of any movie filming on Cape Ann would spend at least one evening at Glenn's restaurant, and the cast of *Mermaids* was no exception. Cher, Winona Ryder, Christina Ricci, and director Richard Benjamin were all expected to attend. The Lobster Hut's restaurant was noted for having the freshest seafood you could get on Rockport's waterfront, and tourists who happened to spot some celebrities walking into the restaurant would wait around for hours to catch them for an autograph or a quick photo when they were leaving, not realizing there was a back door through which all celebrities exited.

While Denny was loading up the donated lobsters to take back to Flannery's to cook, a tourist walked past Denny to the back of Glenn's store where he could see the dock and the ocean beyond. It was a strong low tide, and the seawater had receded to a point where the ocean floor was fully exposed, with no water covering it.

The surprised man asked Glenn, "Where's all the water?"

Glenn shook his head from side to side and rubbed his beard and said, "I know. If this drought doesn't let up, I don't know what we're going to do."

"Well, I hope it rains soon for you," the tourist responded sympathetically, patting Glenn on the shoulder. The tourist ordered two lobster rolls with slaw and chips on the side. Denny could barely keep quiet, waiting for the lobster-roll order to come up and the man to leave.

Denny smiled at Glenn and remarked, "It's low tide, you jerk."

"I know," Glenn replied. "I'm just messing with him. I especially love it when they come back six hours later at high tide, and the water's miraculously reappeared. Then they usually get it and say, 'You ass!' and we have a good laugh."

"Well, good luck with the *Mermaids* cast. If you get a picture with someone famous, I'd love a copy," Denny called, as he was walking out the door.

"Oh, there'll be none of that," Glenn called back. "One of the reasons they always come by is the fact that I'm not star-struck. Half of them I don't even recognize. I don't get to the movies much, so I'm totally unimpressed. To me, they're just good people who've come by for a meal. That's the way I like it, and so do they."

"I can see that," Denny said. "Hey, thanks a million! If we can sell all the lobster rolls, Johnny may be back in business."

"That's the hope," Glenn replied. Then, turning to a customer who had just walked through the door, he bellowed, "Hey, how ya doing today? What can I get for you?"

Denny went back to Flannery's and started the cook. As he waited for the lobsters to steam, Denny used the calculator in the office to figure what their potential take could be. They had enough lobsters to make five hundred lobster rolls. If they sold the rolls for $9.95 each, Johnny would receive a little under $5,000 from the sandwich proceeds alone. That would certainly make a dent in the loss that Johnny suffered.

Denny's train of thought was interrupted when he looked up to see Paul emerging from the freezer. Paul tossed his head from side to side as he walked through the plastic strips of the freezer door, trying to shake his sweatshirt hood off his head. His arms were piled high with three boxes of frozen fish. Each box was labeled with "*Bay State Skye*—25 pounds—Chowder" in black wax crayon.

"I could have gotten that for you," Denny offered.

"No worries," Paul called out. "I knew exactly where they were."

"Are you letting them up?" Denny asked.

"Yes, they're for the congressman's booth," Paul answered. "Would you mind giving me a hand opening the boxes and laying the fillet pieces out on the bench? They need to be thawed by early tomorrow."

"Sure thing," Denny replied.

"Is Contoro's booth making chowder?" Denny asked.

"That's what I heard," Paul replied. "Some local restaurant owners are banding together to make the chowder for the booth. They'll be selling it by the cup."

"Oh, we're going to blow them out of the water," Denny said, extremely pleased with himself. Then he asked, "Are they expecting let-ups?"

"No, but they won't know the difference," Paul replied. "Once they're thawed, it won't be noticeable. The fish was only frozen a couple of weeks ago anyway. I thought it would be fitting for the congressman's chowder to be made with fish from the *Bay State Skye*."

"They aren't frozen; they're quick-chilled," Denny added, with a wink.

"Exactly," Paul said, smiling. Then he asked, "Why do you think you'll blow the congressman's booth out of the water?"

"Have you heard the forecast for Sunday?" Denny asked with a big grin on his face.

"No, I've been so busy I haven't seen the news in days," Paul admitted.

"Well, that meteorologist, Dick Albert, on Channel Five is saying ninety-five degrees for a high in Boston Sunday, with no sea breeze off the water. What would you prefer, a nice cool lobster roll and a bag of chips, or a piping-hot cup of fish chowder on a ninety-five-degree day?" Denny asked jokingly.

"Are you kidding?" Paul questioned. "It's never hotter than the low eighties on Labor Day weekend here. That's why the Schooner Festival's always so popular. It's a great day to be outside."

"Not this Sunday," Denny said with a laugh. "People will come just to see the schooners no matter what the weather, so we'll get a good turnout. But a nice dip in the ocean after a thrilling trip on the greasy pole will be just what the doctor ordered, I think. Top it off with a Virgilio's sub roll filled with lobster meat and mayo, fresh from the icy cooler, and we'll have the most popular activity in Gloucester!"

"I hope you do," Paul said. "But I'd hate to have all this chowder fish go to waste."

"The devil's in the details. Can't overlook the weather!" Denny gloated as he tore open the first box of chowder fish.

Just then, Doug returned from his Friday night deliveries. He parted the plastic dock door strips and walked across the cutting-room floor to grab his time card and punch out. Paul glanced over his shoulder and was delighted to see Doug. Paul still hadn't found a volunteer to work the congressman's booth and was truly hoping that Doug would be willing. He would have preferred to have Doug working in the retail store, but he was desperate.

"Hey, Doug!" Paul called out. Doug sauntered over to where they were laying out the fish.

"You're letting up fish on a Friday night?" Doug asked. "We've got enough fresh fish for tomorrow, you know." Doug gave Paul and Denny a puzzled look.

"This isn't for the retail. It's for Congressman Contoro's chowder booth at the Schooner Festival," Paul said.

"Oh, maybe that explains the sign at the rotary that I just passed," Doug said. "Is the congressman selling chowder? I didn't get a good look at the sign, but I thought it said something about a fishing contest."

"He's doing both, I guess," Paul replied.

"Beauty," said Doug. "After taking care of the orders tomorrow, I may grab my kids and see if we have any luck catching some blues."

"I thought you might want to earn time and a half at the congressman's booth tomorrow," Paul said, trying to entice Doug into working a full day. "Winning the fishing contest isn't a given; time and a half is a sure thing."

"The fishing contest is a slam dunk," Doug said. "I know where they're biting. I just need to catch the biggest one. It would be a good father daughter outing for my three girls too. I think I'll pass, but thanks for the offer." Doug walked over to the time cards, pausing a minute for the clock to read exactly five o'clock, then inserted his card to have the time stamped.

"Oh, crap," Paul said under his breath. He didn't want to work the booth himself, but Rosa had left before he could ask her if she'd like to earn some extra overtime.

"Maybe Contoro has enough volunteers already," Doug said. "You're giving him a lot of fish. They should contact the high school, or maybe call Our Lady of Good Voyage church. They're always willing to help out when a fishing family's in trouble."

"That's not a bad idea," Paul said, surprised he didn't think of that right off the bat. "I think I'll give them a call. It's short notice, but it's been short notice for all of us."

"Good luck. See you tomorrow," Doug called back as he headed for the dock door.

Paul and Denny gave a quick wave in Doug's direction.

Denny took care of laying the rest of the fish out, so Paul walked back to the office where Meredith was finishing up the lobster-room inventory. They had taken so many boats in that day that the lobster counts were off, despite doing a physical inventory of the tiered tanks three times. On the last count, Denny and Meredith discovered a crate of three- to five-pounders that had been overlooked and hadn't been emptied into the tanks yet. Meredith was relieved to find the missing lobsters, which meant as soon as she sent a fax with the figures off to Flannery's Cape Cod home, she would be able to go home herself. Paul walked into the office just as Meredith was setting up the inventory to run through the fax machine.

"Are you heading out now?" Meredith asked.

"Right after I call Our Lady of Good Voyage church to see if they could offer the congressman a couple of volunteers for his chowder booth on Sunday," Paul replied.

"That's a great idea," Meredith said.

"Yeah, Doug thought of it," Paul said. "I just hope we're not too late to get anybody there."

Paul looked through his Rolodex for the church's number. Then he picked up the phone to call. No luck. The office woman had left for the evening—and the weekend, for that matter.

"No one there?" Meredith asked.

"Should have thought of it sooner," Paul replied, rubbing his forehead. "Let's get out of here. We're in for a busy weekend."

"I'm right behind you," said Meredith.

The duo walked to their respective cars, feeling the warm air and sun on their bodies for the first time all day. It felt good. Paul thought to himself, *Working the congressman's booth might not be the worst thing that could happen. At least we'd be warm, extremely warm. There's either a feast or a famine.* Paul got in his car and waved to Meredith as he pulled out of the parking lot.

CHAPTER 7

Sunday came in a blink of an eye. While Jerry Lewis was busily working on his annual Muscular Dystrophy telethon, Cape Ann was buzzing about its own fundraisers. Denny arranged to have the greasy-pole contest included in the entertainment for the day and made sure he drove by early Sunday morning to check to see if it was ready for the event. Denny pulled over on Stacy Boulevard and stopped his car. There it was. Standing majestically two hundred feet off the shore of Pavilion Beach, the forty-five-foot telephone pole attached to a platform glistened in the dawning sunlight. The red flag had already been nailed to a stick and mounted on the end of the pole. Everything looked in order. Denny couldn't wait to have his chance at it. He had won two years ago, and the feeling of exhilaration as his fellow competitors carried him on their shoulders through town was something he'd never forget. It seemed like it was just yesterday, and it might be happening again today. *Who knows?* Denny thought.

Denny had only a day to decide what he would wear, and considering that this was a fundraiser for Johnny, he decided on buying a red Hanes T-shirt. On the back of the shirt, where everyone could see it, Denny used a black Sharpie marker to write, "Johnny's Revenge." His oldest son was put in charge of drawing Johnny's lobster boat on the front, with a few traps in the foreground. When the T-shirt was finished, Denny tried it on, and everyone agreed it was a shame they didn't have some to sell at their booth along with the lobster rolls. But Denny was secretly glad he had the only one. This way it was original, one of a kind. He'd wear it while manning the lobster-roll booth, too. Everyone would know which cause they were supporting when making a purchase—and especially which cause they *weren't* supporting. It was important to Denny and his buddies to take whatever money they could away from the Golini family. After all, you wouldn't have a fundraiser to benefit a couple of thieves. What the hell was Congressman Contoro thinking anyway?

Denny drove to Flannery's to collect the lobster meat that had taken him all day Saturday to pick. Doug was mixing it with a little mayo and salt and pepper when he arrived.

"It's all set to go into containers now. Be sure to keep it cold," Doug said as he put one more dollop of mayo in the bowl of lobster meat and folded it in. Doug had worked in an Ipswich restaurant's kitchen evenings and weekends since he was a kid, and he often made the lobster and crabmeat sandwiches that were sold in Flannery's retail market. He was the natural choice to make the salads for the sandwiches at the event.

"Thanks for doing this, Doug," Denny said.

"No problem, Denny. Anything I can do to help Johnny," Doug said.

"Is that why you didn't want to work in the congressman's booth?" Denny asked as he started to put the puzzle pieces together.

"I think you have to choose a side. I deal with lobstermen enough to understand how devastating it would be to lose all your gear, especially when it was deliberate. I can't volunteer at a fundraiser for the Golini family. I'm staying as far away from that crap storm as possible. Some kind of brawl is bound to happen down there, you know," Doug said, trying to warn Denny.

"Nah," Denny answered. "Nothing's going to happen. We'll have the chowder tent soundly beat, so our tent will be in happy mode.

I doubt the congressman's going to stir up any trouble."

"I hope not," Doug said. "I'll be just as happy fishing in a boat with my kids. Are you bringing your boys fishing?"

"I'm doing the greasy pole, so there's no one to take them. Besides, they'd like to stay and watch their old man win," Denny said, smiling from underneath his lucky Boston Red Sox cap. He grabbed the plastic containers of lobster meat and put them in a cooler. Then he and Doug carried the cooler out to Denny's waiting truck.

Denny drove to the world-famous Fisherman's Memorial on the boulevard and parked his truck. Since it was only eight in the morning, parking wasn't a problem. He chose a spot to the left of the Gloucester fisherman statue and began to set up his tent. It wasn't long before the usual suspects showed up to help, which included Sully, Murph, Jimmy, and of course, Johnny. The tent, table, and chairs were all set up in an instant, and the men were rewarding themselves with a celebratory lobster roll. As they broke open a six-pack of beer, they were anticipating a very successful day.

Denny was in the process of trying on his greasy-pole shirt for the guys to see when Congressman Contoro and Robby arrived to set up the tent for the Gloucester Fisheries Association. Robby, naturally, picked a spot to the left of Denny's tent to set up his own. After all, these were his drinking buddies.

"Hey, what do you think you're doing?" Sully asked gruffly. "Unless you're donating your proceeds to Johnny here, you'd better take your tent and pitch it far away from us."

"Really?" Robby asked, surprised at the hostile reception. "I thought our tents could sit side by side. The day would go by a whole lot faster, and it would be a heck of a lot more fun."

"We're having plenty of fun in our tent already," Sully retorted, sitting back and taking a swig of his beer.

Doug's words were playing in Denny's mind now. "Some kind of brawl is bound to happen down there," Denny recalled Doug saying earlier that morning, followed by, "I'm staying away from that crap storm." Denny hadn't entertained the thought that a fight could break out, but now he was rethinking that. Denny thought as long as everyone chose a side and stayed there, there'd be no problem. He'd forgotten a few people in town had allegiances to both sides. Robby was head of the Gloucester Fisheries Association, which clearly supported the Golini family. That really put Robby between a rock and a hard place because most of his close friends were lobster fishermen.

"I hear you, Robby," said Denny, trying to defuse the situation, "but we've put a lot of time and effort into our fundraiser, and we don't want any competition taking our profits. Sorry, but that's the way it has to be—unless you want your tent to benefit Johnny instead of the Golini family."

Robby approached Denny's tent and said under his breath, "I'm no happier about this than you are, but I have to represent the Gloucester Fisheries Association since I'm the president this year. Unfortunately, they voted for the proceeds to go to the Golini family. Obviously, I had no choice in the matter, or our profits would be going to Johnny, too. In a few months, I won't be an officer anymore. But right now, I have to go with the congressman and support the association's vote."

"In that case, you need to go at least to the other side of the statue," Murph said sympathetically, but firmly. "We need to sell all of our lobster rolls if Johnny's going to keep his boat. We've done the math."

"I get it," said Robby. "No hard feelings?"

"We're good," the men in Denny's tent said in unison. They all understood the dilemma he was in.

Robby directed the congressman to pick up the tent pieces and move them to the other side of the looming Gloucester fisherman.

"Why?" Congressman Contoro confronted Robby. "We have just as much right to be here as they do."

"It'll be better to have our own space," Robby called back. "We all want to have a successful day, and the less competition, the better. Besides, they were here first."

The men inside Denny's tent were happy to hear Robby standing up for them. "When it's all said and done, Robby's a good guy. He's just in a tough situation," Denny said. Everyone nodded in agreement.

Congressman Contoro was clearly aggravated, partially because he had to move the heavy tent frame from where they dropped it off and partially because it was already eighty-five degrees out, and sweat was dripping down the side of his face and continuing down the back of his shirt. Unlike Robby, who wore a light, short-sleeved Cool Max T-shirt and a pair of khaki shorts, the congressman wore his signature navy-blue suit, complete with jacket, tie, cobalt-blue shirt, and of course, his brand-new designer Italian leather loafers.

"You might want to change into something cooler," Denny called to the congressman. "I hear it's going to top off at ninety-five today."

Barry Contoro pretended not to hear Denny.

"Sound advice," Jimmy said quietly to the men in Denny's tent.

"He's going to reek by the end of the day if he doesn't change into some shorts and a T-shirt," Murph added, as he reached for his beer can.

"Nothing better than a chowder salesman dripping with sweat to boost our lobster-roll sales," Johnny joked, and then he became serious. "Did I tell you guys how much I appreciate you setting this up for me?"

"Only a gazillion times," Murph answered.

"Well, I just want you to know how much it means to me," Johnny admitted.

"We know," Jimmy said, and the others nodded in agreement. "At least you're here. I don't see the Golini family showing up to help out and thank people for supporting them. Certainly the wives could scoop chowder, and I'm pretty sure each of them has at least one kid in high school who could help out. I heard Billy Golini's boat was named after his daughter, Skye, who's a freshman at Rockport High. They all should be here."

"That's the truth," Sully said. Then he added, "You're doing good,

Johnny. This whole thing is gonna be behind you in no time." Sully gave Johnny a firm pat on the back as he made his way to the cooler to get another round of beers for everyone.

Denny, Murph, and Jimmy finished attaching the colorful red, white, and blue buntings to the roof of the tent, allowing them to hang down on each side, gently blowing in the day's slight westerly breeze. Not only did the buntings add some much-needed color to the white tent, but they also served as a visor, providing additional sun protection on what was fast becoming a record-breaking hot day. In contrast, Robby and Contoro's tent had a single white banner running along the top front with blue lettering proclaiming, "Piping-Hot Chowder to Benefit the Golini Family." Denny's team could barely contain their gleefulness as the opposing tent's banner was unfurled.

"Ha, piping-hot chowder!" Denny read, chuckling.

"That's gonna sell it," Murph joked.

"Wow, that's going to hurt business," Jimmy said.

"Good enough," said Sully. "May the selling begin!"

Contoro and Robby had just finished setting up their tent in time for the crowd to start arriving for the 10:30 a.m. viewing of the Parade of Sail. Majestic schooners began to arrive to sail from the inner harbor, past the Fisherman's Memorial where Denny and Congressman Contoro's tents were located, to Eastern Point Light where the race was going to start. More than fifteen schooners were expected to compete, and the oohs and ahs from the crowd said it all.

The racing schooners were on average about ninety feet long, with a deck length of about seventy-two feet. The beam, in most cases, was about eighteen and a half inches on most of the schooners, and each boat averaged about five cabins, two for a crew of four, leaving three cabins for guests. Many of the schooners were constructed from local white oak and black locust, with the white oak being used below the waterline. Mahogany was used above the waterline, which gave the schooners a magnificent, rich look. The masts, gaffs, and booms were often constructed of white spruce, and the sight of all fifteen of them in the Parade of Sail was impressive.

The Mayor's Race, where the schooners competed to win the coveted Esperanto Cup, was to begin at 1:00 p.m., which left just about an hour for the greasy-pole event. Denny's tent was crowded from the moment the schooners came into view. Murph lifted the containers of lobster salad out of the cooler while Denny generously filled the freshly baked rolls from Virgilio's and handed them to Sully to wrap. From there, customers would step to the far left to hand their payment, cash only, to Jimmy. Before leaving the tent, each patron received a hearty handshake and a sincere thank-you from Johnny. Denny's tent was operating like a well-oiled machine. Apart from the fact they were serving the best lobster subs at the event, everyone genuinely liked the idea that they were supporting Johnny and helping him get back to lobstering.

In contrast, the piping-hot chowder that was being offered at the congressman's tent wasn't nearly as popular. Had it been a crisp autumn day, the chowder would have given Denny's lobster rolls a run for their money, but steaming-hot chowder being served by a sweaty, middle-aged man, with no presence of the Golini family, just didn't cut the mustard.

Denny and Murph's departure from the tent right at the height of the busy lunch hour wasn't ideal, but they didn't want to miss their second chance at the greasy pole that year. Neither Murph nor Denny made it into the finals during the regular greasy-pole contest at Saint Peter's Fiesta, and they couldn't wait to have another crack at it. They were charging twenty-five dollars for every walk, and instead of giving a cash prize, Denny convinced the administrators to give a hundred-dollar gift certificate to the Gloucester House Restaurant, which was located right on the water, instead. Denny already had his shorts and "Johnny's Revenge" T-shirt on, and Murph was wearing a quick-drying bathing suit. Murph took his T-shirt off. It was the only one he had with him, and he didn't want to be serving up lobster rolls in a wet T-shirt for the rest of the afternoon.

There must have been forty people in line for the greasy pole, and small boats were arriving to get a closer look at the inevitable awkward spills into the tepid water. Of course, the Coast Guard sent a boat from the Gloucester station with a medical team on board, and the Gloucester harbormaster was ready to pluck any contestants out of the sea who couldn't swim back to the greasy-pole platform on their own. Some spectators made their way down to Pavilion Beach to watch, whereas others remained on the boulevard to catch the action. Seasoned spectators came armed with binoculars to score a close-up view of the contestants' facial expressions as they suddenly realized they weren't going to make it to the flag and instead were about to plunge into the sea.

Because the greasy-pole event had to clear out in time for the schooner race starting at one o'clock, the traditional courtesy round was suspended. Normally, the courtesy round gave all contestants the opportunity to take a walk on the pole once, with no one allowed to capture the flag. For today's competition, participants would have to consider their experience at Saint Peter's Fiesta their warm-up round. Although it often took two to four rounds for someone to clear the pole and grab the flag at Saint Peter's Fiesta, for this special fundraiser, everyone was going to have just one crack at walking the pole. If nobody grabbed the flag at the end, then all the money would go to Johnny, and the gift certificate to The Gloucester House wouldn't be awarded. After all, the thrill of walking the greasy pole one more time was reward enough. If by some chance, more than one person managed to grab the red flag, they would continue the greasy-pole contest until everyone had a chance to walk the pole. This would allow officials to collect all the participants' money so that Johnny didn't get shortchanged. There would be a drawing at the end among the winners to see who was awarded the restaurant gift certificate. Of course, everyone who managed to grab the flag would be recorded as a winner for the day's event, which also gave them those all-important bragging rights.

Contestants were shuttled to the greasy-pole platform together in one boat, and the cheers and chants from the contenders added to the excitement building for the event. There were many approaches participants took to navigate the greased-up pole. The first contestant, dressed as Spiderman, took the run-as-fast-as-you-can approach. Clearly this contestant was a marathon runner by day. His gangly body, sporting a form-fitting, blue-and-red outfit, began to streak across the wooden pole like a bullet. However, unlike his sticky, nimble namesake, this Spiderman only made it halfway across and then fell face first, smack-dab into the pole, cracking several ribs. Spiderman clutched his midsection as he fell off the pole. He entered the sea awkwardly on his left side, taking what seemed like hours to reappear on the surface. The first casualty of the day was pulled out of the water by the harbormaster, his ego as badly bruised as his ribs. But true to his superhero persona, he toughed it out and stayed in the harbormaster's boat to watch the rest of the competition.

Next came a more cautious, older man dressed as a great big bluish-green Gumby. "Why didn't I think of that?" Murph commented. "It's like he's wearing a mattress all over his body."

"That could be an advantage on the pole, but I don't think it'll be when he hits the water," Denny replied.

"Oh . . . that's very true," Murph agreed. "I was focusing on the pole."

Gumby took the slow-and-steady, sideways-tight-rope-walker approach to the event. He was able to take about ten tiny steps, one foot beside the other, and then, with a sudden yelp, off the pole and into the water he went. Shortly thereafter, as he began to sink, there was a more serious cry for help from Gumby. The top of Gumby's head was the only thing visible above the water as he almost sank out of sight with the weight of his padded costume. Luckily, the harbormaster saw this coming and was ready to assist immediately after Gumby hit the water.

Then it was Denny's turn. He stood proudly on the platform, showing off his homemade shirt to the crowd. Although it was virtually impossible to read from that distance, most people had seen the shirt when they were waiting in line for a lobster sub and knew what it said. The crowd roared with approval. After all, it was mostly locals watching the greasy-pole contest, as the tourists and East Gloucester residents had already left to view the Mayor's Cup schooner race from the Eastern Point Yacht Club.

Denny stepped cautiously onto the pole. Then with a very controlled quick step, he sprinted to the end and lunged for the stick with the red flag attached. His aim was true, and he relaxed his body to easily drop into the water below with his prize. After disappearing for a moment, everyone cheered to see Denny's right arm rise above the waves, with the red flag in the air, followed by Denny's head bobbing up to the surface behind it. Murph was glad for Denny. He knew how much Denny wanted it. But now Murph had his work cut out for him. Murph's height and mass were an advantage on the basketball court, but it was a hindrance on the greasy pole. Denny's slight body, coupled with his short stature, made him the perfect body type to fly across the pole without slipping.

Murph stood on the platform, looking down at Denny and giving him a thumbs-up. Murph strategized for a moment. The twinkle-toes approach definitely didn't work with big guys, and Murph was too heavy for a quick sprint that barely touched the pole. His wide stride was his strength. *Yes, a quick, wide stride should do the trick*, Murph thought to himself as he waited for the flag's stick to be reattached to the end of the pole.

The owner of a local tuna-fishing boat with an upper-level crow's nest had volunteered for the job of repositioning the flag for this special edition of the greasy-pole contest. This boat was thought to be an essential piece of equipment for today's contest because officials weren't exactly sure how many people would be successful in grabbing the flag. Because there was no practice run, everyone who paid needed to get a chance to walk the pole, or participants would be asking for their money back. But even when the greasy-pole contest was conducted using traditional rules during Saint Peter's Fiesta, a boat with an upper deck or crow's nest was always nearby in case the flag was touched but not securely taken down. A few years back, someone had knocked the flag off its perch at the end of the pole, but the short nails that tentatively secured it in place hadn't been disturbed enough for the flag to fall. Consequently, the flag was left dangling from the edge of the pole, hanging upside down. At that point, it would have been impossible for anyone to grab the flag, and an official boat had to come in to reposition the flag for the contest to continue.

Today it was especially important for officials to mount the flag quickly. Denny had promised organizers of the Schooner Weekend that the greasy-pole contest would be out of the way in time for spectators to see the Mayor's Race for the Esperanto Cup. As officials made short work of reattaching the flag, Murph was entertaining himself by doing a few wide arm circles backward and forward to keep limber for the event. This also served to settle his nerves, which were getting the better of him from having to wait at the edge of the pole for so long. Murph was about to do some deep knee bends when he was finally given the OK to continue the contest.

Murph began his turn by taking one giant stride after another, trying not to commit to any step. He didn't want to put too much weight on the pole, which could cause him to slip. Step by speedy step, Murph approached the flagstick. *One more stride should do it*, Murph thought. Then he felt his left foot slip to the right of the pole. He made a leaping dive to grab the flag with his long left arm. Success! He was clutching the flag in his left hand, which was now attached to only half of the stick. The remaining half was still lodged in the hole on the greasy pole. Murph's muscular left arm had snapped the flagstick in half. He relaxed his body as he catapulted toward the water, preparing for what was sure to be an awkward entry into the sea. Jimmy's eyes were glued to the action at the greasy pole, almost forgetting he had a booth to run. This wasn't really a problem, though, because everybody else was watching the greasy-pole action, too.

"Oh, nuts!" Jimmy jeered. "Good thing he didn't slip to the left, or he'd have been singing soprano for a while." Jimmy was caught up in the moment, not realizing how many people were listening to him. All the men in the crowd winced at Jimmy's remark. Jimmy was relieved to know he'd have a first mate the next day when he left Flannery's to go lobstering. It was crucial to keep up the momentum, now that the lobsters were finally on the move. He didn't need Murph to break a bone right now.

The flag was quickly reattached to a spare stick and mounted once again. The greasy-pole contest was finished exactly at one o'clock, just in time for the Mayor's Race. As it turned out, Murph and Denny were the only ones able to grab the red flag. Officials needed a clear winner because there was only one gift certificate to award. In this case, technique needed to be considered when choosing the winner. Because Denny was able to retrieve the flag in its entirety, whereas Murph had grabbed the flag and only a portion of the stick, the officials threw out the original idea that a drawing would be held in the event of multiple winners. Much to his delight, Denny was declared the winner. Murph didn't mind, recognizing that Denny had the better run. Denny was awarded the gift certificate and that all-important hoist to the shoulders of his fellow competitors and paraded up and down Stacy Boulevard as the victor. As Denny was dropped off at his lobster-roll tent and the crowd's attention turned back toward the sea and the Mayor's Race off in the distance, Denny declared that everyone working the tent was invited to the Gloucester House Restaurant, his treat. The guys in the tent raised their cans of beer to Denny, congratulating him with a somewhat inebriated-sounding, "Here, here!" This day was turning out as phenomenal as Denny had envisioned it, and he beamed from ear to ear. Murph was disappointed that the flagstick broke—he loved to win as much as Denny—but he had to agree the judges made the right call. Soon the tent was in the thick of it again, making lobster subs for hungry spectators and giving them heartfelt thank-yous as they paid for their food.

*   *   *   *   *

For Paul, Meredith, and Rosa, the day had no peaks or valleys. It was a steady stream of people coming into the retail store to select their fish. There were five major holiday times when steak fish ruled, and four of them were in the summertime because steak fish was an excellent choice for grilling. The retail always sold a ton of steak fish on the Fourth of July, Memorial and Labor Day weekends, and Father's Day.

The other holiday period when steak fish was popular might seem a little unusual to some. The fifth prevalent steak fish holiday period was Lent. This didn't include all of Lent, of course. The popularity of steak fish went in very predictable phases. Beginning with Ash Wednesday, the official start of Lent, all the faithful would come into the retail store with large gray spots smudged on their foreheads, ready to repent and buy plain whitefish like haddock, cod, flounder, or chowder fish. For a couple of weeks, Flannery's sold a phenomenal amount of white fish each Friday because there were a lot of Catholics in town. But by the third week of Lent, everyone was sick of eating fish every Friday and longed for a change. That's when steak fish began pulling into the lead. Swordfish, halibut, salmon, and tuna steaks all made a huge comeback during the third and fourth weeks of Lent.

But just as the steak fish popularity was surging, Holy Week would arrive. During Holy Week people would dive right back into the whitefish. Catholics were remembering the history of what happened that week and were once again repenting. But they were also looking toward the bright future ahead, which included Easter and the end of Lent. This often coincided with the beginning of spring and the dusting off of the grill. On Easter weekend, the grilling fish were back, along with shrimp, shellfish, and lobsters.

In some years, Easter was soon followed by Mother's Day, a day that many would expect to be a big grilling day, but it was quite the contrary. The retail store was dead on Mother's Day weekend because everyone was taking his or her mom out to dinner at some swanky restaurant. But not to worry—soon it would be Memorial Day weekend again, and so the cycle would continue. Flannery always said that because they were forced to eat fish, Catholics weren't the backbone of his seafood clientele. Protestants were the real lovers of seafood. They ate fish because they genuinely liked it. Catholics only ate fish when they had to, which may have been why some chose not to eat fish outside those times. Protestants ate fish year-round.

Once most of the orders were picked up and the retail customers were spotty at best, Paul saw his chance to escape to the boulevard to see how things were going with the congressman's booth.

"If you've got this, I'm going to head over to check to see if the congressman's booth needs any help," Paul told Meredith.

"I'm good," said Meredith. "I can't wait to hear how everyone's doing over there."

"I'll be back soon with the dirt," Paul promised.

"Have fun," Meredith called to Paul as he walked out the office door.

Paul met a customer in Flannery's parking lot who offered to drop him off close to Stacy Boulevard. According to the man, the boulevard was packed and finding a parking space would be next to impossible. Paul accepted the invitation, figuring he could hitch a ride with someone ready to leave the event or even walk back to Flannery's. The warmth of the day was such a welcome change from the cold, damp air in the plant. Paul wouldn't mind a long walk back.

As Paul approached the Gloucester Fisherman's Memorial, he saw Congressman Contoro and Denny's tents strategically placed to the right and the left of the statue, respectively. Paul thought they'd want to have all the food venues together, figuring that customers might be enticed to buy cups of chowder to go with their lobster rolls. As Paul got closer, he realized the reason for the separation of tents. The two groups weren't getting along.

Congressman Contoro's tent had sold about twenty-five cups of chowder for the day, and it was already past one thirty in the afternoon. The lunch hour was over, and he was going to have to go back to the Gloucester Fisheries Association reporting that his idea had been a disaster. Barry couldn't let that happen without a fight. His political opponent would surely make a connection between this failed attempt and the congressman's lack of organizing, marketing, and general business skills. This could hurt his bid for reelection. Contoro had almost forgotten the original cause of helping the Golini family. This now had to do with his own political survival. In desperation, and despite Robby strongly urging the congressman to just accept the fact that people didn't want chowder on a humid, ninety-five-degree day, the congressman did the unthinkable. He noticed there were still many people in line at Denny's lobster-roll stand, and Barry thought he might be able to poach—or rather, convince—a few of the customers in line to buy a cup of fish chowder instead.

As Paul arrived at Denny's tent, where all the action was, Sully and Congressman Contoro were chest to chest in a shouting match, arms flailing, hollering at the top of their lungs.

"You son of a bitch," Sully shouted, not caring there were children within earshot. "Get back to your tent and stop trying to steal our customers." Sully shoved Contoro, who was clearly out of his league. Contoro had grown up in Gloucester where the ability to street fight was established at an early age, but he was out of practice having been in politics for so many years. Contoro had lost the roughness that gave a man an edge in a fight and began to back away from Sully.

"I'm not trying to encroach on your business," Contoro lied, trying to save face. "I wanted to let people in line know that there was chowder available to complement your lobster rolls."

"That's not what I heard," Murph interjected, and Jimmy sighed, wishing Murph wouldn't get involved.

A ruddy-faced lobster fisherman who had gotten in the lobster-roll line for the sole purpose of supporting Johnny said, "I didn't hear you say anything about picking up a lobster roll. As a matter of fact, you stood behind me and, leaning in, whispered that you heard the heat had gotten to the lobster salad, and people who ate the lobster rolls were getting sick."

"Come on, Barry," Paul said as he reached out to grab the congressman's arm to escort him back to his booth, trying to defuse the situation. He knew nothing good could come from this, and he wanted to separate the two men as quickly as he could. Paul turned toward Barry, and didn't notice Sully winding up, ready to sucker-punch the congressman. Sully swung, but Contoro was quick and ducked. Sully hit Paul on the left side of his jaw. Paul fell back from the impact, and Murph caught him before he hit the ground. Paul managed to get his footing and stand, holding his jaw with his hand. Denny had already grabbed a plastic bag and had begun filling it with ice. He tied the bag at the top and strode over to Paul.

"See?" Denny said, holding the ice up in front of Contoro and then turning towards the customers in line so that they could clearly see the bag. "We have plenty of ice. Our lobster salad is ice cold." Satisfied he'd made his point, Denny handed the bag to Paul.

"Thanks," Paul said, still stunned by what had just taken place. Paul put the ice to the side of his face that was beginning to throb.

"I'm sorry," said Sully as he touched Paul's forearm. "You shouldn't have come over here. If that congressman didn't have catlike reflexes, that punch would have been planted right where it belonged."

"Seriously, Sully?" Paul asked, understanding the sentiment behind the punch but, under the circumstances, unable to believe Sully was still posturing.

"Well, he deserved it," said Denny, and everyone within earshot was in agreement.

"It's just too bad Sully didn't hit his intended target," Murph added.

Congressman Contoro caused far more damage to his career with this corrupt move than he ever would have by reporting his chowder tent a failure. People would have understood the weather affecting the sale of hot chowder, but now people would be questioning the congressman's temperament and judgment. The fact that a local photographer caught the moment on his camera and was on his way to the *Gloucester Daily Times* to turn the photo in was just the frosting on the cake.

The congressman returned to his chowder booth, and Robby and he began to break the tent down. There was no sense staying. If their tent was unpopular before, it was sure to be deserted once word got around about the fight. It wouldn't be any time at all before nearly everyone in Gloucester heard about the incident, even without the inevitable newspaper story in print. Barry sat in a chair and vigorously rubbed his forehead with his hands.

"I'm usually fairly lucky," Barry thought out loud, trying hard not to lose his composure. "What happened? I'm so screwed now."

Robby wanted to distance himself as far from Contoro as he could. His loyalties always lay with Johnny and the rest of his friends. Why hadn't he just told Contoro he had already made plans with them? Contoro might have been offended, but he'd have gotten over it. Robby hoped that he wasn't linked with Contoro in all of this. If he was, his restaurant could be a virtual ghost town for a while. Robby had as much riding on this as Contoro did. This day had ended up even worse than Robby had anticipated. Hopefully his customers would hear and understand how he wound up in the congressman's chowder tent in the first place.

The lobster-roll tent was still in a jovial mood, however, despite what had just taken place. They had thwarted the congressman's efforts, made a ton of dough for Johnny, and had a greasy-pole winner and runner-up connected to their cause. Paul was collateral damage, but it was all worth it.

Paul sat in a chair under the tent in the shade, a beer in one hand and an ice bag in the other. He hoped more than anything that his picture wasn't smeared all over the front page of the *Gloucester Daily Times* on Tuesday morning. How was he going to explain this to Flannery? Maybe he wouldn't hear. Paul could only hope.

"I bet you wish you'd never heard of the *Bay State Skye*," Denny said as he sat down beside Paul, appearing both exhilarated and exhausted at the same time.

"What does that have to do with anything?" Paul asked in a puzzled tone of voice, almost too sore to care.

"Have you forgotten the chowder fish was from the *Bay State Skye?*" Denny asked. Paul looked forward and thought for a moment.

"I don't believe in all that superstitious rubbish," Paul retorted.

"Neither do I," Denny said. "But there sure have been a lot of bad things happening to people who've come in contact with that dragger's fish—and lobsters, for that matter, although nobody but us, and of course, Jimmy and Murph, knows about that."

"It's just a bunch of coincidences, Denny," Paul replied. "The *Bay State Skye's* chowder fish didn't make the congressman come over here and try to steal your customers, and it certainly didn't make Sully haul off and hit me."

"That's true," Denny said, "but I'll be glad when we get rid of all that boat's fish and lobsters just the same."

"You know, Denny," Paul admitted, "me, too. That boat's been nothing but trouble since the day it was discovered—that's for sure."

"Yup," Denny agreed, then started helping the others take down their tent. "Hey, Paul. A bunch of us are heading to the Gloucester House Restaurant to celebrate our successful day. We think you've earned the right to join us, my treat. What do you say?"

Without hesitation, Paul answered, "No I think I'll take my sorry ass home and see if I can't rest and try to forget the whole incident."

"Are you sure?" Murph piped up. "Getting loaded always helped me way more than resting."

Paul smiled, then regretted it. "I'm sure it probably would, but the hangover would erase any benefit of the alcohol. I'll see you guys later."

Paul started to make his way to his car and then remembered his car was back at Flannery's. He walked over to Robby, who was loading the last of the supplies from his tent into his truck.

"Where's Barry?" Paul asked Robby.

"He ditched me halfway through breaking the tent down," Robby answered, seeming annoyed.

"That wasn't very stand-up of him," Paul added.

"Well, he wasn't really much help anyway. I was better off doing it myself," Robby explained. Then he added, "What can I do you for?"

"Can I hitch a ride to Flannery's with you? I left my car there and don't feel like walking back," Paul admitted.

"Can't blame you there," said Robby. "Hop in. Will you be OK driving home? You're not local, are you?"

"No, but I should be fine. I guess I should've seen it coming, huh?"

"Never turn your back on a fighting man," Robby advised.

"Words to live by," said Paul as he jumped up into Robby's brand-new, red Ram 2500.

*   *   *   *   *

Paul was arriving at Flannery's just about an hour before the time the judging of the bluefish contest was to get under way at Lane's Cove. All the locals loved the idea of a bluefish contest because bluefish were one of the easiest fish to catch, especially this time of year in the Northeast. If you didn't have a boat, it wasn't a problem. Anyone could catch a bluefish straight off the shoreline or a dock. Bluefish most often fed in groups and would wait for schools of prey to become trapped in shallow inlets. Then they'd decimate an entire cluster of fish with their vicious behavior and unrelenting, sharp teeth. Bluefish weren't fussy about water temperature or salinity either. That's why warmer shallow waters and areas around the mouth of a river were often a great place to hunt for bluefish. Bluefish preferred an active tide, but they were also found in slack or flood tides, too. Wherever the prey fish were located, the bluefish would follow. Although bluefish could reach a maximum of twenty pounds, the average fish caught in the Gloucester area was between nine and twelve pounds. Almost any bait could be used to attract a bluefish, with its voracious appetite and aggressive nature.

Doug had been sure to sign up earlier that morning before heading over to Flannery's to work, and he wound up being the first person in line when registration opened at 6:00 a.m. He had been smart to go early because there was no way he'd have gotten away from Flannery's again before 9:00 a.m., which was the official end of sign-ups. Although the majority of contestants had been fishing most of the day, by the time Doug got out of work, over to Lane's Cove, and into his boat with his kids, it was already two in the afternoon. They would have just one hour to head out, fish, and get back in time for the weigh-in.

"We've got this," Doug declared when his girls complained that they were going to lose because of his tardiness. Doug made sure the girls had their life jackets on, then fired up the outboard motor on his fifteen-foot pleasure fishing boat and was off. Waving goodbye to his wife back on shore, Doug and his girls felt set to win this contest. Doug knew that he needed to look at the water for a disturbance on the surface, a spot where many fish were jumping out of the sea, trying to avoid a bluefish bite. But Doug also knew it was important to look up. When bluefish were in a feeding frenzy, it would immediately attract any seagulls in the area. If a colony of seagulls were calling out in excitement and headed in a straight line to a certain area, there was a good chance that there was a massacre of a fish school happening beneath.

As soon as Doug sped out to his favorite, top-secret fishing spot, where it just so happened he had caught two large blues within the last week, he baited everyone's lines with mackerel and helped them to cast off into the water. A lot of fishermen used different kinds of plugs, squid or mackerel lures, or sand eel jigs, but Doug preferred to use simple live mackerel as bait. The rods Doug used were strong enough to hold a two-ounce plug, combined with a twenty-pound test that was tough enough to hold a bluefish but thin enough in diameter to give the length he needed to bring the fish in, all while still fitting on his reel.

Doug helped his ten-year-old daughter with her rod. If she hooked a big blue, he didn't want her to let the rod go out with the fish. His twelve- and fifteen-year-old girls could hold their own with full-size bluefish. And so the boat full of tow-headed, freckle-faced girls waited patiently as their dad got all the lines in the water. Once Doug was able to sit back in the boat and wait, the real game began.

Doug reminded his girls not to strike back too quickly. A bluefish often strikes and misses a few times before becoming hooked. "The best strategy is to steadily retrieve your line," Doug said. "That's what attracted the fish's interest in the first place."

"Or you might want to stop for a moment," Doug's oldest told her sisters, "to make the bluefish think you're a wounded baitfish, right, Dad?"

"That works, too," Doug said with a grin, beaming with pride. Doug loved having a house full of daughters and believed they could achieve anything they wanted if they put their minds to it. He didn't treat his daughters any differently than he would have treated sons if he had them, and this resulted in strong, confident, athletic girls.

Within minutes of dropping the lines in the water, Doug's middle daughter had a fish hooked. Everyone knew it wasn't a bluefish because there wasn't much fight to the fish. When reeled in close to the boat, his middle daughter recognized the fish as a scup. Disappointed, she pulled the fish in, removed the hook, and gently released the fish back into the sea.

Doug looked his daughter square in the eye and said, "This isn't a bad thing. Now we know there are feeder fish in the area. The blues can't be far away. Anywhere there are squid, sand eels, mackerel, scup, butterfish, alewives, or cunners—"

"Basically, anything," his oldest daughter interrupted, adjusting her Coach-brand sunglasses and her navy-blue Red Sox baseball cap.

"Basically," Doug continued, "you know the table's been set for a bluefish feast. Just be patient." All three girls smiled, the youngest wiggling her skinny body back into her father's lap.

Doug baited the hook with a new mackerel and handed the rod

back to his middle daughter, who had just finished collecting her long, blonde hair to tie into a ponytail. "I'm getting serious now," she said with a competitive gleam in her eye and a determined look on her face. With a strong snap of her wrist, she cast the line back into the ocean, far away from the boat. Doug glanced at his watch. There was only a half hour before the judging began. Feeling a little agitated, Doug realized he hadn't eaten since five in the morning, and his stomach felt a little queasy.

"Come on," Doug said under his breath, feeling each wave as it lapped against the side of his boat. Doug knew better than to go out on a boat with an empty stomach. He wouldn't get physically sick, but that didn't mean the feeling wasn't there.

Doug's attention was suddenly drawn to the sky. A line of seagulls was headed right for his boat. The next thing he knew, several fish were jumping out of the water on his starboard side, exactly where he and his daughters had cast their lines. All four rods had a fish hooked, and each rod was bent deeply with the weight of the fish fighting on the other end of the line. The first fish in was Doug's, a beautiful blue that had to go at least twelve or thirteen pounds.

"Beauty," Doug exclaimed proudly as he reached his net out to capture the bluefish and bring it on board. He accomplished this while making sure to support his youngest girl, who had her own large blue hooked on the end of her line.

Doug sat down to encourage his youngest to keep her feet anchored on the side of the boat and lean way back to give her leverage against the large fish. Soon, Doug was reaching his net into the water beside his boat to bring in a blue that was clearly larger than the one he had just caught.

"Wow," his youngest girl exclaimed.

"I think she's beat you, Dad," Doug's eldest said, needling her father.

"I think she has," Doug said happily, rubbing his youngest daughter's shoulders to show how proud he was of her. "And you brought it in yourself, too." Doug high-fived his daughter.

The other two girls pulled in respectable fish, probably in the ten- to eleven-pound range.

"Let's try again," said Doug's middle daughter. They all knew that once you start hitting bluefish, you're bound to catch another as soon as your line hits the water.

Doug looked at his watch. "Man, I'd love to, but if we do, we'll miss the judging, and I think we may have a winner already. We've got ten minutes to get back to Lane's Cove." Doug pulled the cord on his outboard motor and headed back to shore.

"Awww," the girls said in chorus, but they didn't put up much of a fight. They knew their dad was right.

Doug pulled his boat into Lane's Cove and showed the fish they'd caught to his wife, who was sitting under a tree reading a steamy romance novel with a beach setting.

"Hey, you might just have a winner there. I've seen the other fish that have been brought in. That's the biggest fish I've seen all day!" Doug's wife recalled, and she wasn't simply being supportive. The fish their youngest had caught really was the biggest fish she'd seen since she'd arrived.

"Look at his teeth," her daughter exclaimed.

"Frightening," Doug's wife agreed. "I wouldn't want him to have a hold of me."

Doug collected his four fish and grouped his family together. It was precisely 3:00 p.m., and like clockwork, the siren sounded.

"OK, everybody, let's get this weigh-in underway," the judge announced. There was a digital scale that had been calibrated beforehand and checked for accuracy. It was the only scale that would be used for the weigh-in. Each contestant had to present his or her tournament number, which was then checked off on the master list.

"If you could just bring the big fish up, that would be helpful," the middle-aged, dark-haired judge declared after looking at how many people had shown up to have their fish's weight recorded. "We only have an hour for the weigh-in, and there's a lot of you."

After weighing a few fish, the judge declared, "The weight to beat is eleven point two five pounds."

With about forty people remaining to be weighed in, a couple of volunteers began to make their way through the line to eliminate some of the obvious smaller fishes. When it became clear what the volunteers were doing, many contestants who knew their fish were small dropped out of line. Most who were asked to leave agreed they didn't have a chance to win. But not everyone complied.

"That fish couldn't be more than eight pounds," one of the volunteers told a stooped-over elderly man in line.

"I don't care," the old man said defiantly with a thick Portuguese accent, taking a step toward the volunteer in an attempt to intimidate him. "I paid ten dollars to get my fish weighed in, and that's exactly what I intend to do."

The volunteer backed down and walked over to the judge. Shortly after, the judge announced, "We're weighing in the heaviest fish first so that we can award the prizes. The scale will be available afterward for anyone who would like to know the weight of the fish they caught."

The volunteer watched to see if the old man dropped out of line. He didn't. He remained right there, obstinately crossing his arms, with his fish in a plastic bag beside him. Nobody else with a smaller fish left the line either. These contestants were either eternal optimists or they had no idea how to judge the weight and size of a fish.

As Doug approached with his fish, as well as his youngest daughter's catch, the judge was impressed.

"You may have the first- and second-place fish right there," one of the volunteers told Doug as he helped Doug to place the largest fish on the scale. Doug held his breath until he heard his youngest daughter squeal.

"Thirteen point four six pounds! Yippee!" she exclaimed. Doug grinned widely.

"Let's see the other blue," the judge said to Doug. They centered the fish Doug caught on the scale.

"Thirteen point one zero," the judge called out. A volunteer recorded both of Doug's bluefish weights.

"Don't go too far," a volunteer told Doug. "I think we'll be seeing you in the winner's circle, for sure."

Doug tried to conceal his excitement, secretly bragging to himself that he managed to catch the top-two fish in just one hour's time. Most everyone else had fished all day. Doug was as convinced as ever of his skill as a fisherman.

When the weigh-in was complete, the judge announced, "The good news is that no one is going home empty-handed. Everyone was a winner today because everyone who entered caught at least one fish. Even better, the median weight of the fish was ten point two pounds. But the winning fish and the second-place one were caught by this man right here," the judge pointed to Doug, "with a weight of thirteen point four six pounds and thirteen point one zero pounds, respectively." The judge walked up to Doug and handed him two envelopes with the cash prizes enclosed.

Doug handed the first-prize envelope to his youngest daughter and, shaking her hand proudly, said, "She's the one who caught the first-prize fish. This belongs to her."

The few women in the group cheered loudly, and the men and boys clapped politely, although their facial expressions showed more of a frown. "Out fished by a little girl," you could hear them all muttering to themselves. Their pride had taken a beating.

"Where ya from, Doug?" the judge asked. "For the record."

"Born and raised in Rockport," Doug proudly answered.

"Where'd you catch those fish?" one of the volunteers asked Doug.

"Not too far out," Doug said with a wry smile, unwilling to disclose his lucky fishing spot. The volunteer didn't dig any further, recognizing that an answer that vague wasn't going to be followed up with any more details.

The judge turned toward the crowd again and announced, "And the third-place winner is a Gloucester man. Skip, come on up here and collect your third-prize envelope. Skip's bluefish was a close twelve point eight two pounds." The judge handed the third-prize envelope to Skip, a good-looking, suntanned, thirty-five-year-old man, who was an avid sports fisherman. Most people knew him from his small business that specialized in repairing and storing boats in town.

"Where'd you catch your fish, if you don't mind me asking?" inquired the volunteer who posed this same question to Doug.

"Not at all," replied Skip. "I was trolling off Bay View early this morning. The fish hit my boat propeller as I was reeling him in, and it took a big chunk out of him. I almost threw him back. Oh, and I caught him using a Rapala fishing lure."

"You can't beat a slightly off-centered, wobbling Rapala lure," the judge replied. "Lauri Rapala really knew what he was doing when he modeled his fishing lure after a wounded minnow."

"It's my go-to lure whenever I'm trying to catch a big predatory fish," Skip added. Most every fisherman in the crowd concurred.

"If there's anyone here who wants a chance to weigh their fish, help yourself to the scale. I'm going home for a bluefish feed. Happy Labor Day everyone. I hope you had fun. Thanks for coming by to support a great cause. The proceeds will be a big help to the Golini families, and I'm sure the Golini brothers are looking down on us right now and smiling," the judge added with a grin, eyeing the sky. Then he turned to collect his ten-pound bluefish and headed for his truck. Doug, his wife, and their girls headed for the Lobster Hut in Rockport for lobsters in the rough, Doug's treat.

CHAPTER 8

Despite Paul resting for the entire last day of Labor Day weekend, he still went back to work with a large bruised bump on the side of his face.

"What happened to you?" Meredith asked, her eyes following Paul as he walked through the office door about a half hour later than usual.

"Oh, you don't want to know," Paul replied. Paul really didn't want anyone to know. He wanted to forget about the whole Labor Day weekend. But of course, he couldn't. There were too many witnesses, and Paul, being from out of town, wasn't sure what had appeared in the next day's *Gloucester Daily Times.*

He didn't have to wait long for that revelation, however. As he settled into his stool, he caught a glimpse of Denny walking out of the lobster room, headed toward the office with a newspaper stuffed under the arm of his oversize sweatshirt.

"Oh, crap," said Paul, sighing quietly.

"What?" Meredith asked, watching Denny approach the office.

"Oh, man," Denny exclaimed with a smile as he walked through the door and saw Paul's face. "He really got you good!"

"OK, let's see it," Paul said, reaching for the newspaper under Denny's arm.

"It's not as bad as you think," Denny said, handing the paper to Paul. Then he added with a huge grin, "Front page."

"Of course," Paul remarked as he unfolded the *Gloucester Daily Times*.

"Above the fold," Denny added with a smirk.

Paul didn't react. He was focused on learning how much he'd have to explain to Flannery when he called in. Meredith, on the other hand, was sitting on the edge of her seat trying to get a glimpse of the headline.

"Local Man Makes Off with Police Car," was the headline, followed by the subheader, "Officers rush to the aid of Congressman Contoro at Schooner Weekend brawl." Paul read the entire article out loud, word by word, to ensure he knew exactly what it said in case he was asked about it later:

> Gloucester—Police were called to the Gloucester Fisherman's Memorial on Stacy Boulevard on Sunday afternoon in response to several 911 calls reporting a local congressman and several fishermen involved in a brawl. According to eyewitnesses, when Gloucester police arrived, they left their squad car running with the driver's door wide open, in an effort to rush to the aid of the congressman. The officers' attention was quickly redirected, however, when they saw their patrol car slowly rolling toward Main Street. After a short chase down Stacy Boulevard, police were able to stop the squad car and apprehend the culprit, who was identified as Russell Capuci, a local man known to Gloucester police. Capuci was suspected of being heavily intoxicated but refused to take a Breathalyzer test. An additional patrol car was called, and Capuci was taken into police custody. When asked why he took the patrol car, Capuci responded, "I was keeping it safe from the punks." Police returned to the site of the original call, but by then, the parties involved had dispersed.

"See," Denny said, "you kind of lucked out. Nobody knew you were even there. The big story was really the patrol car theft. I think you owe Russell Capuci a drink!"

Paul chuckled, noticeably relieved that his name and face weren't spread across the front page of the local paper. "I believe I do," Paul agreed. "Does anyone know why Russell took the patrol car? I didn't think he was that kind of guy. He kept our alarm system up and running for years, you know."

"I know," Denny said. "I heard he had some health issues and started hitting the sauce pretty hard. Most people I've talked to say Russell had begun drinking that day at the Pilot House and walked down to check out the greasy-pole contest. When it was over, he was headed to the Crow's Nest to continue his bender and saw the opportunity to get a ride there. He was driving very slowly because he was being careful. He didn't want to hit anything. That's how the cops caught up with him so easily."

Paul snickered, and Denny grinned. There was nothing more that needed to be said.

"I'm relieved to have been kept out of the papers," Paul said after a long silence. "I want to forget about the whole thing. Contoro's going to have some explaining to do at the next Gloucester Fisheries Association meeting. From all appearances, his booth was kind of a bust. How did your booth do? It looked busy. Did you make enough money to help Johnny out a bit?"

"Kind of a bust!" Denny blurted out. "More like a ginormous failure, I'd say. That's why he came over to our side to try to pilfer our customers. But he didn't succeed; our customers were loyal to us. They really felt for Johnny and his cause. Not only did we sell out of all the food we prepared for the day, but people were slipping Johnny a few extra bucks as they got to the end of the line. And to top it all off, we had a huge turnout for our greasy-pole event. All and all, Johnny recouped all the money he needed to replace his gear, and he was even able to make a dent in the money he lost from not being able to fish."

"Wow, that's great!" Meredith exclaimed. "I'm glad Cape Ann people really stepped up to the plate for you guys." Because Meredith dealt with the lobstermen every day in her job and seldom saw a dragger fisherman, her favor was clearly with the lobstermen. Then she added, "Who won the greasy-pole contest?"

Denny beamed.

"No way! You won?" Meredith surmised gleefully. "You sure had a lucky weekend."

"No luck necessary," Denny bragged. "It was pure skill." Denny moved his hand steadily in a horizontal straight line and made a grabbing motion at the end of his reach. Then he looked at Meredith with a wide grin and said, "Speaking of luck, did you hear that Doug won the fishing contest? According to Doug, he and his girls had their hooks in the water for about an hour, when everyone else had been fishing all day. Now that's luck."

The clicking sound of a lobster ticket being printed interrupted their conversation. The Boston sales office had woken and begun placing orders. Denny waited for Meredith to jot down instructions about how to best pack the order to assure the lobsters arrived alive.

"Do you want to keep the Gloucester paper, or are you done with it?" Denny asked Paul.

"You'd better let me keep it for a few hours in case Flannery wants to hear about it," Paul replied. "By noon, it's yours."

"Good enough," Denny said as Meredith handed him the completed ticket. Denny went back to the lobster room to get to work.

*　　*　　*　　*　　*

The phone rang about a half hour later on the Boston line. It was Flannery. Much to Paul's relief, he had no interest in hearing about the weekend's events. He was hitting the ground running, just as he had promised, trying to acquire the defunct gurry plant for the newly formed New England Fish Processors' Association. Flannery's first undertaking was to talk to Henry Putnam, owner of the gurry plant that was closed down by the government. Gurry from a couple of weeks ago was being stored at the plant, and this included the fish heads and racks from the *Bay State Skye* catch.

With the warm eighty- and ninety-degree weather Gloucester was enjoying, the stench was only getting worse. The community might have been better served by the government fining the gurry plant's owner but allowing him to keep processing the fish by-products.

Time was of the essence. Flannery had spoken with Henry Putnam several times over the long weekend, and Henry Putnam was very much interested in selling the gurry plant to the New England Fish Processors' Association. Once he knew that Putnam was on the same page he was, Flannery developed a solid plan for how he was going to proceed once the building belonged to the association. A meeting was planned for late that afternoon at an oceanfront restaurant in Gloucester called The Tavern, which was just a stone's throw away from the Gloucester Fisherman's Memorial at Stacy Boulevard, where all the mayhem had broken out over the weekend. Flannery wanted to let Paul know he'd be up to Gloucester that afternoon in case he was early and wanted to stop in at the plant to wait for the meeting.

Paul hung up the phone, thinking to himself that he might just be in the clear, as none of the guys in the New England Fish Processors' Association would have heard about the previous weekend's unfortunate scuffle. Just as he was thinking this, however, his hand inadvertently brushed his bruised face.

"Oh no," Paul said just under his breath, realizing that if Flannery saw his face, he'd be bound to start asking questions. Paul wondered if a touch of makeup Meredith might have with her would help to cover the bruise. After thinking about it for a while, Paul decided to tell the truth if Flannery brought it up. And chances were Flannery would be too focused on the gurry situation to even notice . . . maybe. That might have been wishful thinking on Paul's part, though, and it would look better if he just fessed up rather than ending up caught in a lie if, by some rare chance, one of the guys at the meeting witnessed the event and told Flannery. Besides, the excuse of "I ran into a door" had been vastly over used and was not often believed.

Paul did a lot of worrying for nothing because Flannery arrived at

The Tavern just in time for the meeting, skipping a visit to the plant altogether. He paused at the door of The Tavern to look out at the sea, pondering his early days at the Boston Fish Pier. He reminisced about how almost everyone at the pier was a character in his own right, which made going to work as entertaining as taking in a movie or a good book. Flannery often thought about the winters working at the pier and how it was so cold that by nine in the morning, workers couldn't wait to go up to Fisherman's Grotto to get a drink, not in an effort to get a buzz on but in a desperate effort to keep warm.

While gazing at the sea, Flannery thought nostalgically of *The Adventure* and the *Marjorie Parker*, the last two sailing schooners still fishing the ocean waters when Flannery first began to work at the pier. Whenever they came in under full sail, Flannery's heart would start pounding. Each schooner would have ten or twelve dories, nested inside each other for easy onboard storage as they headed out to George's Banks to fish. Once the schooners arrived at the banks early in the morning, the sixteen- to eighteen-foot dories would be launched into the sea to row out and set baited hooks. To make it easier to fish from the dories, each boat was equipped with a bow on both ends. Although dories were primarily rowed, a sail was part of each dory's equipment in case the need arose. The crew waited until later in the afternoon to check their lines and harvest the fish they caught. Then the dories would return to the mother ship, unload their fish, and ice it down on the schooner. It took quite a crew to man a schooner because each dory generally needed two men to launch. A dory's fish was top shelf, hooked on a line and treated with the utmost care. Flannery would always wind up his stories about the schooners by saying, "Boy, men were men back in those days. You had to be rugged to survive."

One of the many reasons Flannery was attracted to the Gloucester area, when others were urging him to build his second plant in New Bedford, was the colorful history of Cape Ann. Flannery's favorite historical figure was the courageous Captain Howard Blackburn, who hailed from Nova Scotia but found himself fishing on a schooner called the *Grace L. Fears* out of Gloucester. Blackburn had left the schooner in a dory with another fisherman to set his hooks when a winter storm blew up, stranding them apart from the mother ship. Tragically, when Blackburn took his heavy winter mittens off to attempt to tie a knot, they were accidentally bailed overboard by his inexperienced dorymate. Although these mittens were considered essential to the survival of any fisherman in the winter months, Blackburn didn't panic. He pulled his feet out of his boots and attempted to fit his socks onto his hands, but by then his hands were too swollen and the socks wouldn't fit. With no other options, Blackburn positioned his hands in a curve, modeling the posture a hand would take on if holding the oars of a boat. When his hands froze, which Blackburn knew was inevitable, he wanted to be sure he could grasp the oars and row himself and his partner to safety.

After two days at sea, Blackburn's dorymate lost hope that he'd ever see land again and died. On the fifth day of having no food, water, or sleep, Blackburn managed to make it to shore, with his dead dorymate still on board. Despite the efforts of a benevolent Newfoundland family who took Blackburn in and treated his hands and feet with a strong brine solution and poultices of cod-liver oil and flour, Blackburn lost a toe, all of his fingers, and a portion of both of his thumbs. Blackburn proved to be resilient, however, returning to Gloucester to open a cigar shop and serve liquor for some two years before his license was actually issued. Gloucester people turned a blind eye to his bootlegging, however, as Blackburn was a hero in town, and his business thrived. One of Flannery's favorite books was the story of Howard Blackburn, which he never threw out no matter how many times he moved.

For this reason, Flannery was delighted that the starting line for the annual International Dory Race was located right at his back dock, which was across from the State Fish Pier. He would make sure that Paul arranged for the dock to be cleared of any fishing gear and totes to give spectators a great viewing spot for the race.

The concept for the International Dory Race was formulated

in 1951, with a chance winter meeting in a Lunenburg, Nova Scotia, bar of a Gloucester fisherman named Tom Frontiero and a Lunenburg fisherman, Lloyd Heisler. Lunenburg and Gloucester were both bustling fishing communities, and competition between the two locations had never been hotter. When the conversation turned to which city spawned the most powerful dory rowers, both men insisted their rowers were faster. This was a claim that could be easily tested, and so it was arranged for each city to gather their best rowers together for a dory race to be held in Gloucester.

While Lunenburg had no problem choosing their two rowers for the competition, Gloucester scrambled to locate their best rowers out of the men who normally competed in the Seine Rowing Competition at Saint Peter's Fiesta. Unlike the dory races of Lunenburg, the Seine Rowing Competition of Gloucester had four rowers in each boat with the addition of a scuttler at the stern who was responsible for steering. When the Canadians arrived in Gloucester for the race, they wondered why Gloucester had five men on their dory rowers' team. The Canadians said they could beat the Seine race team the way it was, but Gloucester whittled their number of rowers down to two to match the number on the Canadian team to assure a fair race. After sizing up the two men who made up Lunenburg's team, especially Heisler's supersize arms and hands, the Gloucester rowers knew they were in trouble. The race was set to begin that Saturday morning at Saint Peter's Fiesta, and Gloucester hoped for the best.

When race day arrived, the Canadian team was holed up at Saint Peter's Club in the bar, calmly waiting for the match to begin. Heisler was at the bar, drinking, while his partner, Langille, sat drinking soda water at a table, contemplating the race. Meanwhile, the dories were being set to launch from Pavilion Beach. The rules were that each team would travel out to a buoy with a flag, go around the buoy, and head back to the beach. Whoever arrived first was the winner. With Heisler's size, coupled with the new revelation that his teammate Langille had impeccable navigating skills, Gloucester didn't hold out much hope for a victory.

As the race got under way, the Canadian boat made a straight beeline to the buoy, a clear four boat lengths ahead of the Gloucester dory. As they headed back to shore, the Canadian team seemed to hold back, trying not to embarrass the Gloucester team by blowing them out of the water. That was the day that Gloucester rowers learned there was more to rowing than just brute strength. The Lunenburg team had so endeared themselves to the people of Gloucester during their visit that despite their delivering a crushing defeat to Gloucester, the Canadians were invited back each year to compete again. Gloucester rowers had their work cut out for them, however. Inferior strength was a significant factor in their defeat, but they needed to work on their steering, cadence, speed, and plan of action as well. Every spectator could attest to the fact that the Canadians' dory glided through the sea without so much as a splash or a sound as each oar broke the surface of the water. The same couldn't be said of the Gloucester team.

Flannery had always thought that somehow Howard Blackburn's legacy had something to do with the International Dory Races, but the only real connection was the friendly Canadian/American relationship that still existed today. Ever since that first race in June of 1952, the International Dory Races had been held in Gloucester as part of Saint Peter's Fiesta. The race's popularity grew throughout the years, despite moving the start of the race to the State Fish Pier, giving the head of the harbor area of Gloucester a competition to call its own.

On this day, however, as he walked through The Tavern door, Flannery realized his decision to build his plant in Gloucester had led him to this moment, to lead the charge to improve the system of gurry disposal for the entire New England fishing industry. This was definitely nothing Flannery had ever aspired to do, but time was of the essence and with the gurry plant already closed, he needed to expedite the purchase and refurbishing of the plant to keep complaints of the growing stench to a minimum. The gurry already accumulating at the plant needed to be processed as soon as possible, and fish processors needed a place to dump newly produced gurry, which had become a real burden in its own right. No one else had stepped up to the plate to help; thus, Flannery saw no other alternative than to get involved.

The New England Fish Processors' Association meeting got under way, with many of the members speaking up to express their ideas for the new association. Everyone involved considered the plan to purchase the plant a solid course of action. Flannery explained how he planned to install refrigeration to help take the smell down around the plant. As everyone at the meeting was well aware, it was difficult to have any operation involving seafood that didn't include refrigeration. Next, Flannery proposed a plan to insulate the area where the gurry would be stored so that it wouldn't be subjected to the extreme temperature fluctuations for which New England was so famous. All members of the association would have to kick in their fair share of the cost for renovating the plant, which Flannery didn't consider to be a problem, considering the feedback he'd received from the membership. Members knew that in the long run, they'd make money from the plant, which helped ease the pain of the initial investment.

At that time, Flannery introduced Henry Putnam and his attorney. Flannery had spoken to Putnam just that afternoon to iron out the deal. When all parties were in agreement, Flannery told Putnam, "I'm going to tell you right now, we have a deal. Don't pull any funny stuff tonight, 'cause if you do, the deal is off. I'm telling you in advance, anything comes out of the woodwork, and you can forget the whole deal." Putnam told Flannery he understood.

Putnam rose to a quiet room and began to speak to the group with his lawyer at his side. "The whole deal is finalized," he assured the fish processors. "However, I have subordinated debt that's due to me. You'll need to pay me to clean up that debt prior to paying the bank for the plant."

Flannery rose, partly in disbelief and partly knowing something like this would happen considering the parties with which he was dealing. Flannery's lips pursed in a paper-thin line as he spoke to Putnam. "Putnam, I told you this afternoon, don't pull any quickies or it's over. It's over. The deal is off. That's it," Flannery said, and he walked out of the meeting. Flannery knew that the subordinated debt payment would have taken most of the money the processors had chipped in to buy the gurry plant. No one with any sense would have agreed to that deal. Putnam thought the fish processors in the area would have no alternative and would have to agree to pay his subordinated debt, but that wasn't the case. In fact, Putnam and Flannery never spoke again, and Putnam retained ownership of the defunct gurry plant that was closed by the state.

Flannery was tired as he drove home from Gloucester, but his mind was churning through idea after idea at a whirlwind speed. He determined that at the present moment, they had three forty-thousand-pound truckloads of gurry stored over at the State Fish Pier in Gloucester. It had been sitting out there stinking since before the discovery of the abandoned *Bay State Skye*, just teeming with insects, especially maggots. The next day, he would call the Massachusetts state governor and see if he could get some help from the state. After all, this wasn't just Gloucester's problem; it was the state's problem.

The next day, as soon as it opened, Flannery called the governor's office. After introducing himself and citing his credentials, he was put in touch with Tom Herschel, one of the governor's top aides, to explain his situation. "We've got a real problem here, Tom," Flannery began. "It's the fish industry's problem, but it's Boston's problem, and it's the state's problem, too. You have a fishing industry that has to have some help. Right now, we have one hundred and twenty thousand pounds of gurry sitting up in Gloucester in open air and we need help to get rid of it."

"I'm sorry to hear that, Mr. Flannery," Tom said in what appeared to be a well-rehearsed, typical politician's response. "What can the governor do to help?"

"The governor can give the New England Fish Processors'

Association the money it needs to dispose of its industry's by-products," Flannery said.

"How much money would you need?" Tom asked.

"One hundred and twenty-seven thousand dollars a month," Flannery fired back, without hesitation.

"That's a sizeable amount," Tom answered.

"That's what it's going to take to dispose of the gurry," Flannery insisted.

Tom hesitated and then promised, "I'll bring this up when I meet with the governor, and I'll get back to you in a day or two with his response."

"OK," Flannery agreed. "I'll be waiting for your call." With that, both men hung up. It wasn't until Thursday afternoon when Tom finally called Flannery back.

"Mr. Flannery?" Tom asked when Flannery picked up the line.

"Yes, Tom," Flannery replied in as confident a tone as he could muster. "How'd we make out?"

"Well, Mr. Flannery," Tom answered, "the governor understands the position you're in and would really like to help, but unfortunately, there isn't enough money in the discretionary budget at the moment to cover the amount for which you're asking."

"Are you serious?" Flannery asked angrily. "You mean to tell me that our governor doesn't have enough money to help one of the largest industries in his state? Does he know that the Massachusetts seafood industry ranks third in the country for providing jobs and revenue? If Massachusetts fish processors are unable to dispose of their gurry locally they'll have to ship it out of state. That would increase local seafood prices. If processors try to recoup their costs by paying their boats lower prices, the boats would no longer sell their fish in Massachusetts ports. Eventually, the processors would have to close and set up shop in a state that has the resources they need. I don't think the governor fully understands that a grand exodus of seafood processors from the state of Massachusetts would deliver a devastating blow to his state's economy."

The governor's top aid was a good listener, but no matter how hard he tried, Flannery couldn't convince Tom to revisit the issue with the governor. As far as Tom was concerned, the question had been asked and answered, and he had no intentions of bringing the subject up with the governor again.

In desperation, Flannery called the Environmental Protection Agency (EPA) to see if the agency could help in some way. The EPA representatives apparently understood the gravity of the situation better than the governor's office and gave Flannery their permission to take the gurry twelve miles out to sea and dump it. After pinpointing the precise location of the approved dump spot, Flannery finally felt he was making progress. That was a great ace in the hole, but it would take an expensive barge and tugboat combination to put that plan in motion. Flannery needed the governor to cough up some money for the cause. The EPA's plan was too costly for the members of the New England Fish Processors' Association to support on their own. Flannery had to get the governor to pony up some money, or fish processing in the New England area would screech to a halt.

Flannery sat at his desk, trying to think of something he could do to convince Tom and the governor to fund his gurry project. He finally developed a more devious plan, but one that he thought could work. On Friday morning, bright and early, Flannery stopped by the Gloucester Auction House just before it opened. When Vinnie jumped out of his truck and noticed Flannery, he shouted, "Hey, you old son of a gun, what are you doing up here?" Flannery strode over to him, knowing he had his man. When Flannery told Vinnie what he wanted him to do, Vinnie agreed, with a devilish gleam in his eyes.

"I'll probably get arrested, you know," he said to Flannery.

"Don't worry about it," Flannery assured Vinnie. "I'll have someone right there to bail you out."

"I'm in," Vinnie said enthusiastically. It had been a long time since Vinnie had been involved in anything mildly illicit, and he was excited to take part in something that could have a positive outcome for the fishing industry, too.

"I knew I could count on you," Flannery said as he slapped Vinnie on the shoulder.

Flannery gathered as many members of the New England Fish Processors' Association as he could find to let them know about his new plan. "Because we're all members of this association, I wanted to meet with all of you to let you know what our next step will be. I'm about to send word to the governor's office, that unless I've received a letter signed by the governor, in my hand by eleven o'clock this morning, stating that he's going to help us to the tune of one hundred and twenty-seven thousand dollars a month, the gurry is his. We're headed over to the gurry plant right now to load the trucks with aged gurry and drive them up to the statehouse. If there's no word from the governor by eleven, we're going to dump the gurry on the governor's lawn. And we're going to have the Boston Fish Party! Remember the Boston Tea Party? We're going to have the Boston Fish Party—and it's going to go down in history as the governor's Boston Fish Party!"

Everyone loved the idea, and so the plan was etched in stone. The first thing that Flannery did when he got back to his Boston plant, which was nestled in among other fish processors and meat-packers in the Newmarket Square area, was to call Tom at the governor's office to let him know what was coming.

With that, Flannery hung up the phone and immediately dialed up Vinnie, who was waiting at the Gloucester plant for instructions. Meredith answered the phone but didn't get a chance to say her usual "Good morning, Flannery's" before Flannery blurted out, "It's a go!" Flannery sounded like a general rallying his troops.

Vinnie had arrived minutes ago, plunking his large Dunks Styrofoam coffee cup on the counter and pulling himself up into Paul's stool. Meredith had gotten the gist of what was going on by putting two and two together. She knew the governor was holding out on Flannery. When Vinnie said he was there to drive a gurry truck to Boston and dump its contents on the statehouse lawn, most people wouldn't have believed him. But Meredith had worked in the fish business long enough to know this wasn't out of the realm of possibility. People in the fishing industry tended to think outside the box. Flannery wouldn't think twice about dumping a heaping pile of stinking, oozing, maggot-laden gurry on the statehouse lawn if it got his point across. And it was a brilliant idea. The press would be there in a New York minute, and the governor would have to explain why this happened. Hopefully, the focus would turn to the plight of the fishing industry and the disposal of gurry. And if no one got hurt, well, no harm, no foul.

"It's for you," Meredith said with a smile as she set the phone on the counter next to Vinnie. "I believe it's Flannery."

Vinnie eagerly picked up the phone. "I'll be there in a few," Vinnie informed Flannery. Then he quietly added, "This is really happening." Vinnie was trying to wrap his mind around what he was about to do—two hours ago, his biggest concern was figuring out plans for the weekend.

"You're damn right it's really happening!" Flannery shot back. "If that no-good governor of ours won't step up to the plate and do the right thing for the fishing industry, he'll have some explaining to do once the gurry hits the lawn and the story hits the press." Flannery paused, then asked, "You're not getting cold feet on me are you, Vinnie?"

"No way!" Vinnie replied. "You can count on me one hundred percent. No cold feet here. Just don't forget me when I'm cooling my heels in the pokey."

"You know me better than that," Flannery assured him. "I'll have you out before they get a chance to shut the door and turn the key."

"I'm gonna hold you to that," Vinnie replied seriously.

"You've got my word," Flannery assured him. Then he added, "Hey, let me know when you're in position a block or two from the statehouse."

"Will do," Vinnie said and hung up. He started out the office door, but immediately turned back to grab his Dunks cup. "I'd be lost without this," he said to Meredith.

"I hear ya," Meredith answered.

It wasn't long before Vinnie was pulling into the gurry plant and climbing into the driver's seat of a stink bomb on wheels. He pulled the tractor-trailer truck near the gurry plant's empty ten-wheeler dump truck to make loading the gurry easier. Not only would he be transporting decomposing, fermenting fish remains, but many insects had also taken up residence in the goop. The swarm of flies had first led to a crop of creeping maggots, which had now reached adulthood themselves and had contributed to an even larger swarm of flies. The flies weren't going anywhere, either, not as long as their unlimited food supply was around.

*   *   *   *   *

Vinnie was the perfect choice for the job because he was immune to the stench. Before working for Flannery's, Vinnie had made a career out of driving a ten-wheeler to fish-processing plants all around Massachusetts, picking up each processor's gurry and delivering it to cat food and fertilizer companies, to name a few. Vinnie would drive under a hopper full of gurry that was attached to the side of a fish-processing plant and empty the contents of the hopper into his truck. He began filling his bed in the front, and with each pickup, he'd aim the hopper door a little farther toward the back to assure an even load. Usually it went off without a hitch, except for one day that should have been a distant memory, but Vinnie would never forget it.

It was a hot June morning when Vinnie pulled alongside a fish processor's gurry hopper at the Boston Fish Pier. He was careful to position the middle of his truck bed directly under the gurry-hopper door. This was Vinnie's third pickup of the day. His first two pickups hadn't been huge, so they mainly occupied the front of the bed, but they spread out along the bed's bottom as the truck drove along. The hopper Vinnie was about to empty was filled to the brim and would require most of the remaining available space in his bed. Vinnie ran in to grab Billy Golini, who was working at the plant at the time and usually gave Vinnie a hand dumping the gurry. Vinnie told Billy his truck was in place, and therefore it was safe to open the door at the base of the hopper. Billy ran to the lever for the hopper door and pulled it down. Nothing happened. The hopper door released but didn't budge an inch. There was an ooze of fish goo dripping around the edges of the hopper door, which was a good sign. Still hopeful, Billy and Vinnie waited a few minutes, shooting the breeze to pass the time, allowing gravity to work with the weight of the gurry to push against the hopper door enough to completely open it. Still nothing. But Billy and Vinnie weren't giving up so easily. They carried a hose up to the top of the hopper and let the water run into the dried-on mess, hoping to loosen it. Still nothing. Billy looked at Vinnie with a forlorn look, and the two knew what they would have to do. Because the load had been sitting all weekend with the hot sun working on it, much of the exposed gurry had dried out. The two men would have to climb the ladder to the top of the hopper and break the dried gurry free from the hopper sides. They were both equipped with a fish fork with a five-foot-long wooden handle and three widely spaced, curved six-inch prongs that were shorter than a fork used for haying.

Vinnie and Billy climbed up to the hopper top and sat on the rim that encircled the structure. They picked at the dried-on sides while trying to ignore the ample number of maggots and swarming flies. Luckily the day was warm, and the sun was bright. The gentle breeze off the harbor was making the job tolerable, but after twenty minutes had passed with no progress being made other than a few fish parts loosened and thrown over the hopper's side and into the truck bed, Vinnie crept out onto the center of the gurry mass. Billy watched, amazed that the top of the gurry was as solid as it was. This also explained why the gurry hadn't budged. Billy knew they had worked enough on the sides of the hopper, so he carefully stepped out to pick at the center of the mass along with Vinnie. As the two men picked at the dried-up crud, there was an occasional miniature geyser of goopy fish slime that would shoot out of a crack in the gurry crust a couple of inches into the air. Vinnie and Billy both understood that underneath the crusty gurry top lay a gooey mixture of soft decaying fish meat, with more than its share of fish skeletons or racks and an assortment of insects. But neither man had anticipated the horror that was about to happen. As Vinnie and Billy both gave one strong stroke with their forks in unison, they heard a deafening whoosh. With that, the gurry below their feet dropped about five inches. Stunned, Billy looked at Vinnie. Vinnie looked back at Billy, his eyes even wider, quietly saying, "Oh, crap!"

Both men knew what this meant, but Billy was quicker thinking, or maybe positioned better in the hopper than Vinnie, or perhaps both, because Billy twisted around to grab the top lip of the hopper with his right arm as he felt the ground literally fall away underneath him, taking his fish fork with it. As he sprang up off what little solid gurry he had to spring from, Billy's body wasn't quite elevated to the height he needed to reach the side of the hopper. Falling short by a heartbreaking inch, Billy joined Vinnie, whose arms went up over his head in a surrendering position. Vinnie's fish fork went flying in the air and landed on the ground beside the truck bed, and both men barreled into what could only be compared to a trip down a toilet filled with rotten, maggoty gurry, with many sharp bones thrown in to add to the treachery of the trip. Billy's main concern was the heavy metal door that closed the bottom of the hopper. If it were to swing back after emptying and hit either man on the legs or back, the damage could be insurmountable. Luckily, both Vinnie and Billy flowed through the hopper smoothly, plunging into the already half-full truck bed, which helped to break their fall. Of course, that didn't protect the men from the fish bones, many of which now protruded awkwardly from the men's unprotected arms. Billy stood waist high in the gooey fish remains, pulling a small bone from his wrist with a wince. Looking up, Billy had to smile at Vinnie. Vinnie was sitting in the gurry, buried to his chest, flicking a maggot off the end of his nose. Both men's hats had flown off their heads in their travels, but neither cared to go looking for them. Billy made his way over to Vinnie, whose sense of humor was still intact, in spite of the frightening event that he had luckily come through unscathed. As Billy reached a hand out to Vinnie to pull him from the slimy mess, Vinnie tried to recover his footing.

"What a rush, huh?" Vinnie cried out. "Better than an E-ticket ride, I'd say."

Billy couldn't help but smile at the Disneyland reference. "No one would be lining up to take that ride," Billy exclaimed. Both men were trying to be cool, but the adrenaline surge was still appreciable.

Vinnie and Billy carefully navigated the ladder on the outside of the truck bed with their slippery boots. When they reached the ground, one of the dockhands was standing at the ready with a hose that sprayed salt water. The seawater coming straight from the harbor was cold, but it was clean, and the men welcomed the chance to get the fish slime rinsed from their skin and clothes. Billy had a locker at the plant with a fresh uniform in it, and he quickly removed his yellow apron, boots, uniform, underwear, and socks and replaced them all as quickly as he could. He threw everything he was wearing in the trash. There was no way to resurrect that clothing. Vinnie always traveled with a full set of street clothes in his truck, and he, too, scrambled to get out of his nasty work clothes.

"Well that will be one for the boys at the bar tonight," Vinnie said. "Thanks for your help, Billy. Next time I'm in a bind, you're my man!"

Billy shook his head from side to side. "Nobody would understand how scary that was unless they actually lived through it," Billy added. "I think I'll pass on any future hopper walks. You're on your own, Vinnie."

"Oh, Christ, Billy, I'll never do that again!" Vinnie declared as he jumped energetically into the cab of his truck and, giving a wave, drove to his last stop.

*   *   *   *   *

The stink of the month-old gurry plant's load was, of course, a hundred times worse than the norm, but if you're exposed to a strong odor daily, after a while, you simply don't smell it anymore. That's not to say that Vinnie couldn't smell this particular stench; he could. It just didn't induce vomiting in him like it would in most people.

Vinnie climbed into the gurry plant's ten-wheeler and, turning the ignition, backed up just enough to make sure he was in the optimal position to fill his truck with the gurry from the tractor-trailer he'd just moved. Vinnie had chosen the first one filled; that way, he'd be getting the oldest, most obnoxious-smelling gurry possible. He climbed out of his ten-wheeler's cab, carrying with him rubber-gasket material and industrial-strength adhesive. Vinnie meticulously glued strips of rubber gasket to the back door of his dump truck, knowing that without this addition, gurry material would seep through the door and leave a trail of fermenting fish wherever he drove. Once the back door of his dump truck was secured, Vinnie jumped into a backhoe, which was standard equipment at the gurry plant. He positioned the backhoe between his truck and the tractor-trailer truck, and lowered the two stabilizers to steady the backhoe. Then he scooped up the gurry from the first tractor-trailer's bed, and bucketful by bucketful, he filled his dump truck to the top, being sure the load was fairly level with the top of his bed. Then Vinnie added the frosting on the cake—lots of ice with a bit of dry ice thrown in for good measure. Vinnie figured the truck would be sitting in Boston for a while waiting, and the ice would help keep the odor down. It would be a shame to be discovered while awaiting the hour of need.

Satisfied that he'd done the best he could to make his mission a success, Vinnie carefully pulled the canvas top of his dump-truck bed over the icy gurry mixture to ensure no material would fly out and hit the windshield of an unsuspecting driver on the highway. Once the canvas was secure, Vinnie was ready to hit the road.

He fired up his ten-wheeler once again, this time headed straight for the Route 128 rotary. He loved watching pedestrians' reactions as he drove by them. Often it was a simple clothespin grip on their noses and a waving of the free hand to take the odor away from their faces. But on his way out of Gloucester, Vinnie actually saw one man, all dressed up in a business suit and holding a briefcase, vomit all over his newly polished, spit-shined shoes. The man's day had gone seriously south, and to make matters worse, in an instant, the cause of his discomfort would be nowhere to be found. Cars desperately tried to pass Vinnie's truck on the highway, especially when he drove through swanky towns like Beverly Farms, Hamilton, and of course, Manchester-by-the-Sea. Vinnie was careful to do the speed limit, no more and no less. Cars weren't trying to pass him because he was slow. Cars were trying to get ahead of the stink. Vinnie grinned, thinking that it was starting out to be a great day!

Meanwhile, Flannery was taking another step toward accomplishing his mission. Once he had given Vinnie enough time to load his truck, Flannery gave the Gloucester plant a call. Meredith picked up the receiver, but before she could speak, Flannery boisterously called out, "Meredith, put Denny on the phone!" The adrenaline was clearly flowing as Flannery saw his plan coming together.

"I'll go get him," Meredith said, laying the receiver on the counter. Meredith walked into the lobster room where Denny, Doug, and Charlie were busy putting up orders for the midmorning run to the airport.

"Denny," Meredith called out. "Flannery's on the phone. He wants to talk to you."

Denny's smile dropped into a look of concern. "Why would he want to talk to me?" he asked.

"I don't know," Meredith answered. "But if I had to guess, I'd say it has something to do with the whole gurry thing."

"Huh?" Denny looked at Meredith, bewildered, as they both walked to the office. Denny climbed onto Paul's stool and picked up the receiver.

"Hello," Denny said, a little sheepishly, almost as if asking a question.

"Denny, I have a job for you. Grab one of the sales vehicles and shoot down to the statehouse for me. It's still early, yet. If you leave right now, there should be plenty of street parking in the area. Once you're parked, head up to the corner office."

"The governor's office?" Denny asked with furrowed eyebrows, showing concern about what this mission might involve. Denny was most comfortable when his feet were firmly planted within his self-determined triangle in Gloucester, and he had no desire to become the typical strong-willed, think-outside-the-box, fishing-industry type.

"That's right," Flannery answered, unwavering. "I'm sure there are seats right outside the governor's office. Let them know where you're from and take a seat. Be polite and congenial but don't leave, no matter what. As soon as someone in the governor's office hands you a letter, call me immediately."

"Are you sure you want me?" Denny asked. "The last time I was in Boston was years ago when I went to a Sox game with some buddies of mine. I don't know my way around town."

"It's a straight shot down the expressway. Rush-hour traffic is just about over. I'll have Meredith write down some directions for you," Flannery answered.

"All right," Denny replied, giving in.

Flannery was insistent. Denny had no choice in the matter if he wanted to keep his job anyway. But he hated the idea of blindly following orders, not knowing the full scope of what was happening. Men trained in the military were used to taking orders without knowing their purpose. Not Denny. Denny needed to know the whole story, or he wasn't buying into anything. He had his bags packed for Canada with a 1A classification back in the seventies, and if the war hadn't ended in the nick of time, Denny would have been working for a lobster pound in Canada while drinking a double-double and wearing a tuque to keep his ears warm. And he was pretty sure a few of his buddies would have been right there with him.

"And if we reach eleven and you haven't received anything, get your ass out of there, OK?" Flannery added.

Denny flashed Meredith a look of deep concern, with a bit of panic thrown in for good measure. Flannery sensed his discomfort.

"They won't be after you. They'll be too busy arresting Vinnie down on the statehouse lawn," Flannery quipped, quite amused at the cleverness of his undertaking.

"What? Why? You need to tell me a little more before I can do this," Denny responded, respectfully, but fearing he was getting into something he'd rather not.

"Vinnie has a ten-wheeler full of gurry parked and waiting to swing onto Beacon Street. He's going to dump the gurry in front of the statehouse once I give the word. If you get an envelope, Vinnie will drive back to Gloucester and park the truck at the gurry plant. If not, I'll probably be bailing him out of jail. Be sure to call me the minute you get the letter. If I don't hear from you by eleven, the truck is going to roll," Flannery explained, "but you have nothing to worry about. You'll have nothing to do with the dumping."

Denny had a decision to make. Did he trust that he could get out of the statehouse before the gurry was dumped? It would take a few minutes for Vinnie to make his way from a side street in Boston to the statehouse, and then there'd be a little lag time between the dumping and the governor being informed that it had, in fact, happened. Essentially, Denny would be the one putting this whole thing in motion by making or not making the phone call. Denny paused a moment.

"Well, it would be something to break up the day, I suppose," Denny said, finally giving in to Flannery.

"Attaboy," Flannery said.

Denny was pretty sure he could get back to the company car before word got out about the gurry. He'd be anonymous in the whole ordeal, and it would be a great story to tell his grandkids, if he ever had any. Denny ran upstairs to the men's locker room and changed out of his uniform, then grabbed the keys to the older-model Lincoln Flannery kept in the parking lot in case any customers needed transportation from the plant. Then he headed for the expressway and Boston.

Flannery sighed as the operation got underway. He didn't really want to dump the gurry on the statehouse lawn and subsequently bail Vinnie out of jail. But this was the best way to get the governor's attention. When his wife, Elaine, was seeing him off at four that morning, she said in a matter-of-fact tone of voice, "Oh, Jack, you're not going to do that."

Flannery answered, "Oh yes, I am! I just need to mobilize a few key players, and we're good to go. It's all in motion." Flannery's excitement was appreciable. His wife had lived with Flannery long enough to know he was serious, but she still didn't believe he would actually go through with it. She kissed him goodbye and sent him on his way, knowing full well, in her mind, that the gurry would never be dumped and that her husband wouldn't be the topic of the six o'clock news.

Everything seemed to be in place. The governor's office had been informed. Denny had just reached the waiting area for the corner office, announcing that he was there to wait for a letter from the governor. And Vinnie was in position with his very smelly truck, on a side street of Boston that was primarily residential. He hoped he wouldn't have to wait too long because the stench was bound to permeate into the residences that surrounded him. Vinnie's only hope was that most of the people living on this picturesque street had left for work already. He kept checking his side mirrors to be sure no one was approaching. So far, so good. If he was approached, Vinnie planned to say he was just leaving, headed for the gurry plant in Gloucester. Then he'd have to find a new place to wait.

Time seemed to drag as Denny waited for the governor's letter—that is, until it got to be 10:45 a.m. Denny glanced at his watch, and said a barely inaudible, "Oh, crap." He always believed the letter would appear. What if it didn't?

Denny began to become fidgety as he sat a stone's throw from the governor's office. Ten fifty, no envelope. Denny shifted to cross his other leg. Ten fifty-five, no envelope. He caught himself breathing more rapidly than usual. *This was a bad idea*, he thought. *Why did I ever agree to it?*

Just as Denny was about to go down the rabbit hole, Tom walked into the waiting area. "Here you go," the tall, well-dressed man said as he handed Denny an envelope. Denny jumped up to greet the man, who likely had political aspirations himself. He was dripping with diplomacy.

"Sorry it took so long, but glad we made the deadline," Tom said as he reached out to shake Denny's hand with his own manicured one that was smooth as silk.

Denny froze in horror . . . the deadline. He had almost forgotten, being caught up in a glimpse of a lifestyle he'd never get to experience. Denny met the aide's hand with his own rough, clammy one, then wiped a line of perspiration now dripping just beside his left eye. He thanked Tom and turned to leave.

Denny fumbled with the coins in his pocket, almost dropping them, as he fled from the area of the corner office to find a pay phone. Why hadn't he thought to find one before he went upstairs? There was no urgency then. A few minutes here or there wouldn't have mattered at all. But now, every second counted.

As he began to jog down the statehouse stairs, he thought he could meet Vinnie's ten-wheeler at the front of the statehouse, worst-case scenario. He could stop him from dumping the gurry—that is, if he got there in time. Just then, Denny noticed a line of pay phones on the first floor. He speed-walked over, trying not to attract anyone's attention by running. To his horror, every phone was busy, except for one, which had a large "Out of Order" sign attached to its receiver. Denny glanced at the door, then back to the line of phones. He tried to listen to hear if anyone's conversation appeared to be nearing an end. Should he run out to the curb to try to stop Vinnie, or should he remain by the phones? Denny determined that staying by the phones was the optimal solution. After all, there was a time limit to how long someone could talk on a pay phone unless they fed the phone more coins.

Denny was satisfied for a moment with his decision, until he remembered that people could reverse the charges and talk as long as they wanted. What if everyone here had done that? Denny would never think of making a phone call under those terms. Denny always made sure he had the correct change for a three-minute call and stated what he needed succinctly, so as not to require any additional coinage. But he was aware that others could be more frivolous in nature. Denny looked to see if any of the people using the phones appeared frivolous. No, they all appeared to be well-dressed businessmen and women. He was safe. Someone would be hanging up any moment now. But then Denny's thoughts started to spiral. Maybe these people's businesses were paying for the calls, and they could go on forever and he'd never get to use the phone.

Just as he was ready to flee to Beacon Street, a man near him hung up the phone. Denny noticed a woman ready to step in front of him and took three giant steps to grab the receiver before she could reach it. The woman was annoyed at his rudeness, but Denny couldn't help it. He had to make this call. He picked up the receiver and pushed his dime into the slot. He dialed the number that Flannery had given him and was more relieved than he ever thought possible to hear Flannery's voice.

"I have it. It's here. The envelope. I've got it right in my hand," he told Flannery breathing so hard he wasn't sure Flannery would even understand him.

"Oh, that's great!" Flannery said with a noticeable sigh of relief. "Bring it back and we'll see what we've got."

"Don't forget to call your driver off," Denny unnecessarily reminded Flannery.

"I'll do that right now," Flannery assured him. "Come on back to the Boston plant, and head straight up to my office."

"OK," Denny answered back and hung up the phone immediately.

Denny tried to relax as he headed back to where he'd parked the company's Lincoln. For the first time, he felt the warmth of the day and the pleasant feeling of sun on his face. He slowed his pace a bit now that the urgency had passed. Maybe he'd take a quick walk through the Common to the Public Gardens since they were right in front of him. Yes, this might just turn out to be a great day after all.

Meanwhile, Vinnie was sitting a couple of blocks away, looking at his watch, then at his side-view mirrors and straight ahead at the street in front of him. Nothing unusual. Then he gave a long hard look at the bag phone Flannery had given him. "Ring, damn it, ring," he said under his breath. It wasn't a good sign that it was eleven, and he hadn't heard from Flannery yet.

Trying to keep his cool and failing, Vinnie jumped when the bag phone finally rang. "Is it a go?" he blurted out.

"I hate to disappoint you, but we got our letter," Flannery informed Vinnie. "We're going to have to abort the mission. You can bring the gurry back up to Gloucester. When you're done come back to Boston, drop by the plant and I'll take care of you. Thanks for helping me with this."

"Disappointing not to get to dump the gurry, though," Vinnie said.

"I know. That would have been fun, wouldn't it have? But we got what we wanted without actually having to pull that trigger, so we won in the end. It's all good," Flannery said.

"OK, I'll get out of here before someone notices me," Vinnie told Flannery.

"Good enough," said Flannery. "Thanks a million."

Vinnie thought about how much easier it would have been for him to simply dump the gurry in front of the statehouse. Instead, he had to go back to Gloucester and dump the gurry back into the tractor-trailer truck, bucketful by bucketful, basically reversing everything he had done that morning. Feeling a little down, he headed for the expressway and back to Gloucester. But then he remembered there wouldn't be much traffic heading to Gloucester at eleven in the morning, and he knew that Flannery would reward him well for his efforts. Not totally a wasted day, just not as exciting as it could have been. Opportunities like that don't come along every day. It was never a sure thing, but it would have made his day, certainly his week. The truth was, it would have been one of the flashiest things Vinny had done in his life.

CHAPTER 9

After a relaxing stroll through Boston's iconic parks, Denny followed the signs to the southbound side of the expressway, and with the aid of Meredith's directions, he pulled up to the parking area by Flannery's Boston plant. Envelope in hand, he climbed the stairs to the owner's office. Flannery was busy on the phone, which was par for the course. When Flannery noticed Denny awkwardly standing on the threshold of his door, he waved him in, motioning him to take a seat.

"Right now, we have on hand a limited supply of fish by-products that are well suited for field fertilizer," Flannery continued his phone conversation. "We only have three forty-thousand-pound truckloads left, but if you can take them all within the next week, I'll reserve them for you. You'll want to get it turned into your fields before the ground freezes, and next summer you'll be producing crops tenfold to what you did this year." Flannery couldn't resist gilding the lily a bit. "Have you ever heard of the Native American Squanto, who taught the Pilgrims how to grow crops?"

Flannery paused for the farmer's response, then continued, "Well, this was Squanto's secret, the very same thing that Squanto used to help the Pilgrims create that massive feast that became Thanksgiving. You're going to love it. I'll arrange for my driver to get up there by

Sunday. Then your farmhands can start mixing it in with the soil as soon as the new work week begins."

Another pause to hear the farmer's reaction. From what Denny could tell, whomever Flannery was talking to was swallowing his story hook, line, and sinker. "Cost?" Flannery continued, "Well it's your lucky day. I'm willing to let these last truckloads go for the cost of transportation. You pay the trucking, and they're yours."

One last pause and then Flannery closed the deal. "Beautiful! I'll have my driver leave Sunday morning, bright and early. Very good; you're going to wish I had more to give you after you see how good this stuff works."

With that, Flannery hung up the phone and turned to Denny with a gleeful laugh. "If this goes through, I just managed to sell all three truckloads of the old gurry to a six-hundred-and-eighty-nine-acre farm in New York."

"Sweet," Denny remarked.

"So what do you have for me from our governor?" Flannery asked, turning his attention to that all-important envelope. Denny handed it to him, still sealed, and Flannery grabbed a swordfish-shaped letter opener from his drawer to tear the top open.

"Perfect," Flannery said as he scanned the letter. "Hopefully our governor's a man of his word and holds up his end of the bargain. Now I can hire the barge and tugboat out of Boston, and we can move the gurry that's being produced right now."

"I'm glad it all worked out," Denny said as he rose to head out of Flannery's office.

"Hey Denny," Flannery called out, "thanks for your help today. I know it was a little outside your wheelhouse, but you handled it like a pro."

"It was an experience I'll never forget," Denny agreed with a smile as he walked out of Flannery's office, vowing never to do anything like that ever again. But he'd made a few points with Flannery today, and he would have quite a story to tell his family when he got home.

As Denny was leaving, he half expected to run into Vinnie

coming up the stairs, but then he remembered that Vinnie would have to get rid of his truckload of gurry in Gloucester before heading to the Boston plant. It wasn't until later that afternoon that Vinnie had finally returned the gurry to its original tractor-trailer truck and drove down to Flannery's Boston office.

"Vinnie, you old son of a gun," Flannery called out as Vinnie knocked on his open office door. "I thought we'd catch a late lunch at Victoria's Restaurant on Mass Ave. and celebrate our good luck today."

"Sure," Vinnie said, "but I would have felt luckier if I had gotten to dump the gurry. I was really looking forward to everyone's reaction. They would have wanted to arrest me, but I was thinking that as long as I stood near the steaming heap, I don't think anyone would have approached me."

"It would have been something to see—that's for sure," said Flannery. "Let's head out. I've already made reservations. We'll start off with a celebratory beer. You've earned it." He slipped Vinnie an envelope and headed down the stairs to grab the keys to the Boston sales office Lincoln, and then they were off.

Victoria's Restaurant was a stone's throw away from Flannery's Boston plant and was his go-to venue for meetings. Victoria's was also one of his customers, and he had a fierce loyalty to any company that bought fish from him. He seldom ate at any restaurant that didn't buy from his company. After they were seated and had a chance to order, he wasted no time in getting to the real reason for their meeting. "I just got off the phone from talking with a farmer from upstate New York who's interested in taking all of our gurry on hand," Flannery began.

"No kidding!" Vinnie said. "I can't believe anyone would want to have that mess delivered to their door."

"Hey, what better place for it than a seven-hundred-acre farm, give or take an acre? The gurry's already begun the decomposition process. If she tills it into her fields right away, they should be set to go in the spring," he explained. Then he added, "We're doing this woman a tremendous favor."

"Has she ever dealt with fish by-products before?" Vinnie asked. "They can be way more obnoxious than the manure she's probably used to handling."

"If it worked for the Pilgrims, there's no reason it wouldn't work for her farm, too," Flannery said. "Besides, she grows a wide variety of crops and even has some dairy cows. She's the third generation working her farm, so she's no novice. And in all these years, I bet her family's never thought of fertilizing with fish. She's going to love this gurry and wonder why she never used fish by-products before." Flannery excelled at sales because he was able to convince himself that everything he was selling was top-notch. He believed so strongly that his product was the best that people would become blinded by his passion.

"So let me guess the plan. You want me to drive one of those tractor-trailer trucks loaded with gurry up to her farm," Vinnie hypothesized.

"You hit the nail on the head. Only we're going to drive all three up within the week. The first one needs to leave sometime Sunday morning. It's about a four-hour-and-fifteen-minute drive to get to Kinderhook, New York. That's not too bad a trip; just head down 495 to Route 2. It's not too far across the New York border. We'll give the farmhands a couple of days to mix the gurry into the soil, then we'll head up with the next truckload." Flannery paused for a moment to calculate a schedule. Then he continued, "We want to be sure to give her enough time to take care of the first load, so why don't you head up with the next truck early Wednesday morning, arriving just as their work day begins. Then we'll deliver the last load on Friday. With all three truckloads gone, we'll be starting off from scratch with gurry that's freshly cut. That will be a nice starting point for the barge and tugboat I ordered today with the governor's money."

"But, Jack, have you forgotten what those trucks smell like? The first small town I go through, the cops are going to nail me,"

Vinnie insisted.

"No, they won't," Flannery said, anticipating this would be a major concern. "Now, if you take the Mass Pike out, you could get pinched. But if you go through those lovely picturesque towns along Route 2, those cops are going to take one whiff of you and allow you to get out of their town, the quicker, the better. Hells bells, they may even give you a police escort out of town to hurry you along. They aren't going to want to stop you. And they certainly aren't going to arrest you because that would mean they'd have to impound your truck, and no self-respecting cop is going to bring that upon their quaint little town. No, I'm sure you'll have no problem getting out to Kinderhook in record time. Just follow the speed limits so that they have no beef with you. You'll be golden."

Vinnie thought for a minute before he said, "You know, I hate to say it, but you might be right. That really does make sense." Vinnie rubbed his stubbly beard for a moment and then said, "Aw, hell, I didn't have any plans for Sunday anyway. If I hit those small towns right at church time, there might be no one on the streets to smell me coming through anyway. They'd be like virtual ghost towns."

"That's exactly what I was thinking," Flannery said. "That's why Sunday morning is such a perfect time for the first shipment to move through."

"I'll tell you what," Vinnie told Flannery. "I'll drive that first tractor-trailer truck, and we'll see how it goes." Then he met Flannery's steel-gray eyes with his own and said, "But that's all I'm promising. One trip. If it's a piece of cake, I'll try a second truckload. But if there's trouble, and things don't go as we've planned, I'm done. Deal?"

"I don't think you'll have any trouble, but that sounds reasonable. Deal," Flannery said, shaking Vinnie's hand over a basket of bread on the table.

Once that piece of business was finalized, the two men took turns sharing old stories about working at the pier. They both ordered haddock au gratin, ate quickly, and left each other with another handshake.

Flannery was more content than he'd been in weeks as he headed down to his home on the Cape for the weekend. His plan for the gurry was actually taking shape, with all the pieces falling neatly into place. He slid a Frank Sinatra tape into his car's cassette player. Flannery knew the words to most of Sinatra's songs by heart and was singing "My Way" as he took the Route 3 exit, en route to the Sagamore Bridge.

*　　*　　*　　*　　*

Paul and Meredith had spent most of midday Friday taking turns listening to the radio for any news about gurry being dumped at the statehouse. They both had to admit they were just a teeny bit disappointed when they found out it hadn't happened. With all the lobster shipments sent to Logan and Doug back from delivering fish orders to local restaurants, Paul and Meredith were busy working in the retail store with Rosa when Denny appeared at the doorway.

"You wanted to see me?" Denny asked Paul.

"Yes," Paul replied. Then he added, "Let's go into the office."

"Uh-oh," Denny said quietly.

Paul smiled. "You're not in trouble, Denny—that I know of anyway," Paul teased.

As they entered the office and the door closed, Paul told Denny, "I actually have two things I wanted to see you about. It's been a while since we've changed the water in the tanks, hasn't it?"

"It's been about two weeks," Denny answered.

"I don't think they're predicting rain this weekend. It'd be a good time to bring in new water from the harbor. You never know this time of year if you're going to get a week of rain, and then we'd be bringing brackish water into the tanks, so we better get it while the getting's good," Paul said.

"I'll see if Charlie can take care of it on Sunday when he's in," Denny suggested.

"Sounds good," Paul agreed. "The second thing I wanted to talk to you about is more of a favor for Flannery."

"Oh no, Paul!" Denny exclaimed. "I barely got out with my life the last time I did a favor for him!"

"Ha, I think that's a little melodramatic," Paul said, laughing, and then added, "but I think you'll actually enjoy this favor."

"I'll be the judge of that," Denny said suspiciously.

"First, I want you to spend about a half hour cutting fish. Don't worry about getting fishy; that's the point of doing it," Paul said.

"I can do that," Denny said.

"Then I want you to take your fishing rod out to the back dock and fish for another half hour," Paul added.

"Now we're talking," Denny agreed. "But when I get done sitting in the hot sun, I'll need a change of clothes and a shower for sure."

"No you won't. I want you to stink," Paul said.

Denny shot Paul a strange look. "Why?" he asked.

"Because I'm going to send you down to the Captain's Table restaurant at the end of Bearskin Neck in Rockport to collect a check," Paul answered.

"I knew this was too good to be true," Denny declared. "As soon as they get a whiff of me they're going to kick my ass out of there."

"Not if you're sitting at the bar drinking," Paul replied.

"I just got back on board," Denny said jokingly.

"We've gotta do something—and soon," Paul explained. "The Captain's Table is into us for about three months' worth of orders. I first realized why we weren't getting paid a couple of weeks ago when the discovery of the *Bay State Skye* brought to light the Golini brothers' financial problems."

"Did Tony and Billy Golini own the Captain's Table?" Denny asked. "They had their hands in a bunch of things, didn't they?"

"They were fairly successful . . . until they weren't," Paul said. "But at this point, we need some money. I don't know how long they'll stay open. They must have lost their supply of cheap fish since the *Bay State Skye*'s out of commission. We were supplying them with shellfish, shrimp, and seafood that wasn't local, but Billy Golini's boat was providing the restaurant with most of its fresh fish. We're concerned they're going to go belly-up, and then we won't get paid."

"So you just want me to sit at the bar and drink?" Denny asked.

"Go in first and tell them you're there to pick up a check for Flannery's. If they tell you they don't have one, just tell them you'll sit at the bar and wait for them to get you one. Don't leave until you have a check. Just sit there and drink. Be polite, and if they try to kick you out, tell them to call me. When you get a check, I'll send Doug down with their fish order, and he'll drive you back. Sound good?"

"I guess I can do that," Denny said.

"Great, why don't you head over to the cutting line and get as fishy as you can," Paul directed Denny. "Oh, and don't forget to tell Charlie to change some water out on Sunday."

"I won't," Denny said as he left the office.

Denny went to talk to Charlie right away while he was still thinking of it, then strolled over to the cutting line to begin carrying out Paul's instructions. After about an hour, he was ready for his debut at the Captain's Table.

Denny parked his car on Broadway Street and walked up to the tip of the neck with a view of Rockport Harbor. He marched in the front door and announced to the hostess of the swanky, white-tablecloth restaurant that he was there to pick up a check. The manager was called, and in no time, Denny was looking into the chest of a man who was easily ten inches taller than him, with muscles bursting out of his fitted shirt.

"I don't have a check for Flannery's today," the manager told Denny.

"I was told not to leave without one," Denny explained. "I'll just go sit in the bar and wait."

"You can sit wherever you want, but you're still not getting a check today," the manager replied.

"I'm just following orders," Denny said as he made his way to the bar. The bar was nothing like his favorite watering hole, Fitzy's.

This bar was decorated with high-end nautical paraphernalia that would be commonplace on a yacht or a schooner. Feeling very much out of his league, Denny made his way to the most familiar thing he could find, a barstool. He chose a stool between a very well-dressed middle-aged man, sporting a jacket that looked like he was the commander of a fleet, and an older woman dressed from head to toe with designer labels.

"Can I have a beer please?" he asked the bartender.

"Coming right up," the bartender replied; he then took the cap off a locally brewed designer beer and poured it into a glass. Denny thanked the bartender, who insisted on collecting his money right then. Taking out the pile of tens Paul gave him to pay for his drinks, Denny peeled off a bill. When the bartender saw the roll of tens, he relaxed and decided it was safe to start a tab for him.

It wasn't long before both the people on either side of Denny at the bar decided to sit at a table instead. He might have caught the older woman fanning her hand in front of her nose as she stepped away from him. It wasn't long before no one was sitting in the vicinity of where he was perched.

When he was being served his third beer, the bartender told Denny, "You look like a decent guy, but I've gotta tell you, you're a little ripe." The bartender made a fanning motion in front of his face. "Maybe you should head home and shower. You're killing my business."

"I'm just here waiting to pick up a check for Flannery's. As soon as I do, I'll be out your hair," Denny explained as he took a drink of his beer. The bartender called the manager over and asked him how soon the check would be ready.

"As I've already told this gentleman, there is no check. He may as well head out," the manager said, loud enough for Denny to hear.

"I can't leave until I have a check," Denny said, loud enough for the customers to hear.

The manager approached Denny and asked quietly, "Do I need to call the police?"

"I'm not causing any trouble. I'm just sitting here drinking my beer," Denny said as he raised his beer glass to his lips and took a good swig of it. He swallowed hard. "But you can call Paul at Flannery's if you want. If you guys come up with some kind of agreement, I'll be happy to leave."

"That's just what I'm going to do," the manager told Denny. Denny didn't react. He sat calmly and continued drinking his beer.

Back at Flannery's, Paul hurried out the retail door and through the office door to answer the phone. He was expecting a call from the manager and was a little surprised it had taken this long.

"Is this Paul?" the manager at the Captain's Table asked.

"Yes it is," Paul answered.

"I don't know if you're aware of it or not, but one of your guys is sitting in my bar claiming you told him to stay and drink until we provide him with a check for Flannery's," the manager said, half expecting Paul to deny that he'd sent Denny.

"That sounds about right," Paul replied.

"Well, call him off," the annoyed manager told Paul.

"No can do," Paul said. "You're into us for a lot of money at this point, and we need to start being paid."

"Come on—give me a break. I'm sure you heard about what happened with the *Bay State Skye*. Can't you cut me some slack?" the manager asked.

"You owe us money from way before the Golinis were lost at sea. We should have come collecting it long before now," Paul insisted.

The manager's voice got quieter. "Your boy here reeks, you know. He's driving business out of the bar."

"If I were in your shoes," Paul suggested, "I'd get a check to him as quickly as I could."

At this point, the manager saw what Paul was up to. It was no coincidence Flannery's sent an employee with a stench to pick up a check. The manager finally gave in. "OK, what do I need to do to get him out of my bar?"

"Give him a check for at least a third of what you owe, and I'll call him back to the plant," Paul said.

"Done," the manager said.

"Good," Paul declared. "I'll send a man over to deliver your order for this week and collect up my employee."

"OK," the manager said. "I can have him out in fifteen minutes."

"As long as he has a check in his hand," Paul replied.

"He will," the manager promised, and both men hung up.

Paul directed Doug to deliver the Captain Table's order and to give Denny a ride home. Then he called Flannery to tell him he'd be sending a check down to Boston for a third of what the Captain's Table owed. Paul was pretty pleased that his plan had worked. Not a bad way to end the week.

*　　*　　*　　*　　*

When Sunday morning arrived, a very sleepy Charlie unlocked the retail door and punched in the alarm code. He walked over to the second keypad by the lobster-room door and punched in that code as well. Then he lifted the heavy door that was an additional security barrier between the plant floor and the lobster room.

Denny told Charlie to be sure to arrive at 7:00 a.m. sharp. That was when the incoming tide began, which was crucial to bringing in good water. If it was high tide as well, that was even better. Denny managed to plan a time when both occurred simultaneously. The incoming tide was most important because there was a culvert just to the left of Flannery's plant that provided drainage to the streets. If water was brought in during an outgoing tide, the culvert was close enough to Flannery's to allow fresh water to be sucked in on its way out of the harbor.

The worst possible scenario was when there was a sustained period of heavy rain, compromising the city's sewerage system. Normally, water from the street drains emptied directly into the harbor. But if there was too much water in the sewers, the town didn't want sewerage bubbling up into the streets, so they built a safety into the system where raw sewerage could pop over the waste gates and into the street-drainage system. This would allow raw sewerage to flow directly into the harbor before being treated. This didn't happen often, but Paul could remember about a dozen times when he went out back after a significant rainy period and noticed pieces of toilet paper and human waste drifting in the harbor toward the open ocean. Although it was a rare occurrence, if Flannery's happened to be pulling water in at the same time, the potential was there to draw raw sewerage directly into the lobster system, which would compromise their entire inventory.

If the sewerage system was functioning correctly, all the wastewater from Gloucester would flow to the treatment plant, and once treated, it would be pumped out to what was known by local residents as "the bubbler." Treated water would flow through a pipe that ran out the center of the harbor to the outer harbor until it was about three or four miles offshore. Once it reached the end of the line, the treated water would bubble up to the surface. This spot had the reputation of being a great place to fish because the bubbler seemed to attract a multitude of species to the area.

Every now and then, if Flannery's tanks were fairly full of lobsters, as they were that day, it became necessary to dump some water before adding more. The lobsters displaced water in the tanks, which caused the level of the reservoir to rise, so water from the reservoir would empty out into the harbor instead of coming up onto the floor of the lobster room. This limited the amount of water running through the system, which made ammonia levels from the lobsters build at a much more rapid rate. Dumping water before taking more in allowed the ammonia levels to drop much more quickly, which made for a healthier environment for the lobsters. This was the best way to handle the system if it was crowded with lobsters. But there was one drawback. The intake screen area wasn't far from the piping where water was discharged from the system. After water was dumped, it was important to wait for at least a half hour, if not more, to allow the dumped water to leave the area before the new water was drawn in.

No water was going to be dumped that day, though. Charlie was sure of that. He had a hot date planned with his new girlfriend and had no intentions of being late. As far as Charlie was concerned, the lobster system was made up of tanks, a reservoir, a chiller, and a filtration system that would more than take care of any problem a large number of lobsters in the system might cause. Time was of the essence, and he had diligently arrived exactly when Denny had asked.

Charlie knew that when the water in the harbor was warm, which was especially the case in early September, he needed to bring the water into the reservoir first to allow it to mix with the hundred thousand gallons of colder water already there so that when it was sucked up and taken to the top of the tanks, the water would be similar in temperature. This would prevent the lobsters from experiencing any kind of shock when water was changed. The lobsters were normally kept in forty-two degree water, and harbor water was about sixty-eight degrees. If the water was drawn in directly to the top tanks, bypassing the reservoir, that extreme temperature change would cause a lobster to turn upside down and die, a fact of which Charlie was very aware.

But Charlie had places to be and things to do, so he thought of a plan that would speed up his job and still get the task done right. He figured if he opened the valve that pulled water in directly from the harbor to the top tanks about halfway, then opened the valve that drew water out of the harbor and into the reservoir full blast, it would allow enough mixing in the reservoir to balance out the warmer water going directly into the tanks. In the end, he'd be increasing the amount of water he brought in by a third, compared to what he'd be bringing in by fully opening the reservoir valve alone.

Charlie was having a well-deserved cigarette break while the water was being pumped in. When the time was up, Charlie threw his remaining cigarette butt down the hole into the reservoir and walked back to the pump room. He closed the valves, turned on the reservoir pump, pulled the heavy metal door down, and punched in the alarm code. He walked into the retail area, punched the alarm code there, walked out the retail door, being careful to lock up behind him, and left, satisfied he had managed to do what no man had been able to do before him. He had changed the lobster tank water in record time.

*　　*　　*　　*　　*

Meanwhile, Vinnie was over at the gurry plant, firing up the first tractor-trailer truck that contained the oldest gurry. He was uncharacteristically extra-diligent in checking out the safety of his vehicle because he didn't want to have to stop, or even slow down, as he made the trip to New York. When satisfied the truck could do the job, Vinnie paused for a moment, thinking how truly old this batch was. *Imagine*, he said to himself, *some of this gurry was part of the* Bay State Skye's *catch*. It had been close to three weeks since the Golinis' boat was discovered and by now, the two brothers had sunk into anonymity and were all but forgotten by Cape Ann residents. As with everything, time marches on, and as George Harrison so poignantly sung, the world goes on within you and without you. Although the *Bay State Skye* was still docked in Gloucester, no one had seen any of the Golini family in the Cape Ann area since before Labor Day. Following Congressman Contoro's unsuccessful attempt to raise money for the family, the Golinis' name was never spoken in the Gloucester area again, and life truly did go on quite nicely without the Golini brothers.

Vinnie glanced at his watch, dismayed at the time it took him to assure the truck was capable of the trip, and quickly climbed into the cab. He put the truck into gear and once again headed toward the Route 128 rotary. He knew that Cape Ann Ice probably wouldn't supply any free ice for his cause, so Vinnie had to rely on the canvas covering to keep some of the odor in—and on a whole lot of God-fearing people being in church when he came through their lovely New England towns.

Vinnie headed down Route 128 southbound, then headed north on Route 3 until it met up with 495. These were all highways, but there weren't many cars on the road at seven thirty in the morning on a Sunday. The few that were tried to pass as soon as they approached Vinnie's truck. Even when he banged a right onto Route 2 near Littleton and headed out on the Mohawk Trail, everything was still hunky-dory. The Mohawk Trail was a picturesque road anytime, but it was especially popular during leaf-peeping season in the fall. Vinnie was extremely grateful that he was trucking this swill up about two weeks before the first sign of the leaves changing. Vinnie played classic rock on his radio and settled in for a long ride.

The first indication Vinnie had that he'd missed his exit onto Route 112 was when he drove straight down Main Street in Williamstown, Massachusetts, on the New York and Vermont borders. It was a perfect, historic, small New England college town, which of course included a picturesque, white-steepled church. Vinnie passed a red brick building with a hip roof that he assumed housed town offices and a stone church with a sign that read, "Thompson Memorial Chapel," which looked like it might be part of Williams College. Thankfully, the parking places along the streets surrounding the church were packed, and Vinnie could hear hymns being sung from inside. The citizens of the town seemed preoccupied with church, but Vinnie hadn't counted on a bunch of college students without classes on the weekend who were parading up and down Main Street. It wasn't long before he saw young adults dressed in ripped jeans, flannel shirts, and giant shoulder pads gagging by the sidewalk, holding their noses, or running for cover. He wanted to stop and ask a couple of boys who were playing Frisbee on the green for directions to Pittsfield, but when he began to stop, the boys scrambled to pick up their Frisbee and ran in the opposite direction.

This was what Vinnie feared most, getting lost in an unfamiliar area. He should have been paying closer attention to the road signs. It was like he'd put himself into autopilot mode, lulled into a false sense of security while taking in the tranquil scenery and enjoying the deserted trail. He was paying for it now in spades. But Vinnie wasn't the type to obsess over his situation. He was a schemer. He just needed to formulate a plan for the situation. As he slowly rolled on, Vinnie couldn't believe his luck. He looked up and saw a sign for Pittsfield, which would get him right back on track. The green sign stated that Pittsfield was twenty-one miles away on Route 7, with a bold, black arrow pointing left.

Vinnie wiped the sweat from his forehead as he turned his steering wheel a sharp left. "Thank God," he said. He wasn't a praying man by nature, but he'd make this one exception because he was so damned relieved to find his way again. The look of dread immediately drained from his face, being replaced by his signature broad grin. "I'm a lucky son of a bitch just the same," Vinnie said proudly, forgetting that if he was truly lucky, he wouldn't have gotten lost in the first place. "In the end, I always come out smelling like a rose!" The irony of that statement made him smile even broader.

Vinnie was pulling up to the farm in Kinderhook, New York, a little after high noon. He parked his truck as downwind as possible from the traditional white, sprawling farmhouse, which included a classic wraparound porch. The buildings on the property were in tip-top shape, and the farm, in general, appeared to be well maintained. As Vinnie approached the walkway to ring the front bell, a woman in her forties came bouncing out. She was dressed in a pair of fitted, flared Levis and a white turtleneck, with a red flannel shirt over it all, flapping in the breeze that thankfully was blowing away from the farmhouse and toward the truck.

"Are you Flannery's man, Vinnie?" the woman called out in a friendly tone of voice.

"That's me," Vinnie said with a wide smile, trying to put his best foot forward. If the three massive tractor-trailer trucks full of gurry were finally gone from the plant, it would make loading the barge Flannery had just ordered much easier. Not to mention, the air would be a lot sweeter.

"I'm Marge," the woman said as she extended her hand.

"Great to meet you, Marge," Vinnie said as he met her hand with his. Marge had a hearty handshake. They were the hands of someone who wasn't afraid of a good day's work. Vinnie had half expected Marge to be a bit frumpy and was surprised at her fashionable appearance. But the fact that she was forward-thinking enough to try something new and not just follow traditional methods of fertilizing her fields was an indication that, of course, she'd be up-to-date in everything else.

"I've got your first load of gur . . . fish by-product fertilizer," Vinnie told Marge, trying to put the most positive spin that he could on his product. "Where would you like me to put it?"

"If you take a right at the corner, down there where your truck is parked, and follow that road until it ends, the field that's directly in front of you is the one we'll be trying the fish by-product fertilizer out on," Marge said, doing her best to use Vinnie's new term for the gurry he was hauling. "Do you think you can find it all right, or would you like me to send someone with you?"

Vinnie loved the way Marge treated him. She was respectful and knew he was just like most people on this planet, trying to eke out a living for himself. Many people who didn't know Vinnie would have presumed he was a worthless flunky, working an undesirable job because he was capable of doing nothing more. But Vinnie was a smart kid who graduated from high school and had an acceptance letter from Boston University framed on the wall of his den. He chose to do this job because he loved it. He loved the freedom of the job, and he loved the people with whom he worked. They were genuine; they were real. They were the type of people with whom Vinnie wanted to spend his day. Marge appeared to be that type of person.

"I'm sure I can find it," Vinnie replied, not wanting to take anyone with him. "Thanks for your help. I'll spread the load around as much as I can to make it easier for you to till it in. It's a little ripe, you know."

"I do," Marge said with a smile. "Flannery says that's what makes it so good!"

"Very true," Vinnie said with a big grin as he stretched forward to hand Marge a bill of lading. "I'll get right to it. Thanks again."

"Oh, by the way, thanks for coming out on a Sunday," Marge said as she began to turn to go back into her house. Vinnie could smell bacon cooking and imagined Marge's family was having a big country breakfast.

"No problem. I'll let you get back to it," said Vinnie, tipping his baseball cap and turning to begin the walk downhill to meet up with his truck.

Vinnie reached his truck quickly, pushed along by the steep decline of the hill on which he was parked. He bounced into his truck and made his way to Marge's field. The weather had been mostly dry the last two weeks, so Vinnie felt he could drive his heavy tractor-trailer truck onto the field without sinking in. His plan was to drive from one end of the field to the other, stopping many times to dump small amounts of gurry along the way. This would allow the optimal airing of the load, as well as a chance for the many bugs that had hitched a ride in the goop to disperse. Vinnie wound up making three passes at the field to dump the full load. Painstakingly, he stopped, dumped a small amount of gurry, lowered his bed again to keep from tipping on the uneven field, then pulled up a little farther to begin the process all over again. Vinnie made this extra effort because he wanted Flannery's plan to succeed and also because he liked Marge. She obviously knew you make more friends with sugar than vinegar, and it had worked well with Vinnie.

When his truck was empty, Vinnie jumped out of the cab to latch his bed. As he walked back to the driver's side of his truck, he noticed a brand-new tractor with a bucket accessory, as well as a tiller, strategically placed at the ready to push the piles of gurry around and till them into the soil. Vinnie was impressed with Marge's organization. She ran a tight ship.

Vinnie climbed back into his cab and headed for Gloucester, making certain he didn't get lost on the way home. As he reached Route 128, Vinnie breathed a sigh of relief. The first truckload was gone. It was the hardest, in a way, because Vinnie was traveling an unfamiliar route. But Vinnie knew the second truckload would be harder still because he'd be traveling when the roads were busier and people were out and about, carrying on with their day. The potential of discovery and the possibility of being stopped would be heightened on the second trip out. But Vinnie was willing to take the risk. He'd be getting rid of another truckload full of rotten gurry. Vinnie pulled into the gurry plant, hosed down his truck bed, and drove off to salvage what was left of his weekend.

Bay State Skye

CHAPTER 10

While Vinnie was regaling everyone early Monday morning at the Gloucester Display Auction with his tale of ridding the city of one of its infamous gurry truckloads, Charlie was beginning to cull through the lobsters in the tanks at Flannery's. He began, as usual, with the top tanks. He climbed up on the rim of the first tier of tanks, then to the second-tier rim, until he was able to reach inside the top tier of tanks with a three-pronged rake to gently stir up the lobsters. When the rake entered the water, the live lobsters scattered to one side or the other, leaving only weak or dead ones on the bottom. It was important to remove those lobsters immediately to keep the water from spoiling.

Charlie couldn't believe the number of lobsters that weren't moving at the bottom of the tank. When finished, Charlie had removed a little under two hundred pounds of lobsters from the first tank. Then he moved to the second tank on the top tier, a little closer to the back of the room. Gently stirring the water with the rake, he uncovered another two hundred and fifty pounds of lobsters that remained motionless on the tank's bottom. Charlie was in the process of removing them when Denny entered the lobster room, whistling a tune that was stuck in his head from his car radio. Charlie wasted no time in confronting Denny, angry that this mess was waiting for him first thing on a Monday morning.

"What the hell did you do?" Charlie yelled at Denny. "You and Paul must have screwed something up, big-time. Look at all the deads we have. You'd better get some help in here. I'm not doing this alone." He picked up an orange basket that was half-full of rockweed and threw it at the wall.

"What?" Denny said, no longer whistling, eyes wide as he looked at the sea of weak and dead lobsters before him. "How'd we get all these deads?" He picked up a lobster that managed a slight flick of his antenna while his legs and tail hung limply. The deads and weaks were bad, but he knew he had to find out why they died so that he didn't lose the entire lobster inventory. He helped Charlie go through the last two tanks on the upper tier. They discovered that the tank closest to the picking room that backed up to the harbor contained only one hundred live lobsters out of four hundred and seventy-five. The rest were dead or dying.

As soon as Denny saw Paul walk through the plastic strips on the loading dock and take his place in the office, he started to walk toward the office himself. Just as he was about to reach for the doorknob, Charlie brushed past him and flung open the door himself. He knew enough to let Denny walk in first, but he was right on his heels.

"You really messed up this time, Paul," Charlie said arrogantly.

Paul looked at Denny for an explanation, not wishing to dignify Charlie's outburst with an answer.

"Charlie, get back in the lobster room," Denny yelled out. "We need all hands on deck to be ready to pack lobsters when orders start coming in." Then he turned to Meredith and asked, "Can you spare Doug for an hour or two this morning?"

"Sure," Meredith said and jumped down from her stool to reach the loudspeaker mike. She held down the button and said, "Doug, please come to the office; Doug, please come to the office," She placed the mike back on the shelf and settled onto her stool again. This was going to get interesting.

"You can go, Charlie. Doug will be right in," Denny insisted, without his usual carefree grin. Denny almost punched Charlie as he walked by but managed to keep his composure. Reluctantly, Charlie left, trying hard to slam the door behind him, which was virtually impossible with a spring-loaded door. The fact that he and Paul hadn't had any altercations for a while hadn't made him any fonder of Paul, and Paul hadn't softened toward him either. He'd just been preoccupied with more pressing demands on his time.

Once Charlie was out of sight, Denny said in almost a whisper, "I don't know what happened, but we have over a thousand pounds of weaks and deads from the top tier of tanks on the left side, and that may not be all. I haven't had time to go through the rest of the tanks. You didn't do anything over the weekend, did you?"

Paul looked at Denny in disbelief. Both men spoke quietly, as if stating what happened out loud would somehow make it more real. "I haven't been here since Friday night," Paul answered in a low tone. Denny and Paul stood stone still, stunned by the news.

"I came in Saturday and took a couple of boats in," Denny disclosed in a low voice, "but everything was fine when I left."

Paul thought for a minute. "I'd test the water, but it must be full of ammonia with all those deads. It wouldn't really tell us anything."

"There's a lot of foam—that's for sure," Denny replied. Both men knew that foam on the surface of the tanks was a clear indication that ammonia levels were high.

"I'll do a salinity test," Paul said. "Why don't you take a temperature reading? I don't think testing the nitrates and nitrites would be all that helpful right now." Denny agreed as both men headed to the lobster room together.

"Should I still put tickets out to pack lobsters?" Meredith called after them. "I don't want to have to tell Boston what's going on until we know ourselves. They have some lobsters in their pound that could get them through the early morning shipments in a pinch. But I don't think they've got enough to get them through a busy Monday."

"Set up the lobster shipments as usual, and if we have to make changes, we will," Paul called back to Meredith. Then he asked Denny, "How do the right-side tanks look?"

"To tell you the truth, I didn't really notice," said Denny. Paul stopped in his tracks, having just had a revelation.

"Did Charlie come in Sunday and change the water like we asked?" Paul asked Denny.

"I never asked, but I'd assume so. He's usually dependable when it comes to showing up when he should," Denny replied, and in the next moment, Denny knew exactly what Paul was driving at. "Oh, the top-left tanks are the first ones to receive water directly from the harbor if that valve is opened," Denny said quietly.

"That was what I was thinking," replied Paul in the same low voice.

"But Charlie knows better than to bring water directly into the tanks," Denny whispered in a manner that could still be heard over the noise in the plant but not over the cascading water in the lobster room.

"Let's check the right side of the room. If the lobsters are barely affected, then I'll bet that's what happened," Paul surmised.

"In a way, I'm hoping that's it," Denny added. "Sucks that it was preventable, but we should have mostly live lobsters as we move away from the upper-left tanks. And the right side holds the pricier, larger lobsters that aren't so easily replaced."

"Let's hope that's the case. At least then, a simple water change can eliminate most of the ammonia. Glad it didn't rain last night like they predicted," Paul said.

Paul and Denny went through the right-side tanks while Doug and Charlie handled the remaining ones on the left side. Denny pulled out a few weaks and handed them to Paul. The number they found was consistent with what they would have expected coming in after a weekend. This seemed to prove Paul's hypothesis. He didn't want to confront Charlie unless he was absolutely convinced of what happened, and this was all the evidence he needed.

"Hey, Charlie," Denny called out. Charlie came bounding off the lower rim of tanks, happy to leave Doug to finish up his job. Paul thought Charlie would let his guard down more if Denny asked the questions.

"What's up?" he asked. "Did you figure out what happened?"

"We're not sure," Denny replied. Then he commented, "You came in Sunday to change the water in the lobster room, right?"

"Sure did," he answered proudly.

"Did you open the valve that pulls water in from the harbor directly to the upper tanks when you did it?" Denny asked.

"I throttled it," he replied, eager to divulge his timesaving method.

"Throttled it?" Denny parroted his response with a puzzled look.

"That's right. I only opened it halfway, and I opened the valve to the reservoir all the way. Didn't take long at all. You should take water in my way. It's way quicker," he said boastfully. He was waiting for Denny to give him an attaboy. It was an ingenious idea.

Denny sighed. Paul shook his head. "Well, that explains it," Denny quietly said to Paul. Paul nodded in agreement.

"Wait a minute! What? You're not going to blame me for all this," Charlie cried out. "I barely had the tank valve open halfway. Most of the water was going into the reservoir. No way it would cause this."

Paul couldn't keep quiet any longer. "Charlie, the pipe leading from the harbor to the reservoir is two inches in diameter; the pipe leading from the harbor to the upper tanks is four inches in diameter. Even with the valve just halfway open, the pipe leading to the upper tanks took in at least as much water as the reservoir pipe did. That's why the water change happened so quickly. That was the equivalent of suddenly throwing about twenty-five hundred pounds of lobsters into a virtual hot tub."

"Well, how the hell was I supposed to know that?" Charlie answered indignantly.

"You're supposed to follow the procedures you were taught," answered Paul, unable to believe he didn't show one iota of remorse.

"I'll get a cook ready," Denny said. "We need to start going through these lobsters to see if we can salvage some of them for meat. If they show any signs of life, a flick of an antenna or a flip of a swimmeret, put them in a basket to cook."

"Good thinking," Paul told Denny. "If we all work together on this, we should be able to recover the majority of these lobsters for meat."

Paul, Denny, Doug, and Charlie worked as quickly as they could to separate the long-dead lobsters from the ones that would be viable for a cook. Meredith began putting orders out to be filled from the tanks on the right side to be sure they were shipping strong lobsters.

"I can't believe it didn't dawn on Charlie that his new method of bringing in water could have had something to do with all these deads," Paul said. "Clearly, he had no idea or he wouldn't have been bragging so much."

"Charlie's not the sharpest tool in the shed, but to his defense, he didn't know there was a difference in pipe size between the reservoir and upper-tank valves," Denny said.

"That's the only reason I'm not writing him up," Paul said, "even though he didn't follow procedures."

"Who'd of thought he'd have come up with his own idea of how to bring in water more efficiently?" Denny added.

"Who'd of thunk it?" Paul said with a grin as he headed toward the office. "Charlie must have had somewhere to be. Didn't someone say, 'necessity is the mother of invention'? Whoever it was, they were right." It was the first time Paul had smiled since he walked into the plant that morning. Denny began whistling the tune that had come back into his mind from earlier that morning, and he made his way to the back room to start the cook.

As Paul opened the door to the office and climbed up onto his stool, Meredith said, "Plato."

"What?" Paul asked abruptly, turning to her.

"Plato said, 'Necessity is the mother of invention,'" she answered as she completed the lobster order ticket in front of her.

"Oh, really?" Paul said, looking over at her.

Meredith, still working on the ticket, didn't skip a beat. "Yup," she replied matter-of-factly. Paul smiled. He was sure he could take that answer to the bank. He thought back to earlier that summer when he, Doug, Meredith, and Rosa were all working in the retail store on a busy Friday afternoon. A woman and her six-year-old daughter walked into the store to purchase some sushi-grade tuna for her dinner that evening. None of Flannery's crew had seen the pair before and assumed they were new to the area. The young blonde girl, dressed in a pretty yellow sundress, wrapped her hands around her bare arms in an attempt to keep warm in the refrigerated room. She tugged on her mother's white button-down shirt and complained loudly, "Mommy, it smells in here!"

The mother looked lovingly at her daughter and told her, "That's OK. You don't have to worry about working in a place like this. You're going to college."

Meredith ignored the woman and continued helping her customer select the best seafood for her party, but Doug couldn't contain himself. In the most polite, authoritative tone of voice he could muster, he said, "Actually, I have a bachelor of science degree in biology, and she"—he pointed to Meredith—"has a master's degree." Doug would have liked to have thrown the snooty woman and her rude daughter out of the store, telling her there'd be no fish for her today, but he knew that wouldn't have been appropriate. The woman never acknowledged his remarks, which infuriated him even more. She preferred her version of the story and failed to recognize the fact that the fish may have been better at Flannery's because Flannery's had a more educated staff handling it.

Paul was jolted out of his thoughts when the phone rang. "Oh no," he said under his breath, "Flannery. What am I going to tell him?" The phone rang a second time.

"You don't have to say anything now. Wait until the afternoon when we've done the inventory and you've got a total for the cook. The figures might not be as bad as you think," Meredith suggested.

Third ring. Paul knew Meredith was right, but he didn't want to obsess about it all day. Bad news was like a Band-Aid—best to just rip it off and get it over with.

Meredith picked up the phone. "Good morning, Flannery's," she said. Sure enough, it was Flannery at the other end of the line. But he wasn't interested in lobster inventories or even in how the gurry truck operation went on Sunday. She sensed a strangeness in his tone, like something was wrong.

"Hi, Meredith," Flannery said, "Is Paul there?"

"Sitting right beside me," Meredith answered and waited for Paul to pick up the phone.

"Hi Jack," Paul said, "Beautiful weekend. I heard Vinnie's first gurry truck transport was a huge success on Sunday."

"Was it? That's great," Flannery said, sounding preoccupied. It seemed as if he didn't care about the gurry truck, which was uncharacteristic of him. He changed the subject quickly. "Do you have any connections with dealers or boats that fish down south?"

"Do you mean in the Rhode Island and New York area?" Paul asked.

"No, farther south. I mean down in the Bermuda, Florida area?" Flannery answered.

"Maybe a few of our boats or dealers have connections down there. I know Bob Carson took his *Lizzy Jane* to Florida to fish for stone crabs. I'm not sure if he's on the east coast or over on the west coast, though. Why?" Paul didn't have a clue what Flannery was getting at.

"Could you try to get the word out that Wayne Conroy's boat is missing? We're trying to get as many eyes as possible on the sea where he disappeared, to look for any debris from his boat or maybe scope out any of the smaller islands in the area for castaways."

"Of course," Paul said, stunned. "How long's he been missing?"

"He was due back in Jupiter, Florida, on Saturday, but he never arrived. The family reported him missing today," Flannery said. "I was supposed to fly out tomorrow to offer an educational presentation about seafood for some of the staff at Wayne's Crab Royale restaurant. I would imagine they've pushed that off to a later date. We're all hoping that Wayne docked somewhere along the way when the weather got rough or ran aground on one of the islands in the area. So far, there's been no word, but no sign of wreckage either. No one's given up hope. We just need to find him."

"Why did Wayne's kids wait so long to report him missing if he was due in on Saturday?" Paul asked.

"They thought he might have found a quaint harbor to explore, which wasn't uncommon for him," Flannery explained. "It was when he didn't arrive home by Monday morning for work that they knew something was wrong. He loved his work and would never intentionally miss a day."

Flannery was noticeably distraught. Wayne Conroy had been the one to encourage him to start his own business and was one of his biggest moral and financial supporters. It was Wayne who helped him choose a name for his business. Flannery was thinking of a more romantic name having to do with the sea. But Wayne pointed out that Flannery had been in the seafood business for so long, his name would be a recognizable brand in the industry. "Jack, it would be a shame to give up that kind of branding," he told Flannery. Flannery's Fish House was born over a chowder bowl and a gin and tonic at Wayne's iconic restaurant in a restored train station in Pittsburgh.

Flannery told Paul everything he could about Wayne's disappearance, partly hoping that it might help with the search and partly because he was trying to come to grips with the knowledge that his good friend might have perished at sea. "He and a childhood friend from Michigan sailed out to the Bahamas ahead of their wives more than a week ago," Flannery began. "Their wives had stayed behind to celebrate his wife's birthday with their kids in Florida. The two flew out to meet up with their husbands in the Bahamas at the beginning of last week." Flannery paused to take a sip of water.

"It was supposed to be a quick getaway before the Michigan couple returned home. For years, Wayne would take his wife and kids on an annual vacation to the Bahamas, so they all were very familiar with the area and the trip. Thankfully, his kids stayed home this time. Wayne and his friend took the *Liberty* to the Bahamas— you know, the sailboat he talked about when he stopped by the Gloucester plant to pick up some lobster rolls?" Flannery asked, not sure if Paul would recall.

"I remember," Paul said, "Hard to believe it was less than two weeks ago."

"Right," Flannery continued, "Well, Wayne normally had a skipper on board for longer voyages, but for short trips like this one, he often sailed the *Liberty* himself. He knew there was a storm coming. He was in touch with people on the mainland. He had considered staying in the Bahamas until the storm passed but decided to come back anyway. It was his friend's birthday, and he didn't want him to miss his party back in Palm Beach on Saturday night. Seems crazy now, to take a chance with your life for a party, but I guess it's easy to Monday-morning quarterback. The party couldn't be rescheduled because Wayne's friend had to fly home Sunday to be ready for work this morning. Crazy the things you think are so important at the time. His friend never made it to work today anyway," Flannery surmised, knowing that he, himself, had been guilty of going above and beyond to meet his business's call of duty.

"But Wayne's been sailing all his life," Flannery continued. "This wasn't the first storm he'd sailed through, and I'm sure he didn't think it would be his last." Flannery paused, then added, "He may have been wrong about that. I hope not."

Flannery put the phone down on his desk for a moment, and Paul could hear him talking with someone who had stepped into his office. After a minute or so, Flannery picked the phone up again and began talking without skipping a beat. "Anyway, from what I've been told, Wayne's group left the Bahamas for home on Thursday, from a port called Berry's Island, which is about twenty miles from Nassau. As far as everyone knows, the trip was uneventful, and the weather had been calm and sunny for the first day and a half they'd been sailing. But during the early hours of the next day, the storm they'd been warned about blew up much stronger than expected. The National Weather Service clocked seventy-mile-an-hour winds, giving rise to thirty-foot seas. A forty-foot sailboat is no match for weather like that."

"Man, that's awful," said Paul sympathetically. "I feel bad for Wayne and his wife and friends being caught in all that. If he knew it was going to be that bad, I'm sure he never would have left port."

"I know he wouldn't have," Flannery affirmed. Then continued, "I was talking with a seafood dealer in the West Palm Beach area and he said that before the storm, the winds were coming from a southerly direction. But as soon as the storm hit, winds shifted to blowing out of the north, which made the storm much more treacherous for any vessel traveling through the Gulf Stream at the time." Flannery paused again to let Paul fully absorb the devastating meaning of this information.

"The family learned that the Palm Beach County 911 emergency center received a call at four twenty-five in the morning. But it was unclear who the call was from, with only a distinguishable crackle of static coming through. After trying to get a response from the caller, the operator finally gave up and disconnected the call. But another call came in about two minutes later with the same static on the other end. The operator stayed on the line, hoping to make out any words within the static. But it was futile and the line eventually went dead. This may have been Wayne desperately seeking rescue. There's a chance the Coast Guard might be able to trace the call to the bag phone he had on board, but there's been no word yet. That would tell them a lot," Flannery speculated.

"Like his last known location," Paul added.

"Exactly," Flannery agreed. "As soon as the family reported to the Coast Guard that the *Liberty* was missing, they began reaching out to marinas where the boat could have sought shelter. They touched base with the Bahamian search-and-rescue officials to let them know the sailboat hadn't made it home. The Coast Guard also issued a marine alert, trying to gather any information about the missing sailboat." Flannery took another sip of water before continuing.

"The Coast Guard was prepared to do an air-and-sea search but needed to narrow down the vicinity of where the *Liberty* was last seen. The area between Berry Island and Jupiter is vast, and the Gulf Stream moved directly through the route Wayne was taking home. If the two 911 calls were from the *Liberty*, it would have meant that he was almost home. It also would have meant that he might have found himself in the middle of the Gulf Stream at the height of the storm. With the Gulf Stream's strong northerly current meeting up with powerful opposing winds, you would expect waves to build to a fierce height—and quickly," Flannery informed Paul.

Paul actually knew quite a lot about the Gulf Stream because it was the topic of a history report he helped his daughter research not too long ago. The report was about Benjamin Franklin and how he was responsible for studying and naming the Gulf Stream. Although Ponce de León first discovered the Gulf Stream, Benjamin Franklin had taken a keen interest in it as a way to speed up shipping routes in his day. Franklin learned that the Gulf Stream originated at the Straits of Florida while flowing up to Cape Hatteras at great speeds. Although it continued beyond Cape Hatteras, the current wasn't as intense because the Gulf Stream widened as it left the coast and curved toward Western Europe.

The portion of the Gulf Stream from Florida to Cape Hatteras was notorious for being fast, deep, and narrow. Water temperatures in that area commonly read in the mid to high seventies and the current had been clocked at a rapid three miles per hour in the area Wayne was sailing. Franklin discovered that using the Gulf Stream currents could cut days, if not weeks, off passages to Europe compared with voyages that didn't normally take advantage of the Gulf Stream. Although a benefit in transporting people and merchandise by sea quickly, the Gulf Stream was also noted for containing strong winds. If a sailboat—or, more likely, a wreck of a sailboat—like the *Liberty* were to become caught in the Gulf Stream currents, the size of the search zone would increase tremendously, stretching far beyond the confines of the course Wayne was following from the Bahamas to Jupiter. Paul knew all this but thought it wise not to tell Flannery because it wasn't encouraging news. Besides, the chance that Flannery didn't already have this information was pretty slim.

"Wayne always believed that in order to succeed, you have to be willing to take risks," Flannery remembered, "and Wayne held to his belief when it came to sailboat racing and business strategies. But when he was taking passengers out on the *Liberty,* Wayne was levelheaded. He'd never take anyone out if he thought the trip would be risky. I know he had all the latest safety features installed. That included a homing device that was capable of being activated both manually as well as automatically if the *Liberty* were to find herself in trouble." Flannery paused again, as if something had just come to mind.

"Curiously," Flannery continued, "the homing device was never activated. That would have transmitted a signal via satellite to the Coast Guard. No one seems to have an explanation for why the *Liberty's* homing device didn't activate. Without it, the Coast Guard's looking for a needle in a haystack. But they're still planning to carry out a search. It doesn't hurt that one of the people on the missing sailboat is an internationally famous restauranteur. That's probably why officials have to at least attempt a search and rescue, even if they aren't convinced anything will come of it. The Coast Guard tried to tell Wayne's adult kids that when wind and sea currents happen in opposing directions, a forty-foot sailboat, even with the most experienced crew on board, would be no match for the ferocity of the forces of the storm. Of course, the Coast Guard didn't tell Wayne's kids that there was probably a good chance the masts could have been torn from the deck or even the hull of the boat, and the antennae were surely ripped off the sailboat with all that wind. With that kind of catastrophic damage, especially if the motor lost power, there would be no way to steady the *Liberty's* bow to head directly into an oncoming wave. In a matter of minutes, the boat would have capsized if a giant wall of wave rolled up onto the side of the boat."

Paul cringed at the thought of living through such an event and said, "You've just reminded me of why I never took up sailing. I've always liked my feet planted firmly on the ground."

"Funny you should say that. I can't tell you how many times Wayne asked my wife Elaine and I to take a trip on the *Liberty*," Flannery reminisced. "You know, I was always tempted, but my wife immediately put the kibosh on that. She hated sailing on cruise ships, and the thought of being on a relatively small sailboat in the middle of the ocean was something in which she had no interest. As soon as she lost sight of land, that would have been it. And luckily, she and I both knew it. Wayne would have been a gracious host and turned the boat around, but way down deep, he wouldn't have been happy about it."

"Elaine had good reason for not wanting to go sailing, though," Flannery continued. "Her grandmother was attempting to save Elaine's then-thirteen-year-old mother from drowning when she herself became entangled in some water-lily stems when the pond's sandy bottom gave way. Other swimmers rushed to free Elaine's grandmother's ankles from the snarl of vines beneath the water, but they were too late, and she perished. Thankfully, they were able to save Elaine's mother and bring her to shore. Later that day, her grandmother's body was recovered from the pond's bottom. But from that day on, Elaine's mother always feared the water and passed that fear on to her children. My wife never learned to swim. Couple that with the fact that every time she boards a boat of any size she suffers from severe motion sickness, and I knew there wasn't a chance in hell she'd be up for going anywhere on the *Liberty*." Flannery paused and then said, "Who knows, Elaine may have saved both our lives."

Denny walked into the office as Flannery was finishing up his call. He rested against the inside of the door, waiting for Paul to get off the phone. He thought Paul might be talking to Flannery about the extreme loss of lobsters that morning, and from the look on Paul's face, the news wasn't going over very well.

Flannery ended by saying, "Wayne's adult children are funding a search that's basically made up of private planes and helicopters. My heart goes out to Wayne's daughter. She told me she feels like her parents are still on vacation and will come walking through the door at any moment. There's a part of her still holding out hope that her mom and dad are safe but haven't been able to contact her yet. And who knows, that may be the case. We all hope it is. Fifty-five is too young to die. Wayne and his wife were in the prime of their lives. I know they had so much more they wanted to do. I guess we all need to face reality, but it doesn't hurt to cover all our bases. The storm didn't hit Florida until about four twenty on Saturday morning. If those two 911 calls were from Wayne, the *Liberty* couldn't have been far away. I thought if I could get some fishing boats out there looking too, we might just find something. It's very strange that nothing from the boat has washed ashore, especially if the *Liberty* broke up that close to Palm Beach County, which is what the Coast Guard believes. That's what's still giving everyone hope," Flannery concluded, his voice cracking as he tried to hold back tears. "I'd appreciate any help you can give the family with the boats you're in touch with."

"I'll definitely put the word out. I'm so sorry. He seemed like a real down-to-earth guy," Paul sympathized.

"He was the best friend you could ever have hoped for," Flannery said, then added, "but, hey, we aren't giving up the ghost just yet."

"I'll do my best to spread the word," Paul assured Flannery. With that, Flannery hung up.

"How'd he take the lobster catastrophe?" Denny asked.

"I didn't get to tell him about it," Paul replied. Then he added, "Besides, the timing would have been awful."

"Why?" Denny asked.

"Remember that friend of Flannery's who came by a couple of weeks ago? You know, the one who told the story about how he rescued his son who had fallen off his sailboat and into the water?"

Paul asked Denny.

"Yeah," Denny said, "seemed like a good guy."

"Well he's missing at sea," Paul continued. "He got caught in a storm passing through the Gulf Stream. They haven't heard from him, and nothing from his boat has been recovered."

"That's awful," Denny uttered, and he meant it. He had taken a real liking to Wayne, as had everyone the day he visited.

"Well, at least he died doing something he loved," added Paul.

"You know, you hear people say that," Meredith piped up, "but I don't think it's ever given anyone any comfort when the chips are down, and they realize there's no way out, that they were doing something they loved. As a matter of fact, I bet the last thought they had was, 'This sucks! Why did I ever think this was something I wanted to do?' Don't you think?"

"Ha!" Denny exclaimed. "I think you're right there."

Then there was silence. Denny didn't know if anyone else was thinking it, but he just couldn't help himself. "Guess he should have bought lobster rolls up in Maine instead of making a special stop to get them here."

"What difference would that have made?" Meredith asked with a puzzled expression on her face. Denny had forgotten she wasn't in on the theory.

Paul spoke up. "Denny thinks anyone who's come in contact with the *Bay State Skye* or its catch is destined to experience a solid bout of bad luck."

"You've got to admit it's holding true," Denny claimed.

"Yes, I do. But I'd like to think it's just one big coincidence," Paul said, trying to keep things in perspective.

"But wait a minute," Meredith said, after some thought. "The lobster meat that Rosa and I made those subs out of was from Jimmy and Murph's catch. The *Bay State Skye* wasn't involved, except that they discovered the boat the same day the lobsters were caught."

"Oh, but it was involved," Denny pointed out with a gleeful look in his eyes. Then he turned to Paul to ask, "We can trust Meredith, right?"

"I'm sure we can," Paul said.

"Of course you can," Meredith insisted.

"Well," Denny said, "Jimmy and Murph were already coming home with a full catch that day. But when they boarded the Golinis' boat, they found about five hundred extra pounds of lobster the Golini brothers had dragged up."

"Well," Meredith interjected, "I knew the Golinis were dragging illegally through lobster trawl lines, so that's not surprising."

"Yeah, but wait," Denny said impatiently. "So, they decided to help the Golinis out by taking most of the lobsters and putting them in their own totes. That way, the family wouldn't get fined for being over the legal limit for draggers."

"So to make a long story short . . ." Paul said, nudging Denny along.

"OK," Denny said, "long story short, Wayne's lobster rolls more than likely had some of the *Bay State Skye's* lobster meat in them."

"And that caused him to sail into a storm and become lost at sea? You don't really believe that, do you?" Meredith knew fishermen were often superstitious by nature, but she didn't peg Denny for buying into all that.

"You sound skeptical," Paul kidded, teasing Meredith by pointing out the obvious.

"I know it's farfetched, but you never know. There've been a lot of . . . coincidences"—Denny used air quotes as he said the word—"of bad things happening to people who've come in contact with the *Bay State Skye's* catch. That's all. It's beginning to get hard to ignore."

"I'll keep on the lookout for any more incidents," Meredith said, kidding Denny.

"You do that," Denny said, shaking his index finger, "'cause more are on their way."

Meredith smiled. Paul laughed. Denny left the office, headed back to the lobster room, but stopped to tell Murph and Jimmy about Wayne as they came through the loading-dock strips. When he was satisfied he'd told them everything he knew, Denny returned to the lobster room, and Jimmy and Murph came into the office.

"We just heard about Wayne," Jimmy said.

"Good news travels fast," Paul said, shaking his head.

"That's unsettling—we just met the man a couple of weeks ago. Remember when Wayne was talking about how lucky he was to be able to reach into the water and have his son's arm right there to grab when the rogue wave hit his boat?" Murph asked.

"Yes," Paul answered.

"Well, maybe it wasn't luck at all. Maybe it was a warning that Wayne didn't heed," Murph said.

"That's creepy," Paul said, trying to resist taking in the full impact of what Murph said. Paul knew Wayne better than anyone in the room, and the thought of his loss was weighing heavily on him.

"The whole thing is creepy," added Meredith. "I can't shake the feeling that he was just here."

"Have they found anything from the boat?" Jimmy asked.

"Nothing," Paul answered.

"That's strange," Jimmy remarked.

"Isn't that area part of the Bermuda Triangle?" Murph asked.

"I bet you're not the first person to think of that," Meredith replied. "After all, the Bermuda Triangle stretches from Puerto Rico to Bermuda to Miami, so a good part of the *Liberty's* trip would have been in that area. But Jupiter, Florida, isn't part of the Bermuda Triangle. If the 911 calls were from the *Liberty*, then Wayne had made it safely out of the triangle before he got into trouble. He needed to be within the range of the Palm Beach County 911 emergency center to connect with them. But if those calls were from some other source, and Wayne had run into trouble before he got closer to the Florida coast, most of Wayne's trip was in the triangle."

"When I was a kid, I was infatuated with the Bermuda Triangle. You don't hear much about it anymore," Murph said.

"Yes, I was, too," Meredith concurred. "You probably don't hear about it much because they've debunked most of the theories at this point. I read a book a few years ago that was written in the midseventies that claimed to solve the mysteries of the Bermuda Triangle. It maintained that disappearances in the Bermuda Triangle weren't any more numerous than in any other area of the sea that was frequently traveled. It also alleged that unreported, severe storms were often in the area at the time when a lot of the famous shipwrecks and vanishing vessels happened."

"Then I guess the reports of alien abductions, compasses going haywire, and strange magnetic fields were all fictitious?" Murph asked.

"It looks that way, except officials do agree that in the Bermuda Triangle, magnetic compasses will point to true north instead of magnetic north," Meredith said. "If a navigator doesn't adjust for this rarity, it can throw his or her navigation off as much as twenty degrees."

"Well, that's something," Murph argued.

"It would be, except any navigator worth his salt knows about this phenomenon and adjusts for it. It's been a well-known fact since compasses were invented, at least according to what I've read," Meredith said. Then she added, "But I'm no expert on the subject, and I must admit, I loved the old stories from the Bermuda Triangle."

"So did I," Murph agreed. Then he asked, somewhat disappointed, "So there's nothing about the Bermuda Triangle that sets it apart from other areas of the ocean?"

"I wouldn't say that," Meredith answered. "Nowadays the cause of tragedies in the Bermuda Triangle area has been attributed to exactly what Flannery was talking about earlier. Swift, warm, northerly currents in the Gulf Stream often lead to strong winds and turbulent weather. Evidence of a wreck could be swept away or turned under so quickly in those currents, it could seem that they just disappeared."

"Not to mention the water spouts and the fact that hurricane alley is in that area," Paul added.

"And there are shoals and deep trenches that are constantly changing, too," Jimmy remarked.

"If one thing doesn't get you, another will," Paul concluded.

"That's why I'm a land lover. If I'm in a hurricane or a tornado, I want to be sheltered in a well-built house with a cellar. You won't catch me in a flimsy, tippy boat. Catch one wave wrong in a storm and it's all over."

"I'm with you," Meredith agreed.

"Well, I guess we should grab our bait and head out on our flimsy, tippy boat to catch some lobsters," Jimmy joked. "Those lobsters aren't going to jump into the boat by themselves."

With that, Murph and Jimmy left the office and met up with Denny to get their reserved bait, then headed out the same way they came in. Once the live lobster shipments were packed and trucked to Logan, the entire lobster-room crew got to work picking meat from the massive cook. Meredith worked with Denny to help record the figures from the day. When all was said and done, Denny's quick thinking to immediately cook the weak lobsters helped to compensate for the loss of live lobsters. Paul decided not to call Flannery. The loss wasn't going to be as profound as they first thought, and a notation at the bottom of the inventory would probably do the job. Paul called the head of the sales department in Boston to let him know their sales force should think about having a lobster-meat special that week. It had been a long day, and the lobster-room blunder had been all but forgotten in light of the *Liberty* misfortune. Paul and Meredith left Flannery's with the memory of Wayne weighing heavily on each of them.

*   *   *   *   *

Wednesday morning was upon Vinnie before he knew it, and he was anxious to get the second load of old gurry up to New York. Practice made perfect, and Vinnie hit the road before the sun rose, in an effort to avoid rush-hour traffic. It was no time before Vinnie was driving over the town limits of the sleepy little village of Kinderhook and onto Marge's farm. Marge was as happy to see Vinnie as ever. He dumped his load in the usual manner, which Marge mentioned was very kind of him. The extra effort he put into spreading the gurry thinly made the job a lot easier for her farmhands, and they appreciated it. All went well, and Vinnie was on the road back to Gloucester by eleven in the morning.

"Two truckloads gone," Vinnie proudly reported to Flannery after arriving back in Gloucester and cleaning his truck. "Only one more left. We're in the final stretch." Vinnie was delighted to have this task almost behind him, and even more ecstatic to have the gurry plant's yard clear in time for the rented barge to come into play.

"That's great, Vinnie," Flannery began. "Marge told me what a terrific job you've been doing spreading out the gurry for her. She said she'd love to have you as an employee if you ever get sick of the fish business."

"Ha!" Vinnie replied, "I don't see myself ever becoming a farmer, but I appreciate her confidence in me. I've been doing my best to try to please her. After all, she's been doing us a huge favor taking this crap."

"She sure has. She's been a godsend," Flannery commented. Then he added, "But unfortunately, all good things have to come to an end."

"What? No!" Vinnie exclaimed. "I'm all set to take the third truckload up on Friday. We're almost there, Jack. We can't stop now!"

"Oh, if it were up to Marge, she'd have taken the third truckload, no problem," Flannery piped up. "But unfortunately, she's run into a snag."

"She's run into a snag? What kind of snag?" Vinnie asked, repeating Flannery's words.

"Marge was visited by the sheriff today," Flannery began.

"What did he want?" Vinnie asked defensively.

"Oh, relax, Vinnie, it had nothing to do with you," Flannery said. "Well, not directly anyway. He told Marge she could dump all the manure she wanted onto her fields, but there was a law against dumping dead cows on your land in Kinderhook, and he couldn't ignore it if that line had been crossed."

"That's really messed up," Vinnie said. "I didn't see any dead cows lying around. That sheriff must have been mistaken."

"Well, the funny thing is that after you dumped the first load, I asked Marge if she was having any problem with odor from the fish. And she said, 'Well, now and then if the wind was blowing just right and I was walking by the kitchen window, I'd get a little waft of odor from the fields,'" Flannery continued. "But now I guess the odor is permeating the area, and people are accusing her of taking dead cows and dumping them on her land. Evidently, the fish mixed with the manure was starting to smell like dead cows. So, Marge said, 'Mr. Flannery, I was glad to help you out and take the truckloads for you, but I'm afraid I'm going to have to stop.' What could I say? I thanked Marge for taking what she had so far, and unfortunately, we didn't get the last truckload up to her in time. But that's OK. Now that I've gotten some money from the governor, I've hired a barge to come up from Boston tomorrow. We'll load it up with the last truckload and anything else that's accumulated more recently up there. I'll give you the coordinates the Environmental Protection Agency gave me, and we'll be in phase two."

"Then the barge is arriving tomorrow?" Vinnie asked. "That's great news. Loading a barge and taking it out to sea will be way more convenient than driving truckloads of gurry to New York. The last truckload, combined with what we've collected since the New England Fish Processors' Association was formed, should make a full barge. It'll be good to get rid of the rest of the old gurry," Vinnie said.

"The air will be a lot sweeter, I'm sure," said Flannery. "So that's the plan."

"I'll start loading the barge as soon as it arrives," Vinnie said. "By the way, have you gotten any word about the *Liberty*? Paul asked me if I knew anyone fishing around the Jupiter area, but unfortunately all my contacts are up here in New England."

"There's been no word, and nothing's been located from the sailboat," Flannery said. "It's costing Wayne's kids just about a million dollars to hire the search-and-rescue teams, and they aren't going to see a dime of their inheritance if nothing turns up."

"How are they paying for it?" Vinnie asked.

"They're borrowing against the restaurants and taking donations from anyone they can. I sent them a hundred thousand dollars myself. I'm sure Wayne would have done the same if the situation was reversed. If nothing turns up, it could be years before the courts will officially declare Wayne and his wife deceased. That's an extra burden the kids shouldn't have to shoulder," Flannery said. It appeared that Flannery had come to terms with the reality that his longtime friend was gone, and now he had switched to trying to help Wayne's family. "At least officials have projected the area where they think the *Liberty* went down," Flannery added.

"How'd they do that?" Vinnie asked. Vinnie hadn't heard about the 911 calls.

"They were able to trace two 911 calls that came into Palm Beach County's emergency center the morning of the storm. Officials are one hundred percent positive now that the calls came from a bag phone Wayne always took onboard with him. That means he was more than likely in the Gulf Stream by the Jupiter coastline at the height of the storm. It's all but certain that everyone aboard the *Liberty* has perished, but with no body or wreckage, there's no proof the sailboat sank."

"That's one of the worst ways to go," Vinnie said. "My heart goes out to Wayne and his family. You never think it's going to be you, but you just never know, do you?"

"Well, you'd lessen your chances if you stayed off the water, I suppose. But as my wife's father always said, 'You can drown in a teacup if you put your nose in and breathe.'" Flannery always tried to end his conversations with a little levity.

"You've got to love those Down East sayings," Vinnie laughed.

"That you do," Flannery said, "Enjoy the rest of your evening, Vinnie old boy."

"You, too," replied Vinnie, hanging up the phone.

Vinnie walked outside and surveyed the grounds around the

dock. He wanted to be sure he had everything in position and was ready to get to work immediately when the barge arrived the next day. The first thing he did was to back the third tractor-trailer truck in as close as he could to the cement Jersey barriers that lined the dock. The Jersey barriers were essential for keeping trucks from misjudging the distance of their rear wheels to the edge of the dock and rolling into the harbor. This final truckload of gurry would be the first load to christen the newly rented barge. Vinnie couldn't wait. As he jumped into the cab of his truck with newfound energy, Vinnie drove home with a huge grin on his face. A few drinks with the boys and he'd hit the sack early. He had a big day ahead of him tomorrow.

CHAPTER 11

Vinnie drove by Flannery's so early the next day, he caught Doug getting into his truck to head down to the Gloucester auction. Vinnie couldn't resist giving him a playful toot of his horn as he drove by. Doug turned to give Vinnie a tip of his baseball cap and an awkward salute as they both imagined nearby residents cursing the truck that woke them up at five thirty that morning. But Vinnie might as well have stayed in bed for a while longer because the barge didn't arrive until almost nine o'clock. When the barge finally pulled up to the gurry plant at the State Fish Pier, Vinnie was anxious to board her and familiarize himself with her operation.

Even before he set one foot on the barge, however, Vinnie noticed a problem he hadn't anticipated. There was a large space between the barge and the dock that would allow gurry to fall into the harbor when it was dumped from a truck above. The space was caused by a wooden mule, or log, that was chained to the dock pylons. The mule was added to protect the dock from being damaged by the barge constantly hitting each time a strong wave pushed against it sideways. Eliminating the mule wasn't an option because without it, the dock would become damaged and deteriorate. Docks were expensive to repair, and this was an avoidable expense.

Vinnie needed to find a solution to fill this gap—and quickly. The last thing he wanted to do was dump half his truckload of old gurry into the harbor. Not only could it create a dead ocean by the pier, but any businesses drawing in harbor water to support live inventory like lobsters would also suffer a devastating loss if the water was tainted. Flannery's Fish House was one of those businesses. Vinnie knew he had to be careful.

Vinnie boarded the flat-bottomed barge with its riveted metal sides and was immediately drawn to the massive hole in its center. Looking into its depths, Vinnie could see the gigantic doors closed at the bottom of the chamber. Huge hinges and actuators were attached to the doors, allowing them to open and release the barge's load once it had reached its destination.

Vinnie walked to the bow of the barge, where he found large deck plates that covered thirty-foot-wide tanks. These tanks, which were crucial in helping to balance the barge, were in the stern as well. If the load in the center hole was heavier in the aft than the bow, the operator would fill the tanks in the front until the barge evened out, or if the load had shifted closer to the front of the barge, the rear tanks would be filled to create an equilibrium. It was far easier for a tugboat to push a level barge than one that was uneven. Trying to even out the weight of the cargo in the hole would have been extremely difficult, which is why this tank system to create the equivalent of an even load was developed.

Flannery had hired a tugboat/barge combination out of Boston that charged a $10,000 fee every time it made the trip out to the EPA's coordinates. This was a good reason to have the barge's hole filled to the brim before they took the trip out to open ocean. For the most part, the plan was for the tugboat to push the barge, primarily for safety reasons. If the tugboat were to pull the barge, the bobbing up and down of the tugboat and barge in rough seas would create a slackening and then tightening in their tow lines as they dipped in and out of the ocean waters. Towlines were notorious for breaking, which the tugboat captain wanted to avoid at all costs. Pushing a boat was easier and more efficient, and gave the tugboat more control over the direction the barge was headed. But once Vinnie and the tugboat captain had assessed the inner harbor and its calm, sheltered waters—which were crowded with expensive boats—they determined that on the outset, they would tow the barge to keep it from colliding with another vessel.

With the logistics of the trip decided, Vinnie went to work filling the gap between the barge and the dock. He found several two-by-eight boards and placed them side by side, stretching from the dock to the giant hole in the barge. Then he covered the boards with plywood to create a makeshift slide to the barge's hole.

Just as Vinnie was finishing up, Doug drove in with a truck filled to the brim with gurry from Flannery's Boston and Gloucester plants. Flannery's crew had been filling gurry barrels and storing them in their cooler for about two weeks, as were a lot of local fish processors, and they were anxious to free up some space. Doug would have arrived earlier, but he was waiting for a few pounds of haddock that was frozen from the *Bay State Skye's* catch to be let up and skinned so that he could add the skin to his load. It was perfect timing because Vinnie wanted to try out his new system with gurry that wasn't as aged as the gurry in the truck he'd originally planned to dump first. Vinnie quickly moved the third tractor-trailer truck from its first-place position and moved Doug's truck to replace it. He carefully backed to the edge of the dock until the rear tires gently nudged the Jersey barriers.

"Can't get any closer than that," Doug called to Vinnie.

"I sure hope this works," Vinnie replied. Then he added, "I don't want to spend half my day picking gurry out of the harbor."

"At least it's fresh, chilled gurry," Doug called back, "instead of gurry that's already rotten from sitting in the sun for about a decade."

Vinnie gave Doug a thumbs-up as he released the lock on his dump truck and got ready to raise his bed. Then he called out to Doug, "Let me know if it's not going in the hole before I've dumped too much, OK?" Doug held his thumb up in the air so that Vinnie could see it. Both men were excited to be on the ground floor of the new operation.

Vinnie raised the bed higher and higher until it had risen as far as it could go. The load rolled out of the bed, down the plywood slide, and into the hole, just as intended. Vinnie couldn't have asked for a better test run. Doug grabbed a fish fork to pick up a few stray pieces, but all in all, it worked like a charm. Now that the system was proven to be viable, it was time to put it to the ultimate test. Vinnie drove the third tractor-trailer truck back into position, being careful to gently tap the Jersey barriers with his rear wheels. He needed everything to line up perfectly with this load. There was no room for error. He slowly raised the dump bed and the entire load slithered into the hole. Nothing much fell into the harbor except for a small amount of liquid goo that oozed over either side of the ramp. Doug was prepared to help move the load into the hole with a fish fork, but he couldn't stomach the odor that advanced toward him. The stink seemed to move through the air like a dark wave, just as smells were depicted in cartoons when he was a kid. Doug bolted into the gurry plant, upwind from the barge. Vinnie was pretty pleased with the result of his makeshift ramp and grabbed a hose to rinse it before there was no getting the smell out.

Both loads had now been dumped, and Vinnie was amazed at how much room there was left in the barge's hole. Even with the gurry that had arrived in the last few days, Vinnie didn't think he had enough to justify taking the barge out to dump, not at $10,000 a whack—that was for sure. But Vinnie didn't have to wait long for the phone to begin ringing off the hook with seafood companies anxious to get rid of their stored-up gurry. Vinnie couldn't accommodate everyone immediately because he didn't want to run out of room in the barge and end up having to send trucks away after they'd made the trip to Gloucester. Nor did he want to allow them to dump the gurry in a location at the plant; then he'd have to move it with a backhoe. He had just lived through that crap storm and had no desire to revisit it. Because the gurry plant wasn't owned by the New

England Fish Processors' Association, there had been no installation of chillers or coolers, and the fish by-products would be destined to decompose in the sun as had happened with the previous loads from a month ago. Thus, Vinnie agreed to let a truck or two come at a time, and he had a waiting list for the rest. Vinnie worked over the weekend to make sure he had a full barge by Monday morning. This wouldn't be a recurring problem though, because after Vinnie had filled the barge once, he'd be able to estimate better how much gurry would fill the cargo hold in the future. By Monday morning, Vinnie and the tugboat crew were ready for what Flannery called the "shakedown cruise."

*   *   *   *   *

Vinnie was the first to arrive at the barge at the break of dawn Monday morning. Because he was early, he took a quick walk over to Flannery's to catch up with Paul and ask him if he'd like to experience the barge's maiden voyage.

"Are you kidding?" Paul questioned. Then he added, "As much as I'd love to, I'd be barfing all the way out and all the way in again. I love the ocean, but I get violently ill the minute I step onto a boat. And it doesn't matter if it's a rowboat or an ocean liner. That's why I choose jobs around the ocean but not on the ocean. It's worked for me so far, and I'm sticking to it!"

Vinnie understood. He knew that was the scenario for a lot of people who worked in the business but didn't work on a boat. Vinnie tipped his hat and wished Paul good luck at the auction. Paul had been taking Vinnie's place buying fish for Flannery's at the display auction most mornings, and Doug was swinging by to pick the fish up once it was ready for loading on the auction-house dock. Vinnie enjoyed a break from the normal routine and happily walked back to the State Fish Pier.

When the tugboat captain arrived with his six-man crew, he took a walk around the barge to be sure it was properly prepared for the trip to the open ocean. The captain, who appeared to be in his late forties, looked exactly as Vinnie would have expected. His hair was graying, and his well-trimmed beard was snow white. He was a highly skilled man, with years of experience as a deckhand, pilot, and first mate before ever having the opportunity to take the test for his master's license, and the captain had the demeanor of someone who was used to commanding respect. The captain's button-down white shirt was in sharp contrast to Vinnie's Red Sox tee, with the occasional hole that only proved how much he loved his team. Even the captain's crew was a no-nonsense group of men who knew their job and were ready to leap into action at any moment. The hygiene of the captain, as well as the crew, was impeccable and Vinnie felt a little out of his element in what he nonetheless considered to be exactly his element. If anyone had thought the life of a tugboat crew mirrored the occupation of a crew of a fishing vessel, they would have been gravely mistaken. A tugboat crew's job was, for the most part, a clean job, and the fishermen's work was the polar opposite. Looking at the cargo hold that Vinnie had topped off to the brim, the tugboat captain said, "What, you couldn't get any more in?"

Vinnie smiled. "Just trying to get Flannery's money's worth. There's several hundred tons of gurry in there, from what I've calculated. I've kept track so I know what I can take on the next trip."

"Smart man," the tugboat captain conceded. "OK, let's get this show on the road."

"Sounds good," said Vinnie. "What do you need me to do?"

"You can operate the barge doors when we get there," the captain told Vinnie. "Until then, just sit back and relax. We've got it from here."

"Easiest day I've spent at work in years," Vinnie said with a grin. "Like going on my own personal cruise!"

The captain stopped and slowly turned to face Vinnie. "I want to make one thing clear, though," he began. "We're all here to do a job. With any luck this job will go smoothly, but if the need arises, I expect one hundred and ten percent from my crew. If you're on my rig, you're part of my crew. Do we understand each other?"

"Yes sir, we do," Vinnie answered. He suddenly wished he was working his regular job. He didn't have a boss breathing down his neck there, watching his every move. Vinnie felt a little like he'd been drafted into the service, something that he would never voluntarily do. But the truth was that Vinnie preferred a no-nonsense captain to an "anything goes" kind of guy. Although Vinnie felt at home at sea, he had to admit it was outside his comfort zone to be heading to a site the EPA deemed far enough away from civilization to do a gurry dump. But Flannery trusted Vinnie to do a good job and the pay was worth his trouble, so Vinnie settled in on the tugboat and kept his mouth shut.

It was fairly smooth sailing out to the EPA dumpsite coordinates. Once the tugboat had towed the barge past the inner harbor and out into open ocean, it released the towlines. Then the tugboat turned the barge, moving it into a position to make it easy to push. Vinnie had given the tugboat captain a paper with the longitudinal and latitudinal coordination points that Flannery had given to him, to be sure they dumped the gurry in the correct location. Vinnie had no other responsibilities other than to open the barge hull doors and release the gurry into the sea. Easy-peasy. Vinnie felt the sun warming his body, with an occasional salty mist spritzing his skin to keep him from getting too hot. This was turning out to be one of the most perfect days at work he'd ever had. *And imagine*, he thought, *I'm getting paid for this.*

Once the tugboat reached its destination, Vinnie sprang into action, trying to let the tugboat captain know that he was as competent as any other member of the crew on board. With an authoritative stride, Vinnie walked over to the hydraulic controls on the barge, which were located on a console near the electric generator that ran the hydraulic pumps. Vinnie pushed the lever to open the cargo doors below. The whirring sound of the hydraulics could be heard as the immense doors in the barge's hull opened. Content that all was going as planned, Vinnie stood back, away from the giant hole, waiting for the whooshing sound of gurry dropping into the sea. But there was no whooshing sound. The only noise Vinnie heard was the sound of waves slapping against the sides of the barge. The heaping mound of gurry was still peeking out of the barge cargo hold. There was nothing holding the gurry in at this point, yet it hadn't budged an inch. The tugboat captain directed his crew to grab some fish forks and start picking away at the gurry stuck to the sides of the cargo hold. When that didn't work, the tugboat captain directed Vinnie to walk out to the middle and see if he could loosen some of the dried fish there.

Visions of Billy Golini and himself being flushed down the gurry hopper and into his truck bed raced through Vinnie's mind. His compliance with the tugboat captain's demands, absolutely against his nature to begin with, had ended with this order. He suddenly felt lucky to have had that experience with Billy years ago because he knew what the possible outcome of following the tugboat captain's demands could bring. Only this time, he would undoubtedly die. He would go out with the gurry, falling deep into the ocean, and never be heard from again. No way. That wasn't going to happen.

"I've had some experience in situations like these," Vinnie told the captain, then added in an indignant tone of voice, "and I have no intentions of going out with that gurry and becoming fish food. If you want to crawl out on that gurry and poke it with a fork, be my guest. But I'm not doing it."

The tugboat captain was stunned at Vinnie's demeanor. Vinnie had seemed like an independent guy but fairly agreeable just the same. The captain was wise enough to recognize when he'd struck a nerve and took Vinnie's advice.

"Did this happen to you before?" the captain asked.

"It did," Vinnie replied, hearing a softening in the captain's voice. "Not on such a large scale, but the ending was downright terrifying."

"What would you suggest we do to loosen the load?" the captain asked.

"We added water to the sides the last time. It did the trick, but it took forever. And this is at least a hundred times more gurry," Vinnie said.

"Well, we're already out here; let's give it a try," suggested the captain.

The crew immediately attached the hoses to the pumps and began drawing water from the sea into the cargo hold. They spent several hours attempting to rehydrate the gurry with seawater, but their attempts were futile. It was as though someone had poured cement into the cargo hold and allowed it to dry. If Vinnie noticed any man stepping out onto the gurry to reach the center to wet it down, he would call out, "Hey! Trust me, you don't want to go there!"

The man would reluctantly step back onto the solid barge deck, not entirely comprehending the true nature of the danger in which he was putting himself. It wouldn't be long before another man would absentmindedly venture forth on the solid gurry to momentarily reach a spot he couldn't access from the deck. Vinnie spent more of his day warning crewmen to stay on the deck than he did hosing down the gurry. He knew the crewmen would surely perish if the gurry were to suddenly give way out in open ocean. He felt it his duty to supervise the crew, even if it stepped on the captain's toes.

When it became evident the gurry wasn't budging, the captain suggested they head in. They would have to solve this problem at port and then take the barge out again. Vinnie hated to return to the State Fish Pier with the cursed gurry, but he knew he had no choice. That was $10,000 down the damned proverbial toilet. He would have preferred it to be the gurry.

Vinnie closed the hull doors, allowing the tugboat to carefully push the barge back to dock in Gloucester. By the time they disembarked at the State Fish Pier, the captain and Vinnie had gained a working respect for each other. Both men understood that each one held varied experiences that would be invaluable in going forward with this gurry operation. The two men shook hands, and Vinnie headed into his makeshift office at the gurry plant to call Flannery.

Flannery answered the phone on the first ring. "How'd the

shakedown cruise go, Vinnie?" He was way too chipper for the news he was about to receive.

"We didn't have any trouble negotiating the harbor with all those pricey boats to hit, which was a big plus, and we found the dumping ground fairly easily," Vinnie added.

"Great! When will you be able to get another load out?" Flannery asked.

"Well, we ran into a little snag," Vinnie said, waiting to hear a reaction.

"What kind of snag?" Flannery asked, his mood suddenly doing a one-eighty. Vinnie explained what had happened. There was silence from Flannery for a moment.

"Couldn't we treat it like a toilet?" he finally proposed, in a voice that was a little more upbeat. "You know, pump in water around the sides to help flush the gurry out?"

"We tried that for a few hours, but the load didn't budge. The tugboat wound up pushing the full barge back to Gloucester. It was going to get dark soon, and the captain didn't think it was safe to continue," Vinnie said.

"Then it never got dumped? Not only are we blowing our brains out with the cost of this operation, but we still haven't gotten rid of that month-old gurry," Flannery summed up, sighing. "You know, when that barge pulled into the harbor for the first time, I heard that people in all the breakfast joints around Gloucester were saying, 'Have you smelled that barge that's coming in to dock? Doesn't it smell terrible?' I had to laugh because there hadn't been a drop of gurry in that barge yet. It was empty and hadn't been used to transport gurry before. I can only imagine what they'll be saying tomorrow around town when there's really something to complain about."

"It was pretty full over the weekend, so they're probably used to the smell by now," Vinnie replied. "I'm not going to leave the area until I have water around all sides. Hopefully in a day or two, the gurry will have loosened enough to fall out of the cargo hold."

Vinnie knew from past experience that eventually, the barge would empty, just as the small gurry hopper at the Boston Fish Pier did so many years before.

"Vinnie, whatever you do, make sure she's going to dump before you go out again," Flannery warned.

"Understood," Vinnie answered. "I was pretty horrified when it didn't dump this time. And believe me, we all tried hard to get the load out of the barge. It wasn't for lack of effort."

"I'm sure," Flannery said, then hung up. Vinnie knew Flannery was disappointed, and he had a right to be. But not any more so than the entire crew, tugboat captain, and Vinnie himself, who had all spent most of the afternoon struggling to release the cargo from the hold. Flannery had the easy part, Vinnie thought. But Vinnie didn't know that Flannery was struggling with a challenge of his own. Many members of the New England Fish Processors' Association were being slow with their payments, and Flannery hoped and prayed the payments from the governor's office would keep coming in as scheduled.

Vinnie grabbed the saltwater dock hose and added as much water as he could to every side of the cargo hold, until darkness moved in and he couldn't make out the sides of the barge anymore. The full moon was helping for a while, but eventually, clouds overtook the moon, extinguishing its light. It was just as well. Vinnie was exhausted. Slipping into the cargo hold in the dark with no one around to save him would be as close to hell on earth as he could imagine. He decided to call it a night.

* * * * *

Vinnie diligently returned early to continue what he'd started the evening before. He was surprised to feel an aching in his arms and legs as he dragged the dock hose out to the barge hole and turned it on full blast. He realized this was different work than driving a truck or buying fish, but he still thought he was in better shape than he apparently was. The salt water sprayed with the intensity of a fire hose, and Vinnie noticed a softening of the gurry, especially at the sides of the hole. There were even areas where standing water was visible along some of the edges as he continued walking around the circumference of the barge. Vinnie grabbed a six-foot pole and plunged it into the gurry along the side of the hole, almost losing it. He continued testing the edges. With each jab, Vinnie was feeling more and more confident the gurry might slide out of the hole.

Vinnie was concentrating so heavily on the job at hand that he was startled when the phone began ringing over the gurry plant's outside speaker. He was surprised to hear the tugboat captain's voice on the other end of the line.

"You must be telepathic," Vinnie remarked with a broad smile, having just thought of calling the captain to tell him he was ready to try again.

"I was checking in to see if you had any idea when you'd be ready to go out again," the captain said, ignoring Vinnie's opening remark. "I've got another job scheduled, and if you're not needing my services for a few days, I'd like to drop by and take my boat. I'll be back by the end of the week, and we can make another run at it."

"I think we're ready now," Vinnie said, exuding confidence.

"Are you sure?" the captain asked skeptically. "These trips out to the EPA's coordinates don't come cheap."

"You're telling me," Vinnie replied. "But I see a lot of softening in the sides of the load, and in some spots the gurry's actually floating."

"Really? That's hard to believe," the tugboat captain replied.

"I've been working on it since you left yesterday. I believe she's ready to go," Vinnie insisted.

"Well," the captain said hesitating, "if you're sure, I guess we can take another trip today. But you need to be certain. I don't want to have to explain to Flannery why we took two useless trips out. One was bad enough."

"I can relate," Vinnie agreed.

"OK," the captain conceded, "I guess I have to trust you. Clearly you know more about this than I do."

"So you'll be up this morning?" Vinnie asked.

"Give me an hour and a half to round up my crew and get back up there," the captain replied.

"Good enough," Vinnie said. "I'll be ready for you."

The tugboat's crew was already on standby, waiting to hear where they needed to meet up with the tugboat. No one was eager to return to the gurry barge for another run at a sea dump that day, but they made their way back to Gloucester nonetheless. The captain assured his crew that Vinnie was confident there would be no repeat of yesterday.

In contrast, Vinnie felt a twinge of anxiety as he hung up the phone. He hoped he hadn't jumped the gun. Maybe he should have given it a day, just in case. He knew in his gut the load could appear soft enough to dump, but when the moment arrived and the cargo doors opened, something could still be holding the load in place that couldn't have been seen from up above. Vinnie paused for a moment, wondering if he should call the tugboat captain back before he left, but he quickly returned to his senses.

"Of course it's going to dump," Vinnie mumbled to himself and headed out to douse the gurry with one more saltwater hosing, just to hedge his bets.

The captain and crew arrived at the State Fish Pier two hours later, impressed that Vinnie had everything prepared to head out immediately. They boarded the tugboat, checked the towlines, and headed out exactly as they had the day before. The trip was quicker this time because the guesswork had already been taken care of yesterday. Vinnie and the crew knew what to expect and were in position the moment they were needed.

As the tugboat moved into the EPA's approved dumping coordinates, Vinnie made his way to the hydraulic controls, readying himself to open the hull doors. He waited calmly for the captain's signal. It seemed to take forever. Vinnie wasn't a churchgoing man, but remembering his Catholic upbringing, he quickly crossed himself figuring it couldn't hurt.

Finally, the captain raised his arm in the air and gave a thumbs-up to Vinnie. Vinnie could feel the weight of every crewman's stare as he operated the hydraulics. The hull doors creaked open completely, and the load remained in its usual position. He heard a collective sigh from all the crew and avoided looking up to meet the captain's "I told you so" glare. Instead, Vinnie's eyes were fixated on the gurry load. It had to move. The load looked exactly as it did just before he and Billy took a plunge down the Boston Fish Pier hopper. After a couple of minutes had passed, the crew reluctantly started moving to where the fish forks were stored. But all activity ceased when Vinnie raised his left hand in the air, signaling everyone to stop.

"Wait for it," he called out. The men turned to look at Vinnie, and then at the cargo hole. In an instant, the gurry had shifted and dropped about six inches. Vinnie's face beamed with a broad grin. He knew what was coming next. With a sudden jolt, the entire contents of the barge dropped through the hull opening and into the open ocean. There was such an uplift in the barge from the rapid loss of weight that many of the crew grabbed whatever they could to steady themselves in place. Vinnie grasped the side of the control stand, clinging to it with every bit of upper body strength he had. There was no way he was stumbling into the hole and out the doors below. Following the massive elimination of gurry was an instant gush of water, rushing in to displace the missing load in the cargo hold. Once the barge had finally stabilized, the crew erupted in cheers. Vinnie placed his arm across his waist as he bowed in the direction of the tugboat. Then, turning, he closed the hull doors with the hydraulic controls and, raising his hand in the air, gave the captain a victorious thumbs-up.

The captain returned the thumbs-up and nodded at a job well done.

Relieved, Vinnie settled in for the trip home, his mind wandering to under the sea where the gurry had abruptly plunged. He doubted the gurry broke up much on the way to the ocean floor. "That must have been frightening as hell to any sea life in the area," he thought, and then he smiled. The miserable, stinky, gooey gurry was finally gone. From now on, they'd be dealing with fresher by-products. His relief was evident as his body relaxed in his seat, and he drifted off to sleep.

He awoke to the tugboat switching from pushing to towing as it entered Gloucester Harbor. He watched to be sure they didn't approach any of the expensive moored vessels too closely. When the barge was safely docked, the tugboat captain handed him an invoice for the two trips out. The bill totaled a whopping $20,000. The captain told him to give him a call when he was ready to go out with another load. Vinnie thanked the captain for his help and patience and decided to walk over to Fitzy's for a late celebratory lunch.

As the week went forward and each day came to a close, Vinnie would religiously add a layer of salt water to the day's gurry that was dumped in the barge's cargo hold, being sure to rinse the sides down well. As the next few weeks unfolded, trips to empty the barge went off without a hitch. Vinnie had found the secret to a successful dump. As long as he adhered to his system of flushing the cargo hold with water each evening, the barge worked just like a humongous portable toilet.

CHAPTER 12

After the busy summer season when tourists flocked to Gloucester and before the holiday rush that included all kinds of seafood fare, Flannery's workers were enjoying a relaxing fall. The last weekend in September ushered in days that were still warm, but nights were dipping to near freezing, which always heralded the start of the foliage season. Focus shifted from the coastline to apple picking, corn mazes, and of course, the opening of the famous Topsfield Fair. Anyone who had kids, and many who didn't, would make the half-hour drive inland from Cape Ann on a sunny day to enjoy the oldest agricultural fair in the United States. Doug, Denny, Jimmy, and Murph's families loved the rides and carnival section, whereas Meredith and Paul's families, who both lived in the Ipswich/Topsfield area, enjoyed seeing the horse-pulling event and the great pumpkin weigh-in. Of course, everyone couldn't wait to sample the food each year. Curly fries, Billy's loaded baked potatoes, and Winfrey's fudge were at the top of everybody's list of favorites.

Because Saturday morning was expected to be the beginning of a rainy week, Paul felt that Friday evening would be the perfect time to bring new water into the lobster tanks. He'd been putting off pumping water into the tanks for a while, until the gurry plant's barge had a successful dumping or two, just to be sure he wasn't pulling in toxic water. Although the timing was great to pump the best water possible into the tanks, it wasn't perfect, as Friday was opening night at the fair and most of Flannery's crew was planning to attend. Paul could do the job before he headed home to pick up his family, but by the time he finished, opening night at the fair would be winding down. Paul approached Denny, hoping he might be free to stay, but Denny wasn't interested in any overtime that night.

"Are you kidding me?" Denny answered when Paul asked if he'd mind staying behind for an hour or two. "I'm not missing opening night at the fair. My name would be mud with my kids if we got there too late, not to mention the flack I'd take from my wife. Sorry, Paul, no can do."

Paul understood and was resigned to doing the task himself until Charlie, who had overheard Paul asking Denny, stepped forward to volunteer for the job. Charlie had no kids and wasn't a fan of farm animals or carnival rides, so he was available. Besides, he wanted to redeem himself after the fiasco that happened the last time he brought in water and killed off more than a third of the lobsters in the pound. Denny asked Paul if it was all right to have Charlie do the honors, and Paul happily agreed.

While everyone else left the plant precisely at three, Charlie stayed behind to unload the lobsters from a couple of boats that came in late. When he was finishing up, it was nearly five o'clock and he was hungry. As he was putting the last crate of lobsters in the tanks, he noticed a couple of his buddies at the retail door, with their hands pressed against the glass, trying to see if he was inside. Happy to see his friends, he ran to unlock the door and let them in.

"We were headed over to Fitzy's for dinner and pool. You wanna come?" Charlie's best friend asked as he walked into the retail area. Two other men who had graduated from high school with Charlie followed close behind.

"You know it," Charlie answered. "Just let me get this last set of lobsters in the water, and I'll be right with you."

"Great," his friends said in unison and began to peruse the retail store's frozen case. Charlie ran back to the lobster room, newly energized with the opportunity to hang out with his buddies for the night. He hadn't forgotten about changing out the lobster tank water, but at this point, he was starving. As long as he was back by six thirty or so, he'd have plenty of time to bring some water into the plant.

When six thirty rolled around, Charlie found it tougher to leave his friends than he had first thought it would be. It wasn't until another half hour had passed that he dutifully walked back to Flannery's to do his job, promising his buddies he'd be right back. He opened the plant, turned off the alarm, and made his way past the cutting line. As he entered the pump room, his memory flashed back to the last time he'd changed the water. He immediately located the valve he'd opened before that allowed water into the upper tanks from the harbor and made a mental note not to touch it. It helped that Denny had run through the directions before he left, to be sure he remembered what to do. Just as Denny had instructed, he first closed the valve to the chiller and turned off the chiller pump. This kept the water from circulating at too high a pressure, Denny had told him. He could hear Denny's voice in his mind as he executed each step. Then he opened the valve that pumped water from the harbor to the reservoir full blast.

"You're not going to get me this time," Charlie muttered to himself as he checked a second time to be sure the valve to the upper tanks was closed tightly. He waited for what seemed an eternity as he envisioned his buddies at Fitzy's having another round of beer and maybe playing some pool in his absence. But he knew he had to be patient and was bent on doing a good job this time. After all, Christmas was coming and the bonuses Flannery handed out at the end of the year were usually substantial. He wanted to be sure he was in line for a hefty chunk of change this time.

When he was finished, Charlie closed the harbor-to-reservoir-valve, which stopped the flow of water from outside. Then he turned the chiller pump back on. He was confident he had done a great job bringing water in this time. But even more, he had filled the void when no one else was available. He knew his bonus would be at least as large as it was last year, if not more. The keys to that new Ram truck he'd been eyeing would be in his stocking this Christmas Eve for sure. All he needed was a bonus check that matched the amount of the down payment for the truck. He put the alarm on, locked up, and joined his friends back at Fitzy's.

Meanwhile, at the fair, Paul was sitting on the bleachers in the arena with his wife and Meredith and her husband, eating a piece of pumpkin-flavored fudge while watching a 949-pound pumpkin being weighed. As the forklift navigated the dirt floor, being careful not to hit the solid wooden fence that surrounded the ring to help keep livestock and horses contained during competitions, it carefully lifted the pallet holding one of the largest pumpkins in the running.

"That's the winner," Paul declared.

"I don't think size matters," Paul's wife said with a smile, then turned to Meredith and asked, "What do you think?"

Meredith shot a smile back at Paul's wife. "I don't think size matters either. I think that cute little hundred-and-fifty-pound pumpkin they tossed aside over there is much more appealing with its bright orange color and nice round shape than those monstrous blobs with pale coloring that everyone's so excited about. What do you think, honey?" Meredith said, placing her hand on her husband's knee.

"I'm with Paul, the bigger the better. Anyone can grow a little pumpkin with orange color and a nice shape. There's no real contest in that. But growing a massive pumpkin and getting it here in one piece? Now that's an achievement," Meredith's husband declared, reaching out to give Paul a high five. Everybody laughed.

Just then, Paul caught a glimpse of Denny, who appeared to be searching for someone in the stands. He wasn't with his family, so Paul called out, "Hey, Denny!"

Denny scanned the seated crowd to see where the voice was

coming from and saw Paul raising his hand from the top bleacher. Denny made his way up the metal steps and squeezed in to sit on the rail just below him.

"My wife just got home with the kids, and she says there's a call from the alarm company saying there's a tank sensor going off indicating low water levels in the lobster room at Flannery's. They said the building's lost power and someone needs to get up there right away. I'd go, but you know a whole lot more about fixing things than I do," Denny concluded.

"Damn it," Paul remarked under his breath, frustrated he was going to have to leave his family and head to Gloucester.

"I hear ya," Denny said sympathetically. Paul frowned as he looked at his wife.

"That's OK," she said reluctantly. "The kids and I will hitch a ride home with Meredith, if that's alright with you guys?" Paul's wife glanced at Meredith and her husband.

"Course it is," Meredith answered. Then, turning to Paul, she added, "Sorry you have to leave before the end. Hope it's nothing big."

"Sounds like it could be," Paul said. He turned to kiss his wife goodbye, saying, "I'll call you as soon as I know what's up." Then he carefully made his way down the bleacher steps and out into the parking lot. He eyed the Ferris wheel, brightly lit against the night sky. He had intended to take everyone on it as the final ride of the evening. So much for his plans.

When Paul arrived at the plant, it was pitch black. He immediately opened the glove compartment of his car and grabbed a flashlight he had stored there for emergencies. The outside of the plant appeared as it should have. There were no broken windows in the retail market, and the door was locked. Feeling encouraged that no one had broken in and vandalized the plant, he unlocked the door and stepped inside. Aided by his flashlight, he made his way in the dark to the steep metal ship stairs that led to the storage area over the retail store where the main breaker for the entire plant was located. He walked over to the large, thousand-amp main breaker and kicked it back on. The lights in the building flickered for only a moment, followed by a loud boom and then darkness. The main breaker had tripped and the power was off again.

"Oh man, something shorted out big-time!" Paul said, even though there was nobody there to hear him.

He climbed down the stairs and walked to the lobster room. He lifted the metal garage door and crept in a few feet, playing the flashlight off each tank. Everything appeared normal. He turned to examine the main floor, looking for anything blown up or burning. Still nothing. It was eerily quiet in the plant. The only sound he heard was the dripping of water into the practically empty lobster tanks. It put him in mind of a scene from the end of the *Alien* movie. He approached the pump-room door, looking over his shoulder occasionally as if expecting that someone or something was in the room with him. He paused for a moment, then threw open the door and immediately jumped back.

"Holy crap!" he exclaimed, then regained his composure and carefully approached the threshold of the door again, shining a light on the pump room's electrical service. The cover of the electrical panel that held the breakers, which was five feet by two feet and weighed about forty pounds, had been hurled across the room and was lodged in the opposite wall like a meat cleaver. The room smelled of burning wires. Playing his flashlight back on the electrical panel, he could see there was hardly anything in it. There were only wires hanging; the breakers had been blown out of the box. He saw pieces of breakers everywhere as he shined the light on the floor and walls, the biggest piece being about an inch long. Everything in the room was soaking wet. It looked like a massive thunderstorm had converged on it, packing a tornado or two.

"Well, that panel's no good," he said, stating the obvious to himself. Then he asked, "But what the hell caused this?"

He walked back to the lobster room to take a closer look at the tanks. When he shined a light into the first tank, he saw the lobsters huddled at the bottom where about six inches of seawater had collected. There, they competed for the prized position that allowed the most water to cover their gills. Paul checked each tank in turn, and the scenario was the same.

He lifted his shirtsleeve and pointed a beam of light from his flashlight onto the face of his watch. It was almost eleven o'clock. He had to figure out what had happened and fast. That many lobsters wouldn't last very long in only six inches of seawater. He thought of calling Flannery but decided against it. There was nothing Flannery could do, and it would only serve to upset him. Besides, he wouldn't have much to tell him anyway. He could assess the extent of the damage for Flannery, but he wasn't sure of the cause. His priority was to get the power up and running so that he could start filling the lobster tanks again. Flannery would only serve as a distraction, not a solution.

Paul called his regular electrician, who had just returned home from the fair himself. He explained to him the condition of the panel and asked the electrician to gather up as many breakers and panel odds and ends he could find this time of night. It didn't matter whether they were used parts or not. He was desperate.

Thankfully, the electrician was a local Gloucester man and arrived at Flannery's retail door in about twenty minutes. When Paul escorted him across the cutting room to the threshold of the pump-room door, the electrician groaned.

"Geeze Louise, what the hell happened here?" the electrician exclaimed in disbelief, rubbing the side of his head with his free hand.

"Damned if I know," Paul answered, reaching out to take the electrician's toolbox and set it down.

The electrician stood a moment to scan the damage. "You weren't exaggerating, were you?"

"Nope," Paul replied.

Both men studied the room, trying to figure out where to start. They thought of piecing together some breakers, but every one they found fairly intact was drenched with salt water and unusable. The electrician showed Paul the parts he was able to round up.

"Most of these are old parts I took out of people's houses at some point to replace. The system won't be to code, but I think we can fix it up enough to get you through the night so that you can save most of your lobsters."

"That's good enough for me," Paul said, and he and the electrician got to work restoring the panel to make it functional.

Once the panel was deemed safe and operational, Paul climbed up the steep metal stairs to kick the building's main breaker on. He waited for a few minutes, half expecting the breaker to kick off again. But to his relief, the breaker held. He returned to the pump room, and the electrician began to reset each breaker, one at a time. Both men braced themselves for some kind of reaction as the first breaker was switched into working position. Nothing out of the ordinary happened.

"So far, so good," the electrician remarked with a smile. But neither man felt they were out of the woods just yet.

The second breaker was reset, and again, nothing happened. Paul and the electrician began to relax. When the third breaker was switched on, water started gushing up like a geyser from one of the pipes. The electrician rushed to switch the breaker to the off position as quickly as he could, and both men wasted no time in distancing themselves from the open panel.

"Electricity and water don't play well together," the electrician told Paul, something he already knew all too well.

"Is it safe to walk inside?" Paul asked.

"I would think so," the electrician replied. Then he joked, "I'm wearing shockproof boots."

Paul jumped back from the pump-room door.

"I'm just kidding. I was in front of the panel, blocking the spray. I don't think it got wet," the electrician said. Then he added with a smile, "But I do have shockproof boots on."

"I'll be sure to have you stand in all the puddles, then," Paul bantered.

Both men walked cautiously back into the pump room. There were two small lights working now with the top two breakers functioning. This helped, but Paul still needed his flashlight to see the whole picture. He shined the light on the top of the pump that gushed water. It was the chiller pump, but there was no valve on top of it.

"Where's the valve?" Paul asked.

"You mean that valve?" the electrician shined his flashlight on a valve lying on its side on the floor.

"That's the one," Paul said, leaning over to pick it up. Then he exclaimed in astonishment, "It's closed!"

"Sure is," agreed the electrician. "Why the hell would it be closed? No wonder she blew."

"That son of a bitch, Charlie," Paul declared, finally understanding what had happened. "He changed the water, turned the pump to the chiller back on, and never opened the valve to let the water flow to the chiller."

"What a genius!" the electrician quipped. "Didn't you train this guy?"

"You don't know the half of it," Paul explained. "Plus the directions are right here on the wall in case somebody forgets the procedure." Sure enough, the directions were still legible, even after all the destruction in the room.

"This pump must have run for hours without the valve open," Paul surmised. "The water wasn't able to go anywhere, which would have caused the pump to heat, the housing to expand, and the valve to snap off."

"So you had an open pipe with pressurized water flowing out, spraying up, hitting the ceiling, and raining down on everything in the pump room, including the electrical equipment," the electrician concluded. "Salt water mixing with four hundred amps of electricity—no wonder all this happened."

"Water must have seeped into the panel box," Paul continued.

"If you have a two-inch fire hose spraying two hundred and

forty gallons of water a minute, emptying into a twenty-by-twenty closed room, that room's gonna fill up fast. No electrical box would hold up to being submerged in conditions like that," the electrician explained.

"Of course not," Paul replied. "Enough water got into the electrical panel to cause the main breaker to short out and explode into pieces. That created a force so strong that it blew the cover right off the panel."

"Well you can see the bolt holes are ripped off the panel cover," the electrician said, examining the piece of equipment. "Imagine the force that it flew off at. Good thing there was no one in the room at the time."

"They'd be dead for sure," Paul speculated.

"Once the main breaker in the panel blew, it shorted everything else out, including the plant's main breaker," the electrician surmised.

"And that's when the whole building shut down," Paul concluded.

"I guess we've reconstructed the event. Do you know it's daylight outside?" the electrician said.

"Are you kidding? We've been here all night?" Paul asked.

"That's gonna cost you," the electrician joked. "Or I guess Flannery. Does he even know about this?"

"He knows the alarm was going off, but he doesn't know the scope of it. Once he knew I went in to take care of it, he probably went to bed," Paul guessed.

"I think we've got this as good as we can get it for now," the electrician said. "I'll be back with a crew on Monday to replace the used parts with some fresh ones. You should be OK until then, I think."

"I'll need to reconstruct the pipes and start filling lobster tanks at this point," Paul said. Then he added, "Hey, I really appreciate you spending the night with me to get this straightened out."

"No problem," the electrician called back as he walked out the door. "You'll get my bill."

Paul spent a good part of the morning at Flannery's reinstalling piping. When he was sure everything was up and running, he called Denny to see if he could work that afternoon to bring water in to fill the tanks.

"What happened over there anyway?" Denny asked. "When I drove by to take my kids to football practice this morning I noticed your car was still there."

"I'll tell you about it Monday," Paul answered. He had been up for thirty-three hours by this point and really needed to get some sleep.

"I'll be right over," Denny said. "Thanks for going in last night, Paul."

"There was nothing you could have done, Denny," Paul replied. "It's just as well I went in. As soon as you discovered the exploded electrical box in the pump room and that the lobster tanks had drained down, you would have needed to call me in anyway."

"I can't wait to see it. That must have been a real mess!" Denny said.

"Worst electrical explosion I've ever seen," Paul added.

"You know," Denny cautiously continued, "I'll be really glad when all the *Bay State Skye* lobsters are sold and out of the plant. I know you think I'm being superstitious, but you've got to admit, some unusual things have happened since we took those lobsters in."

"You know I've been a disbeliever, and I still am, by the way. But I have to admit, things have been a little rocky in the month and a half since that abandoned boat was discovered," Paul conceded.

"I've been trying to ferret out the lobsters that came in with Jimmy and Murph's load—you know, the larger, more beat-up ones. I'm shipping out as many as I can with orders. But not all of those lobsters were in bad shape, so it's hard to weed them out," Denny admitted.

"Well, keep trying, Denny. Whether there's anything to it or not, I'd just as soon see the last of the lobsters from the *Bay State Skye* go out the door myself," Paul agreed.

With that, Paul hung up the phone and dragged himself over to the retail door to set the alarm and lock up. He was looking forward to sleeping for the rest of the weekend.

When Monday morning came, Charlie arrived bright and cheery, waiting for the powers that be to shower him with appreciation for helping them out at their time of need. He saw the electrician trucks in the parking lot but didn't connect the dots that they might be fixing something he was responsible for breaking.

Paul grabbed Charlie as he walked by the office and asked, "Did you change the water Friday night?"

Charlie answered proudly that he had.

"Did anything happen?" Paul asked.

"No, everything went fine," replied Charlie, still not putting two and two together about the electricians in the building.

"Do you remember turning the chiller pump back on?" Paul asked.

"Yup," Charlie answered.

"Did you open the valve to the chiller after you turned the chiller pump back on?" Paul asked.

"Yup," Charlie answered, still not understanding what Paul was driving at.

"No, you didn't, Charlie," Paul declared.

"Yes, I did," responded Charlie, stepping closer to Paul, looking him square in the eye. Then he added defiantly, "I know I turned that valve on."

"Charlie, the valve was on the floor in the off position," Paul replied.

"Then somebody turned it off after I left," Charlie exclaimed.

"Nobody was here, Charlie. You were the last guy out," Paul fired back. "I got a call at nine thirty Friday night from the alarm company. That pump ran for hours with the valve closed. You're lucky we didn't lose many lobsters, but the electrician bill is going to be steep. We were here fixing the pump room all Friday night and into Saturday noontime. That was a patch job. They're back now to replace everything. Needless to say, you won't be changing the water again."

"Your loss," Charlie declared. Then he added, "I don't care if I ever change the water!" He turned and strode back to the lobster room.

Paul shook his head. Charlie was right. It didn't matter to him whether he changed water or not, but Paul was minus a man who could do the job. He wanted to fire him in the worst way. That man had cost the company a lot of money over the last month or two. But he couldn't fire him for a mistake. Unfortunately, Paul couldn't prove intent, or Charlie would have been out the door right then. Still, his arrogance and lack of remorse were a tough pill to swallow. Paul would be watching. He only had to come up with one more strike, and Charlie would be gone. Then Paul could hire someone with a head on his shoulders whom he could rely on to change the water without incident.

Just then, the phone rang and jolted Paul back from wishful thinking. It was Flannery wondering why the alarm sounded Friday evening. He told Flannery the whole story. There was just no way to candy coat it.

"We need to find a way to get that no-good bastard out," Flannery exploded after Paul had said his piece. "Do you know how much he's cost the company this year?"

"I know," Paul agreed. "I'm working on it. You can't fire him for a mistake, no matter how destructive it turned out to be. There was no malice here. I believe he actually wanted to redeem himself from the last time he took in water."

"Well, don't let him do it again," cried Flannery. "If water needs to be taken in, it's either you or Denny doing it from now on. Understood?"

"Understood," Paul answered, and the two men hung up simultaneously. Paul was surprised at how short Flannery was with him. He would have thought Flannery might have appreciated the fact that he had dropped everything, even left his family at the fair, to check out the plant when the alarm call came in. He then had worked all Friday night into Saturday afternoon, trying to limit the extent of financial damage to the company—and all that after working a full workday that had started at four thirty in the morning. Charlie was well trained and had been taking in water for a long time without incident. There was no rhyme or reason as to why, suddenly, he was botching the job up left and right. Paul had done nothing wrong and had stepped up when he was needed. Since he had no crystal ball to see into the future, he couldn't have anticipated this happening. No one could have.

Deep in thought, Paul hadn't noticed Meredith had just hung up the phone from speaking with the sales office in Boston. When she slid off her stool and headed for the door, he gave her a puzzled look.

"Our salesman received a complaint from one of his customers about last week's lobster order," Meredith informed Paul. "I want to see how today's order's packed in case another complaint comes in next week." Paul nodded in agreement, and Meredith took off toward the lobster room, sales ticket in hand. But as she entered the room and looked up, Meredith froze in her tracks. There was Denny, giving a hand to a very soggy, fully clothed electrician who was attempting to climb out of the lobster-room reservoir below. Denny was apologetic. The electrician was stunned. Meredith listened for a moment to get the gist of what had just happened, then turned back to the office to let Paul know.

"You need to get to the lobster room," Meredith told Paul as she came through the door. "One of the electricians went to check out some wiring and fell into the reservoir. Denny pulled him out, but the electrician's pretty shaken up."

"How'd an electrician fall through the reservoir hatch?" Paul asked.

"I think the hatch was open, and the electrician didn't notice as he walked over it," Meredith said as softly as she could, returning to her seat. She knew this bit of information would make him livid.

"Are you kidding me? There weren't any totes put up as a barrier to block the opening?" Paul exclaimed, jumping out of his seat. His outburst was a cross between anger and fear. The lobster crew knew this safety procedure was crucial, and he couldn't imagine how he was going to tell Flannery. "Was the electrician hurt?"

"I don't think so," Meredith said, "but he's going to need to warm up with a shower and a change of clothes."

Paul flew from the office and met Denny's concerned look as he walked up to the electrician. "I'm so sorry. Let me take you up to the men's locker room where you can get a warm shower and a change of clothes," Paul offered.

"No thanks," the electrician said, shooting Paul an embarrassed grin. "I'm local. I'll go home and change and I'll be back. I'd have brought a change of clothes with me if I'd known I was going for a swim."

Paul smiled. He was relieved to hear the electrician hadn't lost his sense of humor. Spending time in the reservoir was never an enjoyable experience, even when you were expecting it. Paul watched the electrician walk out the retail door, his shockproof boots making a strange squishing sound with every step he took. When the electrician was out of the building, Paul turned to Denny.

"What the hell happened?" Paul asked.

"All I know is I was packing this lobster order when I heard a high-pitched yelp," Denny began. "I turned around and saw nothing. There was no one on the floor but me. But then I heard a muffled 'son of a bitch!' It sounded like it was coming from the reservoir hole, which was open. I don't know when or why it was opened, but somehow it was open."

"Why weren't there totes barricading the opening?" Paul asked.

"I didn't know it was open, Paul," Denny reiterated.

"Where's Charlie?" Paul asked.

"In the meat-picking room," Denny responded.

Paul strode off to the back of the lobster room, with Denny trailing close behind. When he arrived, Paul threw open the door. Charlie jumped, and his arrogant demeanor suddenly shifted to one of anxiousness. Paul seldom lost his cool, but at that moment, Charlie sensed Paul's rage.

"Why did you open the reservoir hole?" Paul cried out, certain Charlie was the guilty party.

"I was going to clean it," Charlie replied cautiously.

"That's bull—we just cleaned it two weeks ago," Denny yelled.

"OK, I might have lost something down there and was about to go get it when I was told to finish picking the meat for this order that had to go out with the next truck," Charlie countered.

"What did you lose?" Denny asked.

"Doesn't matter," Paul said abruptly. Then, turning to Charlie, he said, "You didn't think to cover the hole or put totes around it while the reservoir was open? You know, to follow protocol?"

"I was gonna," Charlie retorted, regaining a bit of his smugness.

"You don't have to worry about it anymore," Paul enlightened Charlie. Paul's anger suddenly melted into elation. He smiled widely. "Denny escort Charlie up to the locker room to get his things while I fill out the third warning. Charlie, you're fired. Done. Terminated! Denny will bring you by to sign the warning on your way out."

Charlie brushed by Paul, slapping the door as he left. Denny caught up with him, following close behind to keep an eye on him. Once he had signed the warning and was out the door, Paul picked up the phone to call Flannery.

Flannery reacted to the news with much less excitement than Paul had anticipated, expecting him to be delighted to see the tail end of Charlie. But what he didn't know was that this wasn't the only crisis Flannery was juggling. At this point, the tugboat captain had made several trips to dump gurry for which he hadn't been paid.

"I know you're in a spot, but I can't keep this up much longer," the captain had informed Flannery in a phone call that morning. "My crew still has to be paid, and my boat has to be fueled every time I go out regardless of whether you pay me or not. And you're not giving me any money."

"I know, I know," Flannery replied sympathetically. Then promised, "I'm working on it, but that son-of-a-bitch governor won't give me my money." Flannery paused and then said, "Look,

I'll get some money to you by the end of the week."

"I hope you can because I can't do any more trips after this week if I don't receive payment," the captain replied, and he meant it.

Flannery hung up the phone, put his head in his hands and covered his eyes. Many of the fish companies hadn't paid their fair share to the New England Fish Processors' Association, and some hadn't made any payments at all. To make matters worse, the governor had missed the last couple of payments he had promised Flannery. It had been a hard weekend and was shaping up to be a harder week.

"I am so screwed," Flannery muttered to himself as he rubbed his face with his hands. It wasn't like him not to be able to brainstorm his way out of a crisis, but this situation seemed to be getting the best of him.

As Flannery sat in his office feeling lost, an idea came to him. He sat up straight in his chair and picked up the phone. He was back in the game again. He called his company's operator.

"Dolly, get me the number for the *Boston Globe*, please. Oh, and while you're at it, look up the number for the *Boston Herald*, too."

"Sure thing," Dolly answered. Within a minute she was calling back with the information. "Would you like me to connect you?"

"That would be great, Dolly," Flannery answered with a new pep in his voice. He was ready to set the world on fire again.

"This is the *Boston Globe*; how can I help you?" Flannery heard the operator say.

"Could I please speak to one of your reporters?"

"One moment, please," said the operator, and after a few rings a man's voice answered the phone.

"Ed Springer, reporter's desk," the voice on the other end of the line stated.

"Hi, Ed," Flannery began. "This is Jack Flannery over at Flannery's Fish House in Boston, and I've got a problem. I've got a deal with the governor. He's supposed to be giving me one hundred and twenty-seven thousand dollars a month to dump the state's fish processors' waste—gurry—at sea. The Environmental Protection Agency has approved it all, and the governor's not coming through with the money. I've got a tugboat to run and I've got a lot of gurry out here, and it's got to get dumped. And I need the money!"

Ed got all excited. This sounded like it could be a great story for the paper, and he would be the one with the scoop. "Oh, is that so? I'll look into this and see what I can find out," he told Flannery. "Can you give me your number so that I can get in touch if I need any more information?"

Flannery gave the reporter his work number and hung up the phone. He paused a moment and then lifted the receiver again to call the *Boston Herald*. The reporter at the *Herald* was as excited to get in on the ground floor of this story as the *Globe* reporter was. Flannery hung up the phone, sat back, and waited. Miraculously, within ten minutes, Flannery's phone rang. The reporters had gotten in touch with the governor's office even faster than he had hoped.

He waited for the third ring to answer, not wanting to appear too anxious, "Hello?"

"This is the governor's office. I'd like to speak to Jack Flannery," the voice on the other end said with a respectable amount of urgency in his voice.

"That's me," Flannery answered.

"Mr. Flannery? The governor would like to see you right away," the voice on the other end insisted.

"I'll be right there," Flannery said nonchalantly, as if he had no idea what the governor would want.

When Flannery arrived at the governor's office, he saw two reporters sitting just outside the corner office. Both men were in their midthirties and hungry for a career-building story. Each reporter wore a medium-gray sport coat with a light-blue, short-sleeved cotton shirt underneath, the top button open. It was as if they had coordinated their wardrobes before leaving their respective offices. Flannery was glad he had chosen his dark-brown sport coat for the occasion, not wishing to match the newspapermen's attire. Flannery smiled as he read each reporter's press credentials. One was from the *Herald*, the other, from the *Globe*. His plan was in motion. The reporters jumped to their feet and rushed over to Flannery.

"Mr. Flannery, Mr. Flannery, we've been waiting for you. Will you sit down with us for a few minutes and give us your story?" they asked simultaneously.

"I'd like to," Flannery said, "but I can't at the moment. The governor just called me, and I have to go in to see him." Disappointed, the reporters returned to their seats while Flannery was ushered into the governor's office. It appeared that Flannery was finally going to meet the governor face to face instead of having to deal with the middlemen that were the governor's aides.

As Flannery walked through the corner-office doorway, he saw the governor sitting behind his massive desk. His jet-black hair and boyish features were true to what Flannery had expected from seeing him in news stories on television. When the governor rose to shake his hand, Flannery was surprised by how tall he was. He had thought the governor's height was around five foot three or four at best, but he actually matched Flannery's own height, eye to eye, at five foot eight.

"Hello, Mr. Flannery," the governor said as the two men shook hands. "It's nice to finally meet you. I can't thank you enough for all you've been doing for the Commonwealth of Massachusetts."

"You should thank me," Flannery fired back, delighted to finally have the opportunity to give the governor a piece of his mind. "You'd have gurry up to your ears if it wasn't for me. I'm not getting my money, and I'll tell you right now, I'm through. I want this money when it's due, and if I don't get it, you're going to get the gurry. I've been doing all this work for nothing. Nobody's paying me for this. I've been working my tail off taking care of your problem. I don't think it's asking too much to get the money to take care of the barge and tugboat crew that's getting rid of your gurry."

If the governor had thought he could intimidate Flannery and then hand him another empty promise, he knew now that would never work. Flannery wasn't a politician who was used to negotiating and then eventually giving a little to take a little. He was from the business world—and from the fish business, no less. Flannery was going to be tough and would push to get his way, just as he would with a boat captain or another fish dealer who was trying to take advantage of him. The governor now realized that deflecting the blame away from himself and giving Flannery his money would be the only way to keep this out of the papers, which the governor desperately wanted. The governor was ready to concede.

"Oh . . . well, I'll take care of this right away. This isn't right!" the governor insisted, inferring that he didn't know the money wasn't being sent out. Then he turned to Tom, his aide, and said, "Tom, tell the treasurer to come in here right now."

Tom disappeared and, like well-rehearsed pageantry, reappeared moments later with the treasurer. "Come in here," the governor ordered the treasurer. "Listen, you need to write a check for Mr. Flannery here"—the governor gestured toward Flannery—"and from now on, make sure he gets his check on time every month."

Without saying a word, the treasurer nodded and left the governor's office, returning moments later with a check made out to the New England Fish Processors' Association for the full amount. The treasurer handed the check to the governor, and the governor handed the check to Flannery. Without saying a word, the treasurer left the office.

"Thank you very much," Flannery said, reaching out to firmly shake the governor's hand. With that, Flannery turned to leave, satisfied that he had gotten the money he needed, with the added bonus of telling the governor just what he thought. Flannery had completely forgotten about the two reporters still seated outside the governor's office. He hadn't taken five steps beyond the corner-office door when both reporters pounced on him to get the story before he could leave.

"Mr. Flannery, Mr. Flannery," both men said at once, "Can we talk now?"

"Well, not really," Flannery sheepishly began. "You see, I just got the money I needed from the governor, so I don't want to be bothering you guys at all."

Frustrated, the reporters turned and left in a huff. They'd been used, and they knew it. Flannery didn't blame them. He felt a little guilty, but the end definitely justified the means in his mind. Besides, if the governor hadn't come up with the money—and quickly—Flannery had full intentions of telling his story to both papers. But that was a last resort. The best-case scenario had just happened. Flannery took the check to the bank, cashed it, and made out his own check to the tugboat captain, sending it off in the evening mail. Another potential catastrophe averted. Flannery sat back in his chair in his Newmarket Square office.

"I was never worried," Flannery said, smiling to himself. "I knew it would all work out in the end."

Bay State Skye

CHAPTER 13

The influx of money from the governor's office was a shot in the arm for the tugboat and gurry-barge operation. They made several more trips over the next few weeks, but even Flannery knew this wasn't going to be sustainable. The EPA's designated dump site would soon create a dead zone in the area of the coordinate points, and there was no doubt in Flannery's mind that the governor's money would dry up again at some point. With the upcoming gubernatorial election closing in and its predicted change in administration, Flannery would more than likely have to begin negotiations all over again with the newly elected governor.

Word of a small gurry plant opening in New Bedford seemed promising, although it wasn't big enough to handle all the gurry the area produced. Many fish processors saw the writing on the wall and had begun experimenting with developing products that would help to use up the waste their fish-cutting lines produced. Pet-food flavor enhancers and plant and crop fertilizers were on the top of most seafood companies' research and development lists. Flannery had already tried selling fish by-products as they came off the line to farms for direct tilling into the fields. All in all, this operation was deemed a failure, although if the gurry had been fresh, there might have been a chance its odor wouldn't have become as unbearable as it did before it was absorbed into the soil. It was clear that some kind of processing had to take place before the gurry was applied to the soil to allow it to become absorbed in a more efficient manner.

Flannery had already begun making arrangements to financially back a pair of scientists who claimed to be able to create viable fertilizer from fish by-products, and equipment was being collected to crank up the opening of Flannery's new "Squanto's Secret" operation in his Gloucester plant. He would have valued a chance to get Wayne Conroy's opinion on this new business venture, but he knew there was little chance of that. It had been almost seven weeks since Wayne and his wife were lost at sea. There was still no sign of any bodies or wreckage from the *Liberty,* and even Wayne's kids had lost hope of ever knowing what truly happened. They were now focused on running Wayne's restaurants and settling in for the seven-year wait to have their parents declared deceased.

*   *   *   *   *

As Paul took his usual forty-five-minute drive through the salt-marsh areas of Ipswich and Essex, his attention shifted from the leftover Halloween decorations from the night before to the weather. A fall storm was brewing. A large weather system had developed that was headed east through the Midwest, reaching as far south as Nashville, while at the same time diving down from Canada and into Michigan and Ohio. This weather system was predicted to hook up with moisture streaming out of the Gulf of Mexico and headed up the Atlantic coastline. Whenever warm moist water from the south clashed with colder, drier air from Canada, nor'easters tended to be the outcome. Although it was still too warm to snow in the Cape Ann area, the tides were astronomically high due to a full beaver moon, and widespread flooding was predicted. It was the perfect setting for cold, biting rains and high winds, which would keep most fishing and lobster boats unproductive. Whenever boats stayed in, seafood would become scarce, and prices would soar, which would make fish and lobsters a tough sell to both nationwide restaurants and local retail customers in the days ahead.

Paul expected to have a full crew in today, and there was plenty of work for the cutting line and lobster room, due to the notorious calm weather before the storm. They needed to pack and ship whatever they could until the airport was closed down, which was more than likely going to happen around noon as the storm bore down on the Boston area.

When Paul arrived at the plant, Denny was already in the office, trying to get whatever orders he could from Meredith. He had begun a cook after going through the lobsters to identify any weaks. Meredith made sure that everything the Boston sales office had requested was waiting for Vinnie at the loading-dock door, including shipments that needed to meet Delta's first flights out. Vinnie was anxious to get on the road to Boston before the weather turned too ugly and welcomed the well-organized greeting he received when he returned from the Gloucester auction. Once Vinnie had loaded up and pulled out to drive across the street and head for the Route 128 rotary, Meredith walked around the plant to the back dock to take a quick look at the surf. It wasn't awful. It was churned up a little more than usual, but she'd seen worse. Then she looked out to the horizon and noted that the sky resembled what her great-grandfather called a snow sky. "It's too warm to snow," she noted as she shook her head and smiled. But when a sudden gust of wind blew around the corner of the building, a biting-cold blast of salty air hit her face. She turned and headed inside, knowing the approaching storm had the potential to pack a punch.

As Meredith passed Denny, she said, "I guess we won't be seeing Jimmy and Murph today."

"I doubt it," Denny remarked. "They're laying traps out in the Nahant Bay and Broad Sound area. They'll probably be up for bait, but they're moored for the month of November somewhere around Nahant."

"Wouldn't they be better off docked here by Flannery's?"

Meredith asked. "We're more sheltered than a river mooring."

"I don't think they were thinking a nor'easter would be barreling up the coast when they booked the mooring for a month. They started setting their traps along the gravel bottom in Nahant about two weeks ago and were having such large hauls from the area that they decided to moor closer to save on fuel," Denny explained.

"I hope that decision doesn't come back to haunt them," Meredith said.

"I hope not," Denny replied. Then he asked, "Are there any more orders to put up?"

"A couple," Meredith said. "Come into the office—I'll get them for you."

As they walked toward the office door, Doug came through the loading-dock strips. "You know there's a nor'easter coming, right?" Doug asked Meredith.

"I do," answered Meredith. What Doug was really asking is if Meredith had done anything to help schedule him in and out of Boston ahead of the storm. "I've given the Boston salesmen a nine forty-five deadline to get all orders in for your second truck run to the airport. I told them you're leaving at ten o'clock sharp. Better to get most of the orders to their flights than to wait for a few indecisive stragglers and have the airport close on us."

"Beauty," Doug remarked. "I don't want the winds to kick up and close the Cape Ann Bridge on me."

"A few of us have to get over that bridge to go home, so you can bet we'll be watching the wind and bridge closings," Meredith told Doug. "We're packing everything as soon as we get the orders, and we'll pile any supplies Boston needs at the loading-dock door. Why don't you ask Denny if he needs a hand packing lobsters, and I'll check with the cutting line to see when they'll have the swordfish portions ready for Boston. The Marriott is going to need them for this afternoon, but a driver from Boston can take care of that delivery while you head for the airport."

"Good enough," Doug replied.

The morning flew by as everyone tried to accomplish as much as they could before Doug's truck left. At five minutes to ten, a salesman called with a last-minute order.

"Has the truck left?" the salesman asked optimistically.

"I don't know. I'll have to check," Meredith answered. Meredith always knew where the trucks were, something of which the Boston sales force was well aware. But she also would do her best to accommodate a last-minute order if it was at all possible, so the question was worth asking. "It's ten minutes past the order deadline anyway," Meredith pointed out.

"I know, but you'd be doing me a huge favor if this order made the truck," the salesman pleaded.

"Is it a big order?" Meredith asked.

"No. It's only for ten lobsters, but they need three- to five-pounders, and we don't have any in Boston," the salesman explained.

Meredith knew Denny would be delighted to pack any order that called for three- to five-pound lobsters; by doing so, there was a good chance he'd be getting rid of some of the *Bay State Skye*'s lobsters.

"Doug's set to go, but I'll check and see if they can get one more order on the truck before ten," Meredith said, putting the salesman on hold. She then ran out to the lobster room.

"Denny, are you up to packing one more order?" Meredith asked.

"Hell no," Doug answered, pointing to his watch. "I have four more minutes, and then I'm out of here."

"I know," said Meredith. Then, turning to Denny, she said, "It's for ten three- to five-pounders."

Denny gave Meredith a knowing smile, then glanced at Doug and said, "Hell yeah, we can do that!"

"What?" Doug asked Denny in disbelief, then shot a questioning look at Meredith.

"It won't take anytime at all to put the order up, especially if you give Denny a hand," Meredith told Doug.

"OK," Doug said, "but I don't know why you two are so gung-ho about filling an order that came in too late."

Reluctantly, Doug began putting a box together to expedite packing the order. Denny jumped up to the edge of the right-side tank that held the three- to five-pounders while Meredith grabbed the ice packs and seaweed. She tossed them in Doug's box and ran back to the phone.

"You're in luck," she told the salesman. "The lobster crew's packing the order right now. But that's it. The truck is gone."

"Thanks for getting the order done for me, Meredith. I appreciate it." The salesman was elated and switched lines to tell his customer in Arizona they'd be getting their lobsters for their celebrity golfing event.

At ten o'clock on the dot, Doug hugged the last lobster order box against his chest and yelled to Meredith, "Are we a go?"

"We are," she said as she gave him a thumbs-up. Then she added, "Careful driving."

Doug hustled out the door and placed the last order in the back of his refrigerated truck. Then he closed and locked the cargo door and jumped into the driver's seat. For a fairly large guy, he was surprisingly quick and agile when the need arose. He fired up his truck and pulled out to the street, following the same route as Vinnie had two and a half hours earlier. As Doug made his way around the first Route 128 rotary, Vinnie was circling around the other side, headed back to the plant. Doug would have loved to have had Vinnie's run that day, but most days, he was glad he had the second run. Vinnie's start time was a little earlier than he wanted to be held to on a daily basis.

When lunch break approached, Paul called Flannery to see if he could release the crew for the day. Most of the cutting line lived in Peabody and Danvers and needed to cross the Cape Ann Bridge before the wind got too strong.

"Everyone's worked their butts off today to get the Marriott order cut and lobster orders on the last truck early," Paul explained. "The truck's long gone, so I wanted to check to see if I could let the crew go for the day. With the nor'easter approaching, the wind is picking up, and there's a chance they might close down the bridge."

"Sure, let them go right before lunch, and close the retail. You and Meredith can get out of there, too. I doubt any boats went out in this wind," Flannery speculated.

"None of ours left," Paul answered. "I'll send everyone home, but I'll wait for Doug to get back and help him unload his truck. Then I'll take off too."

"OK, Paul," Flannery said. "Thanks. Have a safe drive home."

"I will," Paul said, although he wished he could leave with everyone else.

Anticipating an early release, Paul had already told the cutting line to start cleaning up. The men were just winding up the chlorinated water hoses when he gave the word they could leave. Everyone made a mad dash up the stairs to the men's locker room to change their clothes and grab their uneaten lunches. Then, one by one, each man punched his time card and headed out.

Meredith joined Rosa in the retail area to lock the door and help ice down the unsold fish. Then Rosa, Paul, and Meredith carried the fish to the cooler. Once they were finished, Rosa left, too.

Denny was working on the lobster inventory when Meredith walked in to check on him. "Why don't you give me the clipboard? You count, and I'll write down the figures. It'll be faster that way," she suggested. She got no argument from Denny, who quickly gave her the clipboard and began calling out figures. When they finished, Denny punched his time card and headed over to Fitzy's for a storm brew or two. Meredith quickly tallied the lobster figures, which luckily made sense with her starting inventory and what they had shipped that day. She faxed the totals to Flannery and crossed the cutting-room floor to punch out.

"Bye, Paul," she called to the office. "Don't stay too long." Paul gave her a wave back.

"I won't," he said as he picked up the phone to call Boston to find out what time Doug had left the plant to head back to Gloucester. But the phone rang several times before the answering machine picked up. Boston's plant was closed for the day, and even the direct number yielded no response.

Paul walked outside to check on the weather. The sky had gotten really dark, and the wind was howling. Seawater was lapping over the dock at the opposite side of the building and filling in the base of the loading dock that naturally sloped lower than the rest of the parking lot. He looked across at where the *Bay State Skye* was docked. The dragger was listing to one side and looked like it was taking on water. The thought occurred to him that one of the dragger's battery-powered bilge pumps might have quit working, but he had no intentions of investigating on his own. When he got back into the plant, he called the Coast Guard to see if they might want to check on the boat, but they didn't. They were geared up for search-and-rescue calls and had no interest in checking on a privately owned, docked boat. He thought of giving a call to the police but decided he'd more than likely get the same response.

His train of thought was immediately interrupted by Doug pulling into the parking lot, which erased any desire he once had to help the ill-fated fishing boat. He had a forklift at the ready, and he and Doug had the final truck of the day unloaded in no time. Doug immediately punched out and left, and Paul went up to the men's locker room to change his clothes.

As he entered the room, Paul glanced out the locker-room window, where he caught a glimpse of the *Hannah Boden*, which was docked right out back. Normally, he would have had to approach the window and look down to see any sign of a boat tied up at the back dock. He stopped in his tracks, realizing he was looking directly into the *Hannah Boden's* wheelhouse. Running to the window, he found the tide was so high that if it rose another foot, the *Hannah Boden* would be level with the wharf. At that point, a strong gust of wind could easily push her out of the water and onto Flannery's dock. Paul thought for a moment of calling someone, but he figured no one was going to come to help, at least not before the predictable catastrophe happened.

Immediately, he recognized the urgency of heading for home. His attention turned to getting the plant locked up and making it over the bridge before he was stuck spending the night. He ran downstairs, closed the lobster-room door, and locked it. After setting the alarms in the lobster room and retail store, he locked the retail door and left.

Paul waded through at least two feet of seawater to make his way to his car. He was wearing his usual work boots he'd bought at Nelson's to protect his feet from the inevitable water collecting on the cement floor inside Flannery's, but this flood was no match for such everyday footwear. The rain, driven by strong wind gusts, pelted his face as he raised his sweatshirt's hood and looked toward his car, which luckily was parked on the side of the building with the highest point of elevation in the area. He glanced toward the opposite side of the building that was closest to the side dock. Ocean water, which had just begun to spray over the side of the dock when Meredith left, was now in full-fledged flood mode. It had overtaken the parking lot and was beginning to lap onto the upper loading dock that the elderly couple had driven off earlier in the summer.

Paul dove into the driver's side of his white Toyota Camry as he struggled to keep his car door open in the wind. As he was driving out of Flannery's parking lot with the water midway to the top of his tires, he heard a truck horn beep and saw Denny waving as he headed home from Fitzy's.

"What a nut," Paul said to himself, shaking his head and noting Denny's broad smile. As Paul tooted back, a gust of wind hit Denny's truck and noticeably pushed him sideways. He swerved for a moment, then recovered control of his vehicle. This made Paul even more apprehensive about crossing the Cape Ann Bridge. He needed to get going before he couldn't.

Paul made it around the first Route 128 rotary, and then after a short highway stretch, he rounded the second rotary, heading straight for the bridge. He was in luck. Officials hadn't closed the bridge, but judging from the collection of police cars assembled, they were about to. Paul drove onto the bridge and climbed to the crest. As he continued down the other side, he felt a burst of wind push the rear of his car. Paul never touched the gas pedal. He didn't have to. He glanced at the speedometer and noticed he was doing ninety in a fifty-five zone. His first thought was that the cops would be chasing him momentarily, but then he realized they had no desire to make a traffic stop in weather like this. Then he remembered seeing Denny's truck swerve in the wind and began holding his own Toyota's steering wheel with a death grip. Despite all his efforts, his four-cylinder Camry was no match for the seventy-five-mile-an-hour wind gusts this nor'easter was packing. He found himself blown from the high-speed lane to the breakdown lane and managed to recover control just in time to miss a tree in a wooded section by the highway as he came off the ramp from the bridge. Luckily, he was the only fool on that section of the road at the time. He came to a full stop to rest for a moment, then continued on to exit fourteen, which would take him through the back roads of Essex and Ipswich and away from the coastline. He began to relax.

"It should be smooth sailing from here," Paul thought, forgetting that his route took him across the picturesque Essex causeway, which abutted the Essex River on the right side of the road.

As he entered the touristy stretch of road in Essex, he noted the water from the salt marsh and the Essex River encroaching on the main drag. He followed closely behind others who were gingerly navigating the flooding roadway between Woodman's on one side and the Village Restaurant on the other, headed toward Ipswich. The wind was gusting heavily across the open marsh, and everyone's cars were moving to and fro with the gale-force winds. Once he passed the roadway that abutted the Essex River, his route headed slightly more inland, and other than having to avoid a downed tree limb or two, the treacherous part of his route had finally come to an end.

With Paul's arrival back home, everyone connected to Flannery's was out of danger—with one exception. Jimmy was still in the thick of it all. As Doug was making his trek back to Gloucester from Boston, Jimmy was driving in the opposite direction to meet up with his boat, which was located a short distance from Nahant Bay and Lynn Harbor. When he arrived, he launched his dinghy to take him out to the *Anna May*, which was moored among many other commercial and pleasure boats. The moorings were separated sufficiently to avoid any kind of a collision under normal conditions, but there was nothing normal about this storm. The smart choice would have been to sail the *Anna May* back to Gloucester and dock at Flannery's, but the time for that choice had long passed. The weather was beyond safe navigation, and judging from what Paul had observed, the *Anna May* might not have fared well being docked by the *Hannah Boden* anyway. Because it was Jimmy's decision to moor the *Anna May* near Nahant Harbor, he felt that he alone was responsible for the safety of his lobster boat. There was a good chance of a collision in a small body of water with many boats still moored. If he lost his boat, he'd lose both Murph's and his livelihood. He couldn't let that happen without putting up a fight.

When he arrived at his boat, he quickly scanned its sides and deck for any damage sustained. There was none. *So far, so good*, he thought to himself. He lifted the extra cans of fuel that he'd brought with him to weather the storm to the *Anna May*'s deck, along with a couple of coolers of food and drinks he thought he'd need if the storm raged through the night. There was no bathroom on board, which was routine for most lobster boats. Normally, he would hang over the side, but in situations like this where he might be seen, a pail that could be discreetly emptied overboard and rinsed out would do the job. He climbed on board once the dinghy was empty and immediately pulled the small boat into the *Anna May*, flipping it upside down on the deck. He tied a few bowline knots to secure it to the aft deck in order to make certain the boat was still there when the storm ended and he needed to return to shore. Then he gazed out at the building seas, speculating that this storm might become somewhat more ferocious than predicted.

The wheelhouse of the *Anna May* was fully enclosed, with a roof, sturdy walls, and laminated safety glass, which made it a comfortable place to weather the storm. Jimmy's game plan was to fire up the *Anna May's* engine and, while remaining attached to her mooring, dodge any vessels that might come loose and collide with her. He was also there to steer into any rogue waves that could roll her over. Jimmy was confident he could handle this on his own and didn't tell Murph of his plans. He and Murph were very different people, and the thought of spending the night in a storm with Murph was unthinkable to him. One storm was enough to contend with; he didn't need to add any more conflict to the endeavor.

Jimmy turned on the radio to his favorite station; the Vanilla Ice hit "Ice Ice Baby" was playing. Even he couldn't tolerate that song, so he flipped the radio off and turned on his marine radio to keep updated on any chatter about the storm. Then he changed into full Gloucester fisherman gear, which included his orange slicker overalls, knee-high rubber boots, and a yellow slicker and wide-brimmed rain hat. He looked like the original model for the Gloucester Fisherman's Memorial Monument, but he was warm and dry. Careful man that he was, he also had his regulated survival suit and life vest at the ready, just in case.

Because the weather hadn't begun to get too ferocious just yet, Jimmy sat back in his chair and attempted to take a nap. The rolling seas should have been as soothing as a rocking chair, but the impending danger of the storm kept him from drifting off to sleep. Instead, his mind wandered to the years directly after high school, when he was dating his high school sweetheart, Julie Dickens. Julie was a beautiful girl with waist-long dirty-blonde hair and legs that went on forever. He and Julie made a striking couple, and most of their senior class members secretly wished they could have taken one of their places. Of course, they were voted king and queen of the prom, and both planned to go to college after graduation and hold down professional careers.

Jimmy proposed to Julie just before she left for Dartmouth and he took up his studies at Salem State College. Naturally, she said yes, and the date was set for the following summer. During the fall of their freshman year, Jimmy drove up to Hanover, New Hampshire, every weekend, enjoying all the activities that an Ivy League school had to offer. They would sleep on Julie's extra-long twin-size bed in her dorm room, which would have been a problem for her roommate if she had been there on weekends. But Julie's roommate had a job working for a veterinarian in her hometown that she was trying to hold onto for the summers, so she went home most weekends to work. This gave Jimmy and Julie full use of the room, perfect for the engaged couple to really get to know each other. Jimmy smiled.

By midsemester, however, Jimmy had an inkling things weren't going as well as he'd hoped, although he was still largely blind to the lack of reciprocity in the relationship. Julie showed little interest in spending time in his Salem State dorm, and it wasn't long before she became busy most weekends as the holidays approached, giving him excuses as to why he shouldn't bother coming up to stay.

During Thanksgiving break, Jimmy and Julie reconnected, however, attending the traditional Gloucester Thanksgiving Day football game in the morning with everyone they hung out with from high school. A lot of the group made plans to go out for Chinese at the Kowloon, and they both were excited to go. They had a lot of laughs, and things felt right between them again. Jimmy took it as a good sign that Julie was still wearing the engagement ring he gave her. The couple said goodbye to their friends in the parking lot, and everybody vowed to get together over Christmas break. Jimmy put his arm around Julie's waist as he walked her back to his car.

Julie pulled away quickly and ran to the passenger side door, calling back to Jimmy, "It's freezing out here!" And it was, but Jimmy pulling her closer would have kept her warm. He knew something was up.

Jimmy opened the door for Julie, then walked around to the other side of the car and slid into the driver's seat. He didn't have to guess anymore. Julie was holding his engagement ring between her thumb and index finger, waiting for Jimmy to hold out the palm of his hand so that she could drop the ring in it.

"What's going on?" said Jimmy, looking at the ring suspended in midair, trying not to show too much emotion.

"You must have guessed," Julie replied in the most sympathetic tone of voice she could muster.

"You've met someone at Dartmouth," Jimmy retorted, some part of him having known for a long time but not wanting to believe it.

"I have," Julie admitted, "but you know how long-distance relationships go. They seldom work out."

"I guess," Jimmy said, and he put out his hand to collect the ring.

The car was deafeningly silent on the long ride back from Saugus to Gloucester, although Jimmy's mind was silently racing. *Why'd everybody decide to go out for Chinese so far away? OK, Kowloon is the go-to place for catching up in a fun atmosphere, and the food is really good, but it's so far away!* He smelled Julie's bag of leftovers permeating the car, and it was making him nauseated. By the time he finally drove up to Julie's parents' house, Jimmy couldn't wait for Julie to get out.

"I hope we can still be friends," Julie said with a supportive smile.

"Sure," Jimmy responded, with no intentions of seeing her again.

"Well, goodbye," Julie called to Jimmy as she slid out of the passenger side of the car and closed the door. Chivalry was out the window. There'd be no walking her to the screen door tonight. Julie looked relieved as she walked up the path to her childhood home. Jimmy was devastated.

Jimmy opened his eyes with a start and sat up. He'd rather face the storm and rough seas than relive that horrifying past. "That's when I decided, right then and there," he declared as if someone was in the wheelhouse to hear. "The sea never lets you down. Women will abandon you, but the sea is always there for you." He recalled that his next move was to quit school and go to work on his uncle's lobster boat. He'd never regretted leaving Julie behind, but he always wondered, if he'd finished his engineering degree, would his life have been easier?

Jimmy didn't have any time to reflect on that thought. He was suddenly plunged back into reality. Several large waves relentlessly belted *The Life of Riley*, a thirty-foot pleasure boat moored diagonally to the left of his, until the cleats that held its mooring chain became dislodged from its rail, screws and all. Instantly, Jimmy sprang to the captain's wheel and fired up the *Anna May*'s engine. *The Life of Riley* was free from its mooring, with its aft drifting toward the bow of the *Anna May*. Jimmy thrust the *Anna May* into reverse in the nick of time, narrowly missing colliding with the boat. The wind pushed *The Life of Riley* toward the fishing boat to the right of Jimmy's, clipping its bow and turning *The Life of Riley* sideways. Instead of gale-force winds pushing *The Life of Riley* from the side, now the wind was pushing from the aft, which allowed the boat to pick up speed, its bow cutting directly into the surf.

Jimmy watched helplessly as he witnessed the unfolding of a virtual boating demolition derby. *The Life of Riley*'s bow slammed into the bow of a forty-foot pleasure boat that was moored two boats over from the *Anna May*, leaving a gaping foot-and-a-half crack in her hull. Miraculously, *The Life of Riley* came through the collision unscathed, allowing it to continue its course of destruction. One by one, *The Life of Riley* slammed into three more boats as she made her way to shore. Two smaller sailboats were able to turn in the water when *The Life of Riley* connected and only received glancing blows that left scrapes down their sides. But a larger cabin cruiser, the *Lucky So Far*, which was docked near the riverbank, had just run out of luck. Jimmy winced as an eighty-mile-an-hour gust of wind pushed *The Life of Riley*'s bow head-on into the *Lucky So Far*'s side, delivering a catastrophic punch that left a large gouge, causing the boat to instantly take on water. The *Life of Riley*, still in one piece, continued toward the river's edge. Jimmy hoped the batteries in the *Lucky So Far*'s bilge pump were fresh. She was going to need continuous pumping to keep from sinking.

"Who names a boat *Lucky So Far*? They're just asking for it," Jimmy said aloud. "First boat, I bet . . . live and learn."

When all was said and done, two boats were left listing in the water before *The Life of Riley* finally came to rest on the low-lying banks of the river. There she fell to the right, as if exhausted from her ordeal. As far as Jimmy could tell, *The Life of Riley* wasn't damaged.

"Whoa, I'm lucky I was here, or the *Anna May* would have been the first boat taken out," Jimmy said. He focused intently on the rest of the boats surrounding him, making sure they were still attached to their moorings. Although two pleasure boats were in trouble, they were still being held securely in place. Jimmy was glad they weren't working fishermen's boats. He hated to see a man lose his livelihood because of a careless mistake like a set of cleats held on by screws too short to do the job.

Jimmy worked through the night to accelerate at a ninety-degree angle into any large waves that threatened to roll the *Anna May* and alternately threw his boat into reverse to use the mooring to keep straight in the water. When morning came and the storm cleared, he was exhausted. There were a few times during the wee hours of the morning when he had wished he'd taken Murph on this little adventure with him. He had found himself dozing at the wheel. But the *Anna May* had made it through the storm unscathed, and thus, he had achieved his ultimate goal. Very soon, once he got some shuteye, they'd be ready to go out and set traps. After all, the best time to catch lobsters was after a big nor'easter, and this had been a doozy. Jimmy was excited to finish off what had started as a lackluster year with a bonanza.

CHAPTER 14

The next day was a beauty. The quick-moving storm had cleared the coast, leaving behind a picture-perfect cerulean-blue sky. The ocean waters had receded off the roadways, and the lower tide combined with a lack of storm surge made the ocean appear less treacherous and more inviting.

When Paul arrived at Flannery's, he immediately took a walk out back to check on the *Hannah Boden*. Expecting the worst, he was pleasantly surprised to see she had survived the storm unscathed. Her crew was preparing her to ship out because the weather had cleared, which was a welcome sign that things were returning to normal. The day of the storm was an unproductive day for just about everyone involved in the seafood industry. Its impact on everyone's bottom line would be significant, but no one would be affected as severely as the local lobster fishermen.

Doug saw the first signs of devastation when he took a ride past Good Harbor Beach on his way to work. A giant ball of lobster traps had washed up on shore. The traps were entangled with many fishermen's trawl lines, mangled into a new shape that resembled a double boxcar that was about a telephone pole length high. Doug walked over to see if he could make out the tags on any of the traps. Many of the tags were readable, but none of the names sounded familiar. It was possible they were from another area, even another country. Doug remembered a write-up in the *Gloucester Daily Times* about a local lobsterman's trap and buoy washing up on one of the islands of Orkney, Scotland. A fisherman from Rockport happened to be visiting Orkney and recognized the buoy colors as belonging to a lobsterman from Gloucester. Sure enough, when they checked the trap tags, they found the trap had traveled all the way across the pond, a 3,007-mile journey.

No telling where traps will wind up after a storm, Doug thought as he got back in his truck and headed to Flannery's.

Murph stopped by Flannery's around eight that morning to grab some bait and meet up with Jimmy on the *Anna May.*

"Going out already?" Denny called to Murph from the forklift. Murph walked up to Denny, who shut his engine down.

"Jimmy just called. He spent all night on the *Anna May* to make sure nothing happened to her. Good thing, 'cause a boat broke loose from its mooring and did some damage," Murph said.

"Good thing," Denny mimicked, "or you guys would have been up the creek without a paddle. And he's thinking of going out now?"

"I guess," Murph said, scratching his head. "He stopped at some diner to get breakfast this morning, and the locals told him they were finding lobsters on second-story decks in Nahant. He wants to check our traps. The water had to have been pretty stirred up to be hucking lobsters out of the sea and up two stories high."

"I'll say," Denny agreed. "I've never heard of that happening before."

"I'd believe it," Doug declared as he walked into Flannery's through the loading dock's plastic strips. "You should see the giant ball of traps that washed up on Good Harbor Beach."

"There must have been a wicked undertow," Denny thought out loud.

"Good luck finding your traps out there," Doug told Murph sarcastically. "You'll have better luck spotting them in that ball at the beach."

"Maybe you can give us a hand looking," Murph countered. Doug enjoyed tragic things happening to other people a little too much, and it really got on Murph's nerves.

"You'd have a better chance of seeing God than seeing me out there," Doug answered, snickering.

Murph and Denny shook their heads simultaneously. That was Doug, but there was an underlying charm to him that couldn't be ignored. They both knew that if they truly needed something, they could count on Doug. That's how he got away with his cynical demeanor.

Murph decided to take only one barrel of bait instead of his usual two. Jimmy and he had started to move the traps farther out with late fall approaching, but they had only managed to shift the position of about four hundred of them. The other eight hundred were in waters less than a hundred feet deep. To make matters worse, the majority of their traps were wooden. It sounded like they were about to embark on a very frustrating and possibly devastating day. They had twelve hundred traps set before the storm. Murph tried not to think about how many traps they would have by the end of the day. He said goodbye and traveled to meet up with Jimmy and the *Anna May*.

Sully was right behind Murph, buying his usual one barrel of bait for the day. He had heard talk about traps washing up on shore and knew he'd spend most of the day searching for his trawl lines, too. Unlike Jimmy and Murph, he had begun replacing his wooden traps with wire ones which were sturdier. But he didn't have the number of traps that they owned. He could only hope that of the eight hundred traps he'd set, the five hundred wire ones would be found and salvageable.

"Good luck," Denny yelled to Sully over the tooting horn of the forklift. Sully nodded as he made his way to his truck. He drove the short distance to his boat, loaded the barrel of bait, gassed the boat up, and headed out.

Murph had driven as far as Magnolia when he popped a cassette tape into his truck's player from the Phish concert he'd attended at UMass Amherst earlier in the year. He turned the volume up full blast to keep his mind occupied. There was no need to dwell on misfortune that hadn't happened yet. He kept thinking there was a chance they'd luck out. But when he drove into the boatyard parking lot and off-loaded his barrel of bait, he couldn't help but notice *The Life of Riley* lying on its side a bit downriver a piece, and the flurry of activity out by the moorings as owners tried to assess the damage to the boats. Jimmy ran to help Murph haul the bait down from his truck to the dinghy, and Murph filled him in on what he'd heard at Flannery's.

"You know, we wouldn't have been so far inshore if the weather hadn't been so spectacular this fall," Jimmy told him.

"We're always out a ways by now," Murph agreed.

"I hope we don't live to regret it," Jimmy muttered under his breath, already stressed at what he was anticipating to find out there.

The two boarded the *Anna May* from their dinghy and secured the dinghy to the mooring. Having gassed up the engine before Murph arrived, Jimmy immediately headed out to the coordinates of their first trawl line off the coast of Nahant. No matter how much they searched, they couldn't locate their trawl buoy. When he was certain he was directly over one of his trawls, Jimmy used a grappling hook on the end of a long line to see if he could feel anything on the bottom. Nothing. He felt nothing. He pulled the grappling hook in and then paused for a moment.

"This ain't good," Murph said to break the tension. He was stating the obvious. Jimmy glanced at Murph and then back out at the horizon.

Trying to remain hopeful, Jimmy steamed over to where his second trawl line should have been. Just like at the first coordinates, there were no buoy markers. Jimmy grabbed his grappling hook again to see if he could turn up anything. This time, he tried harder. There had to have been something left from all those traps. In an instant, he thought he felt something and managed to raise a mud-laden post from one of his wooden traps. Murph freed the post from the hook and threw it back in the water.

"At least we found something," Jimmy said as he lowered the hook back in the sea. "We had one trawl line with wire traps in this area."

After about fifteen minutes, Jimmy's grappling hook knocked against something that felt like a trap. Jimmy and Murph struggled to pull the object on board because it was anchored in muck. Sure enough, it was one of the *Anna May*'s wire traps, alone, bent out of shape but, amazingly, still holding a lobster. Murph reached inside the twisted trap with his ungloved hand because his wrists were thinner than Jimmy's. As he gently pulled the lobster out, he found it was still in one piece, remarkably, but dead. He turned the lobster over and examined the gills where its legs and carapace met. They were caked with mud and silt.

"This lobster didn't die from the trauma of being tossed around in rough water," Murph noted.

"No, it suffocated in the mud," Jimmy agreed, then leaned back, resting on the side of the boat. "Our traps had been on gravel bottom for a couple of weeks. Now it's muck. The storm surge went so deep it actually changed the landscape of the ocean's bottom. The gravel's been turned under, and mud's replaced it."

"That was some storm," Murph said sighing.

Jimmy and Murph moved into the wheelhouse and melted into their respective seats. Elbows on knees and chins in hands, both men were silent. Neither wanted to admit they might have lost all their gear. By saying it out loud, they felt it somehow made it so.

"At least we have our boat," Jimmy affirmed. "We can replace gear, but the boat . . . not so easily. Not that replacing the gear will be easy."

"Maybe Denny will do another run at the greasy pole to raise us some money," Murph said cheerily. Jimmy cracked a sad smile.

"We'll survive. It won't be easy, but we'll make it back," Jimmy said. "I guess we shouldn't give up all hope. We have a bunch of other coordinates, and not all of them are inshore. We may be able to salvage something yet. Let's head out to deeper water, at least over a hundred feet, where more of our wire traps are sitting. We should have better luck there."

As the *Anna May* got back underway, Murph and Jimmy were listening to the other lobster fishermen chattering on the radio.

"Yeah, I just got here," one lobsterman radioed in. "It's like the storm surge pushed the deeper traps in, and the undertow pushed the inshore traps out, and they all met here. What a mess."

"I've heard Congressman Contoro has already begun working with the Massachusetts Small Business Administration to try to secure loans for fishermen who've lost their gear," another Gloucester fisherman said, joining the conversation.

The radio crackled. "Yeah, but you know how that goes," the first lobsterman replied. "You get a fifty-thousand-dollar loan and wind up paying about three hundred dollars a month for the next twenty years. The replacement traps you've bought are long gone by then, and you're still stuck paying the loan back."

"I hear you," the Gloucester fisherman replied, "but it's good to have it to lean on to get yourself going again if you don't have much behind you."

"True enough," said the first lobsterman.

Murph and Jimmy spent most of the afternoon chasing down their traps set in the deepest water, which yielded some better news. They were able to locate about four hundred and fifty traps that were salvageable. But the traps they had set on gravel bottom in water less than a hundred feet deep were a total loss. They were probably part of the mucky balls of traps and line that washed up on shore. At the end of the day, out of the twelve hundred traps they had set in place before the storm, they had recovered only a third of them. The rest were lost. Jimmy let Murph take the wheel and bring the *Anna May* to dock. He didn't know if he was tired from spending most of the last twenty-four hours up or whether he was dragged down by the losses of the day, but Jimmy was exhausted.

"Should we head back to the mooring?" Murph asked.

"Just to pick up our dinghy—then we'll head up to Flannery's," Jimmy said. "I'm hoping they'll understand our situation and refund the rest of the mooring fee if we leave now. We've got no gear. We won't be able to fish until we can recoup our losses."

"Hey, I wanted to thank you for spending last night protecting the *Anna May*. At least we have a boat, and that's on you," Murph said.

"I appreciate that," Jimmy said, not remembering his brother thanking him for anything, ever. "I must look pretty awful if you're thanking me for something."

"You've got that right," Murph said with a smile. Jimmy leaned back in his chair and fell asleep.

*　　*　　*　　*　　*

Sully steamed out of Gloucester Harbor to a brilliant rising sun, midway in the sky. The water sparkled as he made his way out to check on his traps about six miles off the shores of Swampscott. Although many of the buoys that marked the beginning and end of Sully's trawl lines were missing, he had a lot more success finding his traps than Jimmy and Murph. He used the same combination of grappling hook and line that they used, but he was searching for primarily wire traps in much deeper water. By noontime, he had located about four hundred of his eight hundred traps. As he made his way back to the Gloucester area, Sully checked additional coordinates where he had set traps. The waters were over a hundred feet deep, and he hadn't given up hope of finding a partial trawl line with traps still attached.

Sully took a few bites of a ham and cheese sandwich as he steamed to his next location. Because he fished alone, he didn't have the luxury of taking breaks like Jimmy and Murph did. But he didn't have to share his earnings with a crew either. He set his engine to idle, and immediately, the smooth forward motion of the boat was replaced with a jarring to-and-fro and side-to-side movement. The waves seemed harder and less forgiving than they had been in the past few weeks. Sully knew this meant the seas were cooling, and days were getting shorter. Someone once told him the winter waves were harder because the water's molecules were closer together when the water got cold. The summer's warm air temperatures and long hours of sunlight tended to heat the water and spread out its molecules. Sully wasn't sure if this explanation was true, but he did know that in the winter the waves were choppier and had less give to them.

Sully wasn't exactly at his original coordinates. He had found he was having better luck figuring out the direction the wind was blowing at the time of the storm and adjusting his position accordingly. This strategy was working thus far, so he stuck to it. With no buoy in sight, he grabbed his grappling hook and line and started searching the bottom for a stray trap or trawl line. It wasn't long at all when he hooked a rope that appeared to have been part of a trawl. It was caked with mud, like everything he had pulled up that day. As he examined the rope, he noticed it was shorter than a line connecting one trap to another would have been. The line was cut clean, as if a knife was used to sever it, and the ends appeared distinctly different from the torn, shredded pieces he'd been finding all day.

Sully placed the rope on the deck by the wheelhouse, and this time he threw his grappling hook and line a little farther from his boat, almost as though he was casting a fishing line. The hook instantly grabbed a hold of something weightier.

"A trap," he speculated out loud as he leaned back to pull the grappling line in, hand over hand.

Soon, he saw a slightly contorted wire lobster pot, covered in mud, emerge from the sea. As he pulled the trap out of the water and over his boat's rail, Sully's grin disappeared. The mud had partially washed away as the trap was dragged from the water to reveal a pair of grundgies tangled in the rope around the trap.

"What the hell?" he muttered to himself, noticing the pair of orange waterproof bib pants, identical to the ones he and most of the fishermen from the Cape Ann area wore.

He set the trap down on the deck more gently than usual to get a better look at his find. In an instant, he jumped back. Tangled within the severed lines and marginally damaged wire of the trap was a human skeleton. The skeleton, still wearing the pants that had been bound to the trap, was picked clean by scavengers and bottom feeders.

Sully regained his composure after the initial shock and drew close for a second look. At first he thought he had found a casualty from last night's nor'easter, perhaps a fisherman who had gotten caught in the storm and was desperate to make landfall. But after he was able to collect his thoughts, he realized a body from last night's nor'easter would still have flesh on its skeleton and would more than likely be fully or mostly clothed. No, this skeleton had been submerged for months, maybe even years.

"You were fish food for sure, you poor bastard," Sully said to the skeleton.

Sully was more comfortable with the skeletal remains now that he realized the person the skeleton once belonged to had been dead for some time. He kneeled on his boat's deck to examine the skeleton more closely. He noted the complex knotting of the trawl line around the bones and realized its integration with the trap may have actually helped the bones to remain together.

"Hmm, either you were desperately tangled in your trawl line when you fell overboard, old fellow"—Sully paused to consider the possibility of him becoming entrapped to this extent—"or you were tied to your pot before leaving the deck of your boat."

Sully had forgotten all about the trawl lines he was attempting to recover before dark. This scenario was beginning to seem a little too familiar to him. He carefully attempted to pull the back of the skeleton away from the trap, which was difficult to do with the tightness of the trawl line that bound the trap to the skeleton. But he didn't want to disturb the ropes that secured the skeleton to the trap. He wanted to be sure he could return the remains to the sea if the situation warranted it.

When he managed to get enough slack in the line to get a good look at the back of the skeleton, he reached between the third and fourth ribs on the skeleton's left to pull a black-handled knife from between the bones. Sully smiled. It was a typical knife, with a stainless-steel blade and a soft rubber handle, a tool that every lobsterman would have on board at the ready in case the unthinkable happened and he was snagged by a trawl line as traps were being released into the sea. It was lightweight and elegant, and it felt good in his hand.

With a newly found spring in his step, Sully walked to the side of the wheelhouse where his hydraulic hauler was located. He lifted two sheathed knives off a hook positioned to the side of the hauler, revealing a third, empty sheath. He held the abandoned sheath in one hand and the recovered knife in the other and carefully guided it into place. The knife was a perfect fit.

Sully hung the three sheathed knives back on the hook, being careful to give the most prominent top position to his reunited knife and sheath, and then returned to the skeleton, still entwined with the line and trap. Bending over, Sully grabbed the trap, making certain the skeleton and grundgies were still tightly secured, and heaved the entire ball of wax over the rail. He caught a glimpse of Johnny's tag on the trap as he watched it all splash into the sea, where it lingered for a moment before sinking down to the bottom.

"Go back with your brother, you greedy son of a bitch. I'll see you both in hell," Sully muttered as he turned away from the rail, satisfied there would be one less dragger to deliberately molest another lobsterman's gear.

Sully wiped his hands on an old sweatshirt by the hauler and opened the door of the wheelhouse. Throttling up the engine, he set his course straight for Gloucester. There would be no more stops. Sully was content that he'd already found everything he needed.